The Life & Extraordinary Adventures of

Private Ivan Chonkin

》》》》》》》》》》 《《《《《《《《《《《

Vladimir Voinovich

The Life & Extraordinary Adventures of

PRIVATE IVAN
CHONKIN

TRANSLATED BY RICHARD LOURIE

NORTHWESTERN UNIVERSITY PRESS

EVANSTON, ILLINOIS

》》》》》》》》》》 《《《《《《《《《《《

1

Now, it is impossible to say definitely whether it all really did happen or not, because the incident which set the entire affair in motion (which, until recently, was still in motion) happened in the village of Krasnoye so long ago that there are practically no eyewitnesses left from that time. Those that are tell all kinds of different stories and some can't remember anything at all. Besides, to tell the truth, it was not the kind of incident you'd remember for that long a time. As for me, I've heaped up everything I heard on the subject and added a little something of my own as well, could be I even added more than I heard. But in the end, I was so taken by this story that I decided to set it down in written form. If the story seems uninteresting to you, or boring, or even foolish, then just spit and forget I ever started telling it.

It happened just before the start of the war, the end of May, the beginning of June, 1941, somewhere in there.

It was an ordinary hot day, typical for that time of year. All the kolkhozniks were at work in the fields, but Nyura Belyashova, who worked in the post office and was not directly associated with the kolkhoz, had that day off and was working in her vegetable garden, mounding potatoes.

It was so hot that walking the length of three rows had totally exhausted Nyura. Her dress was drenched in back and under her arms, and as it dried it grew white and stiff from the salt of her sweat. Sweat was running down over her eyes. Nyura stopped to push some loose strands of hair back under her kerchief and to look at the sun to see how long till lunchtime.

She didn't get to see the sun. A big iron bird with a twisted beak that blocked out the sun and the rest of the sky was coming right at her.

"Ai!" she shrieked in terror, and covering her face with her hands, Nyura fell into a furrow in a dead faint.

Borka the hog, rooting about near the porch, scampered out of the way, but seeing that he was in no danger, he went back to the same spot.

After a while Nyura came to. The sun was beating down on her back. She caught the smell of dry earth and manure. Somewhere sparrows were chirping and hens were cackling. Life was still going on. Nyura raised her eyes and saw the lumpy earth beneath her.

What am I doing lying down? she thought, bewildered, and immediately remembered the iron bird.

Nyura was an educated girl. Sometimes she read *The Activist's Notebook*, which the Party organizer, Kilin, ordered regularly. The *Notebook* stated in no uncertain terms that every superstition was an inheritance from the dark past and must be fully uprooted. That idea seemed perfectly correct to Nyura. She turned her head to the right and saw her own porch and Borka the hog still rooting about as he had been before. There was nothing supernatural in that. Borka was always rooting about if he found himself a suitable spot and even if the spot weren't suitable he would root about there anyway. Nyura turned her head farther and saw pure-blue sky and the yellow sun.

Encouraged, she turned her head to the left, and her face fell right back down again. The terrible bird really did exist. It was standing not far from Nyura's garden, its big green wings stretched out wide.

"Get thee hence!" Nyura commanded it with her mind.

She wanted to cross herself, but it was hard to cross your-self lying on your stomach and she was afraid to get up.

Then it hit her like an electric shock. "Of course, it's an airplane!" Which indeed it was. What Nyura had taken for an iron bird was an ordinary biplane and what had seemed a twisted beak was the propeller, now at rest.

Almost skimming Nyura's roof, the plane had touched down, run along the grass, and come to a stop so close to Fedka Reshetov that its right wing had nearly knocked him down. Fedka, a big-faced, red-headed hulk of a man, better known by his nickname "Burly," had been cutting the grass with a scythe.

Catching sight of Burly, the pilot unbuckled his safety belt, leaned out of the cockpit, and shouted: "Hey, mu-zhik, what village is this?"

Burly was not in the least surprised or frightened. He went right over to the plane and readily explained that their village was called Krasnoye, though it used to be called Griaznoye, and that the villages of Kliukvino and New Kliukvino were part of their kolkhoz even though they were on the other side of the river, while Old Kliuk-vino, even though it was on their side of the river, be-longed to another kolkhoz. Their kolkhoz was called "Red Sheaf" and the other one was Voroshilov. There'd been three changes of chairman in the last two years over at Voroshilov. They locked the first one up for stealing, the second one for seducing minors, and the third one, who'd been sent there to straighten things out and who did straighten things out for a while at the beginning, started drinking and kept on drinking until he drank away every-thing he owned and all the kolkhoz funds. Finally things got so bad that during a fit of DT's he went and hung himself and left a note with only one word on it, "Ech," followed by three exclamation points. No one had the slightest idea what this "Ech!!!" was supposed to mean. As for their own chairman, well, he too drank uncontrollably but wasn't what you'd call a hopeless case yet. Burly was about to provide the pilot with further information on the life of the neighboring settlements when people started running up.

As usual, the kids were the first ones on the scene. They were followed by hurrying women, some with little children, some pregnant, and many with their little children and pregnant too. There were even some with one child clinging to their skirts, another holding their hand, a baby cradled in their arm, and yet another ripening in their belly. By the way, in Krasnoye (and is Krasnoye an exception?) the women were glad to have lots of children and were always either pregnant or had just had a baby, and sometimes they had just had a baby and were already pregnant again.

The old men and old women came tottering up next. Then the rest of the kolkhozniks left their work in the outlying fields and came running up, still holding their scythes, rakes, and choppers, presenting a sight that closely resembled the picture "Uprising of the Peasants" which hung in the district club.

Nyura, who was still lying in her garden, opened her eyes again and got up on one elbow.

Lord—an alarming thought flashed through her brain—I'm lying here while everybody else is getting an eyeful.

Teetering on legs that still quivered from fear, Nyura nimbly wriggled through her rail fence and dashed toward the gradually thickening crowd.

The women were in the back rows. Nyura elbowed them aside, groaning: "Oi, girls, let me through!"

And the women made way for Nyura, because they could tell by her voice that she just had to get in there.

Then came a layer of muzhiks. But she elbowed them aside too, saying: "Oi, muzhiks, let me through!"

Finally she found herself in the front row, right up close to the airplane. She could see a broad stripe of oil running the length of the fuselage and the pilot in his leather jacket leaning against the wing, staring in confusion at the crowd and twirling his frayed helmet and smoked glasses on one finger.

Burly was standing next to Nyura. He looked her over from top to bottom, laughed, then said fondly: "Looks like you're still alive, Nyurka. I thought you'd had it. You know, I spotted the plane first. I'm over by the rise cutting hay when I see it coming. Right for your roof, Nyurka, straight for your chimney. Next, I says, it's going to cut old Nyura down."

"Horseshit!" said Nikolai Kurzov, who was standing to Burly's right.

Burly stumbled in mid-speech, gave Nikolai the once-over, easy for Burly to do being a whole head taller than he, then paused for a moment to think, and said: "Horseshit comes from a horse. And I'm no horse. So shut your trap and keep it shut until I say you can open it. You got that? It wasn't me that came butting in."

Burly glanced at the crowd, winked at the pilot, then, satisfied with the impression he had made, went on to say: "Nyurka, that plane was one inch from your chimney, maximum. Minimum's even less. If it had knocked down your chimney, we'd be washing up your dead body tomorrow. I wouldn't have helped wash you, but Kolka Kurzov would have. He's curious about women's bodies. Last year over in Dolgov they locked him up for three days for sneaking into the women's bath and hiding under a bench, that's right."

Everybody broke into laughter, though they knew it was not the truth and that Burly had just thought up the whole thing on the spot. When they had all stopped, Stepan Lukov asked: "Burly! Hey, Burly! When you saw the plane was going to knock over the chimney, were you scared or not?"

Burly's face crinkled in contempt. He wanted to spit but there was no place to, so many people around. So he swallowed his spit and said: "Why should I have been scared? It's not my plane, not my chimney. If it had been mine, maybe I'd have been scared."

Just then, one of the little boys running in and out among the grownups' legs broke away and banged his stick on the wing, making it resound like a drum.

"What are you doing there?" the pilot shouted at the boy.

Frightened, the little boy ducked into the crowd, only to slip back out a moment later, this time, however, without his stick.

Having heard the kind of sound the wing made, Burly shook his head and with concealed malice asked the pilot: "It's covered with pigskin?"

The pilot answered: "With percale."

"What's that?"

"It's some sort of fabric," explained the pilot.

"Funny," said Burly. "I thought they were all made of metal."

"If it was all metal," Kurzov butted in again, "the motor couldn't get it off the ground."

"It isn't the motor that gets it off the ground, it's the lift force," said the warehouseman Gladishev.

Everyone respected Gladishev for his erudition, but this time they doubted what he had to say.

The women paid no attention to these conversations, something else had caught their fancy. They were taking stock of the pilot, staring right at him, discussing the fine points of his attire, not in the least embarrassed by his presence, just as if he were an inanimate object.

"Girls, that leather jacket of his is pure box calf," stated Taika Gorshkova. "Look, it's even pleated. You can see they don't begrudge them good leather."

Ninka Kurzova objected: "That's not box calf, that's kid."

"Oi, I can't believe it!" Taika erupted. "What do you mean, kid? Kid's got blisters."

"And so does his."

"And just where?"

"Go feel, you'll see," said Ninka.

Taika looked doubtfully at the pilot and said: "I would go feel, but he's probably ticklish."

The pilot blushed in embarrassment, without the least idea of how to react to all this.

He was saved by Golubev, the kolkhoz chairman, who drove up to the scene at that moment in his two-wheeled cart.

The whole affair had caught Golubev just as he and Volkov, the one-armed bookkeeper, had been questioning Granny Dunya on the subject of her home brew. The results of the questioning were plain to see: the chairman descended from his cart with special care, his boot tip slowly groping for the iron bracket that was wired to the side and served as a step.

Recently the chairman had been drinking frequently and heavily, on a par with the chairman who had hung himself over in Old Kliukvino. Some people thought he drank because he was a drunkard, while others found the cause in family problems. The chairman had a large family —a wife who suffered constantly from kidney trouble, and six children, who always went around filthy, were always fighting, and who ate a great deal.

All that wouldn't have been so terrible except that, as bad luck would have it, things at the kolkhoz were going poorly. Not what you would call very poorly, you could even say things were going well, except that they were getting worse and worse every year.

In the beginning, when everyone had dragged out all their belongings and piled them up in one great heap, it had been an inspiring sight, and to be in charge of it all seemed a pleasant-enough idea; but later on, somebody had had second thoughts and had gone to get his things back, even though you weren't supposed to. From then on, the chairman felt like the old woman they had stationed on top of the pile to guard it: people surrounded her from all sides, grabbing their belongings every which way; if she grabbed one by the hand, right away another one would start pulling something out from under her—she goes for him, and the first one gets away. What can you do?

It was a trying experience for the chairman since he did not understand that the fault was not his alone. He lived in constant expectation of the arrival of some committee of inspection—then he'd pay for everything, and in full. So far, though, they'd managed to get by. From time to time, various district inspectors, examiners, and instructors would drive down and drink vodka with him while munching on lard and eggs, then they'd sign the documents of certification and drive off, everything still in one piece. The chairman had even ceased to fear them but, since he was no fool, he realized that things couldn't go on like that forever and that someday a Maximum Responsibility Committee of Inspection would suddenly appear and have the final say in the matter.

And so Golubev was not the least surprised to learn that an airplane had landed on the outskirts of the village, near Nyura Belyashova's house. He understood that the day of reckoning had come and made himself ready to meet it with courage and dignity. He ordered Volkov, the bookkeeper, to assemble the staff and then, after gulping down a mouthful of tea to freshen up his breath a bit, he mounted his two-wheeled cart and set off for where the plane had landed, set off to meet his destiny.

When he appeared, the crowd parted, forming a living corridor between him and the pilot. His step quite firm, the chairman walked toward the pilot, extending his arm to him while still some distance off.

"Golubev, Ivan Timofeyevich, chairman of the kolkhoz." He introduced himself without slurring a word, exhaling to the side just to play it safe.

"Lieutenant Meleshko"—the pilot introduced himself.

The chairman was somewhat taken aback that the representative of the Maximum Committee was so young and of such modest rank but didn't let on, and said: "Pleased to meet you. What can I do for you?"

"I'm not sure myself," said the pilot. "My oil line snapped and the motor conked out. So I had to make a forced landing here."

"Following orders?" queried the chairman.

"What do you mean, orders?" said the pilot. "I'm telling you, it was a forced landing. The motor conked out."

That's right, that's right, lay it on thick, thought Ivan

Timofeyevich to himself while saying aloud: "If it's something with the motor, then we can help. Stepan," he said, turning to Lukov, "go poke around in there, see what you find. He works on our tractors," Golubev explained to the pilot. "Takes any machine apart and puts it back together."

"Breaking and fixing are two different things," confirmed Lukov, pulling a monkey wrench from the side pocket of his greasy jacket and making straight for the plane.

"Hey, hey, no, you don't." The pilot was quick to stop him. "That's no tractor, it's a flying machine."

"No difference," continued Lukov hopefully. "Same kind of nuts in both of them. You turn them one way, tightens them up. You turn them the other way, loosens them up."

"You shouldn't have landed here," said the chairman, "but over by Old Kliukvino. They've got a machine and tractor station and workshop over there. They would have fixed you right up."

"When you make a forced landing," explained the pilot patiently, "you don't get to choose the spot. I saw the field wasn't sown and brought her down."

"We practice the grassland system, that's why the field isn't sown," said the chairman in self-justification. "Perhaps you would like to inspect the fields or check our books. My office is open to you."

"What do I need your office for?" asked the pilot, angry that the chairman kept driving at something, yet at what he had no idea. "But hold on a minute. Is there a telephone in your office? I need to make a call."

"Why call right away?" said Golubev, taking offense.

"First you should see what's what, have a little talk with the people."

"Listen," implored the pilot. "Why are you trying to drive me crazy? Why should I talk with the people? I need to talk with my superiors."

What a conversation this turned out to be, observed Golubev to himself. Treats me polite. No swearing. Doesn't want to talk to the people, goes right to his superiors.

"It's up to you," said Golubev, doom in his voice. "It's just that I think it never hurts to have a talk with the people. The people, they see everything, they know everything—who's been here, who's said what, who's been banging his fist on the table. Ai, what's the use of talking!" Golubev waved his hand in disgust and invited the pilot to come with him on his cart. "Get in, I'll take you there. Call as much as you like."

Once again the crowd parted. Golubev obligingly helped the pilot onto the cart, then clambered up himself, causing the spring on his side to buckle and groan.

2

Wilting from the heat, his field shirt unbuttoned, his boots long unpolished and covered with a thick layer of dust, Captain Zavgorodny, the unit duty officer, sat on the porch at headquarters and observed what was happening in front of the entrance to the barracks where the commandant's company was quartered.

And this is what was happening there. Ivan Chonkin, a short, bowlegged private in the Red Army with one year left to serve, his field shirt hanging out over his belt, his forage cap down over his big red ears, his puttees slipping, was standing at attention in front of Company Master Sergeant Peskov and glancing at him in fright, his eyes inflamed from the sun.

The master sergeant, well-fed, rosy-cheeked, and blond, was lounging on an unpainted plank bench with his legs crossed, smoking a cigarette.

"Down!" commanded the sergeant, not very loudly, as if he didn't really feel like commanding, and Chonkin obediently fell to the ground.

"As you were!" Chonkin hopped to his feet. "Down! As you were! Down! Comrade Captain," shouted the sergeant to Zavgorodny, "what time you got there on your gold watch?"

The captain looked at his large watch made at the Kirov works (it wasn't gold, of course, the sergeant was only kidding) and answered lazily: "Ten-thirty."

"That early," lamented the sergeant, "and it's already so hot you could drop." He turned back to Chonkin. "As you were! Down! As you were!"

Alimov the orderly came out onto the porch.

"Comrade Sergeant," he shouted, "you're wanted on the phone."

"Who is it?" asked the sergeant, looking around grumpily.

"I don't know, Comrade Sergeant. The voice was so hoarse, like he had a cold."

"Ask who it is."

The orderly disappeared through the door and the sergeant turned to Chonkin. "Down! As you were! Down!"

The orderly returned, walked over to the bench, and, glancing sympathetically at Chonkin sprawled in the dust, reported: "Comrade Sergeant, they're calling from the bath. They want to know if you're going to pick up the soap yourself or send someone over."

"Can't you see I'm busy?" said the sergeant, keeping his anger in check. "Tell Trofimovich to go get it." Then he returned to Chonkin: "As you were! Down! As you were! Down! As you were!"

"Hey, Sergeant," Zavgorodny said, his curiosity aroused, "why are you giving it to him?"

"This one, Comrade Captain, is a slob," the sergeant was quick to explain, and sent Chonkin back down again. "Down! His term's almost up and he hasn't learned how to salute yet. As you were! Instead of saluting properly he spreads his fingers all the way to his ear. And he doesn't march, he shuffles along like he was out for a walk. Down!" The sergeant took a handkerchief from his pocket and wiped the sweat from his forehead. "They wear you out, Comrade Captain. You put in time with them, train them, ruin your nerves, and it's barely worth it. As you were!"

"Run him out past the post," proposed the captain. "Let him march there and back ten times at parade step, saluting."

"That's a possibility," said the sergeant and spat out his cigarette. "That's a good idea, Comrade Captain. Chonkin, did you hear what the captain said?"

Chonkin just stood there panting and made no answer.

"Look at him! Covered in dust, face filthy; this is no soldier, this is a bad joke. Ten times there and back, as far as the post, and at a . . ." the sergeant drew out his pause, "quick march!"

"That's the way," said the captain, perking up. "Sergeant, order him to point that toe better, forty centimeters from the ground. Ech, what a slob!"

Encouraged by the captain's support, the sergeant barked out his commands: "Get that leg up. Bend that elbow. Fingers to your temple. I'll teach you how to salute your commanding officers. About-face . . . quick march!"

At that moment the telephone rang in the corridor at headquarters. Zavgorodny looked over at it but didn't get up. He had no desire to move. He shouted: "Sergeant, look, his puttees are unwound. Any minute now he's going to trip on them and fall. Watch, you'll die laughing. What does the army need with a scarecrow like that anyway, eh, Sergeant?"

Meanwhile, the telephone in the corridor was ringing louder and more insistently. Zavgorodny got up reluctantly and went into headquarters.

"Hello, Captain Zavgorodny here," he said listlessly into the receiver.

The distance between the village of Krasnoye and the site of the camp was about one hundred and twenty kilometers, maybe more, and the telephone reception was abominable. Lieutenant Meleshko's voice was jammed by crackling and music and it took great effort on Captain Zavgorodny's part to understand what the matter was. From the beginning he did not even attach the proper significance to the lieutenant's message, but wanted to return to the spectacle the call had interrupted. On the way from the telephone to the door, however, the meaning of what he had just heard caught up with him. Then, having realized what had happened, he buttoned up the collar of his field shirt, wiped his boots off against each other, and went to report to the chief of staff.

Zavgorodny knocked on the door with his fist (the chief of staff was a little on the deaf side) and, without waiting for a reply, opened the door halfway, crossed the threshold, and shouted out: "Request permission to enter, Comrade Major."

"Denied," said the major softly, not raising his eyes from his papers.

But Zavgorodny paid no attention to the major's words; he could not recall a case in which the chief of staff had ever granted anyone permission for anything.

"Request permission to report, Comrade Major."

"Denied," said the major, raising his head from his papers. "Is this the way to look, Captain? No shave, buttons and boots not polished."

"Go take a . . ." said the captain in an undertone, playfully looking the major in the eye.

By the movement of the captain's lips the major was able to understand the approximate sense of what had been said to him, but he could not be certain, since he was unable to imagine such impertinence on the part of a junior officer. And so, pretending not to have understood, he continued with what he had been saying. "If you have no money to buy polish in the canteen, I can give you a can as a present."

"Thank you, Comrade Major," said Zavgorodny politely. "I request permission to report that Lieutenant Meleshko's motor has gone out and that he had to make a forced landing."

"Landed? Where?"

"On land."

"Stop your joking. I want to know precisely where Meleshko landed."

"Near the village of Krasnoye."

The major walked over to the map hanging on his wall and searched until he found Krasnoye.

"But what should we do?" He glanced in confusion at Zavgorodny, who just shrugged his shoulders.

"You're the chief, you know best. In my opinion it should be reported to the regimental commander."

The major had never previously distinguished himself by great courage in dealing with his superiors and now, on account of his deafness, feared them all the more, knowing that at any moment they could transfer him to the reserves.

"The commander is occupied right now," he said. "Directing flights."

"A forced landing is a flight matter," Zavgorodny reminded him. "The commander should know about it."

"That means you think it's all right to disturb the commander in this case?"

Zavgorodny said nothing.

"But maybe Meleshko will take care of it himself somehow or other?"

"Request permission to absent myself from the unit, Comrade Major. I will report to the commander myself."

"That's the proper thing," said the major, his spirits rising. "Go there yourself and report to him on your own. As unit duty officer, you have that right. But hold on, Zavgorodny, how can you leave? What if all of a sudden something happens at the unit?"

But Zavgorodny was no longer listening to him; he left the room, shutting the door tightly behind him.

Zavgorodny returned to headquarters about an hour later with the regimental commander, Lieutenant Colonel Opalikov, and with the regimental engineer, Kudlai. Lieutenant Colonel Pakhomov, battalion commander in charge of airfield maintenance, had also come to headquarters. He and the major had cleared up a few matters of their own. When Opalikov appeared, Pakhomov wanted to leave, but Opalikov kept him there. They began discussing what should be done. Kudlai said that there weren't any spare motors in the warehouse and that they couldn't get one from division in less than a week. Zavgorodny proposed that the wings be detached, and the plane be loaded on a vehicle and brought back to camp. The major proposed that they tow it back, which drew a grin of contempt from Zavgorodny. Lieutenant Colonel Pakhomov said nothing at all, but kept making notes in his notebook to display his zeal in service.

Opalikov listened to them scornfully. Then he stood up and walked from one end of the room to the other.

"Having heard and carefully considered all the hogwash which each of you, according to his ability, has proposed, I have come to the conclusion that we will leave the plane where it is until a motor can be brought there. If we drag the plane here over a hundred and twenty kilometers, there'll be nothing left of it but firewood. In the meantime, a guard will be posted there, if only to keep kids from cleaning out the cockpit. Take care of it," said Opalikov, pointing at Pakhomov.

Lieutenant Colonel Pakhomov laid his notebook down on the windowsill and stood up. "Excuse me, but it won't work," he said timidly.

Although he was Opalikov's equal in rank, his senior in age, and not directly subordinate to him, Pakhomov felt Opalikov superior to him; he knew that Opalikov was closer to their superior officers and would become a full colonel ahead of him, which is why he treated him with more respect than he received.

"And just why isn't it going to work?" asked Opalikov impatiently. He did not like any objections, ever.

"The entire commandant's company is already in their second week of guard duty with no one to relieve them."

Pakhomov picked up his notebook and opened it. "Seven in sick bay, twelve out logging, one on leave. That's the lot."

"Not even one man can be found? Some loafer, anyone. Let him snooze by the plane just as long as there's somebody in charge there."

"There's no one, Comrade Lieutenant Colonel," said Pakhomov, with such a baleful look that it was impossible not to believe him.

"Right, it looks bad." Opalikov set to thinking again, then immediately shouted out: "Hurrah! I've got it! Listen, you send that . . . what's his name . . . that smelly soldier of yours that rides the horse."

"Chonkin, you mean?" said Pakhomov incredulously.

"Chonkin. Of course. What a mind I have," marveled Opalikov, clapping the palm of his hand against his forehead.

"But he's . . ." Pakhomov tried to object.

"He's what?"

"There won't be anybody to bring firewood to the kitchen."

"No one is indispensable," said the regimental commander.

His point met with approval. Lieutenant Colonel Pakhomov did not dare object any further.

3

Dear reader! Of course you have already noticed that Ivan Chonkin, the soldier with one year left to serve, was short of stature, bowlegged, and even had red ears. "What a sorry sight he makes!" you will say indignantly. "What kind of example is this for the younger generation? And just where has the author seen a quote unquote hero like this?" And I, the author, my back to the wall and caught, as they say, red-handed, will have to admit that I never saw him anywhere, that I thought him up with my own head, and not to use him as an example but simply to while away the time. "Let's suppose that's so," you'll say without really believing it, "but why think up characters at all? Couldn't the author have taken a military hero from real life, a tall, well-built, disciplined, crack student of military and political theory?" Of course I could have, but I was too late. All the crack students had already been grabbed up and I was left with Chonkin. At first I was upset, then I accepted it. After all, the hero of your book is like your own child, you get what you get, you just don't fling him out the window. Maybe some other people's children are a little better, a little smarter, but still you love your own more just because he's your own.

Before he joined the army, Chonkin's biography contained no pages that would dazzle and arrest your attention, yet it seems somehow fitting to take a few words to tell you where he came from, how life treated him, and what he had done before.

And so, in a certain village by the Volga there once lived a certain Mariana Chonkina, an ordinary country woman, a widow. Her husband, Vasily Chonkin, perished in 1914 in the Imperialist War, which, as everybody knows, later turned into the Civil War and went on for a very long time. During the battle for Tsaritsyn, the village where Mariana lived became a military crossroads used alternately by the Reds and the Whites, both of whom showed a liking for Mariana's spacious and empty house. At one point a certain Ensign Golitsin, who had some rather unclear relation to the illustrious family of Russian princes by the same name, was quartered for an entire week in Mariana's home. Then he left the village and probably never gave it a second thought. But the village did not forget him. When, a year later or maybe more (no one kept track), Mariana gave birth to a son, the whole village had a good chuckle, saying that it couldn't have happened without the aid of the prince. True, the local herdsman, Serega, was also suspected, but he vehemently denied everything.

Mariana named her son Ivan and gave him the patronymic Vasilyevich, after her dead husband, Vasily.

Ivan's first six years, of which he had no recollection at all, were spent in poverty. His mother's health was frail, she neglected the house, yet somehow they kept going, living from hand to mouth until, one day, she drowned in the river. At the beginning of the winter she had gone down to the Volga to rinse out her wash and she fell in. It is at this point that Chonkin's memories of himself and the world around him began.

Ivan was not left totally alone—he was taken in by the neighbors, who might perhaps have been related to him, since their last name was the same as his. They had been childless for many years and had even been considering adopting someone from the orphanage when this perfect opportunity came along. They gave Chonkin clothes and boots and, when he'd grown up a bit, began to train him for farm work. Sometimes he'd be sent to turn the hay or sort potatoes in the cellar or other such work around the farm. For this they would pay.

Then, at a time known to all, a search for kulaks began in the village. Although not a single one could be found, it was mandatory to find some if only to set an example. So they hit on the Chonkins, who were exploiting labor, and child labor at that. The Chonkins were exiled and

Ivan ended up in a Children's Home where, for more than two years, they tormented him with arithmetic. In the beginning he endured it all obediently, but when it came to dividing whole numbers and fractions, he could stand it no longer and hightailed it out of his native village.

By that time he had grown up a bit and was strong enough to tighten the hame strap of a harness. He was given a horse and sent to work on a dairy farm. With his noble origins in mind, people would say to Chonkin: "Prince, go saddle up Roan and haul in some manure."

No one called him Prince in the army because none of them knew his nickname and there was nothing princely in his appearance to tip them off. The battalion commander, Pakhomov, took one look at Chonkin and said: "To the stable."

A perfect choice. The stable was the very place for Chonkin. From then on, he was always on horseback hauling firewood and potatoes to the mess. He got used to the army quickly and quickly mastered its fundamental rules, e.g.: "The less you do the better," "Don't rush to carry out orders, they just might cancel them," and so on.

And although during all his time in the army Chonkin did not become either a machinist or a mechanic as did others his age, he would have been perfectly satisfied with his life if it hadn't been for the master sergeant. Chonkin was not sent on details, did not have to wash the barracks floors, and was relieved of parade drill. He was practically never even in the barracks; in the winter he usually slept in the kitchen and in the summer on a bed of hay in the stables. Since he was directly connected with the kitchen, he received No. 5 rations, that is, the same as flight personnel. There was only one universal obligation from which Chonkin was not exempt—political training.

4

In the summer when the weather was good, political training was usually held not indoors but out at the fringe of a small grove off to one side of the camp. Forever late, Chonkin was late again, but this time it was not his fault. First, the master sergeant had disciplined him; then, at the very last minute, Shurka the cook had sent him to Supply for groats. But the supply master was nowhere to be found and Chonkin had to dash all over camp looking for him. Everyone had already assembled when Chonkin finally came riding up to the grove on horseback. Chonkin's appearance moved the political training instructor, Senior Politruk Yartsev, to remark with delicate sarcasm that since Chonkin had now arrived everything could be considered in order and they might begin.

The soldiers had taken their places on a grassy clearing around the broad tree stump upon which Senior Politruk Yartsev was seated.

Chonkin unbridled his horse, hitched it to a nearby tree where it could nibble the grass, then selected a place for himself down in front but at a safe distance from the politruk. Only after he had sat down and crossed his legs did Chonkin have a look around. Instantly he saw that he could not have chosen a worse spot. Right beside him, staring at him with his light-blue mocking eyes, sat his sworn enemy, Samushkin. This Samushkin would never let a chance go by to play a dirty trick on Chonkin: in the mess hall Samushkin would mix the salt and sugar together, at night in the barracks (on those rare occasions when Chonkin had to sleep there) Samushkin would tie Chonkin's pants to his field shirt to make him late for formation. Once he had even given Chonkin a "bicycle ride"—between the sleeping Chonkin's toes Samushkin had inserted strips of paper which he then set on fire. For this, Samushkin received two days of extra details, while Chonkin was crippled for three.

Chonkin realized that he would have been better off sitting on an anthill than right there next to Samushkin, from whose playful mood no good could possibly come.

The subject being covered was "The Moral Character of the Red Army Soldier." Senior Politruk Yartsev removed his notes from the large yellow briefcase lying on his lap, leafed through them, then briefly reviewed the material already covered.

"Who would like to go first? Chonkin?" he asked, amazed that Chonkin had raised his hand.

Chonkin stood up, pulled his shirt down flat behind his belt, and, shifting from foot to foot, looked directly into Yartsev's eyes. This silent staring continued until Yartsev could not bear it another second.

"Why aren't you summarizing the material?"

"I'm not prepared, Comrade Senior Politruk," Chonkin mumbled hesitantly, dropping his eyes.

"So why did you raise your hand?"

"I didn't raise my hand, Comrade Senior Politruk. I was getting a beetle out. Samushkin put a beetle down my back."

"A beetle?" cross-examined Yartsev, malice in his voice. "And just what are you here for, Comrade Chonkin, to study, or to catch beetles?"

Chonkin said nothing. The senior politruk rose and in his agitation began walking back and forth across the grass.

"We are here," he began, choosing his words carefully, "to study a very important subject—the moral character of the Red Army soldier. In political training, you, Comrade Chonkin, are lagging far behind most of the rest of the men, who pay attention to their instructor in class. The check on political training is getting closer every day and what are you going to have to show when it comes? And while we're on the subject, Chonkin, your discipline leaves much to be desired. The last time I was duty officer you failed to report for calisthenics. Here is a concrete example of weak political training leading to a direct violation of military discipline. Sit down, Comrade Chonkin. Now who would like to speak first?"

Squad Commander Balashov raised his hand.

"Well," said Yartsev, "for some reason Balashov is always the first to raise his hand. And it is always a pleasure to hear what he has to say. Have you made notes, Comrade Balashov?"

"I have," said Balashov modestly, but with a sense of his worth.

"I knew you would," said Yartsev, gazing on Balashov with unconcealed affection. "You may begin."

The senior politruk sat down once again on the tree stump and closed his eyes in anticipation of the genuine delight Balashov's correct, precise reply would bring him.

Balashov opened up a standard cardboard-covered notebook and began to read in a loud, expressive voice without using a single word of his own.

While Balashov read, the soldiers found ways to pass the time. One hid behind another's back and was carried away by *Madame Bovary*, two others played a game of Sea Battle, whereas Chonkin abandoned himself to thought. All sorts of thoughts would visit Chonkin. From his close observation of life and his fathoming of life's laws, Chonkin had understood that it is usually warm in the summer and cold in the winter. But if it was the other way around, he thought, cold in the summer and warm in the winter, then summer would be called winter and winter would be called summer. Then a second, even more serious and interesting thought came into Chonkin's head, but it slipped his mind immediately and he couldn't recall it for the life of him. To know that he had lost a thought grieved Chonkin sorely. Right then he received a poke in the side. He looked over and saw Samushkin, whom he had completely forgotten. Samushkin's index finger was beckoning him to lean closer and hear what Samushkin had to tell him. Chonkin wavered. Samushkin was up to something again. With the senior politruk there, Samushkin wouldn't dare shout in his ear, but he just might spit in it.

"What do you want?" asked Chonkin in a whisper.

"Don't be scared," whispered Samushkin, leaning closer to Chonkin's ear. "Did you know that Stalin had two wives at the same time?"

"Get out of here."

"I'm telling you the truth. Two wives."

"Cut it out," said Chonkin.

"You don't believe me, ask the senior politruk."

"What's it to me?" Chonkin held his ground.

"Go on, ask him, be a friend. I'd do it myself, but I'd feel funny. I asked a lot of questions last time."

It was plain from Samushkin's face how very important it was that Chonkin do him this really very small favor. And kindhearted Chonkin, who didn't know how to refuse anyone or anything, finally gave in.

Balashov was still reading his notes. The senior politruk was only half listening, certain that conscientious Balashov had copied everything straight from the textbook and would not say anything the least bit surprising. But time was running short and Yartsev had to question the other students. He cut Balashov off.

"Thank you, Comrade Balashov," he said. "I have one other question for you—why is our army called a people's army?"

"Because it serves the people," answered Balashov without a moment's hesitation.

"Correct. And the armies of the capitalist countries, who do they serve?"

"A clique of capitalists."

"Correct," said Yartsev with satisfaction. "It has been a pleasure to listen to you. You think correctly and you draw the proper conclusions from the material we have covered. I am giving you an Excellent and will request the battalion leader to have a note of our appreciation entered into your service record."

"I serve the working people," said Balashov softly.

"Be seated, Comrade Balashov." The senior politruk's narrow, piercing eyes scanned the soldiers sitting in front of him. "Who would like to develop the previous speaker's thoughts further?"

Chonkin's hand jerked up, catching Yartsev's attention.

"Comrade Chonkin, how do you wish this gesture of yours to be interpreted? Could you perhaps be battling beetles again?"

Chonkin stood up. "A question, Comrade Senior Politruk."

"Go right ahead." A broad grin spread across the politruk's face: Chonkin's question could at best be very simple, or it might even be quite stupid, but nevertheless he, Yartsev, was duty-bound to descend to the level of any soldier and dispel his ignorance. Yartsev was mistaken. The question may indeed have been stupid, but it was not so simple.

"Is it true," asked Chonkin, "that Stalin used to have two wives?"

Yartsev jumped to his feet as if propelled by a tack.

"What?!" he roared, quivering with fury and fear. "What did you say? You're not getting me mixed up in this." But Yartsev immediately realized that that was the wrong thing to have said and stopped talking altogether.

Chonkin's eyes blinked in confusion. He had no idea what had aroused the senior politruk's fury and attempted to explain himself.

"I didn't mean anything, Comrade Senior Politruk. I only wanted to ask . . . I just heard that Comrade Stalin had . . ."

"Heard? Heard from who?" shouted Yartsev in a frenzy. "From who, I'm asking you. You're singing someone else's tune, Chonkin!"

Chonkin looked hopelessly over at Samushkin, who was serenely leafing through the pages of *The Short History of the All-Union Communist Party* as if the entire incident had nothing at all to do with him. Chonkin could see that Samushkin would deny any reference to himself without batting an eye. And although Chonkin still could not understand the politruk's unbelievable anger, it was clear to him that Samushkin had taken him for another ride, not for a "bicycle ride" this time, but maybe for an even worse kind.

Having started shouting, the senior politruk was unable to stop. He chewed Chonkin out, saying that this was what political immaturity and loss of vigilance can lead to, that people like Chonkin were gold mines for our enemies, who were always on the lookout for the least little crack to worm their way through and start hatching their shameless plots; that people like Chonkin were a disgrace, not only to their unit and company, but to the entire Red Army as well.

There's no telling how Yartsev's monologue would have ended if it hadn't been interrupted by Alimov, the orderly. Alimov had clearly run the whole distance from camp, for it took him a long time to catch his breath. Panting, frozen in a salute, he looked at Yartsev without saying a single word, which made Yartsev lose his train of thought and bark: "What do you want?"

"Comrade Senior Politruk, I request permission to address you," Alimov managed to pant out.

"Permission granted," said Yartsev, lowering himself wearily back onto the stump.

"By order of the battalion commander, Private Chonkin is summoned to the barracks."

This turn of events gladdened both Chonkin and Yartsev.

As he unhitched his horse, Chonkin cursed himself for letting a devil get hold of his tongue. The first question he asks since he's been in the service and what a hornet's nest he stirs up! Chonkin firmly resolved that from there on in he would never ask another question, and that way keep himself from getting into a mess so bad there'd be no getting out.

5

Master Sergeant Peskov was sitting in the storage and supply room slicing soap with a piece of brown thread in preparation for his regiment's forthcoming bath day. It was then that he was called to the phone and ordered by

Battalion Commander Pakhomov to locate Chonkin at once, to issue him a weapon and rations for a week, and to prepare him for a prolonged stretch of guard duty.

Peskov had no idea what kind of duty was involved or why it was to be prolonged, but said "Yes, sir!" because he was accustomed to carrying out orders unquestioningly and by the book. He sent the quartermaster, Trofimovich, who had been helping him slice the soap, to the warehouse, and dispatched the orderly, Alimov, to try to locate Chonkin. That done, he sliced up the remaining soap, wiped his hands on a towel, and sat down to write a letter to his fiancée, who lived in the town of Kotlas.

Peskov had served an additional two years after his first term of duty and now wanted to re-enlist again, but his fiancée did not approve. She considered it better for a married man to work in a factory somewhere than to serve in the army. Master Sergeant Peskov did not agree with her. He wrote:

And, Lyuba, you keep on writing that civilian life is better than the service. Lyuba, you have the wrong idea about it, because the chief thing for every soldier in the Red Army is to endure all the burdens and privations of military service. And also to train his subordinates. You know that our country is encircled on all four sides by a capitalist encirclement and our enemies have but a single aim—to strangle the land of the Soviets and drive our wives and children into slavery. For that reason, every year young soldiers, the sons of workers and the toiling peasantry, are called up to military service. And we veteran soldiers have to pass on to them our battle experience and our military skill. Our cause is training the young generation. But this is a very important question—people need strictness on an everyday basis because you act decent to people and they turn around and act like swine to you. Let's take a regular family, for example. If you don't bring up a child strictly, using the strap on him, then he'll grow up to be a sneak or a hooligan, and children, Lyuba, are our purpose in life. And if you don't have a purpose in life, you can end up hanging yourself or shooting yourself (take Mayakovsky or Esenin, for example).

Peskov put a period at the end of the sentence, dipped his pen in the ink, and began to consider what he would write next. He wanted to unite somehow the question of family and marriage with that of the state's defense capability, but didn't quite see how yet. At that point someone knocking at his door derailed his train of thought.

"Come in," Peskov called out.

Chonkin entered. Fouling up at political training had so distressed Chonkin that he even forgot that regulations required him to report his arrival. Instead, Chonkin said simply: "You called me, Comrade Sergeant?"

"I didn't call you. I ordered you to report," Peskov corrected him. "Go back out, then come back and report your arrival the way a soldier is supposed to."

Chonkin turned toward the door.

"As you were!" said Peskov. "How do you do an about-face?"

Chonkin tried to do a turn correctly but, getting mixed up, he kept turning to the right. It was only on the third try that he managed a turn that was anything like smooth, and this time Peskov finally took pity on him and allowed him to leave, return, and report his arrival. Then he thrust the regulations on guard and garrison duty into Chonkin's hands and dispatched him to the barracks to learn the duties of a sentry. Peskov himself remained in the supply room to finish up his letter, to which he now added new thoughts, inspired by his dealings with Chonkin:

So, Lyuba, at the factory you have an engineer with a higher education, with some ten to twelve men under him. He can order them to do anything at work, but after work or on their days off they're not subordinate to him any more and they can do whatever they want— as the saying goes, you're your own boss and I'm mine. For us, in the army, such a situation is impossible. In my company I have ninety-seven privates and junior command personnel. I can issue them any order at any time and they carry it out unquestioningly, to the letter, on time, and according to the regulations and according to military discipline, even though I have only a fifth-grade education.

At this point Peskov was interrupted again. The door opened and someone entered the storage and supply room. Thinking it was Chonkin again, Peskov said, without turning his head: "Go back out, knock, and come in again."

"I'll knock you" was the answer he received.

Peskov spun around on his stool like a top, jumping to attention at the same time, for it was Lieutenant Colonel Pakhomov he saw before him.

"Comrade Lieutenant Colonel, during your absence there were no incidents in the company . . ." Peskov began, saluting, but Pakhomov cut him short.

"Where is Chonkin?"

"Sent to familiarize himself with the regulations on guard and garrison duty," Peskov reported smartly.

"Sent where?" Pakhomov had not understood.

"To the barracks, Comrade Lieutenant Colonel," Peskov rapped out.

"What, are you crazy?" bellowed Pakhomov. "There's a plane waiting for him and you have him studying regulations. What did I say to you on the telephone? To summon Chonkin at once and prepare him for departure."

"Yes, Comrade Lieutenant Colonel!" said Peskov, dashing for the door.

"Wait a minute! Have you gotten his rations?"

"Trofimovich went for them, but he's still not back. Maybe he's talking with the warehouseman."

"He'll have a talk all right—with me. Go bring him and the rations here at once!"

"I'll send the orderly right away," said Peskov.

"Forget the orderly," said Pakhomov. "You go yourself and on the double! I'll give you five minutes. Twenty-four hours' arrest for every minute over. You understand? On the double!"

The lieutenant colonel spoke quite differently with Master Sergeant Peskov than he had with the regimental commander an hour before. And the way Sergeant Peskov had spoken to Chonkin bore little resemblance to the way he now spoke with Lieutenant Colonel Pakhomov. As for Chonkin, there was no one he could talk to that way except for a horse, because, in rank, a horse was even lower than Chonkin. And lower than a horse there was nothing.

Master Sergeant Peskov dashed outside, where he glanced at his pocket watch and noted the time; he was about to proceed at a walk but looked around and saw the lieutenant colonel watching him from the window. Peskov took off at a run.

He had to run to the opposite end of the camp, some

four hundred meters. There was not a single structure along the way for him to duck behind and catch his breath out of Pakhomov's sight. Peskov felt as if he were on a firing range. He was twenty-five years old, but in the entire two years since his re-enlistment he had run only once, and then it had been fear which had run away with him. The loss of this habit now made itself felt, though it must be said that the heat was something to contend with as well.

As usual the warehouse was cool and shadowy. Scattered rays of sunlight glanced in through the holes in the walls and roof, piercing the darkness, highlighting the boxes, barrels, sacks, and carcasses of beef which hung from a crossbeam. By the half-opened door Dudnik the warehouseman sat dozing, exhausted from the heat, his chin propped on one hand. As soon as he dropped off to sleep, his chin would slip off his sweaty palm and slam against the table. Dudnik would open his eyes, glare with suspicion and hostility at the table, but then, unable to resist the temptation, would once again prop his chin on his hand.

His tongue hanging out, Peskov came dashing up to the warehouse, sank down beside Dudnik on a barley crate, and asked: "Have you seen Trofimovich?"

Once again Dudnik slammed against the table, then looked dazedly over at Peskov.

"What?"

Peskov gazed with respect at Dudnik's chin, which could withstand such blows.

"Your teeth all in one piece?" he asked.

"The teeth are all right," replied Dudnik, shaking his head and yawning. "I'm just afraid the table's going to have to be repaired. Who you looking for?"

"Has Trofimovich been here?"

"Ai, Trofimovich. Trofimovich was here," said Dudnik, closing his eyes and once again propping his chin on his hand.

"Don't go to sleep yet." Peskov shook Dudnik by the shoulder. "Where'd he go?"

Without opening his eyes, Dudnik waved his free hand in the direction of the door. "That way."

Realizing that was as much as he was going to get from Dudnik, Peskov went back outside, then halted in hesitation. Which way to go? He mentally reviewed all the places Trofimovich could possibly be, but he could be anywhere and Peskov found it difficult to come up with one place which was any more likely than another. He took his pocket watch out and glanced at it quickly. More than five minutes had passed since the order had been issued to him. He sighed. He knew that Lieutenant Colonel Pakhomov never spoke idly. Then Peskov suddenly realized that something of the first importance must be going on if Chonkin was being sent somewhere by plane. Maybe Chonkin himself had suddenly become someone very important? He, Peskov, had never been taken anywhere by plane. The realization of the importance of what was happening made Peskov's brain work more efficiently as he once again tried to puzzle out just exactly where Trofimovich could be hiding himself; then without further hesitation he dashed off toward the commissary.

Peskov had not been mistaken. Trofimovich was there, standing beside Tosya the storekeeper in the empty store, telling her the plot of the film *Four People's Hearts*. A knapsack containing Chonkin's rations lay on the floor by Trofimovich's feet.

A minute later Lieutenant Colonel Pakhomov looked out the window and saw the following sight: Trofimovich leaping nimbly down the path to the barracks, the knapsack on his back, with Peskov running behind him, urging him on with his fist.

By evening of that same day, Master Sergeant Peskov was in solitary confinement in the battalion guardhouse continuing his letter to his fiancée from the town of Kotlas.

Naturally, Lyuba, all things considered [he wrote], army life is no lump of sugar. There's a kind of person who doesn't use his position to strengthen military discipline but, just the other way around, uses it to lord it over his subordinates. And of course in civilian life such a situation is impossible because there, after a person's put in his eight hours at the factory, he can think of himself as a free man, and if some engineer or foreman orders him to do anything, he can just tell him where to go and he'd be right to do it.

6

How true it is that a person's life is full of surprises. Had everything taken its usual course that day, Chonkin would have hauled firewood to the kitchen after political training, then had his lunch, his nap, and after his nap, a bath. New uniforms were supposed to be issued at the bath. (Chonkin was already counting on setting aside the uniform and two sets of foot cloths for his upcoming demobilization.) After the bath it would have been back to the stables, then to the warehouse to pick up the food for dinner, then, in the evening, an amateur concert given outdoors on an open platform.

And suddenly—bango—he was summoned to barracks, issued a rifle, a greatcoat roll, and a knapsack, put in an airplane, and an hour and a half later he was already the devil knows where, in some village he had never heard of before, had never suspected even existed.

Chonkin was still queasy from the first plane ride of his life, but the two pilots (the one who had taken him there and the one there waiting) covered the damaged plane with a tarp they lashed to the ground. Then they got into the plane that was working and flew away as if they had never been there at all, leaving Chonkin face to face with the plane and the crowd surrounding it. The crowd, however, gradually began to disperse, leaving Chonkin all by himself.

Chonkin walked around the plane, tugged at the ailerons and rudder bar, and gave the wheel a good kick. Then he spat. Why guard it? Guard it from whom, and for how long? He'd been told nothing. Lieutenant Colonel Pakhomov had said maybe a week, maybe more. In a week you could die from loneliness. Before, he'd been able to talk with his horse and that had been just fine. He even liked talking with horses better than with people, because if you say the wrong thing to a person you can get yourself in hot water, but no matter what you say to a horse it'll accept it. Chonkin chatted with his horse, consulted with it, told it the story of his life, told it about the sergeant, complained about Samushkin and Shurka the cook, and whether the horse understood or not, it would still wave its tail, nod its head—the horse would respond. But how were you supposed to have a talk with a contraption, a bunch of lifeless nuts and bolts? Chonkin spat once again and paced from the nose to the tail, then back from the tail to the nose.

He took a look around. The local scenery did not please Chonkin at all. Three hundred paces from where he stood, a small, lead-colored river (with the odd name of the Tyopa) gleamed through the willows. Chonkin did not have to know the river's name to find the river repulsive. The stunted grove which stretched farther down along the Tyopa was even less to Chonkin's liking, and the rest of the scenery wasn't worth talking about. The ground was bare, uneven, rocky, the village poor. Two houses had board siding, the rest, made of darkened logs, were half sunk into the ground. Some were roofed with shingle, some with straw.

The village was deserted. No matter how much you looked, there wasn't a soul to be seen. In this, there was nothing surprising—everyone was working. And those who weren't had taken refuge from the heat in their huts. Only a skewbald calf that had clearly strayed from the herd was lying in the middle of the road, its tongue hanging out from the heat.

A man with rakes tied to his back bicycled past along the riverbank.

"Hey, hey, hey!" Chonkin shouted out to him, but the rider did not stop or turn around—plainly, he hadn't heard.

Ivan placed his knapsack on the wing of the plane and undid it to see what they'd packed for him. The knapsack contained two loaves of bread, a can of meat, a can of preserved fish, a can of food concentrate, a piece of sausage hard as wood, and a few lumps of sugar wrapped in newspaper. Not what you'd call generous for a week. If he'd known what was coming, he'd have swiped himself something in the pilots' mess, but now what was the use . . .

Chonkin walked the length of the plane again. A few steps forward, a few steps back. Of course his situation had its good side. Now he was not the Chonkin you could just walk up to, slap on the shoulder, and say, "Hey there, Chonkin," and now you couldn't spit in his ear either, to take another example. Now he was a sentry—his person was inviolable. You'd think twice before you spat in *his* ear. The least little thing and it's "Halt! Who goes there?" "Stop, or I'll shoot!" Serious business.

But if you looked at the whole thing from another angle . . .

Chonkin stopped and, resting against the plane, put his mind to work. They had left him alone for a week with no one to relieve him. Then what? According to the regulations, a sentry was forbidden to eat, drink, smoke, laugh, sing, talk, or relieve himself. He was supposed to stand there a week! In a week, like it or not, you're going to break the rules! With that in mind, Chonkin walked back to the tail and broke the rules right then and there. He looked all around. Nothing. Chonkin began to sing:

A Cossack galloped through the valley,
through the Caucasian lands . . .

This was the only song he knew from beginning to end. It was a simple song. Each pair of lines was repeated:

Through the green orchard he did gallop,
a ring was flashing on his hand . . .
Through the green orchard he did gallop,
a ring was flashing on his hand . . .

Chonkin fell silent and cocked an ear. Still nothing! You could sing till you burst and nobody cared. Suddenly he felt even lonelier than before and experienced a genuine need to talk with somebody about anything.

His back to the plane, Chonkin now caught sight of a wagon, which was raising a cloud of dust on the road to the village. Chonkin shaded his eyes with his hand and, looking hard, could make out some ten women sitting in the wagon, their legs dangling over the side, and another one, wearing a red dress and standing, driving the horses. This sight brought Chonkin an indescribable excitement which grew greater the closer the wagon came. When it was fairly close, Chonkin straightened out his uniform, buttoned his collar, and dashed up on the road.

"Hey, girls!" he shouted. "Over here!"

The girls set to hollering and laughing, and the one driving the horses shouted back in reply: "All at once or one at a time?"

"All together and sort things out after," said Chonkin, waving at them.

The girls grew even more boisterous and motioned to Chonkin as if inviting him up on their wagon, but then the driver shouted out something that stopped even Chonkin in his tracks.

"Heeeey, giiiirls," yelped Chonkin from an excess of emotion, but they could no longer hear him. The wagon had disappeared around the bend and all that remained was the white dust that hung a long time in the sweltering air.

All of this had a most pleasant effect on Chonkin. He leaned on his rifle and was overcome by thoughts of the opposite sex, thoughts by no means permitted by the regulations. He looked around again, but not as he had done before, with nothing in mind, just for the sake of a look; now he had something quite definite in mind.

And he found it.

In the vegetable garden closest to him, Chonkin caught

sight of Nyura Belyashova, who, after her afternoon rest, had come out again to mound her potatoes. Her chopper moved in measured rhythms as she turned various sides to Chonkin, who watched her closely, evaluating one by one all the merits of her ample form.

Chonkin was immediately attracted to her, but glancing back at the airplane, he could only sigh. Once again he began pacing the length of the plane—a few steps forward, a few steps back. Somehow or other the steps forward kept getting longer while the steps back kept getting shorter, until finally Chonkin's chest bumped up against a fence made of long, crooked poles. This came as such a surprise for Chonkin himself that, encountering Nyura's inquisitive gaze, he realized that he ought to make some explanation for doing what he'd done and explained himself as follows: "I could use some water." For emphasis he poked his belly with one finger.

"Don't see why not," said Nyura. "Except my water's warm."

"Anything's all right," said Chonkin agreeably.

Nyura lay the chopper down in a furrow, went into her house, and returned at once, holding a black iron ladle. The water really was warm and flat and tasted woody from the barrel. Chonkin took a sip, then bent forward and poured the rest over his head.

"Ai, that's good," he said with exaggerated heartiness. "Ain't it the truth."

"Hang the ladle on the fence," said Nyura, returning to her chopper.

Encountering Chonkin had excited Nyura as well, but she didn't let on, expecting that he would go. But Chonkin didn't feel like leaving. He stood there for a time saying nothing at all, then asked the question that went right to the heart of the matter.

"You live alone or have you got a husband?"

"What do you want to know for?" asked Nyura.

"Just curious," answered Chonkin.

"Married or not, it's none of your business."

This answer satisfied Chonkin. It had to mean that she was alone, but her maidenly pride prevented her from answering such questions directly.

"Maybe I can give you a hand?" offered Chonkin.

"No need," said Nyura. "I can manage."

But Chonkin had already tossed his rifle over the fence and was wriggling his way through the rails. At first Nyura protested for propriety's sake, but then she gave Chonkin her chopper and went and got herself another one from the cow shed. Four hands make light work. Chonkin worked easily and quickly, you could tell it wasn't the first time he'd done that sort of thing. At first Nyura tried to keep up with him, but then, seeing her efforts were useless, she fell hopelessly behind. When they stopped for a break, she remarked with curiosity: "You can tell you're from the country."

"It really shows?" asked Chonkin, surprised.

"Sure does," said Nyura, her eyes dropping in embarrassment. "We've had city folk come here to help us. Made you ashamed just to watch them. Didn't even know how to hold a chopper in their hands. I wonder what they teach them there in the city."

"That's easy," announced Chonkin. "To live off the fat of the countryside."

"That's for sure," agreed Nyura.

Chonkin spat on his hands and set back to work. Every once in a while, as she followed behind him, Nyura would steal a glance at her new acquaintance. Naturally, she had immediately noticed that he was anything but tall, that he wasn't one of the best-looking men she'd ever seen, but after all her long years alone, even someone like Chonkin looked good. She saw he was a handy guy with a kind of a way about him and it was plain to see he'd be a big help. The more she thought about it, the more she liked him, and something like hope began to glimmer in her soul.

7

Nyura was all alone in the world. In the entire village, there was no woman more alone than she, not counting Granny Dunya, but Granny's life was already drawing to a close, while Nyura had scarcely turned twenty-four. She was in the very bloom of life, and yet for marrying it was, let's say, getting a little on the late side. Girls who were quicker at things had jumped into marriage before they were twenty and started right in having children (Taika Gorshkova, who was the same age as Nyura, had had her fifth boy that winter). It wouldn't have been so bad if she'd been worse-looking than the others, but she just wasn't. God had grudged her neither face nor figure, and while she may not have been a beauty she was certainly no freak either. Even Ninka Kurzova, who had a birthmark in the middle of her face, had found her happiness and married Kolka and was already in her fourth or fifth month.

Of course Nyura wasn't the only one who hadn't found anybody, but the others at least had their parents or their brothers and sisters. Nyura had no one. There had been two older brothers, but she didn't remember them. One lost his life in a fire at the age of three and the other one, a bit older, had died from spotted fever.

Nyura's mother had died four years ago. For two years

before, she'd been complaining about the small of her back—something was broken or bent out of shape, maybe from a cold, maybe from hard work, how can you tell? Maybe she should have lain down for a while and taken a good rest, but how could you when the brigade leader does everything but drag you out of the house with a rope—you had to work. And then there was her own house too, little jobs, big jobs, something always needed doing. Sure, you could go see the feldsher, but he was seven kilometers away in Dolgov. That's seven kilometers there and seven back. Besides, he had the same treatment for everyone—soak your feet in hot water, then lie under a quilt. It'll be gone by morning, he'd tell you. You couldn't get off work if you didn't have a fever. They'd tell you: If we let everybody off, who'd do the work?

When it got really bad and she started screaming out loud, Nyura's father went to the chairman (the one before Golubev) to ask for a horse, but the chairman told him: "I can't give you one special, but if there's one going, he's yours." By the time one was going, there was no longer any need for it. The Krasnovskoye cemetery was nearby, just behind where people had their gardens, and they carried the coffin there by hand.

Nyura's father lived on another year in Krasnoye, but once he got a passport on the sly, he went off to the city to try to make a living. He worked as a jack-of-all-trades during the construction of an electric power station, then joined the police. Often when people from his village drove to town to sell produce from the kolkhoz, they would see him in the market walking around with his uniform and his gun, chasing off speculators. At first he wrote Nyura every once in a while but then he got married, his wife had a child, and his letters came even less often, finally stopping completely, and now only rarely did he send her his greetings through a mutual acquaintance.

Maybe another reason nothing had turned out for Nyura in the way of marriage was her timid nature and the fact that she did not have the knack of making herself attractive. Her first prospect broke off with her because she didn't have a word to say, he said you couldn't even sit and talk with her; the second tried to get her to agree to do what he wanted before they were married and his feelings were hurt because she didn't trust him. She trusted the third one, but he too broke off with her—because she went along too easily. Suddenly there weren't that many prospects left and as time passed they grew even fewer and the new crop had their own girls to choose from. And so that is how it happened that Nyura was left alone.

Solitude left its special mark on her life. It could even be seen in her relation to her cow. For other people a cow is a cow. They feed it, they milk it, they drive it to pasture, and that's that. But Nyura just about waited on hers— she'd scrub it clean, pick burrs from its side. And she would speak to her cow with tenderness in her voice as if it were a person and, if she happened to have a treat (a piece of sugar, some piroshki), she would share it with her cow, because the cow also related to her on a person-to-person basis. When the herd was being driven back into the village, Nyura's cow would break away and run home as fast as her legs would carry her, she'd been missing her Nyura so much. She liked to play with her mistress —she'd hook at Nyura with her horn as if she meant it, only it was really done gently, just as a joke. But if she saw someone giving Nyura a hard time, she'd quit playing, lower her head, her eyes would grow bloodshot, she'd go for the offender and, whoever it was, he'd better watch out!

As for Borka the hog, he was always trailing after Nyura like a dog. About two years back Nyura had gotten him from the kolkhoz as a three-day-old suckling, figuring to slaughter him at some point. But the suckling turned out to be sickly and was ill a good deal. Nyura took care of him as if he were a child: she fed him milk with a baby bottle, put hot-water bottles on his belly, bathed him with soap in the trough, wrapped him in her kerchief, and took him to bed with her. Nyura pulled him through, and when he was grown she couldn't bring herself to slaughter him. So Borka lived on with Nyura instead of a dog. Dirty and skinny, he'd dash about the yard, chase chickens, accompany Nyura to the post office, and meet her when she came back. His squeal of joy on her return could be heard throughout the entire village.

Even her chickens were not like other people's chickens. When Nyura sat down on her porch, they'd be right there beside her. One would perch on her shoulder, another on her head, and they'd sit there without stirring a feather, as if on a perch. Afraid to scare them, Nyura wouldn't stir either. A lot of people in the village made fun of her for this but Nyura didn't take it to heart. Instead she would think: Just let her find a man, even if he wasn't much to look at or even not so bright, just as long as he was a good man and good to her, and when she no longer felt obligated to him, then she would open up her whole soul to him. And now this short man, in uniform, his red ears sticking out from his cap, was walking ahead of her down the furrow swinging a chopper as he went. Who was he, this man, and what did he want? Maybe just to pass the time out of boredom, but maybe not. It's always hard to tell right off.

No matter how long it is, even a summer's day comes to an end. The air could be felt stirring, a coolness blew in from the Tyopa, the large red sun, sliced in two by a feathery cloud, had touched the edge of the smoky horizon. The cattle began lowing at the other end of the village and, leaving Chonkin in the garden, Nyura ran off to meet her cow, Beauty. Along the way she met up with Ninka Kurzova, who was carrying a long switch and also going to get her cow. They walked on together.

"And so, get your potatoes in?" asked Ninka with open spite. Needless to say, the entire village was already aware that Nyura was not working her garden alone.

"There's still a little left to do," replied Nyura.

"But now with a helper, it's a little easier." Ninka winked.

"Sure. Many hands make light work," said Nyura and blushed.

"He's a decent guy at least?" asked Ninka, efficiently gathering her information.

"Who knows?" Nyura shrugged her shoulders. "You can't tell much at first. A little on the short side, but he knows how to work. No way I could keep up with him in the garden."

"Hmmmm," approved Ninka. "And what's his name?"

"Ivan," declared Nyura proudly, as if the name were her own.

"Single?"

"I didn't ask."

"Should have. You've got to ask right off."

"But it would make me feel funny to ask right off."

"Of course asking point-blank makes you feel funny," replied Ninka confidently, "but do it sort of offhand, then it's all right. Though he's going to lie to you anyhow."

"Why should he lie?"

"What else can he do?" said Ninka. "That's the story of our life—men tell lies and women believe them. And this one's a soldier to top it off. All he wants is to kill some time. Try to find out when you talk with him and see if you can't get a peek at his papers. But maybe it doesn't tell in their papers, they're not the same as a passport."

"So it looks hopeless?" asked Nyura.

"That's the way it looks."

"I don't know why, but I trust him," said Nyura. "He doesn't look like the lying type."

"If you trust him, that's your business," said Ninka indifferently. "But if I were you, I wouldn't have allowed him anything beforehand."

"Who's allowing him anything?" said Nyura, feeling embarrassed.

"I didn't mean that you are, but that you might. You know how men are, especially soldiers, they get what they want, then they laugh at you."

At that Ninka jumped toward the fence because Beauty was galloping down the road through the village with a little dog yapping desperately behind her. Beauty was racing at Nyura at such speed that it seemed there was no force that could stop her, but then she came to a perfect halt right in front of Nyura.

"She's a devil, that one!" said Ninka in fright. "Careful she doesn't hook you, Nyura."

"Me she wouldn't hook," said Nyura confidently and began scratching Beauty between the horns. Out of breath from running so fast, Beauty's nostrils flared as she panted.

"And now where's that pest of mine?" said Ninka. "I'll go run and see—maybe she got in somebody's garden. Drop by for a chat," she said, her usual invitation. "We'll sing some songs and have a few laughs."

Then Ninka went on down the road swinging her switch.

On the way back, Nyura ran into Granny Dunya's and

bought a half liter of home brew from her. She was afraid that Granny Dunya would start asking her what the drink was for and Nyura thought of saying that it looked like her father might be coming. But Granny Dunya had been sampling her own concoction and had reached the point where absolutely nothing was of any interest to her.

By the time Nyura had milked the cow and come out onto the porch, Chonkin had already finished up the last potato bed and was sitting on the grass smoking.

"Tired?" asked Nyura.

"Hell no," said Chonkin. "I do this kind of work for fun."

"I've got the table set in there," said Nyura, overcoming her shyness.

"The table?" Chonkin's eyes lit up, then he recalled his situation and just sighed. "I can't. I'm sorry but I can't. I've got to stay over there." He waved his hand with annoyance at the plane.

"Lord, but who'd lay a hand on it!" said Nyura heatedly. "Around here people don't even lock their doors."

"They really don't?" asked Chonkin, his hopes up. "You mean it never happened that something belonging to somebody . . ."

"What do you mean," said Nyura. "I've lived here my whole life and I can't remember anything like that. One time when I was very little, this is even before the kolkhoz, Stepan Lukov—he lives over there on the other side of the office—couldn't find his horse and everybody said it was the gypsies. But then they found the horse—she'd just swum over to the other side of the river, that's all."

"But what if the kids get in there and start unscrewing stuff?" he asked, gradually yielding.

"The kids are all in bed by now," said Nyura.

"Well, all right," Ivan decided. "I'll come in for, say, ten minutes or so."

Chonkin picked up his rifle, Nyura collected the choppers.

The front part of her hut was clean and tidy. On the wide table there were a bottle with a rag for a stopper, a dish of fried potatoes, and another of cucumbers. Chonkin realized at once that there wasn't enough meat and, leaving his rifle there, ran back to the plane for his knapsack. Nyura cut the sausage up into thick slices right away but didn't open up any of the canned goods; she didn't want to lose any time.

She seated Chonkin on the bench by the wall and sat herself on a stool opposite him. Chonkin poured out the home brew, a full glass for himself and half a glass for Nyura; she wouldn't allow any more than that.

Chonkin raised his glass and proposed a toast. "To our meeting!"

Chonkin started feeling good after his second glass. He unbuttoned his field shirt, removed his belt, and sat leaning against the wall, all thought of the plane gone from his head. As if in a fog, Nyura's face floated in the gathering dusk, becoming two faces, then reuniting into one again. Chonkin felt cheerful, light, and free. He beckoned Nyura to him with an easy motion of his hand, saying: "Come here."

"What for?" asked Nyura.

"No reason."

"If there's no reason, we can talk just like this," resisted Nyura.

"Come on," said Chonkin dolefully. "I'm not going to bite you."

"This is just stupid," said Nyura, walking around the

table and sitting down on the bench to Chonkin's left, at a distance from him.

They both fell silent. The old clock on the wall opposite them was ticking loudly but couldn't be seen in the darkness of the room. Night had fallen.

Chonkin sighed deeply and moved closer to Nyura. Nyura sighed even more deeply and moved away. Chonkin sighed again and moved closer. Nyura sighed again and moved away. Soon she found herself at the very end of the bench. It wouldn't be safe to move any farther.

"Got cold in here, didn't it?" said Chonkin, placing his left hand on her shoulder.

"Not that cold," objected Nyura, trying to shrug his hand off her shoulder.

"I don't know, but my hands are freezing," said Chonkin, his right hand creeping onto her breasts.

"Do you always go around flying in airplanes?" asked Nyura, making a last desperate attempt to free herself.

"Always," said Chonkin, thrusting his hand under her arm and behind her back to unhook her bra.

8

It wasn't day but it wasn't night either, it wasn't light but it wasn't dark either. Chonkin had woken because he sensed someone was stealing his airplane. He jumped out of the bed—there was no one sleeping beside him—and ran out onto the porch. There he caught sight of Samushkin hitching up a white horse that looked like Roan to the plane. "What are you doing?" shouted Chonkin. Without answering him, Samushkin jumped quickly into the cabin and slapped the horse with the ends of the reins. The horse reared up and, flailing its hooves, began to fly up from the very earth. The same girls who had ridden past

Chonkin that day in the wagon were sitting on the lower wing dangling their feet. Nyura was among them, waving her chopper at Chonkin, signaling him to catch up. Chonkin took off at a run after the plane, and whenever it seemed he was just about there, the plane would again slip away from him. It was getting harder and harder to run, the rolled greatcoat flung over his shoulder and his rifle were keeping him back. He realized that he had no need whatsoever for the rifle because the sergeant had forgotten to issue him any ammunition. Once he threw the rifle away, he began to run much faster. Just when he had almost caught up with the plane and was about to grab hold of the chopper Nyura was holding out to him, the sergeant suddenly appeared before him and asked menacingly: "Why don't you salute?" Chonkin stopped for a moment in front of the sergeant, not knowing whether to answer him or to keep chasing after the plane. The sergeant shouted: "All right, ten times past the post and salute it every time!" Chonkin looked around hurriedly so he could carry out the sergeant's order before the plane flew even farther away, but there wasn't a post to be seen anywhere.

"You mean you don't see the post!" roared the sergeant. "All right then, I'll pull out your eye and show you how a soldier is supposed to see!" With those words, the sergeant walked up to Chonkin, pulled out his right eye, held it out in the air in front of him, and through his pulled-out eye Chonkin actually could see a broken-down post with a bulb burning on top of it. Chonkin thought: I wonder why the bulb's on, there's plenty of light without it. He took his eye back from the sergeant and set off toward the post, but then, remembering the plane, glanced back around.

The plane was right there behind him. It was hovering

motionless in the air while the horse flailed his hooves hopelessly, making no headway. She needs to be shoed, thought Chonkin and then noticed Senior Politruk Yartsev, who had come out from behind a mountain and was beckoning Chonkin with a crooked finger. Chonkin looked back at the sergeant to request his permission, but the sergeant was busy with something else—he was riding on Quartermaster Trofimovich's back around some kind of circular track in the center of which stood Lieutenant Colonel Pakhomov whacking each of them by turns with a long whip.

Chonkin walked up to Yartsev, who bent close to Chonkin's ear. This so frightened Chonkin that he covered his ear with the palm of his hand. "Don't be afraid, he won't spit," said Samushkin from behind him. Ivan took away his hand. Yartsev immediately turned into a beetle and crawled into Chonkin's ear. It tickled. Chonkin was about to shake Yartsev out when Yartsev said softly: "Don't get excited, Comrade Chonkin, your person is inviolable. I can't do anything to you. I have been instructed to inform you that Comrade Stalin never had any wives because he himself is a woman."

Having said that, Yartsev turned back into a man, jumped to the ground, and disappeared behind the mountain.

Just then Comrade Stalin descended slowly from the sky. He had a mustache, a pipe between his teeth, and was wearing a woman's dress. There was a rifle in his hands.

"Is this your rifle?" asked Stalin sternly, with a slight Georgian accent.

"Yes," mumbled Chonkin, tongue-tied, and he reached out for his rifle.

But Comrade Stalin moved away and said: "And where is the sergeant?"

The sergeant dashed over, riding Trofimovich, who pawed at the ground with his hooves, trying to buck the sergeant off, but the sergeant was holding him firmly by the ears.

"Comrade Sergeant," said Stalin. "Private Chonkin has abandoned his post and lost his combat weapon as well. Our Red Army has no need for soldiers like this. I advise you to shoot Comrade Chonkin."

The sergeant slid slowly off Trofimovich, took the rifle from Comrade Stalin, and ordered Chonkin: "Down!"

Chonkin lay down. The marshy dust beneath him was swallowing him up, slipping into his mouth, his ears, his eyes. He tried to rake the dust away with his hands while waiting for the command "As you were!" But the command did not come. Chonkin was sinking in deeper and deeper. Just then something cold touched the back of his neck. He knew it was the barrel of a rifle and that any second a shot would ring out . . .

Chonkin woke up in a cold sweat. There was some woman beside him, her head on his shoulder, but he could not immediately recall just who this woman was and how they came to be sleeping in the same bed. Only when he saw his rifle peacefully hanging on the coat rack did everything come back to him. Chonkin jumped onto the cold floor and raced to the window, stepping on the laces of his pant legs as he ran.

It was light out. The plane was still in the same place, its big ungainly wings clearly silhouetted against the brightening sky. Chonkin sighed in relief. Glancing back around, he met Nyura's gaze. She would have shut her eyes had there been time; now it would be stupid not to look, but she was ashamed to. She was also ashamed that her plump white arm was bare to the shoulder and outside the covers. Nyura slowly pulled her arm to her side in order to hide it, at the same time smiling in embarrassment. Chonkin was also embarrassed but, not wanting to show it and not knowing quite what to do, he strode over to Nyura, took her hand in his, shook it gently, and said: "How do you do."

That morning the women driving the cattle out to pasture saw Chonkin come barefoot and shirtless out of Nyura's house. He went over to the plane and spent quite a while getting it untied. Then he took down part of the fence, rolled the plane into Nyura's garden, and, finally, put the section of fence back in place again.

9

Chairman Golubev was distinguished by an irrepressible tendency to have second thoughts about everything. When his wife would ask him in the morning: "What would you like, an omelet or potatoes?" he would answer: "Give me potatoes."

She'd get the cast-iron pot of potatoes from the oven and at that very second he would realize with absolute certainty that what he really wanted was an omelet. His wife would shove the pot back into the oven and go out to the passageway for eggs. On her return she would be met by her husband's guilty look: he wanted potatoes again.

Sometimes he even grew angry: "Just give me one or the other and don't make me think about such stupid things!"

He was always oppressed by freedom of choice. He

suffered unbearably when pondering which shirt to wear that day, the green or the blue, or which boots, the old or the new. Truly a great deal had been done in Russia over the last twenty-odd years so that Golubev would have no reason to doubt, but all the same the doubts remained and sometimes they even extended to things which at that time were not to be doubted. It was no accident that Borisov, the Secretary of the District Commission Machine and Tractor Station, would sometimes say to Golubev: "Get rid of your doubts. It's time for work, not doubts." And sometimes he would also say: "Remember you are under constant surveillance."

However, this was something he said not only to Golubev but to many other people as well. Borisov wouldn't say what kind of surveillance or how it was being conducted, and perhaps he didn't know himself.

Once Borisov was conducting a District Committee conference for kolkhoz chairmen. The subject was the raising of milk production in the current quarter. Golubev's kolkhoz ranked somewhere in the middle of the indices and he was neither praised nor abused. Golubev just sat looking at the new plaster bust of Stalin which stood by the window on a brown stand. When the conference was over and everyone was beginning to leave, Borisov detained Golubev.

The secretary stopped by the bust of Stalin, stroked it mechanically on the head, and said: "Here's the thing, Ivan Timofeyevich, your Party Organizer, Partorg Kilin, says that you're not paying much attention to visual-aid campaigns. Specifically, you haven't given enough money for the industrial production growth chart."

"I didn't and I won't," said Golubev firmly. "I don't

have the money to build a cow shed, and all Kilin does is draw his diagrams, throwing away all the kolkhoz money."

"What do you mean, he throws away the money?" said the secretary. "Do you know what you're saying?"

"I know," said Ivan Timofeyevich. "I understand everything. It's just that I can't spare the money. The kolkhoz has so little, we don't even know how we're going to plug up the holes. But of course it's all got to come out of my hide because I'm the chairman."

"First you're a Communist, then you're a chairman. And diagrams have great political significance. It's strange to hear a Communist underestimate them. And I still don't know whether what you're saying is just an error or a firm conviction. But if you're going to stick to that position, we'll have to take a good hard look at you again, we'll look right into your very heart, goddamnit!" In his anger Borisov whacked Stalin on the head, then shook his hand in pain. Instantly, the expression of pain on his face changed into one of mortal fear.

Borisov's mouth went dry. He opened his mouth and stared at Golubev as if hypnotized. Golubev, meanwhile, was scared to death himself. He hadn't wanted to see it, but he had seen it, he had! And now what was there to do? Pretend he hadn't noticed? But what if Borisov ran and confessed, then Borisov would be out of trouble and he, Golubev, would catch it for not reporting Borisov in the first place. And if he did report it, they'd be glad to lock him up just because he'd seen what he'd seen.

Both Borisov and Golubev had in mind the story of the schoolboy who aimed his slingshot at his teacher and hit instead a Portrait, breaking the glass. If he had merely knocked the teacher's eye out, they might have let him off as a juvenile, but hitting the Portrait was no more and no less than an attempted assassination. The whereabouts of that schoolboy were presently unknown.

Borisov was the first to find a way out of the predicament. He fumbled a metal cigarette case out of his pocket, opened it, and held it out to Golubev. Golubev hesitated—should I take one or not? He finally decided and took one.

"Yes, and what were we talking about?" asked Borisov as if nothing had happened, though he moved a little farther away from the bust, just to be on the safe side.

"Visual-aid campaigns," Golubev reminded him obligingly, getting a better hold on himself.

"So what I'm saying," said Borisov, his tone of voice quite different now, "is that you must not underestimate the political significance of visual-aid campaigns, Ivan Timofeyevich, and I ask you, as a friend, to please take care of this."

"All right, I will," said Golubev gloomily, anxious to leave.

"So we see eye to eye," said Borisov, in better spirits. He took Golubev by the arm and, while seeing him to the door, said with lowered voice: "And one more thing, Vanyushka, as a comrade I want to warn you, be careful, you are under constant surveillance."

Golubev went outside. The day was still dry and sunny, which the chairman noted with displeasure, since it was high time for some rain. His horse, hitched to an iron fence, was reaching out for a nettle bush, but it was just a little too far away. Golubev clambered up onto his two-wheeled cart and gave the horse its head. The horse went one block and then, without even being told to, stopped from sheer habit across from a wooden building with a sign TEAROOM. A cart full of milk cans stood by the tearoom. The chairman immediately recognized the cart as belonging to his kolkhoz. Golubev tied his own horse to the same post as the other horse, climbed up the rickety porch steps, and opened the door. The tearoom smelled of beer and sauerkraut soup.

The bored woman behind the counter looked up to see who had come in. "Hello, Ivan Timofeyevich."

"Hello, Anyuta," answered the chairman, casting a glance at the corner where Burly sat finishing a beer. When he saw the chairman, Burly stood up.

"It's all right, sit down," motioned Golubev, waiting for Anyuta to pour him his usual—a hundred fifty grams of vodka and a glass of beer. Then he poured the vodka into the beer as he always did and went over to Burly's table. Burly tried to get up again, but Golubev held him down by the shoulder.

"The milk turned in?" asked the chairman, sipping his drink.

"All turned in," said Burly. "They said the fat content was low."

"They'll fix it up," said Golubev, shrugging. "Why are you sitting here?"

"I just met Nyurka from the post office and I promised her a lift back," explained Burly. "That's why I'm waiting."

"Well, so, she still living with her soldier?" asked Ivan Timofeyevich with some curiosity.

"And why shouldn't she be?" said Burly. "He's better than a maid, that's for sure. She goes to work and he fetches the water, chops the firewood, and cooks the soup. Then he puts on her apron and walks around like a woman doing the housework. I haven't seen this myself, but now people are saying he's even embroidering nap-kins." Burly burst out laughing. "I swear, in all my born days I never saw a man go around in a woman's apron and do embroidery too. But here's the interesting part—he was supposed to be sent here for a week and it's been a week and a half already and he's not budging. I don't know, Ivan Timofeyevich, maybe it's just their ignorance talking, but folks have got the notion that that soldier's not here just for nothing and some'll tell you straight out that he's here as part of an investigation."

"What kind of investigation?" The chairman's ears pricked up.

Burly knew how nervous Golubev was on this point and purposely had been egging him on. He noted with pleasure that his words were having the right effect.

"Who knows what kind," said Burly. "One thing's for sure, though, they wouldn't just keep him here for no reason. If the plane is busted, it should be fixed. And if it's in too bad a shape to fix, then you just get rid of it. Why keep a man there for no reason? That's why folks have their doubts, Ivan Timofeyevich. There's a rumor going around"—Burly lowered his voice and leaned to-ward the chairman—"they're going to break the kolkhozes up."

"Forget it," said the chairman angrily. "That'll never happen and don't get your hopes up. It's work that needs doing, not collecting rumors."

Golubev finished off his boilermaker and stood up.

"Here's what you do, Burly," he said in conclusion. "Don't wait for Belyashova if she takes too long. No rea-son to. Let her walk home herself. She's no grand lady."

Having said goodbye to Anyuta, the chairman left, mounted his cart, and set off for home. But Golubev had been struck by Burly's words, especially when taken together with Borisov's warning that he was under constant surveillance. But what kind of surveillance? And how was it being conducted? Maybe by means of that soldier? Hadn't he been sent there specially? True, he didn't look like the sort they'd send, but those who did the sending were no dummies—they wouldn't send somebody you could tell right off had been specially sent. If you could only know for sure. But how could you find out? At that moment a daring thought entered Golubev's mind. And what if I go right up to this soldier, bang my fist on the table, and say to him: What is your assignment and who sent you here? And if that gets me in trouble, better it should happen right away than to sit around waiting, without even knowing what kind of trouble I'm in.

10

So, a week and a half had passed since Chonkin had come to Krasnoye and settled in at Nyura's. He was already used to the place, had gotten to know everybody, and felt right at home. There were no signs that someday Chonkin would be taken away from Krasnoye. It could not be said that Chonkin disliked this life. On the contrary, there was no reveille, no taps, not to mention no calisthenics or political training. Although he had done all right in the army as far as food was concerned, here in Krasnoye he had bread, milk, eggs, all fresh, onions right from the garden, and a woman by his side—what more could you ask? Anyone in Chonkin's position would have been glad to remain at a post like that until his time was up and would even re-enlist for another year. But all the same, there was something in Chonkin's situation which gave him no peace—namely, that he was supposed to have been left there for a week, the week had already passed, and there had been no word from his unit, no further instructions. If they had decided to keep him on there, they should have somehow let him know, and some extra rations wouldn't have hurt either. It was a good thing he'd set himself up so well, otherwise his belt would be going around twice by now.

In the last few days, whenever he went outside, Chonkin would throw his head back and peer into the sky for a slowly enlarging dot and cup his hand to his ear to listen for the murmur of an approaching engine. But no, there was nothing to be seen, nothing to be heard.

Despairing, not knowing what steps to take, Chonkin decided to turn to an intelligent neighbor for advice. Nyura's neighbor, Kuzma Matveyevich Gladishev, was just such a man.

Kuzma Gladishev was known as a learned man not only in Krasnoye but in the entire area. One of the many proofs of his erudition was the wooden outhouse in his garden, on which was written in large black letters, in English, WATER CLOSET.

Though he held the undistinguished and low-paying position of kolkhoz warehouseman, Gladishev did have a lot of free time for supplementing his knowledge, and his mind held such diverse information from such diverse fields that people who knew him could only sigh with envy and respect. He's really something! they'd say. Many people maintained that you could wake Gladishev up at midnight and pose him any question and that without even stopping to think, he would give a very detailed reply and would explain any natural phenomenon from the point of view of modern science without bringing in any otherworldly, divine forces.

Gladishev was an entirely self-educated man, since it would be ridiculous to give any credit to the parish school where he had completed only two grades. The knowledge Gladishev had accumulated might have made its way into his head without making any sense at all, if it hadn't been for the October Revolution, which liberated the people from every form of slavery and permitted any citizen to clamber up the shining, stony heights of science. It should also be mentioned that many original scientific ideas had arisen in Gladishev's liberated mind before the time of our story. Nothing in life passed him by without suggesting all sorts of ideas to him. Say, for instance, Kuzma spots some cockroaches on the stove, his mind goes right to work: Why couldn't you hitch them up together, he thinks, and have them all go in the same direction? The energy thus collected could be put to profitable use in our agriculture. Kuzma spots a cloud and thinks: Why not enclose it in some sort of casing and use it as a balloon? Though this would be difficult to verify now, it is said that it was actually Gladishev who, long before Professor Shklovsky, was the first to propound the theory that the satellites of Mars are artificial in origin.

But beyond all these incidental ideas, there was one Gladishev had decided to dedicate his whole life to, and thereby immortalize his name in the annals of science; inspired by the progressive teachings of Michurin and Lysenko, he had undertaken to create a hybrid of the potato and the tomato; i.e., a plant which would grow the tubers of a potato on the bottom at the same time as tomatoes would grow from the top. In the spirit of that great epoch, Gladishev called his hybrid-to-be the "Path to Socialism" or "PATS" for short. He had intended to spread his experiments across the entire territory of the kolkhoz, but they wouldn't allow him to and he had to limit himself to the confines of his own vegetable garden. For that reason he was sometimes forced to buy both potatoes and tomatoes from his neighbors.

So far these experiments had not produced any actual results, although certain characteristics of the PATS had started to appear: the leaves and stems were potato-like, while the roots were letter-perfect tomato. Despite his numerous failures, Gladishev did not lose heart, understanding that genuine scientific discovery demands labor and no little sacrifice. Those who knew about his experiments didn't put much stock in them, but Gladishev's work had been noticed and given support, which could not ever have happened in the days of the tsars.

At one point the district newspaper, *Bolshevik Tempos,* printed a big, two-column feature about Gladishev, under the general heading "People of the New Village." The column was called "A Born Breeder." It even carried a photograph of him bending over his hybrid as if he could discern there the faint outline of our planet's beautiful future. After the district paper's piece, an article appeared in an all-union paper dealing with the problem of "The Scientific Creativity of the Masses," mentioning Gladishev by name, among others. In his research and in his struggle against the drudgery of it all, Gladishev drew support from the response of a certain agricultural academician, even though that response had been a negative one. In a letter sent personally to Gladishev, the academician had pointed out that Gladishev's experiments were anti-scientific and hopeless as well. Nevertheless, he advised Gladishev to keep his spirits up and, citing the example of the ancient alchemists, pointed out that in science no work is ever done in vain, one thing is sought and another found. In spite of what it had to say, this letter made a strong impression on Gladishev, especially since it had been typed on the official stationery of a respectable institution, had addressed Gladishev as "Esteemed Comrade Gladishev," and had been signed by the academician in his own hand. The letter produced the same impression on everyone who read it. But whenever the "born breeder" would begin to discuss the possibilities the new PATS plant would open up for the world, people would grow bored and withdraw; like many a scientific genius, Gladishev had to live in a state of total isolation until, that is, Chonkin turned up.

Gladishev loved to talk about his work and Chonkin was bored and had nothing against listening to him. This brought them together and they became friends. When Chonkin would go out of the house with something to do or just to get out, there would be Gladishev already working his garden, mounding, weeding, watering, always wearing the exact same outfit: cavalry jodhpurs tucked into worn calfskin boots, an old ragged T-shirt, and a wide-brimmed straw hat that looked like a sombrero. Where he picked that up was anybody's guess.

Chonkin would wave to him. "Hey there, neighbor."

"A good morning to you," Gladishev would answer politely.

"How's life?" Chonkin would ask with interest.

"Working away," the modest reply would follow.

Thus, word by word, their conversation would flow, smooth and unforced.

"So when are those potatoes of yours with the tomatoes going to start coming up?"

"Hold on, it's still early yet. Everything in its own time, as they say. They still have to finish blossoming first."

"But what if nothing comes of them this year again, what are you going to do then?" asked Chonkin curiously.

"This year something should come," said Gladishev with a sigh of hope. "But have a look for yourself. We're getting a stem like a potato and the shape of the leaf is just like a tomato. You see?"

"Yeah, but who knows," said Chonkin dubiously. "Right now you can't tell one from the other."

"What do you mean, you can't tell one from the other?" said Gladishev, offended. "Just look how full these bushes are."

"As far as fullness goes, they're all right," agreed Chonkin. Then his face lit up. An idea had occurred to Chonkin too. "Listen, couldn't you work it so the tomatoes were on the bottom and the potatoes were on the top?"

"No, it couldn't work like that," explained Gladishev patiently. "That would contradict the laws of nature, because the potato is part of the root system while the tomato is an above-ground vegetable."

"But still, that'd really be something," said Chonkin, refusing to give up.

Perhaps Chonkin's questions did seem stupid to Gladishev, but the stupider the question, the more intelligently it can be answered. Their conversations gave them both great pleasure, and their friendship grew stronger with each passing day. They had already decided to get together with their wives, Chonkin and Nyura, and Gladishev and his wife, Aphrodite (that's what Gladishev called her and other people took their cue from him, even though at birth his wife had been given the name Efrosinya).

Chonkin had managed to get a lot of work done that day. He had fetched the water, chopped the firewood, fed Borka his bran, and cooked dinner for himself and Nyura. Usually when all that was done he'd sit by the window, just as he was, still wearing Nyura's apron, and his head propped on his hand, he'd wait there for Nyura to come home. Or, sometimes, to make the time pass more quickly, he'd do his embroidery while he sat there. A soldier sitting by the window in a woman's apron, doing embroidery besides, is a laughable sight, but so what if Chonkin liked to embroider? He enjoyed watching the little cross-stitches form themselves into a picture of a rooster or a rose or some other such thing.

At the moment he had again begun to embroider, but could not get down to work, for thoughts of the uncertainty of his situation kept distracting him. Several times he had gone out onto the porch, hoping for a chat with Gladishev, but Gladishev wasn't around. Chonkin didn't feel right about dropping in on him at home and disturbing him, especially since he had never done it before.

To somehow kill the time, he put himself to work at a job much duller than embroidering, namely, washing the floor. When he was done, Chonkin took the dirty water out past the gate and sent it splashing onto the road.

A girl about five years old, wearing a flower-print cotton dress, was playing with Borka near the fence; she had taken the silk bow out of her hair and tied it around Borka's neck. Borka was twisting his head around, trying to get a look at the bow but not having any success. When she saw Chonkin, the little girl hastily took the bow off Borka and squeezed it in her hand.

"Whose little girl are you?" asked Chonkin.

"I'm the Kilins'. And whose are you?"

"I'm my own." Ivan grinned.

"And I'm my papa's and mama's," boasted the little girl.

"And who do you love more, papa or mama?"

"Stalin," said the little girl, then ran away embarrassed.

"Get on with your Stalin." Chonkin shook his head, watching her go.

However, he too loved Stalin in his own way.

Swinging the empty pail, Chonkin had turned back to the house when Gladishev came out onto his porch, disheveled, with red streaks on his cheeks.

"Hey, neighbor," said Chonkin, glad to see him. "I've been waiting for you here over an hour. Now where's that Gladishev gone to? I says to myself."

"I took a little nap," said Gladishev groggily, stretching and yawning. "I lay down with a book after lunch to read a little bit about plant selection and I guess it just put me right to sleep. Whew, this heat—punishing, isn't it? If we don't get some rain, everything's going to burn right up."

"Listen, neighbor," said Chonkin. "Want some tobacco? I've got some good strong home-grown stuff. Gets you right in the throat. Nyurka bought it over at the market in Dolgov the other day."

Chonkin pushed his apron aside and pulled out a gun-oil can full of tobacco and a little packet of newspaper from his pocket.

"Nothing is more injurious to the health than tobacco," pronounced Gladishev, walking up to the fence which divided the two gardens. "Scientists have calculated that one drop of nicotine can kill a horse."

However, Gladishev did not refuse Chonkin's offer. He lit up and immediately started coughing.

"Sure is strong stuff," he said with approval.

"Strong as Samson. Gets the young ones going and puts the old folks to sleep," chimed in Chonkin. "But listen, neighbor, I've got a little favor to ask you."

"What kind of favor?" Gladishev squinted at him.

"Nothing really, just stupid."

"Let's hear it anyway."

"Oh, it's not even worth talking about."

"All right, if it's not worth talking about, don't talk about it," said Gladishev.

"You're right, of course," agreed Chonkin. "But in another way, I've got to say something. They sent me here for a week and gave me rations for a week, and a week and a half's gone by and no one's come to get me. And not a word about any more rations for me either. So now I'm supposed to live off a woman?"

"You're right, it's not good," said Gladishev. "They're starting to call you Gigolo Chonkin."

"Well, forget that," objected Chonkin. "Listen, you call your own wife what you want, sticks and stones'll break your bones, but you call me Vanya just like always. So here's what I wanted to talk to you about. I've got to make up a short letter to my commander—that I'm still here and what's going to be with me. You're an educated guy. I know my letters pretty good, but I write bad. I had it down all right in school, but then came the kolkhoz and the army; if you're not sleeping you're on a horse pulling reins left and right and you got no use for all that school stuff then."

"Can you sign your name?" asked Gladishev.

"Sure, I can. I can read, and sign my name. You want to hear how I sign my name? First I write the I for Ivan, then the C, then the H, then a little circle and on and on like that, then I put a scrolly line with a couple of slashes through it under the whole thing from one side of the page to the other. Get it?"

"I got it," said Gladishev. "But do you have any paper and ink?"

"What do you think?" said Ivan. "Doesn't Nyura run the post office? I'll tell you something, it's not a job just anybody can do. Takes brains."

"All right." Gladishev finally agreed. "We'll go to your house. My wife's home with the kid, they'll be in the way. And this is an important matter. This letter must be politically correct."

An hour later a politically correct document had been composed. It ran as follows:

To Battalion Commander Comrade Pakhomov
From Red Army Private Comrade Chonkin, Ivan

REPORT

Request permission to report that during your absence
and my presence on my post, specifically, while
guarding the military equipment of the airplane, no
incidents have occurred about which I am now
reporting in written form. Also request permission to
report that, raised in the spirit of wholehearted
devotion to our Party, People, and to the person of the
Great Genius Com. Stalin, J. V., I am ready
unquestioningly to serve further in the defense of our
Socialist Motherland and the protection of her Borders,
for which purpose I request you issue me rations for
an unlimited period of time and also my new uniform
not as yet received by me.

Please do not refuse this request.
I remain . . .

"Good job," said Chonkin, in approval of Gladishev's composition, and set his signature across the entire page, just as he had promised to.

Gladishev added the address onto the stamped envelope Chonkin gave him, then left, satisfied.

Chonkin laid the envelope on the table, picked up the napkin stretched over his embroidery frame, and sat down by the window. It was no longer so hot outside, the sun was close to setting. Nyura should be coming home soon, Borka the hog was already waiting for her on the hillock past the village.

12

Chairman Golubev tied his horse to Nyura's gate and climbed up to the porch. It cannot be said he maintained complete composure; quite the contrary, he was entering Nyura's house with the same sort of trepidation he'd experience when going in to see the First Secretary of the District Committee. But on his way to Nyura's Golubev had resolved to go in and he did not want to back down from his resolution now.

He knocked at the door and opened it without waiting for an answer. At the sight of Golubev, Chonkin's eyes darted around the room in fright and confusion, searching for a place to stick the embroidery frame.

"Doing some embroidery?" asked the chairman politely, but with suspicion in his voice.

"The stuff you do to keep from doing anything," said Chonkin. He tossed the frame on the bench.

"That's for sure," said the chairman, stamping his feet

in the doorway, not knowing how to keep the conversation alive. "Yes, yes," he said.

"Let's not yes around all day," answered Chonkin in jest.

He beats around the bush and leads you astray, the chairman observed to himself. Golubev decided to take a different tack—foreign affairs.

"It says in the papers," he began cautiously, moving closer to the table, "the Germans are bombing London."

"They'll say anything in the papers," said Chonkin, avoiding a direct response.

"What do you mean?" said Golubev. "In our papers everything is there for a reason."

"And what are you here for?" asked Chonkin, sensing something fishy.

"No reason," said the chairman nonchalantly. "I just dropped by to see how you were doing. Writing a dispatch?" he asked, noticing the envelope with the military address on the table.

"Just whatever pops into my mind."

Ooo, what a clever guy! the chairman exclaimed to himself. You try him from one side, you try him from the other, but he just answers like he doesn't understand anything. Probably's got a higher education. Maybe he even understands French.

"Kes-kesay." Golubev surprised himself by suddenly saying aloud the only French he knew.

"Huh?" Chonkin raised his frightened eyes to him and began blinking his eyelids, which had gone red with confusion.

"Kes-kesay," repeated the chairman stubbornly.

"What is this, what are you talking about?" said Chonkin, worried now. In his agitation he began to pace about the room. "Listen, you quit saying those words. Talk like you're supposed to, not that other way. I'm not talking crazy to you."

"I can see you're not talking crazy," said the chairman, deciding to take the offensive. "Surveillance is being conducted here. You think, The fools, they won't understand. But now even the fools have gotten smart. And we understand everything. Maybe everything's not perfect here, but it's no worse than anywhere else. Take the 'Voroshilov,' take 'Ilyich's Legacy'—the same story everywhere you look. And the reason we sowed frozen ground last year was we were ordered to. The orders come from up above, but the kolkhoznik's got to answer for everything. Not to mention the chairman. And then you come flying up in your airplane and start writing!" shouted Golubev, growing more and more incensed. "Go write what you want. Write that the chairman has ruined the kolkhoz, that he's a drunkard. I've been drinking today. Here, smell my breath." He leaned close to Chonkin and exhaled right into his nose. Chonkin recoiled.

"What did I do?" said Chonkin in self-justification. "I just do what I'm ordered to."

"That's what you should have said in the first place, that you were ordered here," said Golubev almost gleefully. "Instead of sitting there like a mouse, disguised as a woman. And what *are* your orders? You want my Party card? Here it is. Prison? All right, I'm ready. Better prison than living like this. I've got six kids. I'll give each one a sack and they can go begging around the villages. But somehow they'll eat. Go ahead, write, write!" In confusion he slammed the door and left.

It was only outside that Golubev understood what a mess he'd made and knew that this time he was really going to catch it.

Whatever happens, he thought irritably, unhitching his horse, better it happens now than to sit around trembling, waiting for it to happen. Whatever happens, happens.

Volkov the bookkeeper was waiting for him in the office with the financial report. The chairman signed the report without even glancing at it, experiencing a vindictive delight. I hope there's something really screwed up in here because it doesn't matter any more. Then he ordered Volkov to write a check for the graph Borisov had spoken to him about. Then Golubev dismissed the accountant.

Left alone, Golubev began to feel more like himself and started to arrange the heap of papers on his desk. They were in no order at all and now the chairman decided to place them in separate piles according to their category. He arranged incoming papers in one pile and outgoing papers (which had not, however, gone out) in another. He made separate piles for financial documents and for reports of the kolkhozniks. Just then Golubev was distracted by overhearing a conversation coming from the other side of the partition which separated his office from the corridor.

"When you come into the cell the first time, they stick a clean towel in front of your feet."

"For what?"

"I'll tell you. If it's your first time, you step over the towel. But if you're a real crook, you wipe your feet on the towel and toss it in the honey pot."

"Tough on the towel."

"Tougher on you if you step over the towel. They start right in on you . . . I forget what they call it . . . Hold on, I got it . . . the initiation."

"What's that all about?"

"For a start, they send you to find the fifth corner. You know what that means?"

"That I know."

"Then comes the parachute jump."

"What kind of parachute jump can you have in a cell?"

"Just you listen . . ."

Golubev found this conversation terribly interesting. And he took it right to heart. It even occurred to him that maybe it was no accident that he was overhearing it, that maybe all this information would be coming in handy in the not-too-distant future. The voices were familiar. The voice asking the questions belonged to Nikolai Kurzov. The voice answering the questions was also familiar but, no matter how hard he tried, Golubev could not place it.

"This is how the parachute jump works. They take you by the arms and legs and throw you to the floor three times, on your back."

"But that would hurt," said Kurzov.

"That's no rest home they're running there," explained the one telling the tale. "Anyway, after that, you're one of the guys, and you get to take part in the elections along with everybody else."

"They really have elections in there?"

"Why not, you've even got them out here, don't you? In there they elect a leader. One man sits with slips of paper with last names on them held between his knees. All the rest are blindfolded and have their hands tied, and they take turns walking up to him and pulling out the slips of paper with their teeth."

"Not so bad," said Kurzov with satisfaction. "Nothing so terrible about that."

"Of course it's nothing so terrible. Except when your

turn comes, you don't get the knees, you get the guy's bare ass."

The chairman was a squeamish person and this detail made his face crinkle up. He wanted to learn who it was telling this interesting story and he went out into the corridor as if he was just going to look in at the brigade office.

On the long bench beneath the wall-newspaper sat Nikolai Kurzov and Lyosha Zharov, who, three years ago, had been given eight years for stealing a sack of flour from the mill. Seeing the chairman, Lyosha sprang to his feet, removing his cap, whose visor had been torn off, and baring his shaved head covered with stubble.

"Hello, Ivan Timofeyevich," he said in the tone of voice people use when meeting someone they haven't seen for a long time.

"Hello," said Chairman Golubev sullenly, as if he had seen Lyosha the day before. "You're out?"

"Got out early," said Lyosha. "I got two days off for every one I served."

"Here to see me?"

"That's right," said Lyosha.

"All right, come on in then."

Lyosha followed the chairman into his office, carefully wiping his ragged boots as if afraid he might wake someone up. Lyosha waited until the chairman had seated himself, and only then did he sit down, on the edge of the stool across from Golubev.

"So, what do you have to say for yourself?" asked the chairman sullenly, after a moment's silence.

"I have come to ask you for work, Ivan Timofeyevich," said Zharov respectfully, nervously pulling at the cap on his knee.

The chairman took a moment to think.

"For work, you say?" said Golubev. "But what kind of work can I give you? You don't have the best reputation, you know, Zharov. Right now I could use a man over at the dairy farm. I'd send you, but you'd start stealing the milk."

"I won't, Ivan Timofeyevich," vowed Lyosha. "I should die on the spot, I won't."

"Skip the promises," said Golubev. "For you, promises are easier than rolling off a log. How many times did I tell you before: Watch it, Zharov, you're acting badly, you're going to come out a loser. Did I tell you or didn't I?"

"You did," agreed Zharov.

"That's right, I did. And what did you use to say back to me. 'It's nothing, we'll get through it.' Now you see what 'nothing' means, don't you?"

"There's no reason to bring up the past, Ivan Timofeyevich," said Lyosha sincerely. He sighed deeply. "I often thought about your words in the camp. I remember one time we were having dinner, and just as they were serving the compote . . ."

"They actually serve compote in there?" asked the chairman with more than a little curiosity.

"Depends on your boss. One'll starve you to death, another one, if he wants to fulfill the plan, will feed you and dress you warm, as long as you give it everything you've got, that's all."

"So, in other words, there are some good bosses?" the chairman asked again, hope in his voice, as he pushed a pack of Delhi cigarettes over toward Zharov. "Have a smoke. And tell me, what do they have in there by way of recreation?"

"Much as you like," said Lyosha. "Movies, amateur shows, a bath every ten days. The amateur shows are better than we've got in the city. We had one People's Artist in the camp and two Honored Artists and I didn't keep track of how many plain regular ones. In general, we had a pretty educated bunch in there." Lyosha lowered his voice. "Lots of them. We had a Member of the Academy. Doing ten. He wanted to foul up the chimes on the Kremlin so they would give the whole country the wrong time."

"Come on!" The chairman looked at Lyosha in disbelief.

"You come on. I tell you, there's a lot of wrecking and sabotage going on in the country, Ivan Timofeyevich. For example, these Delhi cigarettes you smoke, there's sabotage in them too."

"Get out of here," said the chairman, but he took the cigarette from his mouth and looked at it suspiciously. "What kind of sabotage? What are they, poisoned or something?"

"Worse," said Lyosha with conviction. "Can you decipher the word 'Delhi' for me?"

"What's to decipher there? Delhi is Delhi, a city in India."

"Ech," sighed Lyosha. "And you an educated man. Well, if you want to know, if you take it letter by letter, Delhi means Down with the Entire Leninist Humanist International."

"Shhhh, keep it down," said the chairman, looking over at the door. "That's got nothing to do with you and me. I'd rather hear what life's like in there."

At that moment, Nikolai Kurzov, without waiting to be called, came walking right into the chairman's office.

He had to go logging in the morning and asked the chairman to issue him two kilograms of meat.

"Come tomorrow," said the chairman.

"What do you mean, tomorrow?" said Nikolai. "I've got to leave for the train as soon as it's light."

"Doesn't matter. Go the day after tomorrow. I'll write a note saying I detained you here."

The chairman waited until the door had closed behind Nikolai, then immediately returned to Lyosha.

"Let's hear some more."

(Granny Dunya, who worked the minimum amount of workdays and was on duty at the grocery store, noticed that the light was on in the chairman's office until one in the morning.)

The chairman kept on grilling Lyosha about life in the camps, and Lyosha's stories made it clear that life wasn't so terrible in there. In there you worked ten hours, where here Golubev had to run around from dawn till dusk. In there they fed you three times a day, where here it wasn't every day he managed to eat twice. And he hadn't been to the movies in over six months.

As they were parting, Golubev promised to find a good job for Lyosha.

"In the meantime, you'll work as a herdsman," said Golubev. "You'll herd the people's cattle. You know what the pay is, fifteen rubles from the owner and half a workday from the kolkhoz. You get fed in people's houses. One week with one family, the next week another. So you'll work a while as a herdsman, have yourself a look around, then maybe we'll find you something a little better."

The chairman returned home in a good frame of mind that day. He stroked the heads of his sleeping children and even said a tender word to his wife, who was so un-used to affection from her husband that she went out into the passageway and shed a few tears.

Having wiped away her tears, she brought her husband a clay pot full of cold milk from the cellar. Ivan Timo-feyevich drank down almost the entire pot of milk, then got undressed and went to bed. But for a long while he was unable to fall asleep. He sighed and tossed, recalling everything Lyosha had told him, down to the last detail. Then simple fatigue took its toll and his eyelids grew heavy and closed. Even in there people live, thought Golubev as he fell off to sleep.

13

"The earth is shaped like a sphere," explained Gladishev to Chonkin one day. "It is constantly revolving around the sun and around its own axis. We don't feel it revolv-ing because we ourselves are revolving along with the earth."

This wasn't the first time Chonkin had heard about the earth revolving. Someone had told him about it be-fore, though he didn't remember who. What he could not understand was how people stayed on and why the water didn't go flying off.

It was the third week of Chonkin's stay in Krasnoye and there still had been no sign, no word, from his unit. One of his boots was already wearing through and no one had driven or flown there to give him any orders about what to do next. Chonkin, of course, had no idea that Nyura had never mailed the letter he'd given her to send. Hoping that his superiors would forget about Chonkin's existence, and not wishing to remind them of it even at the cost of losing his rations, Nyura had carried the letter around in her tarpaulin bag for several days, then burned it when Ivan wasn't around.

At that time events were occurring in the world which, as yet, bore no direct relation to either Nyura or Chonkin.

On June 14, a conference was held at Hitler's headquarters to put the finishing touches on a plan called "Barbarossa."

Neither Chonkin nor Nyura had the faintest inkling of this plan. They had their own concerns, which seemed more important to them. Nyura, for example, had been looking terrible the last few days; she was shedding hair like a cat, and could barely drag herself around. Although she and Chonkin went to bed early, he wouldn't let her sleep, waking her up at least several times each night to take his pleasure, which he wanted in the daytime as well. As soon as Nyura would cross the threshold of her house, weary from work, Chonkin would pounce on her like a hungry beast and drag her to the bed, mail bag and all. Sometimes she'd hide from him in the hayloft or the hen house, but Chonkin would track her down. There was no escaping the man. She even complained about it to Ninka Kurzova, who just laughed at her, envying Nyura secretly since she had trouble getting her own Nikolai going even once a week.

But on the very day the finishing touches were being put on Operation Barbarossa, Nyura and Chonkin had a misunderstanding, of a sort that's a bit awkward to discuss.

It was evening. Nyura, having returned from the district center, delivered the mail, and twice yielded to Chonkin, was tidying up the house. To be out of her way, Chonkin had gone outside with his hatchet and set to work fixing the fence. He straightened out a post, then took a few steps back; his eyes narrowed; what he saw gave him great joy—what a master I am, thought Chonkin, whatever I try my hand at comes out just fine.

Nyura glanced out the window by chance and also felt a sense of satisfaction. Since Ivan had appeared, her household had been gradually put in order. The stove wasn't smoking any more, the door closed, the scythe had been whetted and sharpened. Even a little nothing like a piece of iron to scrape the mud off your feet— would it have ever been there except for a man?

A good man, a bad man, there for a long time or just passing through, the main thing was—he's yours. And the nice thing was not only that he helped you out around the house and then shared your bed, but just the knowledge that he was there. It was nice to be able to say to a friend or neighbor you ran into: "Yesterday my man fixed the roof, got a chill from the wind, and caught a little cold and had to drink some hot milk." It was even nice to say: "When mine gets pie-eyed, he goes right for the oven tongs or the poker and starts smashing whatever's around until there's not a dish left in one piece in the place." That sounds like a complaint, but in fact it's a form of boasting. Of course you can't say that he invented the steam engine or split the atom, but at least he did something, he proved his worth, and thanks be for that. My man! Mine! Sometimes you might get one that's not much to look at—blind in one eye, hunchbacked, drinks away his money, beats his wife and children half to death. Get rid of him and that's it. But she doesn't get rid of him. He's mine. Good, bad, or indifferent, but not yours, not hers, mine!

Nyura grew pensive as she glanced out the window.

Whether they had lived together a long time or not, she was already attached to him, her heart was his. But was it all worth it? Wouldn't she have to tear her heart away from him all too soon? Could it really be that one day she'd come home and there'd be nothing there but the four walls? You can talk to walls, but walls don't answer.

Chonkin trimmed the last corner post and stepped back two paces, hatchet in hand. It looked good. Even. He planted the hatchet in the fence post and got out his can of rolling tobacco and a piece of newspaper from his pocket, lit up, and knocked at the window.

"Listen, Nyura, make it quick in there. I'll be right in and we can roll around a little."

"Go on, you crazy devil," answered Nyura, swearing fondly. "How much can you do it?"

"Much as you like," Chonkin said. "If it didn't make you so mad, I'd be at you all day long."

Nyura dismissed him with a wave of her hand. Ivan walked away from the window still thinking of what his future might hold. Then he heard someone's voice right behind him and was frightened for a second, even shook from surprise.

"Hey, soldier, can you spare me a smoke?"

Chonkin raised his eyes and saw Burly standing beside him, carrying a fishing pole in one hand and a switch strung with maybe ten little fish in the other. Chonkin got out his shag and newspaper again and, handing them to Burly, asked: "So how's the fishing?"

Burly leaned the pole against the fence, held the switch with the fish tightly under one arm, and, rolling a cigarette, said reluctantly: "The fishing there now! It's a joke. These aren't fish. I'll let the cat gobble these minnows. It used to be you could catch pike there with spoon bait, pike this big . . ." He took a light from Chonkin's cigarette and, touching his left shoulder with his right hand, extended his left arm to demonstrate just how big the pike used to run. "Now you couldn't find a pike there in the daytime with a flashlight. Carp ate them all up, I guess. So you're living with Nyura?" he said, changing the subject abruptly.

"Uh-huh," said Ivan.

"You thinking of staying on with her when you get out?" probed Burly.

"Haven't made up my mind yet," said Chonkin thoughtfully, not sure whether he should confide his doubts to a man he barely knew. "Of course Nyurka's a good girl and nice to look at, but, you know, I'm still a young guy, gotta have a look around first, see what's what, then make it official and settle down to family life."

"What do you need to take a look around for?" said Burly. "Get married, that's. it. After all, Nyurka's got her own house, her own cow. Where are you going to find another girl like that?"

"Well, that sounds pretty true . . ."

"That's what I'm telling you—get married. Nyura's a real good girl, no one'll tell you anything bad about her. No matter how long she lived alone, she never got mixed up with anybody, never had a man in all her born days. The only one she had was Borka, that's right."

"Who's this Borka?" said Chonkin, his ears pricking up.

"Who's this Borka? Her hog, of course," Burly explained readily.

Chonkin choked on his smoke in surprise, started coughing, threw his cigarette down, and ground it out with his heel.

"Quit fooling around," said Chonkin angrily. "What's this about her and a hog?"

Burly looked at Chonkin with his light-blue eyes. "What

did I tell you? Nothing bad's happened here. Everybody knows a woman by herself, she's got needs too, that's right. Judge for yourself—he could have been dinner long ago, but she doesn't want to slaughter him, and why? But how can she slaughter him when he comes to her in bed? They get under the covers and lie there like man and wife. You ask anybody you want in the village, anybody'll tell you—you won't find anybody better than Nyurka."

Satisfied with the impression he'd made, Burly picked up his fishing pole and moved on, taking his time, still puffing on his cigarette. Chonkin, on the other hand, stood there quite a while, his jaw hanging open, his confused eyes following Burly, not knowing how to deal with the news he'd just received.

Her skirt tucked up, Nyura was washing the floor when the door was flung open and Chonkin appeared at the threshold.

"Wait a minute, I'm doing the floor," said Nyura, not noting Chonkin's excited state.

"What do I care?" said Chonkin, and marched with his dirty boots to the rack where his rifle was hanging. Nyura was about to scold him when she realized that something had upset him.

"What's with you?" she asked.

"Nothing." Chonkin grabbed his rifle and slid open the bolt to make sure there was a cartridge inside.

Nyura stood in the doorway, her rag in her hand.

"Let me by!" Chonkin walked up to her and tried to push her out of the way with the butt of his rifle, using it like an oar.

"What's gotten into you?" she cried, looking him right in the eye. "What do you need the rifle for?"

"Let me by, I told you," said Chonkin, shoving her with his shoulder.

"Tell me why," Nyura insisted.

"Well, all right." Chonkin set the rifle by his foot and looked her in the eye. "What went on with you and Borka?"

"What are you talking about? What Borka?"

"Everybody knows what Borka. Borka the hog. You been sleeping with him a long time or what?"

Nyura attempted a smile. "Vanya, you're just making a joke, aren't you?"

For some reason her question entirely deprived him of his composure.

"I'll show you who's joking!" Chonkin threatened her with the butt of his rifle. "Tell me, you bitch, when you started carrying on with him!"

Nyura looked at him in panic, as if trying to figure out whether Chonkin had gone out of his mind. If he hadn't, it meant she was the crazy one, for her poor mind could make no sense of what he was saying.

"Lord, what is going on here!" moaned Nyura.

She let the rag fall, and seizing her head in her wet hands, she walked over to the window. She sat down on the bench and began weeping softly, helplessly, the way sick children do when they don't even have strength enough left to cry.

Chonkin had not anticipated such a reaction. He grew confused and stamped his feet by the open door, not knowing what to do next. Then he leaned the rifle against the wall and walked over to Nyura.

"Listen, Nyurka," he said after a moment's silence. "Even if there was something, I don't care. I'll just shoot him and that'll be the end of it. At least some meat'll come of it, what little he's got. All he does anyway is run around the yard like a dog, it's a waste of food feeding him."

Nyura kept right on crying and Chonkin did not know

whether she had heard him or not. He passed the rough palm of his hand over her hair and, after a moment's thought, put it a different way: "But if there wasn't anything between you, then just say so, Nyura. I wasn't doing it to be mean. I just acted foolish, that's all. Burly was blabbing to me and then I came in here and started blabbing too, without even thinking about it or anything. You know what people are like, Nyura, mean and no good. When a woman or a girl lives alone there's nothing they won't say about her."

His words, however, did not have a soothing effect. Instead, they produced the opposite reaction! Nyura began crying, her voice not her own; she fell onto the bench, clasped both arms around it, and began choking with sobs, her whole body shuddering.

In desperation Chonkin ran around in front of her, trying to do something, then fell to his knees and began pulling Nyura from the bench, shouting directly in her ear: "Listen, Nyura, what's wrong? I didn't mean it. Nobody said anything to me. I made the whole thing up for a joke. I'm a fool, you hear, Nyura, a fool. You want to hit me on the head, use the iron, I don't care, just stop crying."

And in fact Chonkin did grab the iron, which was standing by the bench, and put it into Nyura's hand. Nyura flung the iron aside and Chonkin instinctively hopped away, just escaping injury to his foot. Strange as it may seem, after she had thrown the iron Nyura calmed down and grew quiet; only her shoulders continued to tremble. Chonkin ran out into the passageway and brought back a ladle of water. Her teeth chattering against the ladle, Nyura drank the water down in one gulp, then placed the ladle on the bench in front of her.

She sat down, wiped her tears away with the collar of her dress, and, almost calm now, asked: "Want to eat?"

"Wouldn't hurt," agreed Chonkin joyfully, satisfied that it had all blown over. His doubts now seemed ridiculous to him. He had to go and believe such stupidity. And from who, from Burly, who only knew how to talk nonsense.

Ivan darted outside and brought his hatchet back into the passageway. Just as he was passing the door that led from the house to the cow shed, he heard Borka's muffled grunting and once again a dark doubt stirred in his soul. Though he wished to, he could not suppress it.

Nyura had set two mugs of steaming, still-fragrant cow's milk on the table and was now banging about in the oven with her tongs, trying to pull out the iron pot of potatoes. Chonkin helped her, then sat down at the table.

"Listen, Nyurka," he said, pulling his milk to him. "I don't care if you get mad or not, I'm shooting Borka tomorrow."

"What for?" she asked.

"What does it matter what for? For nothing. Once people start gabbing like that, you've got to shoot him, just so they won't have anything to talk about."

Chonkin looked guardedly at her, but this time Nyura did not break into tears. She dished out the potatoes, pushed one plate over to Chonkin, took the other herself, and said bitterly: "And you think if you kill him, people are going to stop talking? Ech, Vanya, you don't know the people around here. It'll make them jump for joy. Here's what they'll say . . . 'I wonder why he shot the hog all of a sudden?' 'It's clear why. 'Cause Nyura lived with him.' On and on. One person says one thing, the next one adds a couple more, until you can't find a better story in a book. 'One night this Nyurka goes out to milk the cow, leaving Ivan in the house. He waits and waits but no Nyurka. I'll go take a look, he thinks, see if she fell asleep. He goes to the shed and there's Nyurka—' "

"Quiet, you!" Chonkin bellowed suddenly, shoving his mug away from him and splashing milk across the table.

The picture Nyura had drawn had affected Chonkin as strongly as if he'd seen it all with his own eyes and, despite the arguments she used to convince him, he again flew into a rage. He overturned the bench and raced for his rifle, which stood near the door. But Nyura beat him to the door, where she stood like a statue. Chonkin was unable to get her out of the way.

They repeated their earlier scene—Chonkin would bump Nyura with his shoulder and say: "Let me by!" And she would answer him: "I won't!" And he would insist: "Let me by!" But she would stick to her guns: "I won't!"

Finally the whole thing tired Chonkin out and he sat down on the bench, holding his rifle between his knees.

"It's plain to see Burly was telling the truth about you, Nyurka," he said angrily. "If there hadn't been anything between you and Borka, then you wouldn't stick by him like that. He should have been eaten long ago. It's high time to make bacon fat out of that one, and there you go taking his side. And so if that's the way it is, we're not going to live together any more. And so the question right now is—one or the other, me or the hog. I'll give you five minutes to think it over, a little more than five. Then I'll get my stuff and it's pardon me and that's that."

Chonkin glanced up at the wall clock, which hung opposite the window, took note of the time, and, his head in his hands, turned away from Nyura to await her decision. She pulled up the stool and sat down by the door. They both sat in silence as at a train station when all the words you've prepared have been spoken and all that remains is to kiss each other goodbye, which is when they inform you that the train will be two hours late.

Five minutes passed, a little more than five minutes passed, six minutes passed. Chonkin turned to Nyura and asked: "Well, have you made up your mind?"

"What's to make up," she said sadly. "You decided the whole thing yourself, Vanya. Do as you see fit. But I won't let you kill Borka. I've known you only a few days, but you've got to remember he's been living here two years already. I got him from the kolkhoz when he was still so little, just three days old. I fed him milk from a baby bottle and I washed him in the trough and I put a hot-water bottle on his tummy when he was sick. You can laugh if you want to, but now he's like a son to me. And there's nobody dearer to me than him, because he walks me to work and meets me when I come back. No matter what the weather's like, as soon as I start up that little hill he runs to meet me, through snow and even through mud. And, Vanya, at those moments my heart gives such a leap that I have to squat down by him and cry like a fool, whether 'cause I'm so happy or so sad I don't know, but probably both. I've gotten used to your ways, Vanya, and I've gotten real fond of you, like you were my own husband, but you're here today, gone tomorrow, you'll find somebody else, somebody better and prettier than me. And when I'm all alone, Borka'll come over to me and rub his ear on my leg and then I'll feel better right away. He's a living soul, after all."

Her words touched Chonkin, but he wasn't about to back down, because he had a fixed opinion about women—give them an inch and they'll take a mile. "Well, what can we do about it, Nyurka. It's just a shame."

"It's up to you, Vanya."

"Well, all right then," said Chonkin, gathering his rifle, coat, and knapsack in his arms. Then he walked over to Nyura, "I'm going to go, you know, Nyura."

"Go." Nyura was gazing aloofly into the corner.

"Have it your way," said Chonkin and walked out.

Evening had come. The first small stars had appeared in the sky. A radio attached to a post near the kolkhoz office was playing Dunayevsky's songs with lyrics by Lebedev-Kumach.

Chonkin dumped his belongings by the plane, sat down on the wing, and pondered the fickleness of fate. Not long ago, not more than an hour ago, he had been a completely happy man, and though he had known it was all temporary, still he had been the man of the house, the head of the family; but suddenly everything had collapsed and blown away, and once again he was alone, homeless, tied to this broken airplane like a dog to a doghouse. But even a dog tied to a doghouse was better off than Chonkin because it, at least, gets fed because it's a dog, while he, Ivan, had been abandoned to the whims of fate—who knew if they had any intention of ever coming to get him?

It wasn't comfortable sitting on the slanted wing and it was getting cold. Chonkin walked over to the haystack in Nyura's garden, gathered a few armfuls of hay, and began settling in for the night by lying down on the hay and covering himself with his greatcoat.

He didn't feel too bad there. In any case, he was used to sleeping like that, and besides, he thought any minute Nyura would come out and start apologizing to him and ask him to come back. But he'd say: "No. Not for anything. This is the way you wanted it, this is the way it's going to be." He had never thought he'd be jealous over a woman, and look who he was jealous of! The sound of Borka's grunting reached him from the shed and suddenly Chonkin clearly imagined the two of them together and was convulsed with disgust. He should shoot him anyway. That's what Chonkin thought, but, for some reason, he had neither the anger nor the desire to just walk over and do it right then and there.

After Dunayevsky's songs came the latest news, followed by a communication from TASS.

Might be about the blization, thought Chonkin, "demobilization" and "mobilization" were beyond his power to pronounce, even to himself. That, however, was not the subject of the communication.

"Germany," enunciated the announcer, "is observing the conditions of the Soviet-German non-aggression pact just as steadfastly as the Soviet Union is. In view of this, Soviet circles believe that rumors about German intentions of violating the pact and launching an attack on the Soviet Union are completely without ground . . ."

Ground, thought Chonkin. Depends what kind. If the ground's loamy, then it's only good for grasses. But if it's dry and sandy, couldn't be better for potatoes. Though you can't compare it with black earth. That's good for grain, for everything . . .

The very thought of grain and bread got him right in the pit of the stomach.

Sure, he should never have said it at all. When Burly was blabbing, he could have just listened instead of taking it in like a fool. Now look at him. No, he's got to stick by what he said, though there was probably nothing to it anyway and, oi, how he wanted to eat.

By this time it was already dark. Stars were scattered across the entire sky. One yellow star, the brightest among them, hung so low over the horizon that it seemed you could just walk a way, reach out, and touch it. Gladishev said that all the heavenly bodies revolved and moved in space. But this star didn't revolve. It hung in one spot, and no matter how much Chonkin squinted he didn't notice any movement at all.

The radio started wheezing and broke off in the middle of a broadcast of light music, but was replaced by an accordion that someone had started playing nearby and by an unidentified bass, which bellowed out for the whole village to hear:

The mother gave birth to a hooligan
and hooligan was the name she gave him.
She sharpened up a Finnish dagger
and gave it to her hooligan.

And then from some place else came a woman's high voice: "Katka, you miserable bitch, you coming home or not?"

Then the accordionist began to play "Widespread the Sea," shamelessly muddling the melody, probably because he couldn't find the right buttons in the dark.

Then the accordionist fell silent, and other sounds, indiscernible before, could now be heard—the cheep of a field mouse, the chirping of crickets, a cow crunching hay. Somewhere hens started up and cackled in sleepy alarm.

Then a door creaked. Chonkin pricked up his ears. It wasn't Nyura's door but her neighbor's. Gladishev came out onto the porch and stood there a while, sighing, probably getting used to the dark; then he went off toward the outhouse, stumbling among the vegetable beds, puffing on a cigarette. Afterward he stood for a while on the porch again, coughed a bit, then spat out his cigarette and went back inside. A moment later Aphrodite darted out and took a quick piss by the porch. Then Chonkin heard her close the door and spend a long time banging about with the bolt. Nyura did not come out, did not ask his forgiveness, and, it seemed, did not intend to.

14

Someone touched Chonkin's shoulder. He looked up and saw Burly's face, blue in the dim light.

"Let's go," said Burly softly and stretched out his hand to Chonkin.

"Where?" asked Chonkin in surprise.

"Where we must go" came the reply.

Chonkin did not feel like getting up and trudging off into the night with no idea where or why, but he was never able to say no when he heard the word "must."

They walked together, picking their way among tall trees with white trunks that looked like birches. However, these were no birches, but some other kind of tree covered by thick layers of hoarfrost. The grass was also covered with hoarfrost, very odd hoarfrost in which no footprints could be left. Chonkin noticed all this, though he kept hurrying for fear of losing sight of Burly, whose back kept disappearing, then reappearing up ahead. There was one thing Chonkin could not fathom—how you were supposed to get your bearings in this strange forest where there wasn't even the faintest of trails; he was just about to ask Burly about this when, at that very moment, there appeared before them a tall fence with a wicket gate through which Chonkin just managed to squeeze behind his guide. On the other side of the fence was a hut Chonkin recognized at once though he hadn't expected to see it there—the hut was Nyura's.

The people standing by the porch in little groups or by themselves were all strangers to Chonkin. All their identical, dark-colored jackets were unbuttoned. That they were smoking and talking to each other was obvious, since their mouths were opening and closing, but not a single sound issued from them. Even the accordion played by the young man in the high box-calf boots who was sprawled on the porch made no sound. Another young man, wearing sandals, danced squatting and leaping in front of the accordionist, but in such slow motion it looked as if he were swimming underwater. He too made not a sound. There was total silence, even when he whacked his knees.

"What are they doing here?" Chonkin asked Burly and was quite amazed not to hear his own voice.

"Quit gabbing." Burly cut him off severely. This came as the final shock for Chonkin, for Burly's voice had not reached him by means of sound vibration, had not come in through his ears, but had taken some other route.

Indifference on his face, the accordion player made way for them, and Chonkin slowly climbed up the porch steps behind Burly. Then Burly shoved the door open with his foot and let Chonkin in ahead of him. Instead of the passageway Chonkin had expected to see, there was some sort of long corridor with walls inlaid with gleaming white tile and a red carpet spread the length of the floor. Chonkin and Burly proceeded along this carpet, and, at every few steps, silent figures would appear in front of them, emerging from either the wall on the left or the one on the right; they would peer intently into their faces, then retreat, dissolving back into the walls. Then others resembling them, or perhaps it was the same figures returning (Chonkin could not make out their faces), would peer at them again, then again dissolve away. All this was repeated countless times, and the corridor seemed infinitely long, but then Burly stopped Chonkin and pointed to the right, saying: "This way!"

In his confusion Chonkin's feet continued to move without making any progress, since in front of him there was only that same wall inlaid with gleaming white tiles that now reflected the images of Chonkin and Burly. There was no door visible, nothing even remotely resembling a door.

"Why are you standing there? Go on," said Burly impatiently.

"Where?" asked Chonkin.

"Straight ahead. Don't be scared."

Burly nudged him forward, and to his own surprise, Chonkin passed through the wall without brushing up against anything and without snagging on anything either, just as if the wall were woven out of fog.

A spacious, brilliantly lit hall opened up before Chonkin. The source of the pale bluish light could not be seen. The large oblong table standing in the center of the hall had been generously set with drinks and appetizers. The guests swarmed around the table like flies.

By the racket coming from the table, by the mood of the guests, and by the general setting, Chonkin was quick to realize that it was someone's wedding. A look at the head of the table at once confirmed that this was so.

At the head of the table sat Nyura in a white wedding gown, her face radiant with happiness. Enthroned beside her on a tall chair, as custom dictates, sat the groom, a dashing young man in a brown velvet jacket with a "Voroshilov Marksman" button on the right side of his chest. Vigorously waving his short arms and saying something merrily and rapidly to Nyura, the groom flashed his mischievous eyes back and forth until his attention fixed on Chonkin, to whom he gave a simple, friendly nod.

Chonkin stared at the young man—he didn't seem to be one of the locals or anyone from the army and yet Chonkin still felt they'd met somewhere before, had a drink together or something, were somehow already acquainted.

Nyura was embarrassed to see Chonkin and dropped her eyes. Then, realizing she was acting foolishly, she brought her eyes back up again; now they held both a challenge and the desire to justify herself. Her eyes seemed to say: "You never offered me anything like this. You just lived with me, that's all. Why should I have waited, what was there to hope for? After all, time passes, and one day it's too late. That's why it all turned out this way."

All of this had a disturbing effect on Chonkin. It was not that he was jealous (though of course there was some of that too). What he principally felt at that moment was a sense of being wronged and offended. After all, she could have come out and said it right to him, then he could have thought it over and maybe even married her. But she hadn't said a word, and since she hadn't, why invite him to the wedding? Probably just to make fun of him.

However, Chonkin neither expressed any of this in words nor allowed it to show, but bowed to the bride and groom, as custom dictates, and said politely: "Hello."

Then Chonkin bowed to everyone and greeted them with a general hello.

No one answered Chonkin's greeting, but from behind Burly nudged him toward a vacant stool at the table. Chonkin settled himself on this stool, then took a look around.

To his left sat a plump elderly man wearing an embroidered Ukrainian shirt belted with a twisted silk sash. His face was round, with a fat little nose and thick pale eyebrows that hung down over his eyes. The crown of his head was naturally bald and the rest of it had been shaved until it shone. There was a small cut still in the process of healing near his right ear. The several black spots on the top of his head looked as if cigarettes had been stubbed out there. His little eyes swimming in fat, the man looked over good-naturedly at the new arrival and gave him a friendly smile.

The person to Chonkin's right was even more pleasant to behold—a young girl of seventeen or so, her breasts just beginning to develop, the ends of her braids tied in ribbons. Using no spoon, just her mouth, the girl was eating her buttered kasha right off the plate and stealing curious, mischievous glances at Chonkin. It was only then that Chonkin noticed that, like the girl, all the other guests were sticking their faces in their plates and that no forks or spoons had been set before them on the table. I don't get it. A bunch of barbarians, thought Chonkin and glanced inquiringly over at Burly, who had seated himself opposite Chonkin, on the other side of the table. Burly nodded to Chonkin not to be upset, everything was just the way it was supposed to be. However, the red-faced woman in the crepe de chine sarafan sitting next to Burly began winking and making all sorts of faces, which embarrassed Chonkin. He blushed and turned his gaze to the man beside him, who smiled at him and said: "Don't be scared, dear boy, we're all friends here. No one's going to hurt your feelings."

"I'm not scared," said Chonkin, plucking up his courage.

"You're scared," said the man, not believing him. "You're only pretending you're not but, ech, how scared in fact you are. What's your name?"

"Chonkin's my name. Vanya Chonkin."

"And your patronymic?"

"Vasilyevich," Chonkin readily informed the man.

"That's a good name," said his neighbor approvingly. "There once was a tsar named Ivan Vasilyevich, Ivan the Terrible. No doubt you've heard of him?"

"I heard something about him."

"He was a good man, he had heart," said Chonkin's neighbor with real feeling. He moved a glass of vodka toward Chonkin, then took another for himself. "Let's drink, Vanya."

Chonkin intended to drain his glass in one gulp and held his breath as he always did when drinking vodka, so it would go right down, but the vodka turned out to have no taste, no smell, it was just water. Yet, his head started buzzing, his spirits rose at once, and Chonkin began feeling a little freer and easier.

The man beside him pushed a plate of appetizers, pickled cucumbers and fried potatoes, over to Chonkin. Chonkin looked around for a fork and, finding none, was about to eat with his hands, when his neighbor butted in again. "Eat with your mouth, Vanya. It's easier that way."

Chonkin took his advice and tried it. It was true, it was better, and the food tasted better that way too. What did people invent all those forks and spoons for, anyway? You just had to keep washing them. A nuisance.

The man beside Chonkin kept looking at him, smiling good-naturedly, and then asked: "From the badge in your lapel, Vanya, I'd guess you were in the air force."

Ivan was about to make some sort of evasive reply when the girl on the right broke in. "No," she said in a squeaky little voice. "He rides a horse."

Chonkin was surprised. So young, yet she knew everything. But how?

"You really ride a horse," said the man, happy to hear it. "That's wonderful. Horses are so nice. They don't honk at you, they don't rattle, and they don't smell of gasoline. I'd be curious to know how many horses you have in your unit."

"Four," squealed the young girl.

"It's not four at all," said Chonkin. "It's three. The skewbald mare broke her leg and they sent her off to the glue factory."

"The skewbald went to the glue factory all right but the bay had a foal," said the girl in proof of her point.

"Don't argue with her, she knows," said the man to Chonkin's left. "Better you tell me now which goes faster, an airplane or a horse?"

"That's a stupid question," said Chonkin. "When a plane flies low and right at you, zoooom and it's gone, but when it's climbing higher up, then it starts slowing down."

"You don't say," said the man, shaking his head in amazement. He then began to ask Chonkin other questions—how old he was, had he been in the army long, how they fed him there, what kind of clothing they issued, and how long he got his puttees for. Chonkin answered willingly and thoroughly until suddenly he stopped short, realizing that he was blurting out classified military secrets to the first person he'd run into. How could he have done it! How many times had they told him, how often had they warned him: Button your lip! A big mouth is the enemy's best friend!

By this time the enemy in the embroidered shirt had lost all sense of shame and was making no attempt whatsoever to conceal his pencil as it flew across the notebook on his knees.

"Hey, listen, you, what's this all about?" Chonkin flung

himself at the man, making a grab for the notebook. "Gimme that!"

"What's the matter? Why are you shouting?" asked the man, folding up his notebook. "Why the shouting? People will think something's wrong."

"What are you writing for?" There was no holding Chonkin back. "So we've got us a writer here, huh. Give it here, I tell you."

Chonkin threw himself at his opponent and had almost grabbed the notebook away from him when, with surprising swiftness, the man stuck it in his mouth and swallowed it in a flash, pencil and all.

"All gone," he said grinning maliciously, spreading wide his empty hands.

"Don't give me that 'all gone,'" roared Chonkin, attacking with his fists. "I'll tear it out of your throat."

And Chonkin truly would have torn it from his throat, but the man dodged just in time and suddenly began to shout in a frenzy: "Biiiiitter!"

Chonkin remembered that he was at a wedding and, seizing the man's throat, also began shouting for the sake of propriety: "Bitter!" Everyone else picked up the refrain and the entire table began shouting out: "Bitter! Bitter!"

Meanwhile, the man in the embroidered shirt had begun to gag a bit and the very tip of the notebook had appeared at the top of his throat. Chonkin was about to grab it with his free hand, and threw a quick glance at the bride and groom to see if they were watching. But what he saw then immediately deprived him of all his strength and all his desire to struggle for the stupid notebook.

The bride and groom had risen decorously as custom dictates when the guests cry out "Bitter." Their eyes inquired whether they'd really been meant to kiss or whether the guests had simply started up from a lack of anything better to do. Overcoming his embarrassment, the groom hooked his arm around Nyura and, pulling her head abruptly to him, drank in her pale lips with his. Chonkin went cold as he recalled where, when, and under what circumstances he had met the groom. For how could he not recall him when the groom was none other than Borka the hog, who, even though he was wearing a velvet jacket with the marksman button on it and even though he looked like a human being, was a hog all the same.

Chonkin wanted to cry out to the people and draw their attention to what was happening—a hog kissing a human girl—but that would have been a waste of effort, since he would have been drowned out by the roars of "Bitter! Bitter!" that came from every side, though it was not "Bitter!" they were crying but some other word which Chonkin knew as well. He gazed around him and it was only then that he realized with total clarity what was happening, realized that there were no people sitting there at all, only ordinary pigs banging their feet on the table and grunting the way pigs are supposed to.

Chonkin covered his face with his hands and sank back down on his stool. O Lord, what was happening, what had he gotten himself into? Never in his life had he called upon God, but this time there was no getting around it.

The silence made Chonkin come around. He took his hands away from his face. All the pigs were silently staring at him. They seemed to be waiting for him to do something. He felt awful. He shrank from their gaze. Then the spell broke.

"Why are you looking at me, why?" he began shouting desperately, his eyes sliding from snout to snout.

But his words brought no more reply than if they had fallen into a deep well.

Chonkin shifted his gaze to the man on his left. The fat dappled hog in the embroidered Ukrainian shirt was looking at Chonkin without blinking, his dull little eyes swimming in fat.

"You old hog," shouted Chonkin, grabbing him by the shoulders and shaking him. "Why are you staring at me? Why?"

The hog did not answer. He simply grinned and silently pushed Chonkin's hands from his shoulders with his powerful front feet. Chonkin realized that nothing could be accomplished by force and let his head fall onto his chest.

Then the loud voice of Burly the hog rang out through the silence: "Chonkin, why weren't you grunting?"

Chonkin's head jerked up at Burly—what was he talking about?

"You weren't grunting, Chonkin," persisted Burly.

"That's right, he wasn't grunting," corroborated the hog in the Ukrainian shirt as if his sole desire was to get at the truth.

"He wasn't grunting! He wasn't grunting!" the young piggy with the bows near her ears squealed out to the entire hall.

In search of salvation, Chonkin looked over to Nyura, who alone among them all had retained something human about her. Embarrassed, she lowered her eyes and said softly: "Vanya, I don't think you were grunting either."

"It's interesting," said Borka the groom. "Everybody grunts but him. Maybe you don't like to grunt?"

Chonkin's mouth went dry. "But I . . ."

"But you what?"

"I don't know," mumbled Chonkin, his eyes downcast.

"He doesn't know," squealed the little piggy.

"That's right, he doesn't know," confirmed the hog in the embroidered shirt in a bitter tone.

"I don't understand," said Borka, spreading his feet out wide. "Grunting's so enjoyable. Everyone finds such pleasure in it. Grunt, please."

"Grunt, grunt," the young piggy began whispering to Chonkin, nudging him with her elbow.

"Vanya," said Nyura fondly, "grunt. What will it cost you? I didn't know how to before either, but now I've learned and there's nothing to it. Say 'huhn huhn'—that's all there is to it."

"What do you all care?" groaned Chonkin. "What do you need me to grunt for? I don't tell you what to do. Grunt if you like, but why should I? I'm not a pig, I'm a human being."

"He's human," squealed out the young piggy.

"Says he's human," the hog in the shirt repeated in surprise.

"A human being?" cross-examined Borka.

Chonkin's assertion seemed so ridiculous to all the pigs that they banged their feet in unison on the table and then began grunting with delight. The hog in the embroidered shirt stuck his damp snout in Chonkin's ear. Ivan grabbed for his ear but it was no longer there. The hog had turned away and was calmly chewing it as if it were not an ear but, say, a cabbage leaf or something.

The little piggy leaned behind Chonkin and asked the hog: "Taste good?"

"Lousy," said the hog, crinkling up his face as he swallowed the ear.

"What do you mean, lousy?" asked Chonkin, offended. "Yours any better?"

"I have a pig's ears," answered the hog with a superior

air. "Indispensable for the manufacture of jellied meats. And you would be much better off grunting than gabbing."

"Grunt, grunt," whispered the little piggy.

"You were told to grunt," said Burly.

Now Chonkin got angry. "Huhn huhn huhn," he said, mimicking the pigs. "All right? Satisfied?"

"No," said Burly with a frown. "We're not satisfied. You're grunting like you were being forced to. And you should grunt cheerfully, from the bottom of your heart, so that you really enjoy it as we do. C'mon, keep grunting."

"C'mon." The little piggy nudged him with her elbow.

"Huhn huhn," cried Chonkin, a facsimile of extraordinary delight on his face.

"Hold it," interrupted Burly. "You're only pretending you like it, but you're not really satisfied. We don't want you to grunt against your will, we want you to really like it. All right, let's try it together. Huhn huhn!"

Chonkin grunted reluctantly at first, but then, infected by Burly's immense delight, he began to grunt with identical delight; he grunted with everything he had, tears of joy and tenderness welling in his eyes. Swept up by Chonkin's joy, all the pigs began to grunt along with him, pounding their feet on the table. The red-faced pig in the crepe de chine sarafan leaned across the table to kiss Chonkin, when suddenly Borka the hog leaped out of his velvet jacket and now, entirely a pig, began galloping along the table, dashed from one end to the other, then turned around and jumped back into his jacket again. At that very moment golden trays appeared at the far end of the table and were passed from one pig to the next! "Could it be pork?" shuddered Chonkin, but he was seized

by a still greater horror when he saw that it was not
pork at all; quite the contrary, it was humanork.

On the first tray, in a state of total nakedness, quite
ready for consumption, garnished with onions and green
peas, lay Sergeant Peskov. On the trays behind him, simi-
larly garnished, came Quartermaster Trofimovich and Private Samushkin. It's me who betrayed them, Chonkin
realized, feeling the hairs of his head stand up on end.

"Yes, Comrade Chonkin, you gave away a military secret and betrayed us all," confirmed Senior Politruk
Yartsev, wiggling on the next tray, his body blue from
cold. "You betrayed your comrades, your motherland, and
the person of Comrade Stalin."

Thereupon appeared a tray bearing the person of Comrade Stalin. One hand hung from the tray holding the
familiar pipe. Stalin grinned slyly to himself behind his
mustache.

Seized by inexpressible terror, Chonkin knocked over
his stool and bolted for the exit, but he stumbled and fell.
His fingers grabbed the threshold; his fingernails breaking, he tried to claw and crawl his way out, but could not.
Someone was holding him firmly by the legs. Then Chonkin gathered all his strength and with one enormous
effort jerked himself free and slammed his head painfully
against the wing of the plane.

. . . It was a bright and sunny day. Chonkin was sitting
on the hay under the plane, still at a total loss. Someone
was tugging at his leg. Chonkin looked and saw that it
was Borka the hog, not the Borka in the velvet jacket
who'd been sitting at the table, but regular, dirty Borka,
who had obviously just crawled out of a puddle and who
had seized Chonkin's unwound puttees between his teeth

and was tugging at Chonkin's leg, his short front feet braced against the ground, grunting with delight.

"Get out of here, you snake in the grass, you plague!" shouted Chonkin in a frenzy, almost losing consciousness.

15

Hearing his master's voice and thinking he'd been called, Borka rushed to greet Chonkin with a squeal of joy and to lick his ear too if he could. But the only greeting Borka received was a smash in the snout from Chonkin's fist. Surprised by such a welcome, Borka began squealing pitifully. He jumped away to one side and sank to the dusty ground on his chin (that is, what is called a chin when referring to people), stretched his paws out in front of him, and gazed at Chonkin with his little eyes, then began to whimper softly like a dog.

"I'll give you something to whimper about," threatened Chonkin as he started cooling down and began regaining his senses. He looked around. There was an old flannelette blanket on the ground beside him, which he had obviously thrown off while sleeping. There was also a note held down by a rock nearby. It was from Nyura, who, as always, left out the vowels or, if she put them in, more often than not put the wrong ones in: "I've gawn off too work kee beetween kracks in pourch kabudge soop in ovn, eet and bee well, gretings, Nyura." Everything about the note hinted that Nyura bore him no grudge and was ready to make up if Ivan wouldn't stay stubborn.

"Fat chance," said Chonkin aloud and was about to tear up the note, but then thought better of it and, folding it in fours, stuck it in his field-shirt pocket. The mention of the cabbage soup had gotten Ivan right in the pit of his stomach and he remembered that he hadn't had anything to eat since lunch yesterday.

Borka, who by this time had calmed down and fallen silent, again began whimpering as if pleading that some attention be given him, a poor, beaten creature. Ivan looked severely at him out of the corner of his eye, but Borka looked so pitiful and hurt that Ivan couldn't stand it and, slapping his chin, called: "Come here!"

Words would fail any attempt to describe the eagerness with which Borka forgot the wrong unjustly done him and dashed to his master, squealing and grunting so happily that his whole being seemed to say: "I don't know what I did wrong to you, but I did it if you think I did. Beat me for it, kill me if you want, just forgive me."

"All right, all right," grumbled Chonkin and began scratching Borka behind the ear, which made Borka fall immediately to the grass, where he lay first on his side, then, for quite a long time, on his back, his eyes closed in bliss, his short, skinny feet pressed together and held straight up in the air.

Finally Chonkin had enough, punched Borka in the side, and said: "Get outta here!"

In two seconds Borka was on his feet and had dashed off. He looked guardedly back at Chonkin, but, seeing no malice in his master's eyes, felt reassured and chased off after a chicken that had run by.

Chonkin got up, shook the hay off his clothes, wound up his puttees, picked his rifle up off the ground, then had himself a look around. In the neighboring garden loomed the stoop-shouldered figure of Gladishev, as familiar as part of the landscape. He was walking among his beds, bending over each individual PATS bush and mumbling some incantation to it. His wife, Aphrodite, a dirty woman with a sleepy face and uncombed hair, was sitting on the porch, their year-old son, Hercules (another victim of Gladishev's erudition), on her lap. She was peering at her husband with unconcealed disgust.

So that further developments in the relationship between the breeder and his wife be intelligible to the reader, we must pause here, however briefly, to tell the cautionary tale of this ill-matched couple.

Gladishev had married Aphrodite about two years before our story began, when he was pushing forty. For the previous five years, following the death of his mother, Gladishev had lived alone, justly supposing that family life would not be conducive to his creative scientific endeavors. But, as his forties drew near, Gladishev decided to marry (perhaps nature had made its claim on him or perhaps he had tired of solitude). However, this turned out to be no simple matter in spite of there being a surplus of marriageable girls in the village. The girls would put up with his discourses on his remarkable hybrid and would even agree to work hand in hand with him and share the burden of his scientific crusade, meanwhile hoping that given time this foolishness would pass from Gladishev by itself. But just when things would be looking perfect, Gladishev's fiancée would cross the threshold of her future home. It was a rare thing for one of them to last more than half an hour there. They say one fainted dead away in less than two minutes' time. And here's the reason why. In this home Gladishev kept fertilizers for his breeding experiments in special pots. These included both peat-compost pots and pots which contained cow and horse manure, as well as some with chicken droppings. Gladishev ascribed great significance to fertilizers. He would mix them in varying combinations, placing them on the stove and windowsill to ferment at a specific temperature. This went

on not only in the summer but in the winter as well—
with all the windows closed!

And only the future Aphrodite, who had no illusions
whatsoever concerning her charms, was able to put up
with it all. She really wanted a marriage.

When Gladishev realized that she was his only possibility, he decided to forget his dream of marriage once
and for all. But later he reconsidered and took on Efrosinya, who was of no use to anyone else, with the understanding that she would repay his nobility with complete
dedication to him and his science.

But, as they say, man proposes and God disposes. At
first, Efrosinya did truly repay him, but, after she gave
birth to Hercules, she declared war on Gladishev's pots,
using the pretext that they were bad for the baby. She began with hints and attempts at persuasion, then started
making scenes. She would bring the pots out into the passageway. Gladishev would bring them back in. She would
try to smash the pots and Gladishev would give *her* a
smash, though in general he deplored violence. More than
once she took the baby and went home to her parents,
who lived at the other end of the village, but her mother
would send her back every time.

Finally, she reconciled herself to everything, gave up,
and ceased taking care of herself. Never known as a
beauty, God only knew what she'd come to look like now.

And there you have the whole story in a nutshell.

Now let us return to where we left off.

So, Ivan was standing near his airplane, Gladishev was
digging in his garden, and Aphrodite, babe in arms, was
sitting on the porch, looking at her husband with unconcealed disgust.

"Hey, hello there, neighbor," Chonkin called out to
Gladishev, who straightened up from one of his PATS

bushes, tipped his hat with two fingers, and answered politely: "I wish you a good morning."

Chonkin leaned his rifle against the plane and walked up to the fence which divided the two gardens.

"What's this? I see you're still knocking yourself out in your garden. Not fed up yet?"

"How can I put it?" answered Gladishev with dignified reserve. "It's not for myself I do this, not for personal gain, but in the interests of science. But did you by any chance spend the night under your plane?"

"We Tartars don't give a damn where we sleep the night," joked Chonkin. "It's warm now, it's not winter."

"I come out this morning and I see somebody's legs sticking out from under the plane. So I think to myself, Can Vanya really be sleeping out there now? Then I say to Aphrodite, Go look. I say, Seems Vanya's legs are sticking out from under the plane. Listen, Aphrodite," he shouted to his wife to be his witness: "You remember this morning I said to you, Go look. I said, Seems Vanya's legs are sticking out from under the plane."

Aphrodite looked at him with the same expression on her face and neither changed that expression nor reacted in the least to her husband's words.

Chonkin looked over at Gladishev, sighed, then suddenly, to his own surprise, said: "Listen, me and my woman had us a fight. So I left, you know what I mean? That's why I'm sleeping out here now."

"Really?" said Gladishev, disquieted.

"That's right," said Ivan, avoiding a more direct answer. "I says something to her, she says something to me, you know, one thing leads to another, it blows up, and that's it. Listen, I don't give a good goddamn. I grab my coat, my rifle, my sack—what else have I got?—and out I go."

"That's quite a turnabout," said Gladishev, shaking his

head in surprise. "So this morning I go out and I see what looks like your legs sticking out from under the plane. So you had a fight?"

"Yup, we had us a fight," said Chonkin, growing still sadder.

"Maybe you did the right thing," conjectured Gladishev. He glanced apprehensively at his wife, then switched to a whisper. "If you want to know, I'll tell you something. Don't get yourself tied down with these women, Vanya. Get away while you're still young. You know, they're . . . Just take a look at mine sitting there, the rattlesnake. Next time you're talking near her, notice her tongue, it's forked. Stings like a reptile. There's no words for what I've gone through with that one, Vanya. Sure, and am I the only one? The opposite sex has brought men boundless suffering, whether you look at our contemporary epoch of development or at facts from the historical past . . ." Looking out of the corner of his eye at his wife, Gladishev started whispering even softer, as if communicating top-secret information. "When Tsar Nicholas I exiled the Decembrists to Siberia, or wherever the hell it was, their wives weren't content, no, they had to pack up their rags and trudge on after them, even though there was no railroad in those days. They rode the horses to death, they drove the drivers crazy, and they almost kicked the bucket themselves, but finally they got where they wanted to get, you see how it is. I'd never say anything bad about Nyura, Vanya. She's an educated woman, with some understanding of things. But all the same, get away while there's still time."

"I would," said Chonkin. "But this contraption here won't let me." He nodded at the plane; then, after a moment's thought, added sadly: "I'm dying to eat. My stomach's rumbling."

"You want something to eat?" said Gladishev in surprise. "Lord, why didn't you say so before? Let's go to my house. We'll get the primus lit right up and fry an omelet in bacon fat. There's even a little . . ." Gladishev winked at Chonkin . . . "home brew. Let's go. At the same time, you can see how I live."

Chonkin didn't have to be asked twice. He hid his rifle under the straw, crawled through the fence, and, stepping carefully between the beds, followed his host, who walked on ahead with an independent gait. They went up onto the porch. Aphrodite grimaced in pain and turned away.

"You should at least put a piece of oilcloth under the kid," grumbled Gladishev as he passed. "Otherwise he'll piddle and stink up your skirt."

Indifferently, Aphrodite raised her eyes; indifferently, she said: "Better you go take a whiff in the house. And let your guest have a whiff too."

That said, she turned away.

Gladishev opened the door and let Chonkin enter the passageway first.

"You hear how she talks to me?" he said to Ivan. "It's the same thing every day. The filthy fool. My stinks have a scientific purpose, hers are just plain sloppiness."

It was dark inside the passageway. Gladishev struck a match, which lit up the narrow corridor and a door covered with sackcloth. Gladishev opened the door, which immediately released such a smell that Chonkin reeled in surprise. If he had not immediately pinched his nose, Chonkin could well have fallen to the floor. Keeping his nose pinched shut, Chonkin entered the hut behind his host, who then turned to him and said: "Of course, right at the very first it is a little shocking, but I'm already used to it, doesn't bother me a bit. Open up one nostril a little, and when you're used to the smell, open up the other one. You might think the smell is disgusting, but in fact it is healthful and beneficial to the organism and has all sorts of valuable properties. For example, the French firm Coty manufactures the most subtle perfumes from shit. Meantime, you have a look around and I'll whip us up an omelet. We'll have a bite together. I feel like eating something now too."

While Gladishev pumped and kindled the primus, his guest remained in the front room. As he grew used to the smell, Chonkin took Gladishev's advice and opened first one nostril, then the other. He looked about the room, which really was something to see.

First—those pots. There were a great multitude of them and they stood not only on the stove and the windowsill but on the bench by the window, and under the bench, and behind the bedstead of the iron bed, which had not been made—the pillows had been tossed and left where they fell.

Over the bed, as is customary, hung picture frames with flowers and doves at their corners. These frames contained photographs of the master of the house from the years of his youth up through the present time, photographs of his wife, Aphrodite, and of numerous relatives from both sides. Above this iconostasis was fixed a portrait of the Gladishevs together that had been made to order and was executed from various snapshots and so carefully painted by the unknown artist that the faces in the painting bore not the slightest resemblance to the subjects.

The wall opposite the window also served as a museum of sorts—the picture frames hung there contained the letters and articles Gladishev had received about his scientific research, which we have already mentioned. In a frame apart was preserved the letter from the well-known agricultural academician, which we have also previously mentioned.

On the wall between the windows hung a 16-caliber, single-barreled rifle, which the reader of course has already guessed will have to be fired at some point, but whether it will fire or misfire is still uncertain; that, only time will tell.

Chonkin had still not managed to have a proper look at everything in the room when the omelet was ready and Gladishev summoned him to the table.

The back room too was not particularly tidy, but at least it was a bit cleaner than the front room. It contained a cabinet with dishes, a cradle that hung from the ceiling (the couch of Hercules), and an old trunk that had no lid and was crammed full of tattered books mostly scholarly in nature (for example, *Myths of Ancient Greece*, and the popular brochure "The Fly, an Active Spreader of Disease") and an incomplete set of the journal *The Cornfield* from the year 1912 as well. This trunk was the principal source from which Gladishev drew his erudition.

The omelet and bacon fat hissed in the frying pan on the large table, whose oilcloth cover had brown circles burned on it from hot dishes. No matter how giddy the smell made him (though he had in fact grown somewhat used to it), hunger made Chonkin even giddier; he didn't require two invitations and sat down at the table without further formalities.

Gladishev got two forks from the drawer, wiped them off on his T-shirt, placed one before his guest, and took the one with the broken prong for himself. Chonkin was about to poke his fork into the omelet when his host stopped him, saying: "Hold on a minute."

He got two dusty glasses from the cabinet, held them to the light, spat in them, wiped them with his T-shirt too, and placed them on the table. Then he dashed out to the passageway and came back with a partially full bottle of home brew that had a twist of newspaper for a stopper. Gladishev poured his guest half a glass, then poured himself half a glass also.

"There you go, Vanya," he said, pulling the stool up to him and picking up their conversation. "We usually react squeamishly to shit as if it were something bad. But if we look into the matter we see that it could be the most valuable substance on earth, because all life comes from shit and returns to shit."

"In what sense?" Chonkin asked politely, gazing with hungry eyes at the cooling omelet, but then deciding not to begin before his host.

"Any sense you like." Gladishev developed his idea without taking any notice of his guest's impatience. "Judge for yourself. The ground must be fertilized with shit for a good harvest. All the herbs, grains, and fruits that we and the animals eat grow up out of shit. The animals give us milk, meat, wool, and all the rest of it. We use it all and then change it back into shit again. That's the origin of—how should I put it—of the circulation of shit in nature. Let's ask ourselves for a moment why we should use shit in the form of meat or milk or even this bread here, that is, in processed form. A legitimate question arises: Wouldn't it be better to rid ourselves of our biases and false squeamishness and use shit itself in pure form as a sort of wonder vitamin? In the beginning, of course," Gladishev corrected himself, noticing Chonkin wince, "we could remove its natural smell and then, when man was used to it, leave it just the way it is. But, Vanya, that task belongs to the distant future and to future exploits of science. Vanya, I propose we drink a toast to the success of our science, to Soviet power, and to the person of Comrade Stalin, a genius of worldwide fame."

"To our meeting." Chonkin hastily seconded the toast.

They clinked glasses. Ivan downed the contents of his glass and nearly fell off his chair. He instantly lost his breath, just as if he'd been punched in the stomach. Seeing nothing in front of him, Chonkin blindly stuck his fork into the frying pan, tore off a piece of omelet, and, with the aid of his other hand, swallowed the piece, burning himself in the process. Only then did he expel the air that was bursting his lungs.

Gladishev, who had downed his own glass without any difficulty, looked over at Ivan with a sly grin. "Well, Ivan, how's the home brew?"

"First-rate stuff," praised Chonkin, wiping the tears from his eyes with the palm of his hand. "Takes your breath away."

The same grin still on his face, Gladishev pulled the flat tin he used as an ashtray over to himself, spat some home brew into it, then lit it with a match. The home brew blazed up with a murky blue flame.

"See that?"

"You make it from grain or from beetroot?" asked Chonkin curiously.

"From shit, Vanya," said Gladishev with restrained pride.

Chonkin choked. "What do you mean?" he asked, moving away from the table.

"Very simple recipe, Vanya." Gladishev was eager to explain. "You take a kilo of sugar to a kilo of shit . . ."

Knocking his stool over, Chonkin dashed for the door. He almost knocked Aphrodite and the baby down on the porch. Two steps from the porch he braced his forehead against the log wall of the hut, where he vomited himself inside out.

His perplexed host ran out behind him. His feet stomping loudly, Gladishev clambered down the porch.

"Vanya, what's the matter?" he asked sympathetically, touching Chonkin on the shoulder. "That brew was pure, Vanya. You saw how it burned yourself."

Ivan was about to answer, but at the mere mention of the home brew new spasms had seized his stomach and he had barely enough time to spread his legs apart so as not to splatter his boots.

"Oh, Lord!" said Aphrodite suddenly, in hopeless anguish. "You've gone and given another one shit to drink, you goddamned tyrant, there's no getting rid of you. I spit on you!" she said and spat juicily in her husband's direction.

Gladishev, however, did not take offense.

"Instead of spitting you'd be better off bringing a marinated apple up from the cellar. Can't you see the man's not feeling well?"

"Sure, those apples!" groaned Aphrodite. "Those apples stink of shit too. The whole house is stuffed with shit, you should fall in it, you should drown in it, you miserable idiot. I'm leaving you, you bonehead. I'll go begging with the child before I'll be buried in shit."

Without a moment's hesitation, she snatched up Hercules and dashed out the gate. Leaving Chonkin to himself, Gladishev ran off after his wife.

"Where you running to, Aphrodite?" he cried out behind her. "Come back, I say. Don't shame us in front of everybody. Hey, Aphrodite!"

Aphrodite stopped, turned around, and began shouting angrily in Gladishev's face. "I'm not your Aphrodite. I'm Froska, you get that, you lop-eared dunce. Froska!"

Then she turned back around, and holding the child, who was scared half to death, high in the air at the end of her outstretched arms, she ran on farther through the village, leaping and stumbling.

"I'm Froska, people, listen to me, I'm Froska!" she kept shouting with frenzied delight, as if she had just suddenly regained the gift of speech after years of being mute.

16

On June 21, Schulenburg, the German ambassador to the U.S.S.R., was handed a note which read that, according to Soviet information, German troops were massing at the western borders of the Soviet Union. The Soviet government requested the government of Germany to clarify the matter. This note was passed on to Hitler when only minutes remained until the beginning of the war.

At that moment Chonkin, who had made up with Nyura the night before, was still sleeping. Then he was awakened by a call of nature. Chonkin lay without moving for a while, deciding not to get out from under his warm blanket, secretly hoping the need would go away all by itself. But the need did not go away. Chonkin waited until there wasn't a second left to spare. Jamming his feet in his boots and throwing his coat over his bare shoulders, he dashed out to the porch, but there was no time to go any farther than that.

It was a bright, fresh morning. The dew lay thick on the grass, on the leaves of the trees, and on the flat surfaces of the plane. The sun had already broken away from the horizon and was growing visibly smaller. The windows reflected the sun's red light. The perfect silence was broken from time to time by the soft, sleepy mooing of cows. Chonkin was about to wake Nyura up so she could milk Beauty and send her out to pasture, but then he changed his mind and decided to do everything himself. When he was getting the milk pail, Nyura woke and wanted to get up, but Chonkin said to her: "It's all right, sleep a little more."

Chonkin went off to the cow shed.

After milking Beauty, he opened one half of the double gate, but the cow wouldn't go through it. She was used to having both sides of the gate opened up for her. The stupid beast, thought Chonkin and was about to run a bolt across her back, but instead took pity on her.

"Clear out," he muttered peaceably, opening the other half of the gate.

Glancing suspiciously at Chonkin, then shaking her head crowned with short little horns in triumph, Beauty set off for the exit from the yard just as the herd was coming by.

The cows were spread out along the whole broad road, sniffing at the posts and gates as they went, sighing sleepily.

The new herdsman, Lyosha Zharov, came swaying up behind the herd on his horse. An old quilted jacket served him as a saddle. One ripped arm hung down and swung like a pendulum in time to the horse's gait.

Catching sight of the herdsman, Chonkin thought he might enjoy passing the time of day with him. He walked up to the gate and called out: "Hey, you there, how's life treating you?"

Lyosha drew in the reins, stopped the horse, and looked curiously over at Chonkin, whom he was seeing for the first time.

"Not too bad all around," he said after a moment's thought. "Life's pretty good."

They fell silent. Then Chonkin looked up at the clear sky and said: "It looks like we'll have good weather today."

"Good weather, if it doesn't rain."

"You don't get rain without clouds," remarked Chonkin.

"Without clouds, that's right, no rain."

"Sometimes you get clouds and still you don't get rain."

"Sometimes you do," agreed Lyosha.

On that note they parted. Zharov rode on to catch up with the herd and Chonkin went back to the hut.

Nyura was sleeping stretched out across the whole bed. It seemed a shame to wake her. Chonkin walked around the hut for a while, but then, finding nothing to do, ended up walking over to Nyura.

"Listen. Get up," he said, touching her shoulder.

Now the sun was shining right in through the window, its dust-filled rays touching the wall opposite, where the clock with the warped face hung. The clock was old, its works were full of dust, and something in it was always rustling and clacking. The hands showed four o'clock—at that moment the Germans were bombing Kiev.

PART 2

1

The news that war had broken out caught everyone napping, because no one had been paying war the least bit of mind. It's true that about a week and a half earlier Granny Dunya had been spreading word about the dream she had in which her hen Klashka had given birth to a goat with four horns. The experts, however, had judged the vision in question to be harmless; the worst it could mean, in their opinion, was rain. Now everything took on new significance.

Chonkin did not learn about what had happened immediately because he was sitting in the outhouse, in no hurry to leave. Chonkin's time had not been apportioned and allotted for any noble purpose; it was only for living and for him to contemplate the flow of life without drawing any conclusions: simply to eat, drink, sleep, and to answer the calls of nature, not only in those moments determined by the regulations on guard and garrison duty, but as the needs arose.

The summer outhouse stood in the vegetable patch. Rays of sunlight sliced through the flimsy structure. Green flies were buzzing about, a spider was parachuting down from one corner of his web.

Squares of newspaper had been nailed to the wall on Chonkin's right. He tore them off one after the other and read them through, thus acquiring no little fragmentary information on the most diverse matters. He acquainted himself with several headlines:

ERAPY SEASON IN VOLGA HEALTH RESORTS
ILITARY ACTION IN SYR

He read the notice entitled "German Protest to the U.S.A." in its entirety:

> Berlin, 18 July. (TASS) According to a bull
> of the German Information Bureau
> government of the U.S.A. in a note of 6 June
> demanded from the German chargé d'af
> aires in Washington that employ
> of the German Information lib
> in New York, of the Transoc
> ailway Society abandoned
> territory of the United States, Demand
> motivated by the fact that employees w
> cupied with, as it were, inadmissible act
> German government declin
> demands as baseless and lod
> a protest against the activities of the U.S.
> tradicting the treaty.

Chonkin had not yet managed to begin his considerations of the activities of the U.S.A. when Nyura's distant cry reached his ear: "Vaaanya!"

Chonkin pricked up his ears.

"Vanya! Where are you?

"A goblin should come and grab you, Vanya, where are you gone off to now!" fumed Nyura, as she circled closer. There was no way around it, he had to answer her now.

"What's all the fuss about?" Chonkin spoke up, embarrassed in spite of himself. "I'm in here."

Nyura was right beside him. Through a knothole, he caught a glimpse of her face, red with excitement.

"Come out quick!" said Nyura. "It's war!"

"That's all that was missing!" said Chonkin, not so much in surprise as in sorrow. "You mean with America?"

"With Germany!"

Puzzled, Chonkin whistled, and then began to button himself up. Something about it did not strike him quite right and when he came out he asked Nyura who'd been blabbing such nonsense to her.

"They said so on the radio."

"Maybe they're full of it?" said Chonkin hopefully.

"Not too likely," said Nyura. "Everybody's run down to the office for a meeting. Think we ought to go?"

Chonkin grew thoughtful and tilted his head to one side.

"If that's the way things stand, then I guess there's no meeting for me. That's my meeting right there, it should burn to the ground," he said and spat irritably at the airplane.

"Forget it," said Nyura. "Who needs that?"

"Before, nobody. But now it'll come in handy. You go hear what they're saying there, I'll stay here just in case somebody flies in."

A minute later, his rifle on his shoulder, Chonkin was walking around the airplane, twisting his head from side to side in expectation of an attack, either by the Germans or by his commanding officers. His neck had started to hurt and his eyes were dazzled, when Chonkin's keen ears discerned a gradually increasing *zee zee zee* sound.

"It's coming!" Chonkin became excited and craned his neck. A small speck had flashed in front of his eyes and was now increasing in size, gradually assuming the shape of an airplane. But suddenly the speck disappeared and the sound broke off. Right at that very moment something pricked Chonkin; he whacked himself on the forehead and killed a mosquito. "That's not an airplane," he said to himself and wiped the mosquito off on his pants.

Perhaps it was the whack on the forehead, or perhaps it was due to some non-mechanical factor in Chonkin's brain, but something in there moved and this displacement gave rise to the alarming thought that he was wasting his time, that he was of no use to anyone, and that nobody was going to be sent for him. Chonkin had never thought he was destined for anything special, but still, he had never doubted that someday he would be called upon. It would not have to be much, even for some foolish thing, or to give his life freely for something worthwhile, with no thought of reward. But now everything seemed to say that his life was of no use to anyone. (Of course, if looked at from the point of view of world-shaking events, a modest natural phenomenon like Chonkin's life was of the smallest possible worth; yet he had nothing more valuable that he could share with the land of his birth.)

Sadly conscious of his uselessness, Chonkin abandoned the object of his protection and set off toward the office, where the people had gathered and were now awaiting an explanation.

2

People were standing in a broad semicircle in front of the office porch, which was enclosed by a railing. They were patiently watching the door, covered with thick, ragged felt, hoping the authorities would soon come out and supply them with some details. The men were gloomily smoking their cigarettes, the women were weeping softly, and the children were glancing at their parents with no understanding of the sadness that had come over them, since, in a child's imagination, nothing in the world seems more fun than war.

It was midday, the sun was scorching, time stood still, the authorities had not yet appeared. With time on their hands, people began to exchange a few words and ended up talking. Burly was the center of attention, as usual. He consoled his fellow citizens by saying the war wouldn't last past the first rain, when the whole German machine was sure to sink in Russian mud. Kurzov agreed with him, but suggested they not lose sight of the fact that the German was fed on food concentrates and could endure a lot. In spite of his ninety years, failing mind, and total deafness, Grandpa Shapkin was gadding about the crowd trying to find out what the meeting was all about. Nobody would answer him. Finally, Burly took pity on him and, pretending to hold a machine gun by the handles, imitated a long burst of fire in sounds inaudible to Shapkin: "*Bam bam bam bam!*" Then, as if galloping on a valiant steed, Burly began waving an imaginary saber over his head.

Grandpa Shapkin gave all this its proper due, but nevertheless remarked that in the old days they sowed the grain and harvested it *before* they threshed it.

The crowd gradually unraveled into little separate groups, each with its own conversation, none of which had any relation to the war. Stepan Lukov was arguing with Stepan Frolov, saying that if you hitched an elephant to a locomotive, the elephant would win the tug-of-war. Feeling a little sassy, Burly asserted that he could copy the picture of any leader or animal by breaking the picture down into little squares and then copying each square.

Another time Chonkin would have stopped to marvel

at Burly's unusual talent, but he wasn't up to it at that particular moment. Preoccupied with his own unhappy thoughts, he walked around the corner to a tumbledown stack of pine logs. Ivan chose himself a log with no resin on it, sat down, and laid his rifle across his knees. He hadn't even managed to get out his oilcan of shag when Gladishev walked up.

"Say, neighbor, can you spare a piece of newspaper so I can roll up the shag you're treating me to? And I left my matches home."

"Take them," said Chonkin, without looking up.

That was the last of Chonkin's shag.

Gladishev lit up, took a deep drag, spit a shred of tobacco off his tongue, and sighed loudly: "Uh-huh!"

Chonkin said nothing and kept looking straight ahead.

"Uh-huh!" sighed Gladishev still more loudly, in an effort to get Chonkin's attention.

Chonkin said nothing.

"I can't stand it!" said Gladishev, throwing up his hands. "The mind refuses to accept it. They really must have some conscience—they ate our bacon fat and butter and now they play this dirty trick on us, by which I mean their treacherous attack."

Even to these words, Chonkin made no answer.

"No, just you think," said Gladishev heatedly. "You know, Vanya, it's a crying shame. People shouldn't go to war, Vanya, they ought to work for the good of future generations, because it was work and nothing except work that changed the monkey into contemporary man."

Gladishev looked over at Chonkin and suddenly realized something. "But, Vanya, you probably don't know that man is descended from the monkey."

"Me, I'd say from the cow," said Chonkin.

"Man could not descend from the cow," retorted Gladishev with conviction. "And you might ask why."

"I don't ask," said Chonkin.

"Well, but you might," said Gladishev, trying to lure him into a debate in order to demonstrate his own erudition. "I'll tell you why: the cow does not work, but the monkey did."

"Where?" asked Chonkin suddenly, staring hard at Gladishev.

"What do you mean, where?" Gladishev was taken aback.

"I'm asking you, where did your monkey work?" said Chonkin, growing increasingly irritated. "In a plant, a kolkhoz, a factory, where?"

"What a fool you are!" said Gladishev, excited. "What kind of factories, kolkhozes, et cetera could there have been in those primeval conditions? What's wrong with you, friend, are you in your right mind? The things you come out with! The monkey worked in the jungle, that's where. At first it climbed trees for bananas, then it started whacking them down with a stick. It was only later on that it picked up the stone . . ."

Giving Chonkin no chance to gather his wits, Gladishev launched into a brief exposition of the theory of evolution; he got as far as the disappearance of the tail and fur, but was unable to bring his lecture to a close—near the office, people were stirring and buzzing. Partorg Kilin had come out onto the porch.

3

"What's the reason for this gathering?"

Leaning his elbows casually on the railing, Kilin shifted

his small reddish eyes from one face to another, waiting for everyone to settle down and stop talking.

People exchanged glances, at a loss to explain the obvious.

"Well?" Kilin halted his gaze on the field-crop brigade leader. "What do you have to say, Shikalov?"

Shikalov grew confused, moved back, stepped on Burly's foot, and got a cuff on the back of his head. Then Shikalov stopped and stood on the spot, his mouth hanging open.

"I'm waiting, Shikalov," Kilin reminded him.

"You know I . . . I mean, we . . . There was a bulletin," said Shikalov, finally regaining his voice.

"What kind of bulletin?"

"Can you beat that," marveled Shikalov, looking around as if seeking witnesses. "What are you kidding me for? Didn't you hear, or what? There was a bulletin."

"What's the matter with you!" Kilin threw up his hands. "So there was a bulletin. And you mean to tell me that bulletin said people didn't have to work any more but were supposed to assemble and form a crowd. Is that what it said?"

Shikalov hung his head in silence.

"What kind of people are these!" lamented Kilin from the height of his position. "You have no consciousness. I can see even a war's all right with you, if it can get you off work. Everybody disperse, and I don't want to see a single person here in five minutes. Is that clear? I'm placing the responsibility on brigade leaders Shikalov and Taldikin."

"You should have said so right off," said Shikalov, glad things were back to normal. He turned to face the crowd: "All right, disperse. Hey, everybody, you gone deaf or what? Am I talking to myself? What are you standing there with your chops hanging for! Let's move it!" Thrusting out his hairy arms, Shikalov shoved a woman holding a baby. The woman started shouting and the baby began to cry.

"What are you shoving for?" Kurzov tried to stand up for the woman. "She's got a child with her."

"Go on, move it out of here!" Shikalov gave him a shove with his shoulder. "Child or no child, we're not going to stand around here and argue."

Little Taldikin rushed over and attacked Kurzov, jabbing him in the stomach with his little fists.

"All right there, all right," said Shikalov, unloosing a torrent of words. "No cause for a ruckus, save wear and tear on your nerves, go on home, take it easy, drink a little wine . . ."

"Just don't shove!" Kurzov was still resisting. "There's no law says you've got to shove."

"No one's shoving," cooed Taldikin. "I just gave you a little tickle like this."

"And there's no law says you've got to tickle, either," persisted Kurzov.

"Here's the law for you!" concluded Shikalov, sticking his enormous fist under Kurzov's nose.

Meanwhile, Taldikin was scampering through the crowd like a hairy little mutt, coming into view, then vanishing.

"Disperse, everybody, break it up!" he squealed with his sweet little voice. "What are you goggling at? This ain't no zoo. Go to the city if you want a zoo. And you, Grandpa"—he grabbed Shapkin by the sleeve—"you fell asleep or what? Nothing of interest for you here. It's the graveyard that should be on your mind, get it? The graveyard, I'm telling you!" shouted Taldikin into the old man's ears, which were overgrown with gray fluff. "You've already lived three days longer than you was supposed to, you hear me! Move those feet, Grandpa, one in front of the other. That's right, now you've got it!"

Gradually Shikalov and Taldikin achieved complete victory over their fellow villagers. For the time being, the area in front of the office was deserted.

4

The partorg's instructions seemed surprising to many people. They would have seemed surprising to him too, had not . . . But everything in its proper order.

Some three hours before all this happened, Kilin and Golubev had been taking turns cranking the field telephone. The chairman would relieve the partorg, the partorg the chairman, and it was all completely useless. The iron receiver pressed to their ear, they could hear rustling, crackling, clicking, music, the radio announcer's voice repeating the bulletin about the outbreak of war, and some woman cursing out some Mitya who had sold her samovar and quilt to go out drinking. At one point an angry male voice broke in and demanded Sokolov.

"What Sokolov?" asked Golubev.

"You know," said the voice. "You tell him if he doesn't appear tomorrow by zero eight hundred hours, he'll have to answer for it under wartime law."

The chairman was about to explain that there was no Sokolov there, but the angry voice had disappeared and this unknown Sokolov, perhaps without suspecting it in the least, was already setting himself up for a military tribunal.

Golubev yielded his place to the partorg, and walked over to the corner and opened the metal safe where secret and financial documents were kept. He stuck his head in the safe and looked like a photographer about to say: "Hold it! Here goes." He said, however, nothing of the sort. A soft, gurgling sound came from within the safe, then Ivan Timofeyevich withdrew his head and wiped his lips on his sleeve. Encountering the partorg's censorious gaze, Golubev withdrew some sort of record book from the safe, leafed through it without interest, and then replaced it. The hell with it, he thought indifferently, doesn't make any difference now. The war will write everything off. The main thing's to get to the front as fast as possible; there either you get a chest full of medals or a head full of bullets, but either way, at least you can live like an honest man. Unfortunately, due to his flat feet, Ivan Timofeyevich was unfit for military service, although he was hoping to conceal this defect from the examining board.

While Golubev was making plans for the future, Kilin went on stubbornly cranking the handle of the telephone. Everything imaginable could be heard in the receiver, everything except what he needed to hear.

"Allo, allo!" Kilin kept shouting every so often.

Someone said to him: "Go eat a kilo of shit," but Kilin did not take it personally.

"Forget it," advised Ivan Timofeyevich. "We'll hold a meeting, draw up a report, and everything will be fine."

Kilin gave him a long, hard look, then attacked the telephone with still greater frenzy. Suddenly, by sheer magic, the velvety voice of the operator came floating up through the phone: "Exchange!"

Kilin was so taken aback he was unable to utter a single word; all he could do was puff softly into the receiver, which had gotten damp from his sweaty hands.

"Exchange!" she repeated in a tone of voice which said

that all her switchboard had to do was wait for calls from Krasnoye.

"Operator!" cried Kilin, regaining control of himself and afraid to lose her. "Darling, please . . . I've been calling since yesterday . . . Borisov is . . . urgently needed . . ."

"I'll connect you," said the girl simply, and again, as if by magic, a male voice came through the receiver. "Borisov here."

"Sergei Nikanorich," began the partorg hastily, "Kilin here, from Krasnoye. Golubev and I have been trying you, couldn't get through, the people are waiting, work's stopped, it's touchy here, we don't know what to do."

"I don't understand," said Borisov in a tone of surprise. "I don't understand what it is you don't know. Have you held a meeting?"

"Of course not."

"Why?"

"Why?" repeated Kilin. "We didn't know what to do. You know yourself this is a national matter, and there've been no instructions . . ."

"Now I understand." Borisov's voice began to vibrate with irony. "And when you go take a leak, do you unbutton your fly yourself or do you wait for instructions?"

Borisov brought the full weight of his irony down on Kilin's balding head, just as if he himself had not a moment before been ringing up everybody, in the hope of receiving the same sort of saving instructions.

"Well, all right," he said, at last replacing anger with mercy. "You are to hold a spontaneous meeting, using Molotov's speech as your guide. As soon as possible. Assemble the people . . ."

"The people assembled a long time ago," Kilin was glad to report, and he winked at the chairman.

"Now that's good." Borisov began to purr. "Good . . ." he repeated, this time not quite so certain. Then he brought himself up short. "I don't understand!"

"What don't you understand?" asked Kilin in surprise.

"I don't understand how the people assembled. What people, and who assembled them?"

"No one assembled them," Kilin informed him. "They assembled all by themselves. Can you believe that? As soon as they heard the radio, they all came running, the men, the old men, the women and their children . . ."

While saying this, Kilin sensed that Borisov was displeased by something in his report (now Kilin himself was displeased by something about it too), and without completing his grandiloquent sentence, he suddenly fell silent.

"So," said Borisov pensively. "So. So, it means they heard about it themselves and came running themselves . . . Here's what you do, my friend, you wait for me and don't put the receiver down . . ."

Once again, a rustling, a crackling, music, and other sounds, clear and unclear, could be heard through the receiver.

"Well, what's up?" asked the chairman in a whisper.

"He's gone to see what Revkin has to say." The partorg voiced his guess, covering the receiver with the palm of his hand. Kilin went through several changes of expression: he blushed, turned pale, and wiped his uneven bald spot with a dirty handkerchief until it was totally soaked.

The operator broke in twice. "Still talking?"

"We're still talking, still talking," Kilin repeated in haste.

At last he heard a distant clunk, followed by Borisov's insinuating voice: "Listen, old friend, do you have your party card on you?"

"How can you ask, Sergei Nikanorich," Kilin assured him. "As always, right where it belongs, in my left pocket."

"Now, that's good," approved Borisov. "Get on a horse and dash over to the District Committee. And bring your card with you."

"What for?" Kilin did not understand.

"So you can turn it in."

Kilin had never expected such a turn of events. He looked over to the chairman, who had taken advantage of the seriousness of the conversation to head for the safe, but now Golubev stopped midway and answered Kilin's glance with one of feigned concern.

"But what for?" asked Kilin despondently. "What did I do?"

"You unleashed anarchy, that's what you did!" Borisov let his words fall like drops of lead. "Who ever heard of people assembling all by themselves, without any control on the part of the leadership?"

Kilin went cold inside.

"But listen, Sergei Nikanorich, I mean, you said so yourself—a spontaneous meeting . . ."

"Spontaneity, Comrade Kilin, must be controlled!" rapped out Borisov.

Something clicked in the receiver. Music could again be heard and the mysterious woman told her mysterious Mitya that she forgave him the quilt but he better get her a samovar, she didn't care where or how.

"Allo, allo!" shouted Kilin, thinking they'd been cut off. But the operator explained politely that Comrade Borisov had concluded the conversation. Kilin slowly lowered the slippery receiver back onto the cradle and took a deep breath. Wouldn't you know it, he thought, shattered. You think you've done everything right, then you botch it all up with a political mistake. But, of course, it's all so simple, so easy to understand. I could have figured it out myself. Spontaneity must be controlled. Even if it's moving in the desired direction, it's got to be led, otherwise it might decide it can do just what it likes. That's the whole thing right there. Anyhow, it's good that Borisov called me comrade. He could have said "citizen." Political errors are easy to make and hard to correct. Like they say, we have corrective labor camps for correcting mistakes like that.

"Well, what did he say?" The chairman's question finally got through to Kilin.

"Who?" asked Kilin.

"Borisov, who else. Did he give you any instructions?"

"Instructions?" Kilin repeated the question ironically. "And when you go take a leak, do you ask for instructions then too? We must act, that's all the instructions there are."

With those words Kilin went out onto the porch. Taking advantage of the opportunity at hand and, without waiting for any instructions, the chairman plunged his head into the safe once again and did not re-emerge for quite some time.

5

To control the spontaneous is, of course, a difficult matter, but many people have made a habit of doing it.

After the crowd had dispersed—with obvious reluctance, but dispersed all the same—brigade leaders Shikalov and Taldikin returned to the office and sat down on an earthen bench outside to await further orders from the higher authorities.

"What kind of people are they anyway!" marveled Taldikin, who had not cooled down yet from his recent exertions. "You chase them off, but they don't go! Everybody stubborn as a ram, won't budge! You know, I see it like this, if the people in charge say 'Disperse,' you disperse. The people in charge know better what to do, they didn't get where they are with heads like ours. But no, everybody's still up on their high horse, carrying on like they're princes or something."

"What's right is right," agreed Shikalov soberly. "Back when I was still young, we'd chase off the likes of them with our rifles." He grew pensive and smiled, as he recalled a distant time in his life. "I remember, back in 1916, I was stationed in Peterburd, I was a sergeant major at the time. They had the kind of people there that didn't want to go to work, but first thing in the morning they grab rags with all this fooligan stuff written on them, then they fasten these rags onto their sticks and out they go parading to show everybody they know how to read and write. Sometimes you'd go out there and take all that junk away from them and you'd be so angry you'd say: 'You're a fooligan if ever there was one, what're you doing that for?' Then he goes: 'It's not me who's the fooligan,' he goes, 'but you who's the fooligan, I don't grab rags from you,' he goes. 'It's you who grabs them from me.' And I says to him: 'I'm no fooligan, it's you what's the fooligan, because I got the rifle and you don't got nothing.' "

"And what kind of words did they write on those rags?" asked Taldikin, growing interested and hoping the words were dirty.

"The words?" repeated Shikalov. "I'll tell you, fooligan words. Stuff like 'Down with Lenin,' 'Down with Stalin.' "

At this point, Taldikin began to have his doubts.

"Hold on," he stopped Shikalov. "Something's wrong with what you're saying. There wasn't any Lenin or Stalin in 1916. I mean, they were alive but they weren't running the government of the workers and peasants yet."

"Yuh?" asked Shikalov.

"Yuh," answered Taldikin.

"So what you're saying is, we didn't have Lenin or Stalin either then. So who'd we have?"

"Everybody knows that," said Taldikin confidently. "In 1916 it was Tsar Nikolai Alexandrovich, Emperor and Autocrat."

"You're dumb, Taldika," said Shikalov sympathetically. "You a brigade leader and you don't have brains enough to realize that Nikolai, he came later. And Kerensky came before him, too."

"That's really disgusting," said Taldikin, beside himself. "So now Kerensky was a tsar?"

"So what was he then?"

"Primed Minister."

"You got it all screwed up," sighed Shikalov. "What was Kerensky's name?"

"Alexander Fyodorovich."

"Ya see! And the tsar was Nikolai Alexandrovich. So, he had to be Kerensky's son."

Taldikin's head was whirling. He wanted to object but didn't know what to say. "So, all right," he said. "And when do you think the Revolution was?"

"Which revolution?"

"The October one." Taldikin stressed everything he was certain of. "It was in '17."

"I'm not so sure of that." Shikalov shook his head decisively. "In '17, I was stationed in Peterburd too."

"That's where it happened, in Peterburd," said Taldi-kin, his spirits rising.

"No," said Shikalov with conviction. "Maybe it happened some place else, but not in Peterburd."

This last remark finished off the fogging of Taldikin's mind. Until that moment, he had thought himself familiar with the history in question and thought he knew what happened, and where, and in what sequence, but Shikalov put it all in such a different light that Taldikin was forced to think, think, think, but could not think of anything, and ended up saying without much conviction: "But now I heard they don't break up those demonstrations. My nephew happened to be in Moscow last year on May Day and he says a whole mass of people went cheering across the square, and Stalin's right up there on the mamzoleum waving his hand."

Kilin leaned out the window and ordered Shikalov to come in the office. Shikalov got to his feet. Work was in full swing in the chairman's office. The room was dark as a bathhouse from the tobacco smoke. Finding a little room for himself at the very edge of his desk, the partorg had begun penciling out the speaking order for the meeting, determining there and then which points should be interrupted by applause and what type of applause it should be (stormy, prolonged, or just regular). He pushed what he'd written over to the chairman, who, even though he used the one-finger method, banged it all out rather smartly on his typewriter.

"Well, what do you say, Shikalov?" asked Kilin, without tearing himself away from his composition.

"Here's what." Shikalov approached the desk. "Everything's done like you ordered."

"That means you've dispersed them all?"

"All of them," confirmed the brigade leader.

"Down to the last man?"

"Down to the last man. Taldika's the only one left. Should I run him off too?"

"No need for that yet. Take him along to help you. I want every last one of them here in front of the office in half an hour. Make a list of anybody who doesn't come." The partorg raised his head and looked the brigade leader in the eyes. "Anybody who doesn't come better be sick in bed, or else the fine's twenty-five workdays and not one second less. You understand me, Shikalov?"

"Uh-huh." Shikalov nodded gloomily. "Can I start now?"

"Go on." The partorg granted him permission, again returning to his writing.

Shikalov went out. Taldikin was sitting on the porch smoking.

"Let's get going." Shikalov tossed out his words curtly and without breaking stride.

Taldikin stood up and walked along beside him. When they had gone about fifty paces, he thought to ask: "Where we heading?"

"To chase them all back there."

It cannot be said that Taldikin's mouth fell open from surprise or anything of that sort, but still he did express some interest: "So why'd we chase them off in the first place?"

At that point Shikalov stopped and looked at Taldikin. Back in the office, he had not been in the least surprised, since, on the whole, he had no capacity for surprise. They told him to disperse the crowd, he dispersed it. They told him chase them back, he chased them back. But his comrade's question forced him to think, perhaps for the first time in his life. Just why had they chased them off then? Shikalov scratched the back of his head, thought a bit, then made the following conjecture: "I know why. To emancipate the area."

"Emancipate it for who?"

"What do you mean, for who? For the people. So there'd be some place to chase them back to."

That was more than Taldikin could bear and he grew exasperated. "There!" He twirled a finger by his temple. "I may be dumb, but there's nothing cooking in your kettle."

"And in yours there is?"

"That's right, there's something cooking in there."

"All right, let's say there is," agreed Shikalov. "Let's say there's something cooking in there. Then you just eggsplain to me what they chased the people off for?"

"For the fun of it," said Taldikin confidently.

"What a nitwit." Shikalov shook his head. "Who's there any fun for in that?"

"It's fun for the bosses," said Taldikin. "You see, for them it's like with a woman. If you ask her and she agrees right off, well, that's not too interesting. But if she puts up a fight at first, kicks up a little fuss, then after that you take her. Now that's what you call true pleasure."

"What you say is true," said Shikalov, brightening up. "I remember I had this one lady back in Peterburd . . ."

To tell you the truth, after all these years the author can no longer recall what sort of lady Shikalov had or what adventures they shared, but what is known for certain is that, in a short time, a quorum was established near the office porch. And truly, this time people did put up a little resistance (Taldikin was right) and each one had to be influenced personally (some got it in the neck, some in the seat of their pants). But that's the way it was supposed to be (Taldikin was right again): Without some resistance the victor has no pleasure in his victory.

6

A meeting is an arrangement whereby a large number of people gather together, some to say what they really do not think, some not to say what they really do.

The chairman and the partorg came out onto the porch and the usual procedure began. The partorg declared the meeting open, then gave the chairman the floor. The chairman proposed that an honorable presidium be elected, and gave the floor to the partorg. They changed places like this several times, and while one spoke, the other clapped his hands, exhorting the others to do likewise. The people clapped politely but hurriedly, in the hope that something of substance might soon be said.

"Comrades!" The partorg began his speech and immediately heard the sound of sobbing. Displeased, he glanced down to see who was causing the disturbance. What he saw was people's faces.

"Comrades!" he repeated, feeling he could not say another word, for it was only at that moment that he was struck full force by everything that had occurred, the grief that had come down on them all, himself included. Seen against this grief, his recent fears and cunning tricks seemed of no significance to him. And now the text he had written out also seemed insignificant, empty, stupid. What could he say to these people who, at this very moment, were waiting for words which he did not have in him? Just a moment before, he had not thought of himself like everybody else—him, a representative of a higher power that knows and understands when, what, and how to move. Now he knew nothing.

"Comrades!" he began once again, and looked over helplessly at the chairman.

The chairman dashed into the office for water. The water bottle was not in the office and so he went to the tank with the faucet and the cup on a chain. The chairman stepped on the chain and ripped off the cup and half the chain. When the cup appeared in front of Kilin, he grabbed it with both hands and spent a long time taking little swallows in an effort to regain control of himself.

"Comrades!" he began for the fourth time. "The treacherous attack by Fascist Germany . . ." He experienced some relief in pronouncing the first phrase. Gradually he took possession of his text and the text took possession of him. The familiar word patterns dulled his sense of grief, distracted his mind, and soon Kilin's tongue was babbling away all by itself, like a separate and independent part of his body. We shall stand our ground, we shall return blow for blow, with heroic labor we shall meet . . .

The weeping from the crowd had ceased. Kilin's words had shaken their eardrums but had not reached through to their souls. People's thoughts were returning to their ordinary concerns. The only one who stood apart from the crowd was Gladishev, who was standing by the porch; hands apart ready to applaud again, he was paying close attention to the development of the speaker's thought.

"That's right!" he would exclaim with conviction at the proper moments, nodding his head and wide-brimmed straw hat.

Chonkin was standing in back of everybody. His chin resting on the barrel of his rifle, he tried to get at the meat of what Kilin was saying. Having summarized Molotov's speech, Kilin passed from the general to the particular—to the concrete affairs of their own kolkhoz. Recently, the kolkhoz had achieved new and unprecedented successes. Employing advanced agrotechnical methods, the sowing of leguminous plants had been completed in less than the usual time. The partorg reported on how much of what had been sown and on how great an area, how many potatoes and other vegetables had been planted, how much manure and chemical fertilizer had been brought to field. Glancing down at his sheet of paper, Kilin spouted figures like an adding machine.

Chonkin was drinking in the partorg with his eyes, but some vague thought prevented him from concentrating on the figures and from comparing them. Lifting his head forlornly, Chonkin looked back and suddenly noticed in the far distance, on the low road by the river, a bay horse wearily pulling a wagon in which Raisa, the girl from the village general store, was sitting on top of a pile of goods. This sight suddenly made Ivan realize that what he hadn't been able to recall was somehow connected with Raisa, or the wagon, or the horse.

When it finally dawned on him, Chonkin began to jostle his way through the crowd toward his neighbor and friend, who was standing in plain view in front of everybody, hands ready to applaud.

"Say, listen, neighbor," said Chonkin, nudging Gladishev's elbow. "What I want to ask you is, what about the horse?"

"What kind of horse?" Gladishev turned to him, a bit bewildered.

"You know, a horse, a horse." Gladishev's slow-wittedness angered Chonkin. "A four-legged animal. It does work too. So why didn't a horse turn into a man?"

"Bah, you really are something!" Gladishev even spat he was so annoyed, just at the wrong moment too, for the crowd now broke into applause. Catching hold of himself, the breeder quickly began to applaud as well, gazing in devotion at the speaker so that his spitting would not be construed as having anything to do with the speech.

Meanwhile, having concluded the positive portion of his speech, the speaker now switched to the part containing the criticisms.

"But, comrades," he said, "side by side with our great successes in raising crop yields, there are individual shortcomings which, if taken all together, look rather, I would say, ominous. For example, Gorshkova, Evdokiya, constantly delays paying either her income tax or the local tax. Reshetov, Fyodor, permitted damage to be done to a kolkhoz field by letting his private cattle graze there, for which the administration has fined him forty workdays. Shameful, comrades, that's what it is, shameful. We don't have to go very far for examples when even our brigade leader Taldikin displayed an uncomradelike attitude toward a woman. Specifically, on the day popularly referred to as Ivan's day, Taldikin, while under the influence of alcohol, struck his wife with a wagon shaft. Taldikin, did this actually happen or not? Nothing to say? Shame on you. And we are all ashamed for you. Look, if your wife does something wrong, give her a whack on the butt. [Animation. Laughter.] You can even use a strap and no one'll say anything to you. But a wagon shaft—that's a pretty heavy thing.

"And now, comrades, I will pass to the next matter. For us this is a painful, a very painful matter. What I have in mind is the failure to work the minimum number of workdays. The situation looks so bad we feel like tearing our hair and screaming. Unfortunately, there are still certain people among us who divide things up—this is mine, and that's the kolkhoz's—and there are people who don't want to work, and flaunt their age and their illnesses. Bringing up the rear in this respect is Zhikin, Ilya. You could even say that he has established something of a record, having worked from the beginning of the year up to the present a total of no whole and 75 percent of one workday. [Animation. Laughter. Exclamation by Gladishev: "Disgraceful!"] Of course I realize that Zhikin is a disabled Civil War veteran and has no legs. But now he's cashing in on those legs of his. The leadership of the kolkhoz and the party is not composed of beasts and we feel for other people. Comrades, no one is forcing Zhikin to work as a courier or to help out with haymaking. But he's perfectly able to help with the weeding. Let him sit himself down in a furrow and crawl from bush to bush at his own speed, weeding as he goes and thereby fulfilling the minimum workday requirements. It's no use his sticking those missing legs of his in our faces. [Exclamation by Gladishev: "That's right!"]

The speaker fell silent, evaluating the impression that he had made on the people assembled before him, and then, in his own good time, continued: "Comrades, I recently read Nikolai Ostrovsky's novel *How the Steel Was Tempered*. This is a very good book and I recommend it to anyone who can read. It tells the story of a man who went through the fire and water of the Revolution and the Civil War, and ended up not only without arms and legs but blinded in both eyes as well, and who, chained to his bed by pain, found the strength and courage in himself to serve his people and write that book. No one demands this of you. You're not about to write any books. Though I do advise you to read a little. You in particular, Comrade Zhikin. Is he present or not? [Shikalov's voice: "Not here."] There, you see, he didn't comply, he didn't even come on an occasion like this. You'll tell me: But he has no legs. I don't need to be told. But when Zhikin needs to, he gets around on his board and casters as well as a lot of people on their bicycles. As Ivan Timofeyevich is my witness, one time we ran after Zhikin and couldn't catch him. So could he have gotten here on his casters? He could have. Of course, Zhikin is a worthy man and no one is trying to take that away from him. But past services do not give anyone the right to rest on his laurels, legs or no legs. [Exclamation by Gladishev: "That's right!"]"

Having concluded his criticism of their shortcomings, the partorg once again buried his nose in his sheet of paper, because it was now time to deliver the triumphant conclusion to his speech and it wouldn't do to make any mistakes.

The more the partorg spoke, the more anxiety was expressed on the chairman's face. The crowd was thinning out noticeably. First, Granny Dunya snuck off around the corner of the office. She was followed a short while later by Ninka Kurzova, who also disappeared. All this did not escape the eyes of Taika Gorshkova, who, nudging her husband, Mishka, with her elbow, indicated Ninka with a movement of her eyes. Taika and Mishka began to shift toward the corner while applauding the speaker's last remark. When Stepan Lukov moved off in that same direction, the chairman did not say a word but simply made a fist at Lukov. Lukov stopped. But it was enough for Ivan Timofeyevich to look away for a minute for

Lukov and Frolov and even the chairman's own wife to
slip away from the crowd. The chairman beckoned to
Shikalov, who was looking around nervously. Shikalov
tiptoed up to the porch, listened to the orders whispered
to him, nodded his head, and disappeared, not to re-
appear.

Partorg Kilin noticed none of this as he delivered the
concluding portion of his speech. But, when approaching
the end he raised his head to greet the inevitable burst
of applause, all that greeted his eyes were the backs of
his listeners as they sauntered amiably away. The only
person standing in the dusty square in front of the office
was Ivan Chonkin. His chin on his rifle, Chonkin was
lost in unhappy thoughts about the origins of man.

7

Raisa the storekeeper was sitting by herself in the store
pondering the imponderable. The day before, she had
picked up a batch of goods at the District Consumers'
Union and, deciding to take advantage of having a horse
that day, did not drive straight home but set off in the
other direction, to her sister-in-law's, who lived about
twelve kilometers from Dolgov. At her sister-in-law's,
Raisa drank some red wine, listened to the gramophone,
sang a little bit herself, went to bed late, and got up late.
By the time she had breakfast (which also included red
wine) and harnessed up the horse, it was after twelve
before she finally drove away. She was on the road quite
a while, but she didn't run into anyone. Finally, she arrived back at the village, totally unaware of the events
transpiring in the great world. She did, of course, see a
large crowd near the office as she drove into the village,

but she didn't attach any significance to it, thinking: It could just be nothing.

Raisa had driven up to the store, unloaded the goods, and had begun setting them out on the shelves. It was just then that Granny Dunya popped up in front of her, asking to buy fifty bars of soap.

"How many?" asked Raisa, dumbfounded.

"Fifty."

"What do you need so many for?" asked Raisa, still at a loss.

"You know how it is, Raiushka, what with all that's happening," she said fawningly. "You've got to stock up."

"All what that's happening?"

"You know . . ." Granny Dunya was about to make reference to the treacherous attack but, realizing in time that Raisa had no idea what was going on, started mumbling about some guests she was expecting. Raisa didn't find this explanation satisfactory.

"Why so much soap for guests?" she asked, unable to grasp what was really happening. "Two bars, all right; three bars, all right; even ten. But fifty bars? For what?"

"You never know." Granny Dunya shook her head evasively, with no intention, however, of yielding an inch.

"Well, go on, take them if that's what you need," Raisa yielded. She dragged an unsealed soap box out from the corner. In all, the box contained thirty-eight bars of soap, of which Raisa took two for herself.

"Can't you give me a little sack for them?" asked Granny Dunya, watching regretfully as the two bars were set aside.

"Will you give it back?" asked Raisa.

"Naturally I'll give it back!" said Granny Dunya, taking offense. "I've got no need for other people's stuff, Raiushka. I'm no crook, you know."

Raisa helped her pack it all in the dirty sack and then threw it onto the counter.

"Something else?"

"Some salt," she said, releasing the breath she'd been holding.

"How much?"

"A pood and a half should do me."

"What's the matter with you, woman, have you gone daft? What are you going to do with that much salt?"

"I've got cabbage to pickle, cucumbers, tomatoes."

"So now it's cucumbers and tomatoes? And how about beet tops, you going to pickle them too?"

"Could be them too," agreed Granny Dunya. "Then you know how it goes—one day there's salt, next day no salt, or else there's salt but you haven't got the money. It's nothing to get all worked up about, just let me have a little salt."

"Well, all right," yielded Raisa. "I'll give you a pood, but don't ask me for more."

"A pood'll be fine." Sensing that time was running short, Granny Dunya in her turn yielded.

There wasn't room in the sack for the salt. They had to unload the soap, pour in the salt, cover it over with newspaper, then put the soap back in on top.

"That it?" asked Raisa hopefully.

Granny Dunya hesitated, then asked uncertainly: "I could use some matches too."

"How many?" asked Raisa wearily. "A thousand boxes?"

"Get on with your thousand," said the old woman with noble indignation. "A hundred boxes'll do me fine."

"I'll give you ten," said Raisa.

They agreed on twenty. Granny Dunya was not about to quarrel any further, and she threw the matches into her sack. Using an abacus, Raisa called out the total due her. Granny Dunya dipped her hand inside her knit breeches, rummaged about for some time, then pulled out a little bundle made from a dirty, flower-print rag, stuffed with a neat stack of rubles. Granny Dunya wasn't highly educated but she did know how to count. Nevertheless, she laid her rubles down on the counter one at a time, stopping each time and looking up at Raisa in the mystical hope that she would say "That's enough." But Raisa was a patient woman, and she waited until Granny Dunya had laid out every last ruble that she owed. With the leftover money, the old woman bought two kilograms of dry yeast, six packets of Georgian tea, two packages of "Morning" tooth powder, and, for her niece, a little doll in a cardboard box that was marked "Tanya Doll No. 5 with Hat."

Not wanting to waste an extra second, the old woman hoisted the sack onto her shoulder.

"Watch out now your belly button doesn't come untied!" Raisa shouted after her.

"Don't worry," answered the old woman, as she closed the door behind her and was gone.

Raisa had not even had time to give any thought to Granny Dunya's odd behavior when the door burst open and in rushed Ninka Kurzova. Her kerchief had fallen to one side, her hair was disheveled, her face red. Without even saying hello, she began running her inflamed eyes along the shelves.

"What can you use today, Ninka?" asked Raisa in a kindly voice.

"What?" Ninka feverishly began trying to remember just what it was she needed, but everything she had thought of on the way to the store had now suddenly flown out of her head.

"That's all you have to say?"

"Do you have soap?" said Ninka, recalling what she wanted.

"Need much?" asked Raisa, carefully casting a side-long glance at the two bars she had kept for herself.

"A hundred bars," blurted out Ninka.

"Have you gone daft or something?" said Raisa, unable to restrain herself.

"All right, ninety," said Ninka, knocking off ten.

"Sure you don't want a hundred and ninety?"

"Give me whatever you've got, just make it quick."

"And where am I going to get all that for you, when Granny Dunya just cleaned out the store?"

"Ah, Granny Dunya!"

Ninka raced for the door, but Raisa got there first and barred the doorway.

"Let me by!" said Ninka, knocking against her.

"Hold on! Ninka, tell me why everybody's running around for soap? Has something happened?"

For something like an instant Ninka was struck speechless and stared in amazement at Raisa. "You don't know what's happened?"

"No."

"Then you're a dope!" said Ninka, and pushing Raisa aside, she leaped from the store.

8

Granny Dunya was lugging her booty home. It was no light burden. The pood of salt alone was thirty-six pounds, then there were the thirty-six bars of soap, four hundred grams each. Plus two kilograms of yeast, the tooth powder, and the No. 5 Tanya Doll with Hat. And you had to throw in a kilogram for the sack, too. No matter what you say, a respectable load. The farther she went, the more often the old woman stopped to rest, leaning the sack against the nearest fence. However, as the saying goes, burdens you choose don't weigh you down. Besides, her sense of achievement gave her added strength. And so, having rested for the last time, Dunya was already at her own hut, with ten steps, fifteen at the most, left to go, when someone pulled sharply at her sack.

Granny Dunya turned around and there was Ninka Kurzova.

"Granny, let's see that sack. We'll divvy it up," said Ninka rapidly.

"Eh?" In moments of personal disaster Granny Dunya would immediately be struck deaf in both ears.

"Let's go halves," repeated Ninka.

"Ninushka, how could I have any calves?" complained the old woman. "It's been more than a year since I sold my cow. I had nothing to feed her. The goat had babies in the winter, but then it died in the spring." She shook her head sadly and smiled.

"Don't bother my head with your goat, just give me some soap," said Ninka.

"You're right, it's fools live on hope," said Granny Dunya.

"Listen." Ninka screwed her eyes up wearily. "Let's divvy it up the easy way. So's I don't have to take all of it away from you. Understand?"

"It's hard for me to stand," sighed Dunya. "My legs've been paining me lately . . ."

"Old woman!" Nearly beside herself, Ninka let go of the sack, grabbed Granny Dunya by the front of her dress, and began shouting right in her ear. "You blab all you want, just give me the soap. What do you need it all

for? I've got a family and children . . . I will soon anyway. Stop pulling, let me have the sack."

"Oh, so it's soap you want!" the old woman said, reluctantly admitting that she understood. "Go see Raisa,
she's got some."

"Liar!" shouted Ninka.

"Don't you shout at me," said Granny Dunya, offended.
"I'm not deaf, you know. Just ask and I'll give. Naturally.
Aren't we neighbors? If we don't help each other out,
then who's going to?"

Granny Dunya lowered the sack to the ground and
spent a long time untying it with fingers suddenly dis-
obedient, trying Ninka's patience. Then she slipped one
hand inside and began rummaging about, squeezing each
bar for size. She wanted to choose the smallest possible
bar, but each bar seemed larger than the one before.
Finally she sighed, pulled out one bar, and put it down
in front of her on the grass. Sadness in her eyes, she
looked at it—naturally it was much too big. In her mind's
eye she cut the bar in half, but Ninka's imagination drew
quite a different picture. Granny Dunya sighed once
again and began tying up the sack.

"Hold on there, Granny!" Ninka grabbed hold of the
sack again. "Let's drop all this and divvy it up fair and
square. Half of what's there is yours, the other half's
mine. Otherwise, I'm taking the whole thing."

"Ninka, what are you saying?" The old woman was
becoming seriously worried. "You're insulting an old
woman. You know, I used to rock you in your cradle.
Better let go before I start shouting."

"Shout all you want!" said Ninka and shoved the old
woman.

"Saints alive!" Granny Dunya burst into tears, as she
fell to the ground on her back.

Ninka paid no attention to her, grabbed the sack, and dashed away. She ran several feet, then stopped, turned back, and picked up the bar of soap that Granny Dunya had set down on the grass, and then she ran off again. But just then someone grabbed hold of the sack from behind.

"Now you're going to get it, you old pest!" threatened Ninka, thinking it was Granny Dunya. But when she turned around, it was Mishka Gorshkov she saw, with Taika right behind him.

"What's the big hurry?" Mishka smiled. "Let's divvy it up."

"Right away," said Ninka, pulling the sack to herself. "Fast as I can."

"Eeeeeee!" screeched Taika and grabbed Ninka by the hair.

"I'm being robbed!" screeched Ninka and kicked Taika in the stomach. By then a huge crowd was already approaching them from Stepan Frolov's vegetable patch. Charging out in front, Burly was brandishing a picket he'd ripped out of somebody's fence.

When Chairman Golubev and Partorg Kilin, with Chonkin bringing up the rear, arrived at the scene of the incident, an incredible spectacle greeted their eyes. The citizens of Krasnoye were all tangled up in one immense ball that looked like a many-headed, many-armed, and many-legged hydra, droning, breathing, and shaking its limbs as if trying to rip something from its own insides. Only parts of people could be seen, and those in a most confused fashion. The few hairs he had left stood up on the chairman's head when he saw Stepan Lukov with a woman's breasts come crawling out of the pile. Upon closer examination, the breasts turned out to belong to Taika Gorshkova. Two feet in canvas boots belonging to two widely spread legs were struggling to get back into the pile. A third leg, visible through ripped pants, was sticking straight up like an antenna; this leg had been tattooed from ankle to knee in blue ink, which had faded in time and which read: *Right leg.*

This sorry sight was completed by the dogs who had come running from all ends of the village. They were dashing about in the general pandemonium, barking wildly. To his surprise, Chonkin noticed Borka among them, running about, grunting and squealing more than all the rest of them, as if trying to prove himself top dog.

Chonkin found his friend and neighbor Gladishev close by, standing to one side of the melee. His hands crossed behind his back, Kuzma Matveyevich stood and felt pained for his fellow villagers, as he observed their storming passions.

"Vanya, here's a perfect exhibit for you, now you see where that animal who so proudly calls himself man comes from."

Gladishev looked over at Chonkin and shook his head sadly. Just then, the hydra spat out a half-squashed bar of soap which landed right at the feet of the breeder.

"And for this, people will cease to be human," said Gladishev, pointing down at the object of so much unhappiness, and nudging it fastidiously with the tip of his boot. Gladishev walked off, nudging the object of his contempt with his feet as if he were lost in scientific reverie. But he had not taken five steps when a boy came wriggling out from the side, grabbed the miserable bar of soap on the run, and, slipping past the breeder's rough hand, took to his heels.

"There they are, the young generation," announced Gladishev, having walked back to Chonkin. "Our successors and our hope. Look what we fought for and now look what we're running up against. A treacherous enemy attacks the country, people are dying for Russia, and that brat snatches the last bar of soap from an old man."

Gladishev sighed heavily and pulled his hat down over his forehead, waiting in vain for another gift from fate.

10

After a moment's confusion, Kilin and Golubev began an unequal battle with the unconscious mass. Having advised the partorg to enter from the other side, the chairman dashed headlong into the fray and, in a short while, had dragged out Nikolai Kurzov, a chunk of soap stuck to one shoulder of his tattered shirt, his head white from tooth powder.

"Stay right here!" Ivan Timofeyevich ordered him and once again plunged into the heap, but by the time he had made his way to the very bottom, he found the selfsame Kurzov there and now not only was his shirt in tatters but his nose had been smashed and there was the distinct imprint of someone's heel on his right cheek.

In spite of his usually mild nature, Golubev went wild with rage. Emerging with Kurzov, he led him over to Chonkin.

"Vanya, be a buddy and guard this one. Anything happens, just shoot. I'll answer for it," said Golubev.

For the third time the chairman dashed over to the hydra, which immediately swallowed him up.

Kurzov calmed down as soon as he was placed under guard, and made no attempt to break away but just stood there, breathing heavily, touching his swollen nose with one finger.

Meanwhile, Chonkin's eyes were searching for Nyura, who was somewhere in the free-for-all. It made Chonkin nervous to think that she might get crushed in there. When the dress he knew so well flashed before his eyes, Chonkin could not hold back.

"Here, take this," said Chonkin, shoving the rifle at Kurzov. He ran over to the melee, hoping that he could grab hold of Nyura and pull her out. Just then, someone gave him a hard shove in the side. Chonkin staggered and pulled one leg from the ground in an effort to regain his balance, but someone pulled his other leg and Chonkin tumbled into the general heap. He was spun around like a chip of wood in a whirlpool. One minute he'd be at the very bottom, the next he'd swim his way to the top, and then he'd again fall back into the middle among bodies smelling of sweat and kerosene. Somebody grabbed him by the throat, somebody was biting and scratching him, and Chonkin too was biting and scratching somebody else.

Now Chonkin found himself at the very bottom, being dragged along the ground by the back of his head, his mouth filled with dust and his eyes with tooth powder; coughing, sneezing, and spitting, he had just about gotten it all out when his face sank into something soft, warm, and familiar.

"Nyura, that you?" he could barely gasp out.

"Vanya!" cried Nyura in joy, kicking herself free of someone.

Neither Vanya nor Nyura was in any condition to talk and so they just lay against each other at the bottom of the raging elements until someone drove his heel into

Chonkin's chin. At that point Chonkin realized that it was time to get out of there, and he started backing his way out, dragging Nyura by the feet.

11

"So," said Partorg Kilin, holding the sack containing what was left of the provisions. "Now it's a different story. Now you will all reassemble by the office and we'll put an end to this meeting. Anybody who thinks otherwise gets nothing from this sack. Let's go, Ivan Timofeyevich."

Kilin flung the considerably lightened sack over his shoulder and set off first.

Granny Dunya was sitting in the dust of the battle site, crying. Clutching her head in her dark hands, crooked from gout, she wept and wept. A little off to one side lay a cardboard box ripped to pieces, and near it was the No. 5 Tanya Doll, now without hat, the head slightly torn.

Burly took the old woman by the elbow and helped her to her feet. "Let's go, Granny," he said. "Nothing to cry over. Let's go do some hand-clapping."

12

They had not even managed to crowd back together by the office when a column of dust arose at the outskirts of town and began heading rapidly toward them. The people rushed to one side. The column whirled up close to the office and then subsided. An MK jeep emerged from the dust. The people were surprised, the authorities were uneasy. An MK meant nothing less than somebody from the province. In the district, even First Secretary Revkin never got to drive anything like that.

People with notebooks and cameras came pouring out of the MK. One of them ran up to the rear door and flung it open. First, an enormous backside covered in dark-blue material emerged from the door, followed by the rest of the backside's owner, a hefty woman in a wool suit and white blouse, with a medal on her left breast.

"Lyushka, Lyushka." A sound like dry leaves went rustling through the crowd.

"Greetings, neighbors," the newly arrived woman said loudly and made her way toward the porch through the crowd, which had parted respectfully. As she went she nodded a separate greeting to Burly, who was eyeing her ironically.

"Hello, brother," she said.

"Hello to you too, if we're being friends," answered Burly.

At that moment the woman noticed puny Egor Miakishev skulking in the crowd.

"Egor!" She rushed into the crowd and dragged Egor into the very middle of everyone. "Why didn't you come greet your beloved spouse? Aren't you glad to see her?"

"Well," mumbled Miakishev in embarrassment and dropped his eyes.

"Don't you 'well' me," said Lyushka. "Kiss your wife who you haven't seen for so long. Only first wipe off your lips, I can see you've been eating raw eggs again." She bent forward and presented first one cheek to Miakishev, then the other. Miakishev wiped his lips on his dirty sleeve and kissed her where he'd been instructed. Lyushka's face crinkled up.

"God help us, the smell of tobacco on him is something. Almost as good as the smell of a man. But I've been missing you, more than I can tell. I kept thinking, Wonder how that husband of mine is getting on back there. Isn't he bored all alone in his cold bed? Or maybe he's already dragged somebody in there with him?"

Intimidated, Miakishev looked at his wife without blinking.

"What does he have to drag somebody in there for," Burly said loudly, "when he sleeps with a horse in the stable?"

Someone in the crowd snorted, everyone else fell silent. The reporters exchanged glances. Lyushka stopped and stared hard at her brother.

"Up to your old tricks, brother?" she asked, with hidden menace in her voice.

"Sure am," Burly was quick to agree.

"Well," said Lyushka. "Better watch out, the joke may end up on you."

She slowly climbed the porch steps, then disappeared behind the door that had been flung open by Kilin.

All the visitors had made the office crowded. Lyushka immediately seated herself at the chairman's desk, Kilin found himself a place off to one side, the reporters took seats along the wall, and Golubev stood by the safe, pressing the door shut with his shoulder.

"And so, comrades," said Lyushka in a brisk and cheerful voice. "How's life?"

"How's life?" the partorg repeated, spreading his hands. "We live simply here, country-style. Right now, we've just been having a little tiff with the people."

"What's the problem?" asked Lyushka.

"Nothing much." Kilin avoided the question. "Let's hear about you. You spend all your time in the capital. I guess you must have tea with Stalin at least once a day."

"Well, maybe not that often, but we do get together sometimes."

"And so what kind of guy is he?" asked Golubev quickly.

"What can I tell you," said Lyushka, growing pensive. "A very simple man," she said, throwing a sidelong glance at the reporters. "And very modest. When there's a reception in the Kremlin he never fails to call me over and greet me and take my hand and say: 'Hello, Lyushka. How are you? How's your health?' A very sympathetic human being."

"Sympathetic?" the chairman repeated quickly. "And so, how has he been looking lately?"

"He looks good," said Lyushka and then suddenly broke into tears. "It's so hard for him right now. Having to think for us all by himself."

13

Lyushka had been born and raised in a poor peasant family. In the summertime she had worked as a farmhand and she had spent the winters without getting off the stove, since she owned neither felt boots nor pants. Without collectivization she could not have become a famous milkmaid, because the half-dead cow on her farm did not give record milk yields. When, as a result of skimpy feeding, the cow became entirely dead, it ceased to be of any use at all. Lyushka's own life might have come to the same sort of sad end, but favorable changes occurred just in time. Lyushka was one of the first to register for the kolkhoz. After signing up, she was given cows that had once belonged to kulaks, and although these cows did not give milk as they had before, they continued to yield in abundance from inertia. Gradually Lyushka got on her feet. She acquired shoes, some nice clothes; she married Egor; she joined the Party. Soon thereafter workers and heroes of labor began to emerge everywhere, and by all accounts Lyushka fell squarely in this category. The first notices about her achievements began appearing in the local and regional press. But Lyushka's real ascent began when a reporter wrote a sensational article (either it was based on her own words or else he made the whole thing up himself) which reported that Lyushka had broken with the age-old way of milking cows and from now on was going to grab four udders at the same time, two in each hand. That's how it all began. Delivering a speech at the Kremlin at a conference of collective farmers, Lyushka assured those present, as well as Comrade Stalin personally, that they were finished with their outmoded technique once and for all. And to Comrade Stalin's reply of "Cadres! Cadres!" she pledged to teach her method to all milkmaids on her kolkhoz. "Will it work for all of them?" asked Comrade Stalin slyly. "Of course, Comrade Stalin, because every milkmaid's got two hands," said Lyushka smartly, and held her own two hands out in front of her. "Right you are." Comrade Stalin smiled and nodded his head. From that time on, Lyushka was never to be found at her own kolkhoz. She was either taking part in the Supreme Soviet or attending a conference or receiving a delegation of English dockworkers, chatting with the writer Lion Feuchtwanger or being presented with a decoration in the Kremlin. Great fame came to Lyushka. The newspapers wrote about her, the radio talked about her, newsreels featured her. The magazine *Ogonyok* printed her portrait on its cover. Red Army soldiers wrote her letters proposing marriage.

Lyushka was completely exhausted. One day, racing to her native village to have her picture taken pulling on a cow's udders, then going on to a session at the Academy of Agriculture, a meeting with writers, a speech before the veterans of the Revolution . . . No rest from the reporters. Wherever Lyushka went, they were sure to go. Lyushka herself had become something of a milk cow for them. Sketches and articles were written about her, songs were composed about her. Even Lyushka herself, at her wit's end, had already started to believe that all these reporters had been created only to prepare reports on her, to write about her life and take her picture.

A so-called Miakishev movement arose and grew very popular. The Miakishevites (that's what they were called) pledged greater achievements, filled the highest governmental bodies, shared their experiences in the newspapers, and appeared on movie screens. There was nobody left to milk the cows.

14

"What are we going to do with you!" the partorg addressed the crowd in irritation. "So now you're standing here assembled. And you think you're standing in an organized manner. But from where I'm standing up here, I don't notice any organization. All I see is everyone trying to stand in back so they can be the first to run off to the store. None of you has any shame. Even Lyushka being here doesn't make you ashamed. Our legendary Lyushka. Who has often met with Comrade Stalin personally. Who's got reporters with her. Who can write about all this in the papers, you know. Comrade reporters"—Kilin turned to one of the reporters—"I personally request that you write about all of this and print it throughout the whole Soviet Union. Write that in our kolkhoz the people have no consciousness. People are conscious everywhere but here. Let them learn some shame. I swear they sprawl and straggle like a herd of cattle. All right now, bring it in closer together. And if you don't know how to stand right, then I'll tell you how—all you men join hands, women in the middle. That's how you should stand. But that's no good either. How are you going to clap? Join arms. Now, that's a different story."

Having thus created order, Kilin gave the floor to Lyushka. She came forward, said nothing for a moment, then began speaking quietly in her homespun way.

"Men, women!" she said. "A great misfortune has come down on us all. A treacherous enemy has attacked our country without declaring war. It wasn't so long ago they were pretending to be our friends. Two years ago I was in Moscow and I had the chance of seeing their Ribbentrop up close. I'll tell you the truth, he didn't make much of an impression on me. Not much to look at, sort of like our, let's say"—she cast about for someone to compare him to, though she had prepared the comparison beforehand—"like our Stepan Frolov, except, of course, with a little more on the ball. He smiles and he makes his sprechen Sie Deutsch toasts, but meanwhile, Kliment Efremovich Voroshilov whispered in my ear: 'Lyushka, don't think he's all that friendly, he's got a stone behind his back and you should see the size of it.' Now I remember Kliment Efremovich's words often and I think, Yes, it's true, they were hiding a stone behind their backs, a cobblestone. Men, women, now, when misfortune is already upon us, there's nothing left to do but close ranks around our Party and around the person of Comrade Stalin. When I'm in Moscow and see him, our own, our very own Stalin, allow me to tell him on your behalf that all the workers of your kolkhoz will give every last drop of their strength . . . Get your camera away from my face"—unexpectedly, and to the delight of all, Lyushka addressed the reporter hanging over the railing taking her picture. "Take it from the side . . . Every last drop of their strength to increase our harvest. Everything for the front, everything for victory!" Lyushka fell silent and took a moment to gather her thoughts. Then she continued: "To you, the women, we make a special appeal. Any day now our men, our fathers, our husbands, our brothers will be going off to defend our freedom. War is war and it could be that not all of them will be coming home again. But while they're away we'll be left here by ourselves. It won't be easy. There'll be the children and you'll have to clean and cook and do the wash at home and look after your gardens and not forget the kolkhoz either. Whether we like it or not, each of us has to do the work of two or three now. For ourselves and for our men. We've got to see this thing through and we will. Men, go to the front! Do your duty as men, defend our country from the foe until there's not a single one of them left. And don't you be worried about us. We'll take your place . . ."

Lyushka spoke simply and clearly, and those standing down below her were either crying or smiling through their tears. Lyushka herself had to bring her handkerchief to her eyes several times. After her speech she got into the MK with all the reporters, and raising a column of dust, they wheeled off into higher spheres.

As had been promised, the salt, matches, and soap were divided up after the meeting. Nyura too got her share—a half bar of soap, a bag of salt, and about two boxes of matches. Night had already fallen by the time she returned home. Chonkin was sitting by the window using an awl and plain brown thread (he didn't have any waxed thread) in an attempt to get his boots in shape.

"Here's what they gave us," said Nyura, laying out her share on the table.

Chonkin glanced at the stuff without interest. "So anyhow, maybe they'll come tomorrow," he said with a sigh.

"Who?" asked Nyura.

"Who, who." Chonkin grew angry. "There's a war on and I'm stuck here . . ."

Nyura didn't say anything. She took the pea soup from the oven, brought it to the table, and burst into tears.

"What's with you?" asked Chonkin, surprised.

"What's the big hurry to run off to war?" said Nyura through her tears. "You're going to be better off there than here with me?"

15

Gladishev couldn't get to sleep. He stared into the darkness, sighing, groaning, catching bedbugs on himself. But it wasn't the bedbugs that were keeping him from sleep, it was thoughts. They all turned around the same thing. Chonkin's stupid question at the meeting had disturbed him and had even, it would seem, shaken his unshakable faith in science and scientific authorities. "Why doesn't a horse turn into a man?" And, indeed, why doesn't it?

Pressed up against the wall by Aphrodite, Gladishev lay there and thought. True, every horse did a great deal of work, more than any monkey ever did. You can ride them, plow with them, they can pull all sorts of loads. The horse works long hours summer and winter and never has a holiday or a day off. By no means the stupidest of animals, still, out of all the horses Gladishev had ever known, not one had turned into a human being yet. Unable to find any sort of convenient explanation for this mystery of nature, Gladishev sighed noisily.

"Aren't you asleep?" asked Aphrodite in a loud whisper.

"I'm sleeping," answered Gladishev angrily and turned away toward the wall.

Sleep had just begun to overcome Gladishev when Hercules woke up and started crying.

"Sh sh sh shshsh sh," Aphrodite hissed at him, and she began to rock the cradle noisily without getting up out of bed. Hercules did not quiet down. Aphrodite slipped her legs out of bed, took Hercules from the cradle, and gave him her breast. The baby calmed down and began smacking his lips. While feeding him, Aphrodite fussed about with her free hand in the cradle, no doubt changing his swaddling clothes. But when she put him back in the cradle, Hercules started crying again. Aphrodite rocked the cradle and began singing:

Lullaby and good night,
With Herky bedight . . .

She didn't know any more of the words and kept on repeating the same two lines over and over again:

Lullaby and good night,
With Herky bedight . . .

Finally, the child fell off to sleep, Aphrodite quieted down again, and the master of the house was at the brink of sleep. But no sooner had he closed his eyes than he was absolutely sure that he'd heard the outer door being opened. Gladishev was surprised. Could he really have forgotten to lock it on his way to bed? And even if he had, who would disturb people at such a late hour, especially when there was no light in the window? Gladishev pricked up his ears. Maybe he'd just been imagining things? No. Someone had come down the passageway and was now fumbling his way blindly down the corridor. The footsteps grew nearer and nearer, until finally the bedroom door itself opened with a creak. Gladishev drew himself up on one elbow, peered intently into the darkness, and, to his great surprise, recognized the intruder as the gelding Osoaviakhim.* Gladishev shook his head to get hold of himself and to convince himself that it wasn't all just his imagination but was actually happening. It really was Osoaviakhim (whom Gladishev knew well, since he used him to haul provisions to the warehouse) who was now standing in person in the middle of Gladishev's room, breathing noisily.

"Hello, Kuzma Matveyevich," he said unexpectedly, in a human voice.

"Hello, hello," answered Gladishev with self-restraint, well aware of how odd the proceedings were.

"I've come to inform you, Kuzma Matveyevich, that I now have become a human being and will not haul provisions any longer."

For some reason the gelding sighed and banged his hooves against the floor as he shifted his weight.

"Shhh, quiet," hissed Gladishev. "You'll wake the child." Moving Aphrodite slightly, he sat up in bed and, feeling an uncommon joy in being perhaps the first human being to witness such a remarkable phenomenon, asked impatiently: "How did you manage to turn into a human being, Osya?"

* Acronym of Society for Assistance to the Defense, Aviation, and Chemical Construction of the U.S.S.R.

"Here's the way it happened," said Osoaviakhim pensively. "I've been working a lot lately, you know that yourself—hauling provisions from the warehouse, not even turning up my nose at hauling manure, not to mention plowing. I didn't say no to any of it and so, as a result of all my painstaking work, I finally turned into a human being."

"Interesting," said Gladishev. "This is very interesting, only now who am I going to use for hauling provisions?"

"That's your problem, Kuzma Matveyevich," said the gelding, shaking its head. "You'll have to find a replacement. You can even take Tulip, he won't be turning human for a good long time."

"Why's that?" asked Gladishev in surprise.

"He's lazy, that's why, he'll only work under the lash. Long as you don't hit him, he won't budge from his place. And do you know what you've got to run like to turn into a human being?" Osoaviakhim suddenly began neighing, but caught himself at once. "Forgive me, Kuzma Matveyevich, certain survivals from my horse past still crop up."

"It's all right, it happens." Kuzma Matveyevich granted his pardon. "But what I'd like to know is, what do you propose to do now? Will you stay on at the kolkhoz or what?"

"Hardly," sighed Osoaviakhim. "With my talent there's nothing for me here now. I think I'll head for, say, Moscow and let the professors there have a look at me. Maybe I can do a lecture series. Ech, Kuzma Matveyevich, life is just beginning for me. I'd like to get married and have children to aid the further progress of science and here I am, unable to."

"Why's that?"

"You, you're asking?" Osoaviakhim grinned bitterly.

"What was it that you yourself did to me eight years back? Deprived me of those very parts of the body indispensable for the propagation of the species."

It was an awkward moment for Gladishev. He felt embarrassed and it seemed he even blushed, a good thing it was too dark for it to be seen.

"Forgive me, friend Osya," he said sincerely. "Had I known that you were going to turn into a human being, I'd never have allowed it. I thought, He's a horse, and a horse is a horse. If I'd known . . ."

"If I'd known," mimicked Osoaviakhim. "And what is a horse? Not a living creature too? Someone whose last joy you can take away just like that? We don't go to the movies, we don't read books, only one pleasure is left us, and along you come with your knife . . ."

Gladishev's ears pricked up. Something was not quite right in what this Osoaviakhim was saying. No sooner does he turn into a human being than he starts criticizing. Of course this was a significant achievement from the biological point of view but, from a political standpoint, to change a horse into a human being is only half the problem. The main thing was, into what kind of human being—the Soviet kind or the other kind? Having displayed proper and timely vigilance, Gladishev now posed the gelding a question of the sort known as "stumpers."

"Now answer me this, Osya: If, for example, they send you to the front, who are you going to fight for, us or the Germans?"

The gelding looked at Gladishev with sympathy and shook his head as if to say, What a dumb person. "For me to go to the front is totally out of the question, Kuzma Matveyevich."

"And why is that so totally out of the question for you?" asked Gladishev insinuatingly.

"Because," said the gelding angrily, "I have nothing to pull a trigger with. I have no fingers."

"Now I've got it!" Gladishev whacked himself on the forehead and woke up.

He opened his eyes, totally unable to understand where the gelding had gone. Everything in the room was just the same as it had been before, and he, Gladishev, was still lying in his own bed on his down feather bedding, still pressed to the wall by Aphrodite. She was now bringing her full weight to bear on him, smacking her lips and whistling in her sleep with repulsive gusto. The room was hot and stuffy. Gladishev pushed on his wife with his shoulder—nothing. He pushed a second time, with the same lack of success. He grew angry, and bracing his arms and legs against the wall, he slammed his butt into Aphrodite so that she almost went rolling off the bed. She leaped up, saying: "Huh? What?" unable to comprehend what was going on.

"You hear me, Aphrodite?" Gladishev asked in a whisper. "Where's that gelding gotten himself to?"

"What gelding?" Aphrodite shook her head, trying to wake up fully.

"You know the gelding Osoaviakhim," said Gladishev, irritated by his wife's slowness.

"Oh, Lord!" muttered Aphrodite. "God only knows what he's babbling about now. Now he's gone and invented some gelding. Go back to sleep."

Aphrodite turned over on her stomach, buried her face in the pillow, and immediately fell back to sleep.

Gladishev lay beside her, staring up at the ceiling. Consciousness was gradually returning to him and at last he understood that the gelding had come to him in a dream. Gladishev was no stranger to books. He had read *Sleep and Dreams*, which now aided him in properly evaluating this most recent dream. Yesterday, Chonkin was spouting all kinds of hogwash, that's why I had the dream, he thought to himself. But still, there was some sort of strange thought that had not yet found words for itself, that kept drilling away and tormenting him, and he had no idea whatsoever what it meant. He couldn't drop back off to sleep again. He lay tossing and turning until the first gleam of day came in through the window. Then he crawled over Aphrodite and, deep in thought, pulled on his breeches.

That morning Nyura had woken up before Ivan and before daybreak. She'd been tossing and turning and then finally gave up and decided to get out of bed. It was early yet to milk the cow and she thought of going down to the river for water before it grew light. She got her pails and yoke in the passageway, opened the door, and nearly died—someone was sitting on her porch.

"Who's that?" she asked in fear and, just to be on the safe side, pulled the door in closer to herself.

"Don't be afraid, Nyura. It's me, Gladishev."

Surprised, Nyura opened the door halfway again.

"What are you doing sitting there?"

"Just sitting," answered Gladishev vaguely. "Your man up yet?"

"Fat chance," laughed Nyura. "Sleeping like a log. What's the matter?"

"I need to see him," answered Gladishev, evasively again.

"Maybe I should wake him?" Nyura esteemed her neighbor as a learned man and figured he wouldn't disturb anybody over nothing at all.

"No, no, it's not worth it."

"Why isn't it? I'll go wake him. Let him get up. In the

night he's rushing off to war, but in the morning you've got your hands full to wake him up."

Gladishev did not particularly object, since the idea he wished to convey to his friend, while not terribly serious in nature, would still have been hard to keep all to himself.

A minute later Chonkin came out onto the porch, wearing only his pants.

"You wanted me?" he asked, yawning and scratching himself.

Gladishev delayed answering. He waited until Nyura had picked up her pails and had gone a good distance from them; only then, embarrassed that he'd gotten a man out of bed for such a trifle, did he begin uncertainly: "Remember yesterday you were asking about the horse?"

"About what horse?" Ivan had not understood.

"About the horse in general, why it doesn't turn into a human being."

"Aaahhh." Ivan recalled that indeed there had been some sort of conversation like that the day before.

"Here's the point," said Gladishev proudly. "I have understood why the horse does not turn into a human being. It does not turn into a human being because it doesn't have any fingers."

"Aw, you surprise me," said Chonkin. "I knew since I was a little kid horses don't have fingers."

"That's not the point. I'm not telling you they don't have fingers, I'm telling you they don't turn into human beings because they don't have fingers."

"And I'm telling you that everybody knows horses don't have fingers."

At that point they began quarreling in the way people often quarrel, each trying to prove something quite different to the other and neither attempting to understand what the other was saying. The quarrel was just on the verge of turning nasty when Aphrodite came out onto her porch in her underclothing and called her husband home for breakfast. Kuzma Matveyevich set off for home, the quarrel unfinished. On the table he found a bacon-fat omelet, so hot it was still sizzling. Gladishev pulled the frying pan over to himself, sat down on the bench, and immediately felt something under him, not so much sharp as hard and uneven. He jumped up and turned around. There was a horseshoe on the bench.

"What's this?" he asked his wife severely, showing her the horseshoe.

"How should I know?" She shrugged her shoulders. "It was lying by the door. First I was going to throw it out, but I thought, Maybe it'll come in—"

Aphrodite did not get to finish her sentence. Gladishev grabbed the horseshoe, jumped up from the table, and dashed out of the house, his shirt untucked and flying.

Even from some distance away Gladishev noticed a gathering near the stables which included, among others, Chairman Golubev, Partorg Kilin, both brigade leaders, and the stableman, Egor Miakishev.

"What's going on here?" asked Gladishev.

"A horse ran off," explained Miakishev.

"Which one?" Gladishev went cold as his mind made its own guess.

"Osoaviakhim." The stableman spat in annoyance. "We'd been here figuring out which horses to turn over to the army, that one included, so last night he breaks the fence and off he goes. Or else maybe gypsies stole him."

"That could well be," Gladishev hastened to agree.

16

Lieutenant Colonel Opalikov stood with his arms and legs spread, while Regimental Engineer Kudlai and two senior technicians fitted him into his parachute. Opalikov frowned gloomily. In a few minutes he would have to take his regiment into the air and direct them to the district of Tiraspol as ordered. The route had been adjusted and delineated, the instructions had been gone over with the flight personnel. Squadron commanders had reported their flight readiness. Tiraspol, all right Tiraspol, thought Opalikov. What's the difference where they shoot you down? And they've got to shoot you down, there's no place to hide up there. The donkeys we fly are no match for those Messerschmitts. All right, he said to himself, that's not the point. He'd lived thirty-four years, that was enough. Not everybody got even that much. He'd seen a little bit of the world. But, Nadka, Nadka . . . At the thought of his wife, his mood went from bad to worse. "I will wait for you," she had said. Sure, let's hear about it. She'll wait all right, in some other guy's bed. Bitch! When other women heard it was war, they started sobbing, that one barely managed to squeeze out one little tear. The barren fig tree! It must have even made her happy. Her husband at the front and total freedom for her. Not that she didn't have enough freedom before. She'd drag anyone she could get her hands on down on top of her. Sometimes he'd walk through town and feel nothing but shame. It seemed as though everybody was pointing a finger at him. Here he comes, the regimental commander. He can command a regiment, but he can't even keep his own wife in line. In the army everything's out in plain view. Worse than in a village. Everybody knows everything about everybody. Even about the time she and the quartermaster, at the warehouse, on a pile of old coats . . . How low can you get! That time, he was going to shoot her dead, he'd drawn his pistol from his holster . . . But his hand wouldn't obey him. Of course the whole thing was his own fault. As Kudlai said: 'You have to look close when you're buying . . ." Obviously, that was the way she was. An insatiable creature, all right the hell with her, thought Lieutenant Colonel Opalikov as Pakhomov drove up in a sidecar.

"Comrade Lieutenant Colonel." Pakhomov's hand flew to his temple in salute as soon as he had hopped out of the sidecar.

"What's happening on your end?" interrupted Opalikov, raising one leg slightly to make it easier for Kudlai to pull the parachute strap through and around.

"Loading of airfield echelon equipment completed," Pakhomov reported. "I think it'll take us about four days to get to Tiraspol."

"Good, good," said Opalikov, and assisted by the engineer, he climbed up onto the wing. "So then we'll be waiting for you in Tiraspol."

Opalikov got into the cockpit and began fidgeting about for a comfortable position. He laid his map case across his knees and ran through the first part of his route again in his mind. Takeoff. Assemble in rendezvous zone. Then a course of 257 degrees, 4 degrees wind correction. After passing control point, a 20-degree turn to the left. Everything normal, everything correct, except for that Nadka . . . Opalikov raised his head.

Pakhomov was still standing by the plane, shifting from foot to foot.

"What else is there, Pakhomov?" said Opalikov, turning his attention to Pakhomov.

"It's just that I don't know what to do with Chonkin," said the battalion commander uncertainly.

"With Chonkin who?" Opalikov's brows rose in bewilderment.

"The soldier guarding the plane."

"Ah." Opalikov put his feet on the pedals, checked the rudders and ailerons, then switched on the ignition. "You mean he hasn't been relieved yet?"

"Not yet," said Pakhomov. "And the plane's still there too."

"That's not a plane," said Opalikov, dismissing it with a flick of his hand. "It's a coffin. And what's that Chonkin doing there?"

"Standing guard." Pakhomov shrugged his shoulders. "I heard he even got himself sort of married there." He smiled, unsure how to express his attitude toward what the soldier had done.

"Married?" gasped Opalikov. His brain simply could not accommodate such a thought—getting married at a time like this! For what? Here he was with a wife and he didn't know what to do with her. "Well, since he got himself married, let him be," Opalikov decided. "I've got no time to worry about him now. Kudlai!" he shouted out to the engineer, "tell each regiment to start their motors."

Chonkin's fate had been decided.

17

"I'll put the cabbage soup on, you go get the cow and bring her home," said Nyura. She put her head in the oven and began blowing noisily on the fire.

"In two shakes." Chonkin was scouring the buttons on his field jacket with tooth powder and didn't feel like going anywhere.

"Shake it now," remarked Nyura. "You can clean your buttons after."

She had just dragged herself back from Dolgov with a full pouch, then delivered the mail; now she was tired and upset that Chonkin hadn't fixed any dinner.

Chonkin laid his field shirt and brush aside, walked up to Nyura from behind, and grabbed her with both hands.

"Get out of here." Nyura wiggled her butt in displeasure.

They squabbled a bit, Chonkin pointing out that it was early yet and that he had a pain in the small of his back, all to no avail—in the end he had to give in.

He played a little with Borka out in the yard, had a chat with Granny Dunya in the street, then another with Grandpa Shapkin, who was sitting outside on an earthen bench, and had finally gotten as far as the office when he spotted a large crowd consisting mostly of womenfolk. The only men there were Burly, Volkov the bookkeeper, and one other, a stranger to Chonkin. Everybody else was at the front. The town had been nearly cleaned out during the first week of the war. The people gathered by the office were looking in silence at the loudspeaker, which was issuing a crackly sound.

"What're you standing here for?" Ivan asked Ninka Kurzova.

But Ninka didn't answer and only touched a finger to her lips. At that point somebody coughed from within the loudspeaker and a voice with a distinct Georgian accent said softly: "Comrades! Citizens! Brothers and sisters! Fighting men of our army and navy! I address you, my friends!"

Chonkin sighed and stood perfectly still, his eyes never leaving the loudspeaker.

The loudspeaker coughed once again, then something began to gurgle, as if the person standing at the microphone was either pouring water or choking with sobs. This gurgling lasted quite some time and had an oppressive effect on the listeners. Then it was over and the voice with the accent began speaking again, quietly and reasonably: "The treacherous armed attack by Hitler's Germany on our motherland, begun on June 22, still continues. In spite of heroic resistance by the Red Army, in spite of the fact that the enemy's best divisions and the best units of his air force have already been smashed and have found their graves on the field of battle, the enemy continues to creep forward, thrusting fresh forces to the front. Hitler's troops have succeeded in seizing Lithuania, a significant portion of Latvia, the western part of Belorussia, and part of the western Ukraine. The Fascist air force is expanding the area of its bomber operations and bombing the cities of Murmansk, Orsha, Mogilev, Smolensk, Kiev, Odessa, Sevastopol. Our motherland stands in grave danger . . ."

Granny Dunya, who was standing behind Chonkin, began sobbing. Ninka Kurzova, who'd just seen her husband off to the front the day before, began pulling at her lips. The others began stirring and sniffling.

Chonkin listened to the words spoken with the noticeable Georgian accent, and believed in them implicitly, but there still were certain things he could not understand. If the enemy's best divisions and the best units of his air force had been smashed and had found their graves, what was there worth getting so upset about? It'd be even easier to smash his weaker units and divisions. Besides that, he could not understand the expression "found their graves on the field of battle." Why there and not some place else? And who dug those graves for them? Chonkin visualized a vast throng of people walking through unknown fields in search of their graves. For a second or two he even felt sorry for them, although he knew full well he mustn't. Reflecting on such things, Chonkin missed a good deal of what the speaker had been saying, and now he lifted his head back up to catch the jist again.

"The Red Army, the Red Navy, and all citizens of the Soviet Union must hold every inch of Soviet land, must fight to the last drop of their blood for our cities and villages, and display the courage, initiative, and gumption characteristic of our people . . ."

Everyone listened, nodding their heads, Chonkin as well. He was ready to fight, but he didn't know who and how. When the men were being taken off to the front, the captain from the military commissariat had been sitting on the office porch having a chat with the chairman. Chonkin had walked over to him, addressed him with all proper respect, request this and permission that, but the captain didn't even listen to what he had to say, instead he barked: "Are you at your post? Who gave you the right to abandon your post? About-face! To your post, on the double!" That was their entire conversation. But Stalin, he wouldn't have said that, he was smart, he could understand and see how things were for you. No wonder the people loved him. And he sang good too. "Valenki, valenki." But how come he sings in a woman's voice? Then the song ended, followed by a burst of applause.

"That was something!" Chonkin heard from behind. He started and turned around. Toying with her whip, her mouth gaping open, Taika Gorshkova was staring at the loudspeaker. She was the herdsman, now that Lyosha Zharov had been taken off to the front.

Chonkin looked around and, not seeing anyone but Taika there, fixed his eyes on her again.

"That Ruslanova's singing, I tell you, that's really something," repeated Taika.

"What, did you drive the cows back in already?" asked Chonkin in surprise.

"A long time ago. What of it?"

"It's all right, nothing."

Surprised that he'd missed the cows being driven in, Chonkin set off for home. Of course, the cow would get back on its own, it knew the way. But still, it was strange that he'd been so busy thinking that he hadn't noticed everybody going home. Now it seemed that they hadn't all gone home but were still together, except that for some reason they'd moved to a different spot. Looked like they were over by Gladishev's. Yes, that's right, that's what it was.

"What're you standing here for?" Chonkin asked Ninka Kurzova again. Ninka turned and looked at Chonkin somewhat strangely, as if something had happened to him. Then everybody else began turning their heads in Chonkin's direction and looking at him with some sort of vague anticipation. Chonkin grew confused, he had no idea what the matter was, and he started looking down at himself to see if he hadn't somehow gotten himself all dirty. Just then Burly came out of the crowd and walked toward Chonkin with outstretched arms.

"Vanya, buddy, what're you standing here for?" he called out. "Come here quick. I've got something to show you. A real sight to see."

He took Chonkin by the arm and led him through the crowd, which was quick to make way for them. When he finally reached his neighbor's fence, Chonkin could not believe his eyes. The remarkable garden created by Gladishev's daily toil and genius was now a scene of terrible devastation. It had been as thoroughly gouged and trampled as if a herd of elephants had passed through it. Here and there the tattered remains of what had once been PATS bushes jutted up from the ground and the sole bush that had been miraculously spared showed luxuriantly green against a backdrop of utter destruction.

The culprit responsible for the entire catastrophe, Beauty the cow, had probably left this last bush for a final treat. Standing in the middle of the garden, she was now reaching out for the bush and would certainly have gotten it, but the owner of the garden was holding her by the horns; filled with despair and blind rage, he was determined to save at least this one pitiful remnant of the miracle he had created.

His dirty tarpaulin boots planted wide apart, Gladishev stood in front of the cow like a toreador. He strained his every sinew struggling to repel the horned barbarian.

Right beside Gladishev, pulling at his sleeve, Nyura was sobbing inconsolably.

"Matveyevich." The tears were streaming down her face. "Let go of the cow. Please, please. What are you going to do to her?"

"Cut her throat," said Gladishev sullenly.

"Oh, my God!" wailed Nyura. "She's my only one. Let her go!"

"I'll cut her throat," insisted Gladishev, and he started dragging the cow to the barn. The cow dug in and kept reaching out for the last remaining PATS bush. On the porch, indifferent to it all, Aphrodite was breast-feeding Hercules. Chonkin looked around in confusion, with no idea what to do.

"Why are you just standing there, Vanya?" Burly smiled approval at him. "Go save the cow. He'll kill it, you know. One slash and that's it."

Burly winked at Volkov the bookkeeper, who was standing beside him.

Chonkin had no desire to get himself mixed up in this mess, but Gladishev would not let go and Nyura was weeping. Reluctantly, Ivan stuck his head between the fence rails.

"Oi!" squealed a thin voice belonging to Zinaida Volkova, the bookkeeper's wife. "Oi, girls, now it's going to be murder!"

The sight of Chonkin coming emboldened Nyura and she took the offensive. "You damn tyrant!" she cried, and grabbed hold of her enemy's red right ear.

"So that's it!" Gladishev was outraged and gave Nyura a shove in the stomach with his foot.

Nyura fell back into a furrow and began howling at the top of her lungs.

Chonkin raced over to Nyura, bent down to her, and saw that nothing terrible had happened. She was alive and not even hurt.

"What are you howling about?" he asked quite soberly as he helped Nyura back up on her feet and brushed off her dress. "Nobody did anything to you. Sure, Kuzma Matveyevich gave you a little shove, but you can understand that. Anybody would have taken it just as hard. The man worked all summer watering, looking after the garden like it was his own child, and now just look what happened. And you, Kuzma Matveyevich," Chonkin addressed his neighbor, "for God's sake, forgive the cow, you know yourself a cow's not a human being. It's got no idea this is yours and that's somebody else's, it just sees something green and gobbles it up, that's all there is to it. Why, day before yesterday, Nyura hung a green jacket out on the fence, the cow goes over and gobbles it right down, all except for the left sleeve. Now you've had it, you pain in the ass," said Chonkin, brandishing his fist at the cow. "Let her go, neighbor. I'm going to punish her so she'll never put her nose in anybody else's garden again."

With these words, Chonkin placed his hands on top of Gladishev's, around Beauty's horns.

"Get out of here," said Gladishev, and he gave Chonkin a shove with his shoulder.

"I will like hell," said Chonkin, and he gave his neighbor one back. "No, you Kuzma Matveyevich, let go of the cow, and Nyurka and me'll pay you back for your garden."

"Moron!" said Gladishev, with tears in his eyes. "How can you pay back a scientific quest? I was going to grow a hybrid of world significance, a cross between a potato and a tomato."

"We'll make it up to you," Chonkin assured him. "I swear we will. Anyway, what do you really care if they grow together or separate?"

Chonkin continued to shoulder his stubborn neighbor and had already gained complete control of one horn. Now they were pulling the cow in opposite directions, which was easier for the cow to bear, due to the even distribution of forces.

The moment of truth had come. Chonkin was shoving Gladishev with his left shoulder and Gladishev was responding with his right.

Leaning against the fence, the crowd now held its breath. Having switched breasts, Aphrodite went right on feeding Hercules. Everything was quiet. The only sound to be heard was the heavy puffing of the warring factions and the indifferent sighs of the cow, who had not lost its desire to chomp the last remaining bush of the ill-fated hybrid.

The crowd awaited the next development in silence.

"Hey, soldier, sock 'im in the eye," advised Burly, his voice startlingly loud.

"Oi, women, close your eyes, it's gonna be murder!" Zinaida Volkova cried out shrilly.

Her husband, standing not too far away, began to make his way through the crowd toward his wife.

"Murder, murder, it's going to be murder," she muttered feverishly, as if repeating an incantation.

Finally the bookkeeper reached his wife, moved Ninka Kurzova out of the way, took her place, and then, taking his time, wound up carefully and, with his one remaining hand, gave Zinaida such a slap in the face that without other people to support her she would hardly have remained standing on her feet. Silently grabbing her cheek with both hands, Zinaida began to make her way out of the crowd while the bookkeeper turned to Burly and calmly began to explain what he'd done.

"How many times have I told her, Keep your nose out of other people's business. The time Kolka Kurzov had the fight with Stepan from over Kliukvino, she was watching that one too, moaning and groaning, and so they took down her name as a witness. So, of course, when the judge calls her, the first thing she does is faint dead away and they had to bring her back with artificial respiration."

"You should just polish her off yourself," advised Burly merrily. "That would put an end to her witness days."

"Murder!" Zinaida howled in a frenzied voice, now that she had finally worked her way out of the crowd. Then, still holding her cheek in both hands, she raced off through the village.

In response to her howl, Chonkin and Gladishev slackened their grip at the same time. The cow felt this, shook its head, and the two opponents, not expecting any such treachery, went tumbling back in opposite directions.

Without wasting a second and without breaking stride, the cow whisked up the last of the miraculous hybrid, roots and all, and set its jaws casually to work.

Now on his hands and knees, Gladishev watched the cow as if spellbound. "Oh, mother!" In a passion he reached out for the cow, hobbling toward it on his knees. "That's a good girl, let go now, please, let go of it!"

Smacking her lips, sighing, and staring guardedly at Gladishev, the cow took a step back.

"Let go of it!" Without rising from his knees, Gladishev reached out for the cow's face. A green shredded clump flashed for an instant from the cow's open jaws. Gladishev made a grab for it, but at that very moment the cow swallowed deeply and the last of the remarkable hybrid vanished forever into its bottomless belly. Overcoming his momentary paralysis, Gladishev jumped to his feet and ran to his house, howling wildly.

Then Chonkin too got up from the ground. Without so much as a glance at anyone, he shook the dust off his pants and, with one hand, grabbed the cow by the horn, made a fist, and punched Beauty in the face with all his might. The cow yanked its head back, but did not put up much of a struggle. Chonkin began pulling her into the barn, having yelled out to Nyura to run ahead and open the gate.

"So that's that," said Burly regretfully. But Burly was mistaken.

At that very moment, disheveled, his eyes flashing savagely, Gladishev ran out onto his porch holding a 16-caliber Berdan rifle in his hands. The crowd gasped.

"I said it was going to be murder," said Zinaida, who had returned just in time.

Gladishev brought the rifle to his shoulder and aimed it at Chonkin.

"Vanya!" screamed Nyura in desperation.

Chonkin turned around. Fingers wrapped around the cow's horns, he stood looking straight down the barrel of the Berdan rifle. Chonkin seemed rooted to the spot, unable to move. A foolish thought—I'm thirsty—flashed through his mind. Chonkin licked his lips.

The hammer's dry click sounded like a twig being snapped. That's it, thought Chonkin. But then, why wasn't he feeling any pain? Why wasn't he falling down? Why was Gladishev cocking the rifle again? Another click.

Suddenly the loud, sober, reasonable voice of Aphrodite rang out: "You numbskull! Where are you shooting? And with what? You used up all the powder for fertilizer a long time ago."

A murmur passed through the crowd. Gladishev cocked the rifle yet another time, peered down the barrel, and then, convinced there was no powder there, flung the rifle crashing to the ground, sat down on the porch, and began weeping bitterly, holding his head in his hands.

Chonkin still had his fingers wrapped around Beauty's

horns, and he was still standing on the same spot as if stuck there. Nyura walked up to him and laid a hand on his shoulder.

"Let's go, Vanya," she said tenderly.

He looked at her blankly, not comprehending what it was she wanted.

"Home, I'm telling you. Let's go now!" Nyura shouted as if she were talking to a deaf man.

"Oh, home." Chonkin shook his head as his awareness returned. The two of them set to work. Chonkin took one horn and Nyura the other and they began pulling the cow, now quite full and in a docile mood.

Meanwhile, Gladishev was still weeping loudly and vociferously on his porch. Exposing the white woolly hair on his stomach, Gladishev used the hem of his tattered T-shirt to wipe his eyes.

That was more than Chonkin could bear, and leaving the cow and Nyura behind, he went back over toward his recently defeated enemy.

"Say, neighbor," he said, touching the tip of his boot to the tip of Gladishev's. "Don't, you know—it's going to be all right, don't take it so hard. When the war's over, I'll be demoblizized and then we'll plant your garden back up with those PATS, Nyura's too."

He touched Gladishev's shoulder as a sign of reconciliation. Gladishev shuddered, broke into a roar, grabbed Chonkin's outstretched hand and was about to bite it, but Chonkin pulled it away just in time and jumped off to the side. Keeping his distance, Chonkin looked at the breeder with apprehension and pity, with no idea what to do next.

Nyura came up to Chonkin and started in on him. "Ach, Vanya, you blunderer. Whose mind are you trying to change, who are you feeling sorry for? Was he feeling sorry for you when he aimed the gun at your head? He wanted to kill you!"

"So what if he wanted to," said Chonkin. "You know how it is when a man gets all worked up. Matveyevich, you weren't really going to . . ." Chonkin shifted from one foot to the other but could not bring himself to move any closer to Gladishev.

18

On Sunday, at the kolkhoz market in the town of Dolgov, an elderly man who had been selling box-calf boot tops was arrested. It was not only a question of his selling boot tops, and the fact that they were made of box calf had nothing to do with it at all. The point was that, when asked his last name, his reply was such that Klim Svintsov, who had been sent to the marketplace to uncover anyone maliciously spreading false rumors, had no other choice but to take the old rogue by that place popularly known as the scruff of the neck and bring him to the Right Place. Especially since it was precisely there, at the Right Place, that Svintsov served as a sergeant. To readers from distant galaxies, unfamiliar with our earthly customs, a legitimate question might occur—what does the Right Place mean? Right for whom and for what? In this connection, the author offers the following explanation: In the bygone times described by the author, there existed everywhere a certain Institution, which was not so much military as militant. Over the years it waged a crippling war against its own citizens and waged it with unfailing success. Its enemy was numerous but unarmed—the constancy of these two factors made the Institution's victory both impressive and inevitable. The chastising sword of the Institution hung constantly over everyone, ready to come down whenever necessary or even without any reason at all. This Institution acquired the reputation of seeing everything, hearing everything, knowing everything, and, if something was out of line, the Institution would be there in a flash. For this reason people would say, If you're too smart, you'll end up in the Right Place; if you chatter too much, you'll end up in the Right Place. Such a state of affairs was considered completely normal, though, come to think of it, why shouldn't a person be too smart if that was the way he came into the world? And why shouldn't a person chatter away if he's got someone to talk to and something to talk about? On his way through life the author has personally met large numbers of people who seemed to have been designed by nature for the express purpose of chattering away. Besides, there are many different varieties of chatter. One person says what he ought to and another says something he's not supposed to. If you say what you're supposed to, you'll have everything you need and even a little bit extra. But if you say what you are not supposed to say, you'll end up in the Right Place—that is, in the very Institution which we were discussing above. We will further add that this Institution operates on the principle of "beat your own so that outsiders will fear you." I will not say anything about outsiders, but their own really did grow to be afraid of them. In fact, as soon as there was an exacerbation of contradictions in a foreign country or a crisis of their entire system or an all-pervasive decay, this Institution would grab their own and drag them off to the Right Place, where there was not room enough for them all.

But, at the particular moment when Sergeant Klim Svintsov caught the malicious chatterbox at the marketplace, there was more than enough room at the Right Place. The last four who had come to the Right Place, each in his own way, had been dispatched elsewhere even before the war had started. The Institution had speedily reorganized its operations, adapting them to the needs of wartime in response to orders issued by the head of the Institution, Captain Afanasy Milyaga, who had received his instructions from those even higher up than he, and they in turn had received theirs from the highest authorities. The fulfilling of the instructions was to be guided by Comrade Stalin's historic speech. In that historic speech, among other things, it had been said: "We must organize a merciless struggle against all disorganizers of the rear, panicmongers, rumormongers, we must wipe out spies, saboteurs, enemy paratroops, and render all speedy assistance to our fighting men."

This quotation, in the form of a colorfully designed poster, hung in Captain Milyaga's office in a direct line with his eyes. And behind Captain Milyaga hung the well-known photograph of Stalin holding a little girl in his arms. The little girl was smiling at Stalin, Stalin was smiling at the little girl. But at the same time he was squinting one eye at the back of Milyaga's head as if trying to determine whether any unnecessary thoughts might be swarming about in there.

On Monday the captain appeared at work, as always right on time.

"Punctuality is the politeness of kings," he was fond of saying to his staff, never failing to add, "figuratively speaking, of course" (so that no one would suspect him of monarchist sentiments).

The captain found Sergeant Svintsov in his waiting

room telling his troubles to Kapa the secretary. Svintsov's wife had gone with their children to her mother in Altai, where she would stay for quite some time. He himself had written her not to come back, that she'd be safer there. He told Kapa all this as a lead into the next part of their conversation.

"Kapitolina," he said urgently, staring at the secretary with his bestial eyes, "a man without a woman's just like a bull without a cow." His comparisons were always direct and crude. "A man can't go long without a woman. You come live with me a little while, I'll give you a length of real crepe de chine. So besides all the pleasure, you'll get a dress out of it too."

Kapa was used to his approach and not offended by it. "Klim," she laughed. "Go to the bathhouse and douse yourself with cold water."

"Won't help." Klim's face darkened. "I need a woman. And don't you think I'm not a real man either."

"Klim, what are you saying!" Kapa was horrified.

"I'm just talking straight from the shoulder. I know you sleep with your husband and with the captain too. So come put in a little time with me. Better to live with three men than with two."

"Klim, you're an idiot!" Kapa did not like allusions to her relations with the captain.

Svintsov frowned and looked sullenly up at Kapa.

"If you don't want to live with me," he said after a moment's thought, "why call me names? Have you got a friend?"

"Klim, can you live with just any woman?"

"Sure, any woman."

The conversation was interrupted by the appearance of Captain Milyaga. Captain Milyaga was distinguished from other people by the fact that he was always smiling. His smile was nice and pleasant and fully corresponded to the last name he bore.* The captain smiled when he said hello, he smiled while interrogating prisoners, he smiled when others were sobbing; in brief, he was constantly smiling. Now, too, smiling, he greeted Kapa and then turned with a smile to Svintsov, who had overturned his chair when Milyaga appeared, to stand at attention by the door.

"You here to see me?"

"Yes."

"Come in, then."

Milyaga took the key to his office from Kapa and entered first. He drew the blinds, flung open the window, which gave onto a small interior court, and inhaled a chestful of fresh air.

Down in the courtyard Lieutenant Filippov was busy drilling the staff. In addition to Filippov, the staff consisted of five men. In normal times there was never enough time for drill. There was always too much work to do. But now, in this short period of transition when they were switching over to a wartime footing, a free day had turned up. Not to mention the fact that there had also been instructions to pay special attention to drill.

The five men, having formed a single-file column, were practicing their parade drill. Lieutenant Filippov was walking down one side and, inspiring his subordinates with his own example, lifted his legs in their flashing box-calf boots high in the air.

"Well, what do you have to say, Svintsov?" asked the captain without turning around.

* *Milyaga has the flavor of "nice guy" in Russian.*

"Not much." Svintsov yawned lazily into his fist. "Our boys found a stray horse."

"What kind of horse?"

"A gelding. They asked around, no one knows whose it is."

"And where is this gelding now?"

"They tied it to a tree in the yard."

"Was it given hay?"

"Why feed somebody else's horse?"

The captain turned around and looked reproachfully at Svintsov. "Ech, Svintsov, you can tell right off you don't like animals."

"I'm not too fond of people either," confessed Svintsov.

"All right, all right, what else?"

"Yesterday, Comrade Captain, I caught me a spy."

"A spy?" The captain brightened up. "Where is he?"

"I'll bring him right in."

Svintsov left the room. The captain sat down at his desk. A spy would come in very handy right now. The captain glanced over at the poster hanging across from him: ". . . to wipe out spies, saboteurs, enemy paratroops . . ." Well, if it's wipe them out, then wipe them out it is, thought the captain and smiled to himself.

In order not to waste time until Svintsov returned, Captain Milyaga set to examining his secret mail. The mail consisted of all manner of circulars, excerpts from the orders of higher government bodies, the decisions of executive committees and from the minutes of certain top-level meetings. The subjects were highly varied: tightening control over grain collection; the preparation of a new wartime bond plan; tightening control over persons evading their military obligations; tightening control over the selection of personnel; gearing up industrial enterprises for wartime production; the battle against rumors and the need to spread counter-rumors.

The door fl w open. Nudged by Svintsov, a poorly dressed elderly man whose nationality could be told at a single glance entered the office. Having appraised the office and its contents, the old man smiled affably and, his hand extended, walked up to the captain.

"Khow do you do, Chief!" he said, his pronunciation of Russian less than perfect.

"Khow do you do, khow do you do!" joked the captain, bringing his hands out from behind his back.

The prisoner was pleasantly surprised by this and inquired as to whether the captain belonged to the same national minority as he. The captain was not offended, but answered in the negative.

"You can't mean it!" The prisoner threw up his hands. "And such an intelligent look to your face."

The prisoner looked around, took the chair standing by the wall, moved it over to Captain Milyaga's desk, and sat down. As a rule, visitors to this office were usually more reserved in their behavior. Obviously, the old man has not yet quite understood where's he's landed, thought the captain merrily, but he did not let on. He did not say anything even when his guest placed his elbows on the captain's desk, as if he were the host there, and looked trustingly into the captain's face.

"I'm ready to listen," said the old man benevolently.

"To listen to me?" The captain smiled. "I think it'd be better the other way around—if I listened to you."

The guest turned out to be quite obliging and agreed with the captain's proposal. "In the first place," he began, "please send somebody to my wife, Tsilya—she's sitting on the bench by the gate—and tell her I'll be back soon."

The captain was somewhat surprised and asked his prisoner how he had gotten the information that Tsilya was sitting on the bench by the gate and was not some place else.

"I'll be glad to explain," said the old man. "I'm no longer such a young man that my Tsilya might think I'm spending the night with some shiksa."

"That's quite natural," the captain readily agreed, "but your age might cause your wife worries of a different sort. She might think you've had a heart attack or that you . . . God forbid, I would never wish this on you . . . but she might think"—the captain's eyes began to sparkle happily—"that you might have fallen, for example, in front of a car. Eh? Such things do happen, you know. After all, you've got to agree, in life anything can happen."

"What are you talking about?" The prisoner waved his hand. "My Tsilya is so panicky, she always imagines the worst."

"Aha." The captain broke into a smile of complete satisfaction. "That means you think ending up here is even worse than falling in front of a car. I can see that you are a very intelligent man and I like how you evaluate your situation so accurately. But, that being so, you ought to agree that to send someone to your wife and allow her the hope that you'll be coming back soon would be premature. You know, we don't like to part with our guests so quickly, and taking that into account, would it really be worthwhile to upset an old woman for no good reason? To a certain degree this would even be, I'd say, inhumane."

"I understand you," the old man agreed. "I understand you very well. It's also a pleasure for me to see your face, Chief, but all the same we'll have to say our goodbyes soon, and I'll tell you why. But first of all, please dismiss this idiot." The old man pointed his thumb at Svintsov, who was standing behind him.

"What did you say?" asked the captain, anticipating great fun. "You said—this idiot?"

"Then you tell me what else he is. Ask him why he started pestering me at the market. What did I do to him?"

"Yes, as a matter of fact"—the captain turned his head toward his subordinate—"Svintsov, what did he do to you?"

"Let him tell you himself," growled Svintsov sullenly.

"And I will," threatened the prisoner. "I'll tell it all just the way it was."

"And I'll be very glad to hear what you have to say," said the captain sincerely.

He reached behind him on the safe for a pile of lined paper and placed it on the desk in front of him. The first sheet read:

MINUTES OF INTERROGATION NO.

Citizen (ess)...
(*Last name. First name. Patronymic.*)
Year of Birth...
Place of Birth..
Social Origin...
Nationality..
Party Membership...
Education ....
Job and Place of Work....................................
Accused, Suspected (Underline one)
of crimes cited in the statutes of the Criminal Code of the
RSFSR; article numbers...................................

The captain removed his gold-tipped fountain pen

from an iron cup on his desk, underlined "Accused," and then benevolently looked up at the man seated across from him. "And so?" said the captain.

"You mean you're really going to write down what I say?" asked the guest, almost flattered.

"Naturally." The captain nodded.

"All right then, go ahead," sighed the accused. "I'm an old man, I get a pension of twelve rubles a month, but I've got eyes, I see what's what. On Sunday morning, my wife, Tsilya, woke me up at twenty past seven. Have you got that? She said to me: 'Moishe, we've got nothing to eat. You've got to go to the market and sell something.' I'm a shoemaker by profession and I always have a little leather around, so I took some old box-calf tops and went to the market. Then this idiot of yours walks up to me and asks me what right I have to be profiteering. I explained to him that profiteering—make a note of this—means when you buy cheap and you sell dear. But I'm not buying anything, I'm only selling. Then he asked me what my last name was and I told him. Then he grabbed me by the collar and starts dragging me here to your department. Meanwhile, a crowd forms and everybody starts saying they've just caught a spy. I must tell you quite frankly that I'm no spy. I have a very good profession and I always earn my crust of bread. And if he doesn't like my last name . . ."

"What is your last name?" interrupted Milyaga, his pen poised above the document.

"My last name is Stalin."

The captain shuddered, but even now did not forget to smile. "What did you say?"

"You heard what I said well enough."

The captain regained control over himself. He had en-

countered all sorts of madmen, including those suffering
from delusions of grandeur. He winked at Svintsov, who
flicked out his hand (how hard do you have to hit an old
man?) and the impostor fell to the floor.

"Oi, oi," the old man groaned as he began to get back
up on his feet. "Oi, Chief, that idiot of yours is after me
again! Look, blood's coming out of my nose. Please make
a note of that in your records."

Having struggled to his feet, the old man stood in front
of the captain, holding his nose, from which, in fact,
large red drops were falling to the floor.

"It's nothing." The captain smiled. "The man got a
little excited. But maybe he had good reason to. Maybe
he's the nervous type and you insult him by calling him
an idiot. And when you insult him, you also insult those
agencies which he represents. Not to mention the fact
that you dared use that name so very dear to us all, that
name only one man in our country can use, and you know
who I'm talking about."

"Oi, Chief!" The impostor shook his head. "Why are
you talking so harshly to me? You can't even begin to
imagine what's going to happen when you look at my
papers. You'll lick my blood off the floor with your tongue,
you and your idiot too. Then I'll walk over to you, pull
down my pants, and you and your idiot will kiss my rear
end."

This time Svintsov's blow knocked the old man clear
off his feet. A denture went flying from his mouth, knocked
against the doorjamb, and split into two pieces. Clutching
his head in his hands, the impostor began to groan and
utter incoherent cries.

"As a matter of fact, Svintsov, where are his papers?"
asked the captain.

"I don't know," said Svintsov. "I didn't look."

"Then look."

Svintsov bent over the victim, rummaged through his clothes, then laid an old greasy passport on the captain's desk.

Faintly disgusted, the captain opened the passport and could not believe his eyes. Perhaps for the first time in his life the smile slipped from the captain's face. It suddenly seemed dark in the office, and he switched on his desk lamp. The letters, painstakingly traced out in the India ink of the bureaucracy, were dancing about in front of Milyaga's eyes and he was totally unable to order them. Slatin, Satlin, Saltin . . . No, there was no way around it, Stalin. Stalin, Moisei Solomonovich. Could he really be a relative? The captain shivered. He could already see himself up against the wall. Oh, my God, what's going on here! Of course, and wasn't Stalin's father a shoemaker!

"Svintsov!" said the captain, without hearing his own voice, "get out of this office!"

Svintsov left. But this did not make the captain's position any easier. For a short period of time, Milyaga simply went out of his mind and engaged in completely meaningless activity, pulling papers over to him, then pushing them away again. Finally, he grabbed a paperweight and set it down on the passport, blew on the passport, and, with both hands, carefully moved it to the edge of his desk.

Meanwhile, the prisoner was still lying on the floor in his previous posture, still writhing, holding his head in both hands as if afraid it might otherwise completely fall off.

The captain moved his chair aside and, standing at

attention, pronounced at the top of his lungs, as if barking out an order: "Hello, Comrade Stalin!"

Stalin took one hand away from his face and squinted mistrustfully at the captain. "Khello, khello," he said cautiously. "We've already met."

He should have helped the old man to his feet, but the captain could not make up his mind. His knees were trembling and there was a taste like kerosene in his mouth.

"You . . ." he said, swallowing his saliva, "you . . ." he licked his lips . . . "you are Stalin's papa?"

"Oi, I hurt all over!" Stalin crawled along the floor on his hands and knees; he picked up, first one half of his denture, then the other. "My teeth!" he groaned, gazing at the pieces. "My God, what will I do without them?"

He struggled to his feet, sat down across from the captain, and looked him in the eye. "So, scared now, you bastard?" he asked with malicious joy. "Sit down, you bastard, a hundred sores on your head. Now where am I going to get teeth like these?"

"We'll have new ones made for you," the captain hastened to assure him.

"New ones," mimicked the old man. "Where are you going to get new ones like these, I'd like to know. My son made me these teeth. Do you think anyone in this town knows how to make teeth like that?"

"Those teeth were made personally by Comrade Stalin?" The captain was moved and reached out his hand. "May I touch them?"

"Fool," said Stalin, pushing the pieces out of reach. "Your hands are all bloody and you want to touch my teeth with them."

At that moment a life-saving flash of memory gleamed

in the captain's brain. If this was Stalin's father, that meant that Stalin himself should be named Joseph Moiseyevich. But, after all, Stalin's name was . . . his name was . . . Milyaga found himself totally unable to recall the beloved leader's patronymic.

"I'm sorry," he began indecisively, "but it seems to me that Stalin's papa's last name wasn't Stalin. And Solomon wasn't his first name either." The captain was gradually regaining control of his faculties. "And so just why are you trying to pass yourself off as Comrade Stalin's papa?"

"Because I am the father of Comrade Stalin. My son, Comrade Zinovy Stalin, is the most-well-known dental technician in Gomel."

"So that's it!" The captain's playful mood returned to him. "Anyhow, our dental technicians don't do such a bad job either."

The captain pressed the button on his bell. Kapa appeared in the door. "Svintsov!" the captain ordered.

"You're not going to call that idiot back in here?" said Stalin, beginning to get worried. "You know, I don't advise you to do it. You're still a young man, you've got everything ahead of you. Why should you ruin your career? Listen to an old man's advice."

"I've already listened to you." The captain smiled.

"So listen some more. I won't charge for my advice. I only want to tell you that if anyone finds out you arrested Stalin and beat him up, even if it wasn't *that* Stalin, or even his father, but just plain Stalin, my God, you couldn't begin to imagine what'll happen to you!"

The captain grew thoughtful. Could be the old man was right. It really was a ticklish situation.

Svintsov entered. "You summoned me, Comrade Captain?"

"Leave," said Milyaga.

Svintsov left.

"Listen," said the captain. "Moisei . . . uh, uh . . ."

"Solomonovich," Stalin prompted him, not without a sense of his own dignity.

"Moisei Solomonovich, why do you have this last name? After all, you know who it belongs to."

"In the first place, it belongs to me," said Moisei Solomonovich. "And because my father was a Stalin and my grandfather before him was a Stalin too. My grandfather had a small factory where he made steel. And for that reason he got the name Stalin."*

"But, all the same, it's an awkward coincidence."

"Awkward for you, but quite comfortable for me. Because if my last name was Shpulman or, let's say, Ivanov, then your idiot could knock my teeth out whenever he pleased. The chief over in Gomel suggested many times that I change my last name, but I always answered him in one word—no. By the way, he looked a lot like you. He couldn't be your brother, by any chance?"

"I don't have any brothers," said the captain. "I was an only child."

"I feel sorry for you," sympathized Stalin. "An only child, that's never good. He can grow up an egotist."

The captain made no reply to this observation. He tore up the minutes of the interrogation and threw them in the wastebasket. Then he rose, extended his hand, and announced to his guest that he was very glad to have made his acquaintance. But his guest was in no hurry to depart. He requested that before leaving the Institution

* Stal *means steel in Russian. Stalin can either mean "man of steel," as it does in the case of Joseph Stalin, or something like Steelman, as it does here.*

his boot tops be returned to him and that a permit be written out to the district polyclinic for the repair of his dentures.

"We'll arrange it." The captain summoned Kapa and ordered her to fill out the proper form.

Kapa was shaken by this order, not knowing what had dictated it. The Institution always displayed concern for people, but never to that degree! "Maybe next you'll be sending him to a health resort?" she asked mockingly.

The old man perked up and requested that for the time being he not be sent to any health resort.

"I like health resorts very much, especially the Crimea," he said. "The Crimea is the pearl of the South, sweet as tsimmes. But I'm afraid the Germans will be getting there soon."

"The Germans would cure you all right," said Kapa significantly.

She was to regret her imprudent remark immediately.

"It seems this girl is a bit of an anti-Semite," said Stalin, with obvious concern about her future. "But she's young, I don't imagine she grew up under the old regime, and she's probably in the Party or the Komsomol." Glancing at Kapa as if she were an unfortunate cripple, he sighed, moaned, shook his head, and said bitterly that if she didn't change her convictions she too would have to kiss his "rear end." However, before beginning the ceremony, she would have to wipe her lips. "Because of my wife, Tsilya," he explained. "She's very jealous. And if she catches sight of any lipstick, there'll be hell to pay, such trouble in the family."

With no idea whatsoever of what was happening, Kapa looked to the captain. Why was he permitting this impudent old man to talk like this? Why didn't he order him shot immediately?

"Kapochka"—the captain smiled at her in an obvious hurry to brush the incident aside—"please write out the form for this comrade."

Offended, her lips pressed tightly together, Kapa set off to carry out the order. She returned at once and, without looking at the old man, asked him his last name. The old man opened his mouth willingly enough but the captain cut him off. "No last name is needed," he said quickly. "Fill it out to—the bearer."

"I don't understand any of this," said Kapa. "What kind of person is this that doesn't have a last name?"

"I have a last name," said the old man.

"Yes, he has a last name," confirmed the captain, "but it is a secret." He smiled to Kapa and the old man respectively. "Go write what you were told to. The bearer of this note is being referred . . ."

Several minutes later the captain was accompanying the old man to the gate, just as if he were an honored guest. And in truth there was an old woman sitting on the bench by the gate. She was holding a torn wicker purse on her lap and staring straight ahead. You could tell at once that waiting was her normal condition. She was in the habit of filling the minutes and hours of her waiting by enumerating the great men her people had given the world. At this moment she was staring straight ahead, counting the names by bending down her fingers as she mumbled: ". . . Marx, Einstein, Spinoza, Lincoln, Trotsky, Sverdlov, Rothschild . . ."

"Tsilya," Stalin said to her. "I want to introduce you to this young man. He is a very interesting young man."

"Is he Jewish?" Tsilya perked up.

"He isn't Jewish, but he's a very interesting young . . ."

"Och!" Tsilya shook her head, having lost interest in Milyaga. "Where did you get that bad habit of yours?

As soon as we come to a new place, right away you start up with the goyim. Can't you find yourself any other kind of company?"

"Tsilya, what you're saying is wrong. This is a very fine young man. He's even a little bit better than the one in Gomel. The one in Gomel kept me in jail for three full days, and for three full days I explained to him why he shouldn't keep me in jail. But this one understood everything right away."

Having returned to his office, Captain Milyaga said something conciliatory to Kapa and took a letter from her that had come in that day's mail. Probably an anonymous letter. The Institution's address had been written with the left hand and there was no return address. There was nothing out of the ordinary in this. Citizens almost always wrote letters to the Institution headed by Milyaga without a return address, and these letters were, with rare exceptions, written with the left hand. (The exceptions were the lefties, who used their right hand.) As a rule, such letters contained petty denunciations. Someone was criticizing the rationing system. Someone was expressing some doubts about our swift victory over the Germans. Someone had told a story of dubious content in the kitchen. One vigilant comrade requested that attention be paid to the work of the poet Isakovsky. "The poet's words," wrote the vigilant comrade, "in the song 'No World's Better than This One' are heard on records and are broadcast on the radio throughout the Soviet Union. Among other lines, there is the well-known one, 'At dawn she glimpsed a cockatoo.' But if you listen carefully, you'll hear something else: 'At dawn she glimpsed a cock or two.' That's what the line says if you listen closely." The vigilant comrade suggested that the poet be invited to the Right Place and that he be asked directly: "What is this, a mistake or malicious intent?" At the same time the author of the letter reported that he had already asked the local newspaper about this scandalous matter, but had as yet received no reply. "The paper's persistent silence," concluded the vigilant comrade, "forces one to think that the editor may well be in criminal collusion with the poet Isakovsky, and if that is so, is this not an indication of a far-flung organization of wreckers and saboteurs?"

It must be said, to the Institution's credit, that very few such letters ever caused it to take measures; otherwise there would not have been a single person left free in the country.

And so the letter which had arrived in the latest mail seemed totally run-of-the-mill at first glance. But for some reason it occurred to the captain that this very letter might contain an important message. He opened the letter and realized after the first few lines that he had not been mistaken.

We hereby inform you that the deserter and betrayer of the motherland, Comrade Chonkin, Ivan, is hiding in our village of Krasnoye and that he is residing in the home of the postmistress, Belyashova, Nyura, that his person is armed and that he has combat matériel as well, in the form of an airplane which is not flying into battle against the German Fascist aggressors but is standing in a vegetable patch serving no purpose whatsoever in a period of grave trials for our country. Although his place is at the front, Red Army soldier Chonkin, Ivan, is not fighting at the front but occupies himself with debauchery and all manner of drunkenness

and hooliganism. The above-mentioned Chonkin,
Ivan, has been expressing immature ideas and disbelief
in the teachings of Marxism-Leninism and also in the
teachings of C. Darwin concerning the origin of man,
according to which teachings the monkey turned into a
man by means of labor and intelligent actions. In
addition to the above-mentioned, he has permitted the
cow of Belyashova, Nyura, to do criminal damage to the
garden of the well-known local breeder and naturalist,
Gladishev, Kuzma Matveyevich, and by these acts
Chonkin has undoubtedly caused a great loss to our
Soviet agricultural science in the virgin territory of
hybridization. We request that you repress this
high-handed deserter and call him to account in
accordance with all the severity of Soviet law. We
remain yours truly, the residents of the village of
Krasnoye.

The captain read the letter through and underlined the words "deserter, betrayer, Chonkin" with a red pencil. He underlined the name "Gladishev" in blue pencil, then wrote "sender" off to one side and followed that with a question mark.

The letter could not have come at a better moment. It was time to begin carrying out the Supreme Commander's orders. The captain summoned Lieutenant Filippov.

"Filippov," he said to him, "get as many men as you need. Tomorrow you're going to Krasnoye to arrest a deserter by the name of Chonkin. You'll get a warrant from the procurator. And find out who this Gladishev is. He might prove useful to us later on."

19

Since evening, the sky had been completely filled with storm clouds and it had begun raining. It rained all night without letting up and by morning the road was so bad it was unthinkable to use it. Nyura walked down the side of the road; her big boots, once her father's, kept slipping down and she had to hold them up by the tops. Her bag was heavy from the rain and kept slipping off her shoulder. Having slogged through two and a half kilometers like this, she came to the first fork in the road, at which point she caught sight of a tarpaulin-covered one-and-a-half-ton truck. Several men were busy digging beside the truck. Drenched, covered with dirt from head to foot, they were clearing the road in front of the truck, some with shovels, some with their bare hands. One man, with two small bars on his lapels, was standing a little off to the side and smoking, shielding his disintegrating cigarette from the rain with the palm of his hand. An enormous, gangly man came out from behind the truck, holding a piece of plywood which he used instead of a shovel. Catching sight of Nyura, who was passing on one side of the truck, he stopped and stared at her from under his reddish eyebrows with bestial eyes.

"A woman!" he shouted in wonder, as if the encounter were taking place on an uninhabited island.

The men in gray uniforms quit working, swung around in Nyura's direction, and began looking her over in total silence. Nyura shrunk from their gaze.

"Hey, girl!" shouted the one who was smoking. "Is it far to Krasnoye?"

"No, not that far," said Nyura. "You drive another kilometer or so; go over the little hill, and from there you can already see the village. Who you looking for over there?" she asked, plucking up her courage.

"You've got some son-of-a-bitch deserter living over there," confided a soldier with a shovel, standing near the lieutenant.

"Prokopov," the lieutenant cut him off sternly. "Button your lip."

"What did I say wrong?" Prokopov threw down his shovel, went over to the truck, and got behind the wheel. The truck started moving, went a short ways, then got stuck in the mud again. Nyura went on her way. She walked along the road for a while, then went off to the right, then dashed down and along the river back to Krasnoye.

Chonkin was sleeping so soundly she couldn't wake him at first. She even had to splash some cold water on his face. Nyura told him about the men stuck on the road and what they'd said about a deserter.

"So let them catch their deserter," said Chonkin, shaking his sleepy head, unable to make any sense out of any of it. "What's it got to do with me?"

"Oh, Lord!" Nyura threw up her hands. "You really don't see who the deserter is? You!"

"Me a deserter?" marveled Chonkin.

"No, maybe me."

Chonkin lowered his feet from the bed. "Something's wrong in what you're saying, Nyurka," he said with displeasure. "Just think for yourself—what kind of deserter can I be? I was stationed here to guard that airplane. Since I wrote to my unit, nobody's come to relieve me. I can't quit my post all by myself, it's against regulations. So how can I be a deserter, then, huh?"

Nyura began to weep and implored Chonkin to take

some urgent measures, because there was no way of proving any of that to them.

Chonkin thought a minute, then shook his head decisively. "No, Nyura, I'm not about to hide, because I don't have the right to abandon my post. And no one can relieve me of it except the corporal of the guard, the commander of the guard, the duty officer or . . ." Chonkin thought for a while about what other responsible person could relieve him of his post and decided that, after the duty officer, he could not be subordinate to anyone lower than a general . . . "Or a general," he concluded, and then began getting dressed.

"So what are you going to do then?" asked Nyura.

"What can I do?" He shrugged his shoulders. "I'll go stand guard—and just let anybody try and come near."

It was still raining. Chonkin slipped his overcoat on and slung his cartridge belt over it.

"You're going to shoot at them?" Nyura asked fearfully.

"If they leave me alone I won't," promised Chonkin. "But if they don't, they shouldn't blame me."

Nyura rushed over to Ivan, threw her arms around his neck, and burst into tears. "Vanya," she begged, choking with tears, "Please, don't resist them. They'll kill you."

Chonkin ran his hand across her hair. It was wet. "What can you do, Nyurka," he sighed. "I'm still the sentry. Let's say our goodbyes now, just in case."

They kissed three times. Then Nyura, without quite knowing how to do it, made the sign of the cross over him.

Chonkin slung his rifle over his shoulder, pulled his forage cap down over his eyes, and went outside. The rain seemed to have let up and a faint rainbow had begun to shine somewhere on the other side of New Kliukvino.

Ivan made his way to the plane, his feet sticking in the mud, feeling the water ooze into his bad right boot. The rain was rustling like wheat. Heavy raindrops quivered on the taut edges of the greasy tarpaulin wing covering. Chonkin climbed up on the right lower wing, the upper wing shielding him from the rain. It was not especially comfortable sitting there, since the wing was sloping and slippery. On the other hand, the view was good; both roads, the upper one and the one that ran along the Tyopa, were in plain view.

An hour passed, no one appeared. Another half hour passed and Nyura brought him breakfast, potatoes and milk. Just then the rain stopped and the sun peeped out. The sun was reflected in the puddles, sparkling brightly in every drop. Perhaps it was the sun, perhaps it was breakfast, perhaps it was both of them together, but Chonkin's mood took a turn for the better and the sense of impending danger left him. He even began to doze off a little.

"Hey, soldier!"

Chonkin started and grabbed hold of his rifle. It was Burly, standing by the gate. He was barefoot and both of his pant legs had been rolled up almost to the knee. He had a dragnet flung over his shoulder.

"I'm looking for somebody to go net-fishing with," he explained, gazing curiously at Chonkin.

"Move back!" said Chonkin and turned away, still keeping one eye on Burly.

"What's wrong with you?" said Burly in surprise. "Have you got something against me? If it's from what I told you about Borka, you're way off. I didn't see it myself, maybe she wasn't sleeping with him." Burly hung the dragnet on the fence, bent down, and stuck one foot through the slats. He was just about to bring the other foot through when Chonkin hopped down from the wing.

"Hey, hey, don't you come through there or I'll shoot," he shouted, and aimed his rifle at Burly.

Burly retreated and hurriedly pulled the net from the fence.

"I swear you're cracked, buddy."

At that moment a covered truck came over the hill. The driver stepped on the gas and turned the wheel hard. Standing beside him on the running board, holding on to the door, the lieutenant, who was covered in mud, was issuing orders. The other men in gray uniform, smeared with mud from head to foot and lathered with sweat, were nudging the truck forward. The truck still kept skidding, its rear end swerving from side to side. Observing this unexpected sight with great curiosity, Burly kept off to one side.

"Hey, comrade, give us a hand!" the lieutenant shouted hoarsely to him.

"You think I got nothing better to do," muttered Burly. He turned around and went slowly on his way. But then he was overcome with curiosity, doubled back, and started after the truck, which by this time had already pulled up in front of the kolkhoz office.

20

Ivan Timofeyevich Golubev was sitting in his office, toiling over the composition of a report concerning haymaking in the last ten-day period. Needless to say, the report was a fraud, since there had been practically no haymaking at all during the last ten-day period. The men were leaving for the front, the women were getting them ready, some harvest that was! The District Committee, however, did not consider such reasons valid. Borisov cursed him out on the telephone and demanded that the plan be fulfilled. Naturally he knew that, in times like these, he was demanding the impossible, but the paper signifying work completed was more important to him than the work itself—Borisov was also being cursed out by those over him. And so Borisov collected papers from all the kolkhozes, compiled the figures, and sent them off to the province, where further reports were compiled on the basis of the district reports, and so it went, all the way to the top.

That is why at that very moment Golubev was sitting in his office doing his bit for the great cause of paper work. He ruled sheets of paper into squares, in which he entered the hectares, metric centners, percentages, and workdays opposite the names of the brigade leaders. Then he called Volkov the bookkeeper, who was sitting in the next room. Volkov swiftly tallied up the figures in each column on his abacus, and the chairman entered them in the column marked Total. After he had dismissed the bookkeeper, the chairman put his quite legible signature to the report, blew on the freshly baked document, and pushed it away in order to admire it from afar. The figures looked impressive and the chairman caught himself starting to half-believe them. His work done, Golubev got up to stretch. Still stretching, he walked over to the window and froze, his hands in the air.

A covered one-and-a-half-ton truck was parked in front of his office. There was a group of muddy men in gray uniforms standing by the truck, and two of them were already mounting the stairs. "This is it!" groaned the chairman to himself. No matter how much he had prepared himself for his fate, the sudden appearance of the men in gray had caught him off guard. All the more so, since he had requested to be sent to the front and it looked like his request was going to be granted. Now it was all over. The chairman began rushing around the office. What could he do? It was pointless to run; besides, there was no time—he could already hear their footsteps next door in the bookkeeper's office. Hide? Ridiculous. Suddenly his gaze fell on the report he had just composed. There it was, the evidence! He had signed his own sentence. What now? Burn it? No time. Rip it up? They'd paste it back together. There was only one way out. Ivan Timofeyevich rolled the paper into a ball and jammed it into his mouth. But there was not time enough for him to swallow it.

The door opened, revealing the two men. The first one, the runty one, had two bars on his lapels, the one with the bestial face had triangles on his.

The lieutenant used his sleeve to wipe the sweat from his forehead, smearing it with mud in the process, then said hello. A faint moo-like sound was his reply.

Assuming that he was dealing with an ordinary deaf-mute, the lieutenant grimaced involuntarily, for he did not like people who were unable to answer his questions.

"Where is the chairman?" he asked sternly. "The head!" He used his hands to depict a large head.

"Moooo," mooed the chairman, humbly poking one finger to his chest.

The lieutenant was surprised at first, he had never seen a deaf-and-dumb chairman before (how can he speak at meetings?), but if that's the way it was, that's the way it was supposed to be and he began trying to communicate with the help of his hands. "You understand, there's a certain person here . . . a deserter, you understand?" Doing the best he could, the lieutenant first imitated a battle (*bang bang*), then a man running from the battlefield.

"And what we have to do is . . ." He whipped his pistol from his holster and stuck it in the chairman's stomach. "Hands up!"

The chairman's jaw dropped open, the saliva-covered ball of paper fell out of his mouth; he began to stagger, and then collapsed on the floor, hitting the back of his head on the way down.

The lieutenant lost his composure. He looked down at the chairman, then over at the soldier who was standing motionless and silent by the door. "What the hell . . ." he muttered in confusion. "Soon as he sees a gun, he faints. And for some reason the guy eats paper." He picked up the crumpled ball of paper from the floor, unfolded it fastidiously, looked it over, then threw it on the desk. He nudged the chairman with the tip of his boot, bent down, and started slapping his cheeks. "Hey, get up, you hear me, get up. Stop making believe." He took the chairman's hand and felt his wrist. "I can't tell if there's any pulse or not."

He unbuttoned the chairman's field jacket and shirt, and put an ear to his chest.

"Svintsov, keep your feet still," he said, then listened intently. If the heart was beating it was beating so softly he couldn't hear it.

"So?" asked Svintsov, curious.

"I can't tell." The lieutenant got up from his knees and

was about to brush them off, but one look at his pants convinced him not to waste the energy. "Go on, you take a listen, maybe your hearing's better than mine."

Svintsov bent down and put his ear to Golubev's chest. Then he raised his head and said: "Mice."

"What mice?" The lieutenant did not understand.

"Mice scraping around under the floor," explained Svintsov. "Could be rats too. The squeaking's too low for a mouse. I had something down in my cellar last year. At first I got it wrong, thought it was mice and like a fool I throw my cat down there. They just pounced right on her, ate off her tail. She barely got out alive."

"Svintsov, did I order you to listen for mice? Is his heart beating or isn't it?"

"Who knows," answered Svintsov. "I'm no doctor. I don't know much about this kind of stuff. I think we ought to open the window and let in some fresh air. If he's alive he'll come to; if he's dead he'll start turning blue, nose first. Isn't that how you tell?"

"Who the hell knows," said the lieutenant in a fit of temper. "People's nerves are starting to go. Why are they so afraid of us? We just don't grab anybody we bump into, there's got to be a warrant. All right, the hell with him, let him lie there. Go in the other office and bring the one-armed guy in here. Just don't be too rough on him. If he croaks, where are we going to find another one to be a witness for us?"

Svintsov opened the door to the next office and called the bookkeeper. Volkov timidly stepped across the threshold. As soon as he spotted the chairman lying on the floor under the desk, Volkov turned completely green and began shaking in terror.

"Do you know this man?" The lieutenant nodded at the body sprawled motionless on the floor.

"Never met him!" cried Volkov, biting his tongue in fright.

"What do you mean?" The lieutenant was amazed. "Who is this man?"

"Chairman Golubev," babbled Volkov, flustered by the absurdity of his own answers. "But I only see him at work, and as for personal relations, we've never even talked."

"So you've never even talked?" The lieutenant looked suspiciously at Volkov. "You mean you see him every day and you never exchanged a single word?"

"Not one word . . . I swear it, not one. I'm not a Party member of course . . . I didn't get much education, I don't understand anything about this sort of thing."

"We'll teach you to understand," said Svintsov from where he stood.

"Though one time he did say to me that the works of Marx and Engels were hard for a worker to understand. He said you need special political training for them."

"So," said the lieutenant. "And that's it?"

"That's it."

Svintsov lurched at Volkov and put his huge red fist, spattered with birthmarks or freckles, right up against his nose.

"You quit clamming up or else I'll flatten your nose on your face. The lieutenant questions you polite, you answer him polite, you scum."

There is no telling how it all might have ended had not the lieutenant recalled that he had not come there to interrogate Volkov. Cutting Svintsov's crude remarks short, he informed Volkov that he was being entrusted with the role of official witness at the arrest of the deserter Chonkin.

21

The seven men in gray walked in line formation down Krasnoye's one wide street. The eighth man was the bookkeeper Volkov, who lagged as far behind as he could, gazing about in fright as if expecting a sudden blow.

As soon as the villagers caught sight of the men coming, they hid in their huts, peeking out cautiously from behind their curtains. The children stopped crying, even the dogs were not barking at the gates.

There was a silence like that before dawn, when all those who go to bed late have already gone to bed and those who get up early have not yet gotten up.

The people watching from behind their curtains would freeze in position when the line approached their hut and they would heave a sigh of relief when it passed by. Once again they would hold their breath in fear and curiosity—where were they going? Whose house?

When the grays had passed Gladishev's it became clear to everybody that they were going to Chonkin's; it had to be him, there was only one hut left, the last one in the village.

"Stop! Who goes there?" Chonkin's voice rang out, startling everyone. After the preceding silence, it sounded so loud the entire village could hear it.

"Friend," barked out the lieutenant, without breaking stride, and he signaled his men to move forward immediately.

"Stop or I'll shoot!" Chonkin clicked the bolt of his rifle shut.

"Don't shoot, you're under arrest!" shouted the lieutenant, unsnapping his holster as he advanced.

"Stop or I'll shoot!" repeated Chonkin and, taking up a firing position, he fired a warning shot in the air.

"Throw down your arms!" In one swift motion the lieutenant snatched the pistol from his holster and, without taking aim, fired a shot in Chonkin's direction. Chonkin dove nimbly beneath the fuselage and crawled out on the other side of the plane. The bullet had pierced the hood of the engine and lodged somewhere inside.

Chonkin set his rifle at the end of the fuselage near the tail fin and carefully stuck out his head. The grays were drawing nearer. Now they had all drawn their pistols. The unarmed bookkeeper Volkov kept lagging farther and farther behind, increasing the distance between himself and the lieutenant, at the same time trying to hide behind Svintsov's broad back. Without losing a second, Chonkin sighted in on the lieutenant's chin and pulled the trigger. But at that precise moment somebody nudged his elbow, which in turn saved the lieutenant's life. The bullet went whistling right past his ear.

"Down!" cried the lieutenant and selflessly threw himself first into the mud.

Chonkin shuddered and turned around. Frightened by the shot, Borka the hog had scampered off to one side but was now approaching Chonkin again with wary friendliness.

"Shoo!" Chonkin threatened Borka with the butt of his rifle, but thinking Chonkin was just playing, Borka pounced on him and it did not prove easy to get him quieted down. Although the grays were still lying side by side in the mud with their commanding officer, they could get to their feet at any moment and rush to the attack.

The lieutenant was the first to get hold of himself. "Hey, you!" Ungluing himself from the ground, the lieutenant raised some sort of paper over his head. "You are under arrest. Here is the warrant for your arrest, signed by the procurator."

"Did the procurator really sign it himself?" asked Chonkin in some amazement.

"What do you think, I'd try and trick you?" said the lieutenant, offended not so much for himself as for the Institution which he served. "We don't make arrests without the procurator's sanction."

"The procurator knows my name?"

"But of course. Aren't you Chonkin?"

"That's me. Who else." He even broke into laughter, embarrassed that such important people would tear themselves away from their important affairs, that they had remembered his name and entered it on an official document.

"So, you going to surrender then?" asked the lieutenant.

Chonkin gave it some thought. No matter what you say, a warrant was a serious document. But regulations didn't say you can take a sentry off his post with a warrant.

"I can't, Comrade Lieutenant, I just can't," said Chonkin, his voice full of sympathy. "Of course, I understand you've got a job to do. But if you were a corporal of the guard or a commander of the guard or even a duty officer . . ."

"Consider me your duty officer," conceded the lieutenant.

"No," said Chonkin. "There's nobody looks like you in our unit. I know all the commanding officers personally, I used to work in the mess, see what I mean? And you're not wearing the right kind of uniform either."

"All right then," said the lieutenant angrily. "If you don't want to give yourself up the easy way, we'll make you do it the hard way."

He rose decisively to his feet and began moving toward Chonkin, his pistol in one hand and the warrant above his head in the other. His men also got to their feet and began carefully advancing behind the lieutenant. Volkov the bookkeeper stayed where he was.

"Hey! Hey!" shouted Chonkin. "Better stay where you are. I'll shoot! I'm at my post, you know!"

Chonkin wished to avoid bloodshed at all costs, but they were no longer responding to him. Chonkin realized that the negotiations had broken down and once again he flung his rifle across the fuselage. Borka kept getting in his way, grabbing the hem of Chonkin's overcoat in his teeth, until Chonkin began to scratch Borka's side with his left hand, repeating over and over: "Borya-Bor-Bor-Bor." It was awkward holding the rifle with just one hand, but at least Borka was out of his way now. Borka had quieted down and was lying in the mud, his feet in the air. Like all pigs, he loved to be petted.

"Chonkin!" warned the lieutenant as he drew nearer, brandishing the warrant and the pistol. "Don't even think of shooting, it'll go harder on you."

A shot rang out; the bullet pierced the warrant in the very place where the procurator had affixed his seal and signature. This time, without waiting for a command, the men hit the ground, followed by their lieutenant.

"Now look what you've done, you crum!" shouted the lieutenant, on the verge of tears. "You've ruined a document signed by the procurator. You shot through a seal with the emblem of the Soviet Union on it! You'll pay for that!"

The next shot again forced the lieutenant to slam his nose back into the mud. Trying not to raise his head, the lieutenant turned his face to Svintsov. "Svintsov, crawl around to the right. We've got to distract him."

"Yes, sir!" answered Svintsov, raising his backside slightly. At that very moment a bullet dispatched by Chonkin stung into that backside like a bumblebee.

Svintsov rammed himself back into the wet earth and began roaring in an inhuman voice.

"What's the matter, Svintsov?" asked the lieutenant, worried. "You wounded?"

"Wa-wa-wa-wa!" howled Svintsov, not from pain but from fear the wound was fatal.

From his cover, Chonkin kept a vigilant eye on his enemies. They were all lying in the mud now and, with the exception of the one with the red hair, gave no signs of life. Behind all of them lay the bookkeeper Volkov, who'd gotten into the whole mess purely by accident.

Chonkin caught the sound of someone's footsteps coming up slowly behind him. "Who's that?" Chonkin started.

"It's me, Vanya." It was Nyura's voice.

"Ah, Nyurka." Chonkin was overjoyed. "Come here. Just don't stick your head out. They'll kill you. And scratch Borka a little, will you?"

Nyura squatted down by Borka and began scratching him behind the ear.

"So you see," said Chonkin with some satisfaction. "And you were scared."

"But what's going to happen now?" asked Nyura dolefully.

"Now?" Chonkin did not remove his eyes from the men lying in the mud. "They can lie there until someone relieves me."

"But what if you have to go to the outhouse?"

"If I have to . . ." Chonkin grew thoughtful and immediately found a way out of his predicament. "Then you can stand guard a few minutes."

"What about when it gets dark?" asked Nyura.

"We'll stand guard when it's dark."

"You big dope," sighed Nyura. "They're in gray. You can't even see them in the mud now. And when it's dark you won't be able to see anything."

"There you go, cackling around me again." Chonkin was angry at her, displaying the peculiarly human habit of venting anger at those who tell the unpleasant truth, as if keeping it quiet would make everything better. Deep in thought, Chonkin began sorting through all the possible alternatives. Finally he came up with the solution.

"Nyurka," he said, his mood more cheerful. "Run to the house and get your mail bag and a good length of rope. Understand?"

"No," said Nyura.

"You'll see why later. Just go."

22

Shortly thereafter, those who wanted to could see the following sight: Nyura came out of her house with a long piece of rope and her tarpaulin mail bag. She walked up behind the men lying in the mud and signaled Chonkin with her hand.

"Hey, you!" shouted Chonkin from his cover. "Nyura's going to come around now. Surrender your revolvers to her. If anyone puts up a fight, I'll shoot him on the spot. You got that?"

No one answered. Since when Nyura scaled a fish she

started with the head, she went over to the lieutenant first.

"Get out of here, you bitch, or I'll shoot you," hissed the lieutenant without raising his head.

Nyura came to a halt. "Vanya!" she cried.

"What?"

"He's calling me names."

"All right, move off to the side!" Chonkin aimed at the lieutenant, squinting his left eye.

"Hey, don't shoot! I was only kidding! Here's my pistol."

The lieutenant flung his pistol over his back and high enough in the air so that Chonkin could see it. The pistol splashed at Nyura's feet. She cleaned the mud from it and tossed it into her bag.

"Hey, you, what are you waiting for?" Nyura walked over to Svintsov, who seemed to be trying to embrace the whole earth.

"I'm not waiting for anything, sweetheart," said Svintsov with a groan. "It's over there." And indeed his Nagan pistol was lying far from its owner, on top of a drying hummock. Nyura tossed that gun as well into her bag.

"Oi," moaned Svintsov. "Oi, I can't stand it."

"Are you wounded?" asked Nyura with concern.

"That's right, sweetheart. I've got to get bandaged up. I'm bleeding to death here. I've got three kids. Who'll take care of them?"

"Right away, soon as I can, just a little more patience," said Nyura and she began to hurry. Although to all appearances Svintsov was nothing but a beast, even a beast, if suffering, will arouse pity in a normal person.

It was easy from then on. The remaining members of the task force, following their senior officer's good example, obeyed unquestioningly and surrendered their arms.

They didn't offer any resistance when Nyura tied them all together with a single piece of rope, the way mountain climbers do before a difficult ascent.

23

The workday was coming to a close. There had been no news at all from the detail dispatched to capture the deserter and Captain Milyaga was starting to feel nervous. Kapa the secretary had been on the phone a good two hours, driving the exchange operators to distraction, but no one was picking up the phone in Krasnoye.

"Any luck?" Milyaga kept leaning out of his office.

Kapa would shrug her delicate shoulders guiltily, as if she were to blame for it all, and then once again would start cranking the handle on the telephone.

When there were ten minutes left till the end of work, Kapa began fixing her hair, uncertain whether it was worth the trouble or not. If the boss called her in, her hair would just get messed up anyway. But he probably wouldn't call her in today, since those dummies led by Filippov had gotten themselves lost somewhere along the line and the boss wouldn't be in any mood for her. Precisely at eighteen hundred hours the bell over her door rang out shrilly. Kapa got herself together and, wiggling her fanny a bit more than usual, walked into the captain's office, blossoming into an unofficial smile at the sight of him.

The captain replied with a smile and the suggestion that she take a little stroll over to the village of Krasnoye, since no one else was left and he was unable to leave the Institution right at that particular time.

"Some horse has strayed here, take him if you want," said the captain.

"I don't know how to ride horseback," said Kapa timidly.

"In that case, just run over there. You're young, seven kilometers is not much out of your way."

"What are you talking about, Afanasy Petrovich," said Kapa, her feelings hurt. "How am I supposed to walk through mud like that?"

"Nothing to it, put on your rubber boots," said the captain. "You'll only have to go one way, you can come back with them in the truck. Besides, I bet you run into them halfway there."

Kapa attempted to make further objections, but the captain smiled icily and, addressing her by her last name (a sign of extreme irritation), made it perfectly clear to Kapa that although she was a civilian her position in a military institution during wartime obliged her to carry out orders unquestioningly, to the letter and to the minute, all of which she had agreed to and signed her name to when she was hired for the job.

Lips trembling, Kapa said: "Yes, sir!" and rushed weeping from the office. She set off for home at a run to get her rubber boots and on her way made the most terrible vow—that no argument and no threat (including being fired) could ever force her to lie down again with that heartless man on that nightmare of a tattered, squashed, and ink-splattered office couch.

She did not, however, succeed in carrying out her orders. Her husband, the director of the local milk factory, who had long suspected her of cheating on him, threw a fit of jealousy and locked her in a storeroom.

The sun was setting when Captain Milyaga, still staffless, with no news from Kapa, locked up the Institution entrusted to his care with a large padlock, saddled the stray, and set off after the missing party.

24

Along the road, which had dried out by day's end, the horse carried Captain Milyaga swiftly forward into the unknown. At times, from an excess of energy, it would break into a trot, but the captain would restrain it, wishing to prolong the unexpected pleasure of the ride. Milyaga was in a better mood. He glanced lightheartedly from one side to the other, taking the dusk-darkened countryside for something quite special. Ech, he thought. How beautiful nature is here! In what other country can you find such pines and birches? Milyaga had never been in any other country, yet, because of his innate patriotism, he was convinced that there was no vegetation worthy of attention anywhere else. So fine! he rejoiced, filling his smoke-saturated lungs with air. You'd think the oxygen content was higher here than in the office. Lately Milyaga had been spending night and day in his office, thereby doing the maximum possible damage both to himself and to the fatherland. True, he had never been especially zealous. He always strove for mediocrity, understanding it was just as dangerous to be a shock worker on the invisible front as it was to be a laggard. In the life of those who serve the Institution there are sometimes moments of anxiety when legality triumphs. In the space of his career Afanasy Milyaga had twice to experience that particular unpleasantness. Both times, everyone from top to bottom had been sheared away, but both times Milyaga managed to come out in one piece and even to advance in the service, from senior supervisor to chief of the district division. This allowed him to look on the future with guarded optimism and the hope that he would survive the next triumph of legality.

Musing in such fashion, Milyaga did not notice that it was growing dark. By the time he rode into Krasnoye, it was already night. Stopping at the first hut, the captain heard a woman scolding somebody behind the gate. "Borka, you little devil, are you coming home or do you want me to warm your butt with my switch?"

A merry grunting could be heard in response, from which the captain, with his penchant for analyzing and comparing facts of every sort, surmised that Borka was not human.

"Hey, girl," the captain called into the dark, "do you know where our workers are?"

"What workers?"

"You know," said Milyaga shyly.

A moment of silence ensued behind the gate, then the woman's voice said warily: "And who might you be?"

"You know too much, you grow old too soon," joked the captain.

"They're all here, in the hut," said the girl indecisively, after a moment's thought.

"May I come in?" he asked.

The girl hesitated and once again answered uncertainly: "All right."

The captain jumped nimbly to the ground, tied his horse to the fence, and passed through the gate. The woman, who was young (even in the dark he'd managed to notice that), called the invisible Borka a parasite, opened the door, and let the captain in ahead of her.

He walked through a dark passageway, brushing up against clattering objects, then went down a corridor, fumbling his hand along the wall.

"Door's to the right," said the girl.

Groping until he found the doorknob, Milyaga entered

some sort of room and squinted his eyes—an oil lamp was burning on the table. When he'd grown somewhat used to the light, Milyaga was able to make out all his men, seven strong. Five of them were sitting on a bench by the wall. Lieutenant Filippov, his cheek on his fist, was sleeping on the floor, and the seventh, Svintsov, was lying on a bed, his butt in the air, groaning softly. A soldier with light-blue insignia was sitting on a stool in the middle of the room, holding a rifle with its bayonet fixed. As soon as the soldier saw Milyaga enter, he pointed his bayonet at him.

"What is going on here?" the captain asked severely.

"Cut the shouting," said the soldier. "There's a wounded man sleeping."

"And who are you?" shouted Milyaga, grabbing for his holster.

At that moment the soldier jumped up from the stool and brought the bayonet to the captain's stomach. "Hands up!"

"I'll give you 'hands up' in a minute." The captain smiled, attempting to unsnap his holster.

"I'll stick it right in you," warned the soldier.

Encountering the soldier's merciless gaze, the captain realized that he was in trouble and slowly raised his hands.

"Nyurka," said the soldier to the girl, who was still standing by the door, "take his revolver and throw it in the bag."

25

Several days had passed since Captain Milyaga's department had vanished, but nobody in the district seemed to notice. And after all it wasn't a needle that had vanished in a haystack but a reputable Institution which occupied a prominent place among other institutions. An Institution without which you could barely take a single step. Now here it was, totally gone, and nobody even gave a hoot. People were living, working, having children, and dying, and all without the knowledge of the proper agencies. Things were just drifting along by themselves.

No one knows how long this disgraceful state of affairs might have continued had not the First Secretary of the District Committee, Comrade Revkin, gradually begun to sense that somehow something was missing in the world around him. This odd sensation grew gradually stronger; it stuck in him like a splinter and, wherever he was, Revkin thought about it—at his office at the District Committee, at a conference of outstanding workers, at a session of the District Soviet, even at home. Having failed to come to any understanding of his condition, he lost his appetite, grew distracted, and one time he even went so far as to put his long johns on over his riding breeches and was about to go to work like that, but Motya, his personal chauffeur, tactfully restrained him.

And so one night when Revkin was lying in bed, staring up at the ceiling, sighing, and smoking cigarette after cigarette, his wife Aglaya, who was lying there beside him, asked: "What's the matter with you, Andrei?"

He had thought she was sleeping and her unexpected question made him gag on the smoke. "How do you mean?" he asked, clearing his throat.

"The last few days you've gotten, I don't know, nervous; you look terrible, you're not eating, and you never stop smoking. Are you having some trouble at work?"

"No," he said. "Everything's fine there."

"You feeling well?"

"Fit as a fiddle."

Neither of them said anything for a moment.

"Andrei," his wife said, troubled, "tell me, as one Communist to another, are you by any chance having unwholesome thoughts?"

Revkin had first met Aglaya more than ten years ago when they were both helping to carry out the policy of collectivization. Aglaya, then still a twenty-five-year-old Komsomol girl with fire in her eyes, won Revkin's heart because she could spend whole days and nights in the saddle dashing madly about the district hunting down and unmasking kulaks and wreckers. Her heart, young but strong, knew no mercy for her enemies, who at that time were being dispatched into the cold earth in great numbers. She did not always understand the humane party line, which did not permit one to kill them all right on the spot. Now she managed a Children's Home.

Her question made Revkin thoughtful. He put out one cigarette and lit up another. "Yes, Glashka," he said, finished with his thinking. "It looks like you're right. I really am having unwholesome thoughts."

Again they both fell silent.

"Andrei," Aglaya said softly and inexorably, "if you yourself feel these unwholesome thoughts in you, then you should make a clean breast of it to the Party."

"Yes, I should," agreed Andrei. "But what's going to happen to our son? He's only seven, after all."

"Don't you worry. I'll raise him to be a true Bolshevik. He'll even forget what your name was."

She helped her husband pack his suitcase but refused to spend the rest of the night in the same bed with him, out of ideological considerations.

In the morning, when his car arrived, Revkin ordered his chauffeur, Motya, to drive him to the Institution, because he had grown unused to walking and could not have found his way there on foot.

To his great surprise, there were none of the Right People at the Right Place. There were no sentries, no one was on duty, and a massive lock was hanging on the big green gate. Revkin knocked at the door and at the gate and tried to peep in the first-floor window—there was no one to be seen.

Strange, thought Revkin. How is it possible there's no one working in an Institution like this?

"That lock's probably been there a week," said Motya, as if reading Revkin's thoughts. "Maybe they were fired."

"Not fired, liquidated," Revkin corrected severely and ordered Motya to drive him to the District Committee.

On the way there Revkin did think that, indeed, the disappearance of such an important Institution could not be explained by anything but its liquidation. But if that was so, why hadn't he been informed? Anyway, was it possible, in wartime especially, to liquidate an organization which aids the state in protecting itself from internal enemies? And where was the explanation for this disappearance to be found if not in the intrigues of those very enemies who had obviously now stepped up their activities?

Having locked himself in his office, Revkin called around to the neighboring districts and, by means of careful questions, learned that the Institution was still in existence and in full operation. This information did not make things any easier for him. Now the situation seemed even more muddled. An immediate investigation would have to be launched.

Revkin picked up the phone and asked to be connected with Captain Milyaga.

"He doesn't answer," said the operator and it was only then that Revkin realized the complete absurdity of the call. For if Milyaga were there, there wouldn't be any reason to call him. But, on the other hand, who else could fathom the complex problem of the disappearance of the Right People, especially when it was they who were supposed to deal with such problems?

A resolution should be submitted, thought the Secretary, that there be two Institutions in each district. The first would carry out its usual functions and the second would keep an eye on the first so that it wouldn't disappear.

Revkin had no sooner noted down this idea on his desk calendar than another idea occurred to him: But who's going to keep their eye on the second Institution? That means a third will have to be created, and a fourth for the third and so on, ad infinitum, and then who would be left to do anything else? It had turned into a vicious cycle.

There was no time, however, for prolonged meditation. Action was required.

Revkin sent his chauffeur, Motya, to the marketplace to find out what the old women were saying. Motya returned shortly and informed him that the women were saying that, apparently, the entire personnel of the Institution had driven off to the village of Krasnoye to arrest some deserter. A thread had been found. Once again Revkin felt right with the world and the strange feeling, that splinter in his side, vanished as if it had been extracted by tweezers.

Revkin called Krasnoye. Chairman Golubev (back, apparently, among the living) came to the phone.

To Revkin's question concerning the whereabouts of

the party that had gone to Krasnoye Golubev answered: "Chonkin and his girl arrested them."

Needless to say, the connection was rotten. Moreover, it was difficult to imagine that some Chonkin and some girl could have arrested all of them and all at once. That simply could not be. And so it seemed to Revkin that Golubev had not said "girl" but "gang."

"And how big is his gang?" inquired Revkin.

"Now let me see . . ." Golubev hesitated, summoning up Nyura's image in his mind. ". . . Pretty good-sized on the whole."

Revkin had no sooner hung up the phone than the entire district began crawling with ominous rumors. People were saying that Chonkin's gang was active in their area and that it was numerous and well armed. As regards the person of Chonkin himself, there were the most contrary opinions. Some people said that Chonkin was a criminal who had escaped from prison with his gang. Others contended that Chonkin was a White general who had been living in China until recently and who now planned to attack the Soviet Union; he was assembling countless troops and all people with a grudge against Soviet power were flocking to his side from every corner of the land.

A third group refuted the two preceding versions, claiming that, having fled from the Germans, Stalin had gone into hiding under the name Chonkin. They said that his guard consisted exclusively of persons of Georgian nationality, but that his woman was Russian, from the common folk. They went on to say that Stalin had grown extremely indignant upon observing what was going on in the district and that he was summoning all the different chiefs and punishing them severely for wrecking and sabotage. In particular, he had arrested the entire personnel of the Institution with Captain Milyaga at their head and ordered them shot on the spot.

Tsilya Stalin brought this news home from a line where she'd been standing waiting for kerosene.

"Moishe, have you heard the news?" she said to her husband, who was sitting by the window, hammering nails into the sole of a shoe. "People are saying that some Chonkin or other has shot that goy of yours . . ."

"Yes, I heard," said Moisei Solomonovich, having first taken the nails from his mouth. "He was an interesting young man and I feel very sorry for him."

Tsilya went off to kindle the kerosene stove, but returned immediately. "Moishe," she said emotionally, "you think this Chonkin could be Jewish?"

Moisei Solomonovich put his little hammer aside. "Chonkin?" he repeated in surprise. "That sounds like one of their names to me."

"Chonkin?" Tsilya looked at her husband as if he were a fool. "Ha! Listen to you! So then what about Rivkin and Zuskin?"

Returning to her kerosene stove, she kept repeating the name Chonkin in various ways, shaking her gray head in doubt.

In order to somehow neutralize these ominous rumors, the local newspaper, *Bolshevik Tempos*, featured a series of items in a section of the paper called "Amusing Information." For example, there was a story about a triton that had been frozen for five thousand years and had revived after it had been warmed up; and another about a certain skilled folk craftsman, a metal worker from the town of Cheboksara, who had scratched the entire text of Gorky's article "Whose Side Are You On, Masters of

Culture?" onto a kernel of wheat. But since the rumors continued to spread, the newspaper, in an effort to redirect people's attention, began running a debate in its pages, under the general heading "The Rules of Etiquette —Necessary or Not?" In the first article to appear in that section, Neuzhelev, a reader from the District Committee, wrote that the victory of the October Revolution, of worldwide historical significance, not only brought the peoples of our boundless country liberation from the rule of the capitalists and landowners, but negated the old ethical and moral standards and replaced them with ones that reflected the radical changes that had taken place in social relations. The new standards were primarily distinguished by their clear class approach. The society of victorious socialism, he wrote, does not accept the bourgeois rules of etiquette which are tainted by exploitation. Expressions like "Mister," "Sir," "Your humble servant," and so on, have vanished forever. The word "comrade," with which we address each other, not only testifies to the equality among the various groups of the population but to the equality between men and women as well. At the same time, we reject any manifestation of nihilism in the sphere of workers' relationships. Neuzhelev maintained that, in spite of the new principles, certain traditional standards of behavior ought to be preserved even in our socialist community. For example, as regards public transportation (which, by the way, had never existed in Dolgov), one should give up one's seat to invalids, people advanced in years, pregnant women, and women with children. A man should greet the woman first, but should not be first to offer his hand; he should let the woman enter a room first and should remove any headgear when indoors. Naturally, it was not obligatory to kiss a lady's hand, but it was necessary to display courtesy and sensitivity to one's neighbors and to one's comrades at work. In this connection such vestiges of the past as social crudeness and foul language were completely intolerable. To play musical instruments after eleven o'clock was also inadmissible. Having cited several negative examples, the author concluded his article with the thought that mutual courtesy was the foundation of the healthy attitude on which, in the final analysis, our labor productivity depended. And, since victory at the front depended on our work in the rear, the inevitable conclusion suggested itself.

This article made a strong impression on quite a few people.

By the way, two outstanding citizens were residing in the town of Dolgov at that time. It has been years since anyone has remembered their names, their ranks, or what posts they held. The old-timers say that these two were somewhat eccentric types who, wearing straw hats in summer and tall gray sheepskin hats in winter, would meet on Collectivization Square and leisurely stroll down Post Office Cross Street to the kolkhoz market and back. During their strolls they would keep looking back over their shoulders while conversing in whispers about the most current topics. The fact that they were in Dolgov at the height of military operations and not with the army in the field leads one to assume that they were not then of draftable age.

On the evening of the day when the newspaper carried Neuzhelev's article, these two thinkers met as usual on the square and greeted each other by tipping their hats.

"So what do you have to say about all this?" asked the First Thinker straight off and then immediately spun his head to the left, the right, the rear, and then again to the left and the right, to make sure no one was following them and eavesdropping.

The Second Thinker did not even ask him what he meant. Since they constantly communicated, it took only the merest allusion for them to understand each other. The Second Thinker also performed the almost ritual act of turning his head to the left, right, and rear, and then said: "Ech, forget it! They have to fill up the space in the newspaper with something . . ."

"Is that what you think?" said the First Thinker, squinting craftily. "They've got nothing else to write about, is that it? The Germans have seized the Baltic states, Belorussia, the Ukraine, and are now outside Moscow, not to mention total confusion in the district. The harvest hasn't been gathered, the cattle have no feed, that Chonkin gang is on the loose, and the district paper has nothing better to write about than good manners?"

"Forget it," repeated the Second Thinker. "One of the readers had an idea . . ."

"It is precisely there that you are mistaken!" screeched the First Thinker gleefully. This was his crowning phrase. In every argument with his friend he would wait with palpitating heart for a moment like this in order to say: "It is precisely there that you are mistaken!"

"I am not mistaken about anything," the Second Thinker muttered with displeasure.

"I assure you that you are mistaken. Believe me, I know the system. Nobody gets any ideas without orders from above. Here everything is at once both more complicated and simpler. They have finally realized"—the First Thinker spun his head around and then lowered his voice—"that without a return to the old values we will lose the war."

"Because we are not kissing ladies' hands?"

"Yes, exactly!" exclaimed the First Thinker. "Precisely for that reason. You do not comprehend these elementary things. This is not a war between two systems, but between two civilizations. Whichever turns out to be the higher will survive."

"Hold on there!" The Second Thinker spread his hands. "That's going too far. At one time, the Huns . . ."

"What are you bringing in the Huns for? Remember Alexander the Great!"

And they were off! The Huns, Alexander the Great, the war with the Philistines, the Crusades, the Crossing of the Alps, the battle at Marathon, the storming of Izmail, the breaching of the Maginot Line . . .

"You just don't understand!" The First Thinker began swinging his arms about. "There is a great difference between Verdun and Austerlitz."

"What are you dragging in your Austerlitz for? Take Trafalgar."

"Take him yourself."

In such fashion they quarreled their way through several hours, waving their arms, stopping, lowering them, raising their voices again as they walked from the square to the market and back. They did not reach any agreement, but still they did have a breath of fresh air, which as everyone knows is of great value to the body. Parting long after midnight, neither of them was able to fall asleep for quite a while, each turning over in his memory the particulars of their conversation and each meanwhile thinking: "Now I know what I'll tell him tomorrow . . ."

The article on good manners made quite a strong impression on other residents of the town as well. In a polemical notice entitled "And Just Why Not?" an old schoolteacher, while giving class interpretation its due, nevertheless maintained that ladies' hands not only may be kissed but should be. "It is beautiful, elegant, and chivalrous," she wrote. And chivalry, was, in her words, an inherent characteristic of Soviet man. The teacher was answered by a biting rebuff written by the distinguished cattle butcher Terenty Knish, entitled "Look What They Want Now!" What reason is there, he wrote, for a workingman to kiss some lady's hand? And what if her hands haven't been washed, or, even worse, have scabs on them? "That's enough, I'm sorry," wrote Knish. "I'll put it straight to you like a worker—if you don't have a certificate from the doctor, I won't kiss your hand." The local poet Serafim Butilko expressed his feelings in a long poem entitled "I See Communism Clearly in the Distance," which, by the way, had no direct bearing on the topic under discussion.

In summing up the debate, the newspaper thanked everyone who had participated, scolded the schoolteacher and Knish for their extremism, and finally concluded that the very existence of such divergent points of view on the question at hand testified to the seriousness and timeliness of the issue raised by Neuzhelev, that this issue was not to be brushed aside, nor would solving it prove a simple matter.

While the newspaper was distracting the populace, the district leaders were sorting through all the more probable stories to arrive at the conclusion that in all likelihood Chonkin was the commander of German paratroops who had landed in the district in order to disrupt work in the rear and to prepare for a troop attack in that sector.

Not knowing how to proceed, the district authorities rushed to the provincial authorities, and they in turn went to the military authorities. An infantry unit was taken from an echelon on its way to the front and flung into the campaign to liquidate Chonkin's gang (the "so-called Chonkin," as the secret documents now referred to him).

A gray dusk was gathering when, observing all the rules of camouflage, the regiment arrived at the village of Krasnoye and surrounded it. Two battalions blocked off either end of the road and the third entrenched itself along the vegetable patches (there was a natural barrier on the fourth side, the river Tyopa).

Two scouts were sent out on reconnaissance.

26

It had not been an especially complicated matter for Chonkin to arrest the entire staff of the district Institution. The real difficulties arose afterward. It is a known fact that every person is in the habit of going to sleep from time to time, and while in that state he loses awareness and anyone who wants to can take advantage of him.

Nyura began relieving Chonkin, but this wasn't very easy for her to do since no one had relieved her of her duties as postmistress and she still had to take care of the house.

On top of this, it turned out that the workers of the Institution, just like ordinary mortals, had to answer the call of nature several times a day. For some reason, none of them ever had to answer that call at the same time. This was no problem when Nyura was there. While Chonkin escorted the next prisoner needing to go, Nyura would guard the rest. But when Nyura was not there or when she was sleeping, the others could escape, even though their hands were tied. At first Chonkin took them all out together each time; then he came up with another method. He found an old dog collar in the hayloft and fastened a strong rope to it. The problem had been conclusively and irrevocably solved. If someone had to go, first he had to put on the dog collar, and then he was free to move within the limits prescribed by the length of the rope. The winter outhouse was located right in the covered cattleyard, which was connected to the main hut by a narrow little corridor. (Later on, witnesses would testify that any time you peeped in the window you'd see the same sight—Chonkin sitting on a stool near the half-open door, holding his rifle in one hand, and in the other a piece of rope wound around his wrist and stretched out tight from the other end.)

But then a new difficulty arose. Nyura's scanty food supply was on the way down. It turned out that the workers of the Institution had as much appetite as any other social group. At first Nyura stanchly endured all the burdens and privations of military service, but there came a point when she could stand it no more.

She had returned home at the usual hour. The sun was setting, but night was still far away. As usual Chonkin was sitting on the stool by the door, leaning back up against the doorjamb, his feet stretched out, his rifle in his hands. The prisoners had settled down in their place in the corner. Three of them were on the floor playing a furious game of Old Maid, a fourth was waiting his turn for the outhouse, two were sleeping, each using part of Nyura's old quilted jacket for a pillow, and the seventh prisoner was sitting on the bench, staring wistfully out the window at the river, the forest, freedom.

Aside from Chonkin, no one paid Nyura any attention. Even Chonkin said nothing to her but only raised his head and gave her a long, sympathetic glance. Without saying a word, she threw her bag over the threshold and stepped over Chonkin's outstretched legs. Sticking her head into the stove, she removed her cast-iron pot, which contained the grand total of one potato cooked in its skin. Nyura turned the potato over in her hand, flung it into the far corner, and burst into tears. This didn't seem to surprise anyone either. Only Captain Milyaga, who was sitting with his back to Nyura and did not wish to turn around, asked Svintsov: "What's going on there?"

"The woman's crying," said Svintsov, with something like sympathy as he looked at her.

"And why's she crying?"

"She wants some chow," said Svintsov gloomily.

"That's all right, we'll be feeding her soon enough," promised the captain, throwing down the jack of diamonds.

"That's for sure." Svintsov threw down his cards and started for the corner.

"What's with you?" asked the captain, surprised.

"Enough," said Svintsov. "I'm sick of cards."

He spread his overcoat out on the floor, lay down on his back, and stared up at the ceiling. Recently some sort of vague feelings had begun to stir in Svintsov's dense soul, to oppress and alarm him.

These feelings are usually called pangs of conscience, but Svintsov, never having experienced anything of the sort before, was unable to identify them. (Previously, Svintsov had related to people as if they were trees—if he were told to cut them down he cut them down; if he were not told to, he wouldn't touch them.) But once, recently, having woken up in the middle of the night, he suddenly began thinking about himself: Good Lord, he thought, how did it ever come to pass that he, Svintsov, a simple, gentle village muzhik, had become a murderer?

Had Svintsov been better educated he would have found the explanation of his life in historical expediency, but he was an ignorant man and his conscience, once awakened, would not go back to sleep. It gnawed at him and gave him no peace.

Svintsov lay in the corner and stared up at the ceiling while his comrades continued to discuss Nyura. Edrenkov said: "Maybe she's afraid we'll torture her when we get out of this."

"Could be," said Captain Milyaga. "But she's wrong not to believe we're humane. We don't use special methods on women. That is, on women," he added after a moment's thought, "who do not persist in their errors."

"Yes," said Edrenkov. "I feel bad for the woman. If she doesn't get the firing squad, she won't do any less than ten years. And it's hard on the women in the camps. Put out for the chief, give it to the supervisor . . ."

"I'll give you something this minute, a crack on the noggin with this pot!" said Nyura in a fury, picking up the cast-iron pot.

"Hey, careful there!" said Lieutenant Filippov in a fluster. "Private Chonkin, order her to put the pot back where it belongs. The Geneva Convention provides for the humane treatment of prisoners of war."

The lieutenant was a great lawyer and was continually pestering Chonkin with this convention, according to which, it seemed, you had to supply prisoners with ample food, drink, and clothing and treat them courteously. Chonkin would have been happy to live like that himself but didn't know how to go about getting Geneva-type treatment.

"Forget it, Nyurka, don't get mixed up with them," he said. "Your pot'll just get busted anyway. Hold this. I'll be right back." He handed Nyura the rifle and ran out into the passageway. He returned with a glass of milk and a piece of black, crumbly cookie that he had baked specially for Nyura that day from Borka's bran.

Nyura tore at the cookie with her teeth, but tears were flowing down her cheeks and dropping into her milk.

Chonkin looked at her with pity and realized that something had to be done. It wasn't enough that she had him on her back, now he'd saddled her with this bunch too. Maybe she might just get fed up with the lot of them and kick them all out together. But where would he go with them then? As soon as he arrested them, Chonkin thought that somewhere some higher-up would catch on. If they forgot about a private, you'd think at least a whole district organization disappearing would have some effect on somebody, that they'd jump to find out how such a thing could possibly happen. But no, day after day passed and everything was just as quiet and peaceful as if nothing had happened anywhere. *Bolshevik Tempos,* aside from Sovinformbureau's summary of world events, was printing all sorts of rubbish, but that the Institution had vanished, not one peep. This made Chonkin conclude that people notice what is right in front of their eyes, but that what is not there does not get noticed.

"Nyurka," said Ivan, having made his decision. "You guard them a while. I'll be right back."

"Where you going?" asked Nyura in surprise.

"You'll see afterward."

Chonkin smoothed his field shirt down behind his belt, wiped off his boots with a rag, and left. In the passageway he grabbed an 800-gram flask and made straight for Granny Dunya's.

27

Chairman Golubev was sitting in his office looking through some official papers in his usual state of depression. The sun was setting. Houses, trees, fences, people, and dogs were all casting long shadows, stimulating melancholy thoughts and the desire for a drink. He had not had one since the day before when he had driven to the district center and requested that he be sent to the front. For a good hour he tried to prove to the red-haired woman doctor that being flatfooted was insufficient grounds for being forced to idle in the rear. He raised his voice to her, tried flattery, and even attempted to seduce her, without, however, any particular enthusiasm. Toward the end she had begun to waver, but when she thrust her long thin fingers under his ribs, she was horrified and clutched her head.

"My God!" she said. "Your liver is twice normal size. Do you drink?"

"From time to time," said Golubev, avoiding her eyes.

"You should quit," she said decisively. "Can a person really have such a devil-may-care attitude toward their own health?"

"Absolutely not," agreed Golubev.

"It's simply barbarous!" she continued.

"Yes, it really is," affirmed Golubev. "I'll quit today."

"Well, all right then," she relented. "In two weeks' time you can face the board again, and if the District Committee isn't opposed, you can go."

After their conversation, Golubev set off for home. As usual, his horse stopped across from the teahouse, but Golubev lashed it with the tips of the reins and continued on his way. In the last day and a half he hadn't had a drop to drink. Yes, he thought with some satisfaction, gazing out the window, I've still got my will power left. At that very moment Chonkin appeared in the chairman's field of vision. He was walking across the square toward the office, carrying a certain streamlined object which Ivan Timofeyevich's experienced eyes recognized immediately. A flask. Ivan Timofeyevich swallowed his saliva and held his breath. Chonkin was now at the office, his boots banging loudly as he mounted the steps. The chairman arranged the papers on his desk and assumed his official expression. A knock came at the door.

"Yes," said the chairman and reached for a cigarette.

Chonkin entered, said hello, and stopped by the door, shifting from foot to foot.

"Come on in, Vanya," invited the chairman, his eyes never leaving the flask. "Come in, sit down."

Chonkin walked uncertainly up to the desk and sat down at the very edge of the creaking chair.

"Come on, Vanya, don't be shy," encouraged the chairman. "Sit regular, Vanya, get your whole ass on the chair."

"We're all right like this." Referring to himself as "we" in his confusion, Chonkin fidgeted with that very part of his anatomy to which the chairman had just so delicately referred. Still, Chonkin did not dare move any farther back on the chair.

A long and painful silence ensued. Golubev gazed expectantly at his visitor, but it seemed the cat had gotten Chonkin's tongue. Finally, Chonkin got hold of himself and began. "Listen, here's the thing . . ." said Chonkin, straining so hard he turned red, and then he fell silent, not knowing what to say next.

"I see," said the chairman, without waiting for Chonkin to go on. "Vanya, don't get excited, just spell out why you came. You want a smoke?" The chairman pushed a pack of Kazbek cigarettes (he hadn't been smoking Delhis for quite some time) over to Chonkin.

"No," said Chonkin, but took a cigarette anyway. He lit the filter instead of the tobacco, threw the cigarette to the floor, and crushed it out with his heel.

"Listen, here's the thing . . ." Chonkin began again, and then with sudden decisiveness banged the flask down in front of Golubev. "You want a drink?"

The chairman looked at the flask, licked his lips, then looked mistrustfully back up at Chonkin. "You doing this out of friendship or as a bribe?"

"As a bribe," confirmed Chonkin.

"In that case, don't." Ivan Timofeyevich carefully pushed the flask back to Chonkin.

"If it's don't, then it's don't," agreed Chonkin readily, and he took the flask and stood up.

"Hold on there," said the chairman, beginning to feel uneasy. "Why don't we say you have a problem that can be solved through regular channels. Then we can drink out of friendship and not because there's a bribe involved. What do you think?"

Chonkin put the flask back down on the desk and pushed it over to the chairman. "Drink," he said.

"How about you?"

"You pour, I'll drink."

Half an hour later, the contents of the flask drastically decreased, Golubev and Chonkin were already bosom buddies. They sat smoking Kazbek cigarettes, while the chairman complained about his life: "Before, Vanya, it was tough," he said. "But now it's worse than ever. They took the men to the front. There's only the women left. Of course women are a great force too, especially in a system like ours, but they took my hammer man to the front and what woman can lift a big hammer like that? I'm talking about healthy women now, but there aren't any healthy women in a village. One's pregnant, another one's nursing, another one, rain or shine, she grabs the small of her back and tells me, 'This weather's murder on my back.' The higher-ups have no idea what we go through. Everything for the front, everything for the victory, that's what they're demanding now. They come, they curse me out, they call me on the phone, they curse me out. Borisov curses me out, Revkin curses me out, my mother this, my mother that. The Regional Committee calls me up and they can't say a word without swearing their heads off either. So I ask you, Vanya, how can I go on like this? That's why I'm requesting they send me to the front, or even to prison, or even into the devil's mouth, anything to get free of this kolkhoz. Let somebody else take over, I've had it. But to tell the truth, Vanya, I really want to finish up by putting things straight here, so that somebody'll remember me a little kindly. But that's not the way it's working out."

The chairman shook his head in despair and drained a half glass of home brew in a single gulp. Their conversation had now reached the point most advantageous for Chonkin and he could not let the moment slip by.

"If things really are so tough for you," said Chonkin casually, "I can help you out."

"How are you going to help me out?" said Golubev, with a negative wave of the hand.

"I can," insisted Chonkin, filling their glasses. "Here, take it, wet your whistle. If you want, tomorrow morning I'll bring my prisoners out to the field and they can dig up the whole kolkhoz for you."

The chairman shuddered. He pushed his own glass over to Chonkin, then pushed himself away from his desk. He shook his head and fixed a long, unblinking gaze on Chonkin. Chonkin smiled.

"What?" said Golubev, fear in his voice. "Where'd you get that idea?"

"It's up to you." Chonkin shrugged his shoulders. "I just wanted to help you out. You should go take a look at their faces; you make them work right, they can move mountains for you."

"No, Vanya," said the chairman sadly. "I can't go for that. I'll tell you, as a Communist, I'm afraid of them."

"Lord, why be scared of them?" Chonkin threw up his hands. "You just give me a flat field so I can see them all at the same time and keep guard on them. If you don't want them, I can go to any other kolkhoz with them. Anybody'd take us on now and thank me for it too. You know, I'm not asking you for any workdays, just three squares a day, that's all."

His initial fear over, Golubev now grew thoughtful. On the whole it was a tempting proposition, but still the chairman vacillated.

"The classics of Marxism," he said uncertainly, "say there is no great profit to be gained from slave labor. But to tell you the truth, Vanya, we're in no position to turn up our noses at even a little profit. Let's keep on drinking."

Some time later, Chonkin left the chairman rocking slightly from drink and from his fine frame of mind. In the left-hand pocket of his field shirt was a scrap of paper on which the chairman had written in a drunken, uneven hand: "To Brigade Leader Comrade Shikalov: Comrade Chonkin's team is to be taken on for temporary work. Register them as volunteers." There was also another piece of paper in that same pocket—instructions that Chonkin's team be issued a week's worth of provisions in advance.

28

Waking up the next morning with an aching head, Ivan Timofeyevich Golubev dimly recalled individual details of the previous evening but could not bring himself to believe it all. "It couldn't be," he said to himself. "I'm a doomed man, of course, but still I couldn't do anything like that. It must have just been a dream or something I imagined when I was plastered."

Nevertheless, whatever it was, Golubev did not go to work. He called in sick and sent his wife to the office to find out what was going on. His wife soon returned and gave him Shikalov's message that everything was going according to plan and that Chonkin's team had been allotted the front line of work. The chairman groaned inwardly, but the message came to him in such a way that it all seemed quite normal to him (and why not?). Finally he grew somewhat calmer, dressed, had his breakfast, went to the stable, got a horse, and rode off to have a look at what was going on. Chonkin's team (now even the chairman had started calling it that) was working in full strength on the large potato field. Four of them were digging up the potatoes, two were loading sacks, and two others (Captain Milyaga and Lieutenant Filippov) were dragging the sacks out to the road. His rifle across his knees, Chonkin was sitting calmly on an old abandoned seeding machine and lazily watching them work, shaking his small head from time to time to keep from falling asleep.

Catching sight of the chairman, Chonkin gave him a friendly wave of the hand, but Ivan Timofeyevich rode on by, as if he had not noticed anything at all.

29

Work ennobles a man. But it depends on who. Chonkin's prisoners perceived their new fate in various ways. Some were indifferent, figuring work was work. Some were even happy—it was nicer to pass the time out in the open air than in a stuffy hut crammed with bedbugs. Lieutenant Filippov stanchly endured his privations, but fought against Chonkin's violations of the international laws concerned with the treatment of prisoners of war (commanding officers, the lieutenant insisted, must not be used for manual labor).

The change of situation had the most unexpected effect on Svintsov. Falling greedily on the simple peasant labor he had known since childhood, he suddenly began to experience an inexplicable delight. He worked harder than anyone, driving himself to the point of exhaustion. He dug potatoes, poured them in the sacks, dragged the sacks out to the road; he tortured himself with work and could not get enough of it. After dinner he would spread his overcoat on the floor and sleep like the dead but, first thing in the morning, he would jump up before everyone else and wait impatiently to go back out to the field again.

In the beginning, even Captain Milyaga was pleased by this new turn of events, for beyond any shadow of a doubt this act had earned Chonkin the supreme penalty. In his fantasies, the captain would imagine how zestfully he would interrogate Chonkin; the very thought made

Milyaga's thin lips curl into a vengeful smile. But, in the last few days, the captain had suddenly grown terribly worried. He experienced a feeling similar to the one Chonkin had felt on the first day of the war, when he became convinced that he was of no use to anyone. But Chonkin had never especially believed himself one of the chosen few, which could hardly be said of the captain. The fact that no one had been sent to his rescue in so long a time greatly troubled Milyaga. What could be happening? Could the town of Dolgov have been taken by the Germans? Could the Institution have already been liquidated? Could the order to use the Institution on the labor front have been issued to Chonkin from higher up? Milyaga searched for answers to all his questions, but found none. Then one fine day a resolution formed within the captain's ingenious head: he must escape. Escape no matter what. The captain set to familiarizing himself with Chonkin, studying his habits and ways, for, in order to defeat an enemy, first you must know him. The captain made observations of the surrounding terrain, but it was flat, making it difficult to escape without the risk of being shot, a risk the captain did not yet wish to run. But in the captain's head another boldly conceived plan was now ripening.

30

Although science contends that slave labor is not self-justifying, the practice of using the Institution's workers at the Red Sheaf kolkhoz proved the contrary. The district organizations began receiving reports of a potato harvest described in such figures that even Borisov was disturbed and phoned Golubev to say, Lie, all right, but

don't overdo it. Golubev replied that he was not about
to deceive his own government and the documents only
reflected the actual state of affairs. The District Committee's adviser, Chmikalov, was dispatched by Borisov
to Krasnoye, and he returned to the district and confirmed that the reports reflected the actual truth, that he
had seen with his own eyes the mountains of potatoes,
which corresponded to the reports they'd been receiving.
As he was informed at the kolkhoz, such productivity had
been achieved by fully utilizing the reserve labor force.
Finally, the district accepted it as the truth and the newspaper was ordered to run an article generalizing on the
experience of this outstanding farm. Golubev's farm was
held up as an example for others and the question was
posed: "Why is it Golubev can and you can't?" News
about the kolkhoz reached as far as the province capital
and Golubev was even mentioned in an official report in
Moscow.

Shortly thereafter Golubev learned that somebody on
the district level had gotten the bright idea of sending a
report on the potato harvest that had been completed
ahead of schedule to Comrade Stalin personally. Realizing
that now his doom was sealed, Ivan Timofeyevich invited
Chonkin over and set out two bottles of the purest, first-
class home brew. "Well, Vanya," he said, almost gleefully, "Now we've had it."

"What's the matter?" asked Chonkin.

Golubev told him everything. Chonkin scratched the
back of his head, said there was nothing to lose, and
insisted that the chairman send him to a new labor front.
The chairman agreed and promised to send Chonkin's
team to the silo. The agreement was sealed with a drink
and when, at twilight, the two of them left the office,

they were both experiencing some difficulty staying on their feet. The chairman stopped on the porch to lock the door. Chonkin stood beside Golubev, marking time with his feet.

"Vanya, you're a very smart person," said the chairman thickly, while fumbling with the bolt in the dark. "At first glance you look like a perfect ninny, but look a little closer, you see the mind of a statesman. You shouldn't be a private, you ought to be commanding a company."

"I'd go for a division," boasted Chonkin. Holding on to the railing with one hand, he was taking a leak over the side of the porch.

"Well, a division might be overshooting the mark a little." Having abandoned the attempt to find the lock, the chairman was now standing beside Chonkin and had begun taking a leak himself.

"All right then, a regiment," said Chonkin, knocking down his price while buttoning up his fly. Just then a step appeared under his foot, which he hadn't noticed, and he rolled crashing off the porch.

The chairman stood on the porch and held on to the railing, waiting for Chonkin to get up. Chonkin did not get up.

"Ivan," Golubev called into the darkness.

No answer came.

To keep from falling, the chairman lay down and crawled from the porch on his stomach. Then he began crawling on all fours, fumbling around in the dewy grass until he ran across Chonkin. Chonkin was lying on his back, his arms spread out wide, snuffling serenely. Golubev climbed onto Chonkin and lay down across him. "Ivan," he called.

"Eh?" Chonkin stirred.

"You alive?" asked the chairman.

"I don't know," said Chonkin. "What's that lying on me?"

"Must be me," said Golubev after a moment's thought.

"And who are you?"

"Me?" The chairman was about to take offense but, straining his memory, realized that as a matter of fact he wasn't quite sure himself who he was. Nevertheless, with great effort, he recalled: "I'm Golubev, Ivan Timofeyevich."

"And what's that lying on top of me?"

"It's me lying there." Golubev was starting to get angry.

"Can you get off?" asked Chonkin.

"Get off?" Golubev attempted to get up on all fours, but his arms buckled and once again he tumbled down on top of Chonkin.

"Hold it," said the chairman. "In a second I'm going to get up and then you put your legs up against me. And don't stick them in my kisser either, you bastard. Put them against my chest. That's the way."

Chonkin finally managed to shove him off. Now they were lying side by side.

"Ivan," called Golubev after a period of silence.

"Yah?"

"The hell with this. Let's go."

"All right, let's go."

Ivan got up on his feet but did not last there very long and fell back down on the ground.

"This is how you should walk," said Ivan Timofeyevich, getting back up on all fours. Chonkin assumed the same position and the two friends set off for parts unknown.

"Well, how do you like it this way?" asked the chairman after a little while.

"Fine," said Chonkin.

"This way of walking's even better than regular," said the chairman with conviction. "If you fall you don't get hurt. Jean Jacques Rousseau said man should walk on all fours and go back to nature."

"Who's this Zhan Zhak?" asked Chonkin, who found the strange name hard to pronounce.

"Who the hell knows," said the chairman. "Some Frenchman."

Then he inhaled a chestful of air and began to sing:

From hut to hut along the village
the rushing poles began to move . . .

Chonkin joined in:

The wires hummed and played a tune.
We'd never seen such a sight before . . .

"Ivan," said the chairman, suddenly remembering something.

"What?"

"Did I close up the office or not?"

"Who the hell knows," said Chonkin with complete unconcern.

"Let's go back."

"Fine by me."

Walking on all fours was very nice indeed, though the dew chilled their hands and soaked through their pants at the knees.

"Ivan!"

"Yah?"

"Let's sing some more."

"All right," said Chonkin and began singing the only other song he knew:

A Cossack galloped through the valley,
through the Caucasian lands . . .

The chairman joined in:

A Cossack galloped through the valley,
through the Caucasian lands . . .

Chonkin began the next verse:

Through the green orchard he did gallop . . .

Just then a thought entered Chonkin's mind and brought him to a halt. "Listen," he asked the chairman. "You scared?"

"Of who?"

"My prisoners."

"Why should I be scared of them?" said the chairman, flinging all caution to the wind. "I'm leaving for the front anyway. You know what I do with them. I—"

Here Ivan Timofeyevich employed a verb which might cause a foreigner unfamiliar with the subtleties of our language to conclude that Golubev's relations with the employees of the Institution were of an intimate nature.

But Chonkin was no foreigner and understood that Golubev was speaking figuratively. The chairman went on to enumerate certain government, party, and social organizations, as well as a series of leading comrades with whom his relations were also, figuratively speaking, intimate.

"Ivan!" The chairman suddenly remembered something else.

"Yah?"

"Where we going?"

"The office, I thought," said Chonkin, not particularly sure.

"Where is it?"

"How the hell am I supposed to know."

"Hold on, I think we're lost. We've got to figure out our direction."

The chairman turned over on his back and began searching the night sky for the North Star.

"What for?" asked Chonkin.

"Don't bother me," said the chairman. "First we locate the Great Bear and from there it's four inches to the North Star. If you find the North Star, you find north."

"The office is in the north?" asked Chonkin.

"Don't bother me." The chairman was still lying on his back. Some of the stars were partially obscured by rain clouds and the rest of the stars kept doubling, tripling, and quadrupling; besides, there were so many stars that, to judge by them, north was located in every direction, which suited the chairman just fine, for it allowed him to crawl off anywhere he wanted.

While he was getting back up on his hands and knees, Chonkin lurched forward and suddenly his head came into contact with something hard. Chonkin began groping about in the dark.

What he felt was the wheel of a truck, most likely the one the grays had come in. That meant the office had to be right next to it. And so it was. Skirting the truck, Chonkin crawled a little farther until he ran into a wall, misty white in the darkness.

"Looks like the office, Timofeyevich," Chonkin called out.

The chairman crawled up. He ran the palm of his hand down the rough wall.

"There, you see," he said with pleasure. "And you ask, why consult the North Star. Look around, the bolt's got to be there some place."

As they fumbled along the wall, they kept bumping into each other and crawling off in opposite directions, repeating the process several times. Chonkin was first to take in the situation.

"Listen, Timofeyevich, the lock has to be on the door and the door has to be on the porch."

The chairman took a moment to think it through, then found himself in agreement with Chonkin's reasoning.

It is not to laugh at a drunken man one more time, but solely for truth's sake, that we report that, even when they located the door, Chonkin and the chairman were not able to cope with it for quite some time. Like a living creature, the lock kept slipping out of their hands, and each time it slipped it banged the chairman's knee so painfully that a sober man would have lost the use of his leg, but, as everyone knows, God gives a drunk a little extra protection.

They each went their separate way home. It remains a mystery how Chonkin found the road; one can only assume that crawling around on all fours had sobered him a little.

While going in the gate, Chonkin caught the muffled sounds of men's voices coming from behind the vegetable patches and noticed the glimmer of a lit cigarette.

"Hey, who's there?" shouted Chonkin.

The glimmer vanished. Chonkin stood, straining his eyes and ears, but now there was nothing to be seen, nothing to be heard.

"Must be so drunk I'm seeing things," Chonkin reassured himself and entered the hut.

31

The wick on the oil lamp had been burned down almost to the very end; the small flame's weak light barely filled the room.

Nyura was sitting on the stool by the door, the rifle pressed tight between her knees. The prisoners, exhausted from their day's work, were sleeping side by side on the floor.

"Where've you been?" asked Nyura angrily, but in a whisper so as not to wake the sleeping prisoners.

"Wherever I was I ain't there now," answered Chonkin and grabbed hold of the doorjamb to keep from falling.

"Oi, did you get yourself soused?" gasped Nyura.

"Soused." Chonkin nodded, with a foolish grin. "I just had to get soused, Nyura, tomorrow they're flinging us into a new sector."

"What are you talking about!" said Nyura.

With two fingers of his free hand, Chonkin extracted the chairman's note, issuing him supplementary provisions, from the pocket of his field shirt and handed it to Nyura. Nyura held the note up to the lamp and, her lips moving, began pondering its contents.

"Lie down and get yourself some rest, you haven't slept yet, you know," she said, letting the tenderness color her voice.

Chonkin's reply was a whack from behind. "Nah, you get yourself some. I'll grab an hour in the morning."

He took the rifle from Nyura, sat down on the stool, and leaned back up against the doorpost. Nyura lay down with her clothes on, her face to the wall, and was soon asleep. Everything was quiet. Only the lieutenant was squealing like a puppy in his sleep, smacking his lips loudly. A gray moth circling above the oil lamp kept knocking against the glass, then flying away. It was stuffy and humid and soon rain could be heard rustling through the leaves.

To keep from falling asleep, Chonkin went over to the bucket in the corner, ladled out a handful of water, and splashed it on his face. No sooner had he resumed his former position than he again began to drift off to sleep. He was holding the rifle squeezed tight between his knees and hands, but his fingers kept unclenching by themselves and heroic efforts were required to keep from falling off the stool. Several times he caught himself at the very last second, and then would bug out his eyes to stare vigilantly about the room, but everything would still be calm and quiet, the only sounds the rain rustling outside and a mouse gnawing wood.

Finally, weary of struggling with himself, Chonkin blocked the door with the table, laid his head down on it, and sank into oblivion. But he did not sleep peacefully. He dreamed of Kuzma Gladishev, Chairman Golubev, the Great Bear, and Jean Jacques Rousseau, drunk and crawling backwards on all fours from Granny Dunya's house. Chonkin realized Rousseau was his prisoner and that he was preparing to escape.

"Stop!" Chonkin ordered him. "Where are you going?"

"Back," said Jean Jacques hoarsely. "Back to nature." Then he crawled farther back into the bushes.

"Stop!" Chonkin shouted, grabbing Rousseau by his slippery elbows. "Stop or I'll shoot!"

Chonkin was amazed at not being able to hear his own voice, and that also made him afraid. But Jean Jacques was afraid of Chonkin too. Suddenly he made a pitiful face, began to whimper, and said with childlike capriciousness: "I have to go! I have to go! I have to go!"

Chonkin opened his eyes. Jean Jacques had gotten up onto his feet and assumed the appearance of Captain Milyaga. The captain was pulling on Chonkin from across the table with his two bound hands, demanding insistently: "Hey, you dummy, wake up! I have to go!"

Chonkin looked dumbfounded at his furious prisoner, unable to decide whether he was dreaming or awake. When he realized that he was awake, Chonkin shook himself and rose reluctantly to his feet. He pushed the table away, took the dog collar off the nail, and muttered: "They have to go, they have to go. The day wasn't long enough for them. Let's see your neck."

The captain bent forward. Chonkin fastened the collar on the third hole so that it would be tight enough without choking Milyaga, tugged the rope to make sure it was fast, then dismissed Milyaga: "All right, go, but make it snappy."

Chonkin wound the free end of the rope around his hand and sank into thought. His thoughts were simple ones. Looking at the fly crawling across the ceiling, he thought: There goes a fly. Looking at the lamp, he thought: Lamp's on. He dozed off. Once again he dreamed of Jean Jacques Rousseau, who was grazing in Gladishev's garden. Chonkin shouted out to Gladishev: "Hey, listen, that's no cow that gobbled up your PATS, that's Jean Jacques."

Gladishev grinned maliciously and said, tipping his hat: "Don't you worry about the PATS, better you watch out, he's untying himself and running away."

Chonkin awoke with fright. Everything was quiet. Svintsov was snoring, the lamp was burning, now the fly was crawling in the other direction. Chonkin pulled lightly at the rope. The captain was still there.

What is he, constipated or something? thought Chonkin, closing his eyes.

Jean Jacques had disappeared somewhere. A young woman was lugging a basket of laundry back up from the river. As she approached she smiled so radiantly that Chonkin had to smile back at her. He was not surprised when she set the basket down on the ground, took him in her arms light as fluff, and began rocking him and singing:

Lullaby,
birds will fly.
Birds will fly
to Vanya's cradle.

"Who are you?" asked Chonkin.

"You don't recognize me?" The woman smiled. "I'm your mother."

"Mama." Chonkin reached out to put his arms around her.

But just then men in gray field shirts sprang out from behind the bushes. Chonkin could distinguish Svintsov, Lieutenant Filippov, and Captain Milyaga among them. The captain reached out for Chonkin.

"That's him! That's him!" Milyaga started shouting, his face twisted into a terrible smile.

Clutching her son to her breast, Chonkin's mother started screaming blue murder. Chonkin wanted to cry out too, but could not and woke up. He looked around, his mind boggled.

Everything was calm and quiet. The lamp with the short wick was burning with a feeble flame. The prisoners were sleeping on the floor. Nyura was sleeping on the bed, her back to the wall now.

Chonkin looked at the clock, which had stopped. He didn't know how long he'd been asleep, but felt that it had been quite a while. Captain Milyaga was still out there in the toilet, the proof of which was the rope wound around Chonkin's hand.

"That's it, you'll sit out there forever," said Chonkin aloud, and he tugged on the rope to let the captain know that his time was up. Chonkin waited for what he considered sufficient time for the captain to pull up his pants, then he tugged on the rope again. No one was responding at the other end. Chonkin roused himself and tugged the rope harder. This time it began to yield, but not easily.

"Come on, come on, why give me a hard time!" muttered Chonkin, pulling in more and more rope. Now footsteps could be heard in the corridor. But they didn't sound like Captain Milyaga's soft footfall. These steps were short and quick as if someone in hard shoes were mincing down the corridor.

A terrible suspicion flashed through Chonkin's brain. He jerked the rope in with all his might. The door flew open, and smeared with dung from head to foot, a puzzled expression on his sleepy face, Borka the hog tumbled into the room.

32

Having escaped to freedom, Captain Milyaga experienced both tremendous excitement and complete physical collapse. His heartbeat was a totally irregular flutter, his hands were trembling, his legs would not obey him at all. Escaping now made no sense to the captain. It had been warm and kind of comfortable back in the hut but out here, there was the rain and the cold and it was pitch black and he did not know where to run, or for what.

He had not been the least nervous while cutting the rope with the scythe he'd found earlier in the day or while he was coolly placing the collar on the hog, even though the hog had kicked up a struggle. The gate to the cow barn had been locked from the outside, but the captain had found a small hole right beneath the roof and had crawled through with great effort, tearing the shoulder of his field shirt in the process. Now here he was with no idea why he'd done it. It was dark, it was pouring, cold drops of rain were rolling off the roof, falling down his neck, and sliding slowly down his back. But that was the furthest thing from his mind as he stood with the back of his head against the log wall, crying.

If someone had walked up to him and asked: "Hey, what are you crying for?" Milyaga could not have answered. From joy that he was free again? But there was no joy. From fury? From the desire for revenge? At that moment he felt neither one nor the other. All he felt was complete indifference to his fate, hopelessness, and the utter pointlessness of anything he might do. For Captain Milyaga, this was an unfamiliar state. He did not budge from where he stood, even at the risk of being caught by Chonkin any second, and he continued crying without knowing why. Perhaps it was simply a fit of hysterics coming in the wake of the captain's recent trying experiences.

Suddenly he started. He no longer felt alone in the yard. Peering into the darkness, he could make out the outline of some strange creature, some enormous thing. He did not realize immediately that this was the very airplane which had started the whole crazy business. When he did realize what it was, Milyaga calmed down somewhat, and as he grew calmer, he began to think things through.

The plane was standing at the edge of the garden, its tail pointing toward the hut. So the town of Dolgov must be located in approximately the same direction that the plane's right wing was pointing, which meant he should run in that direction. But what good would Dolgov do him if there was no one left from the Institution but Kapa the secretary? That meant he should go right to the province, to Luzhin, the head of the provincial office. And tell him what? That a single soldier with an 1891/1930 model rifle had arrested the entire staff of the district office? These days, that guaranteed a military tribunal and a firing squad. However, if he appraised the situation soberly, he might just wriggle his way out of it. Especially since Milyaga knew a little something about Luzhin. In particular, a little something about the provincial chief's background. Maybe Luzhin himself had forgotten that before the Revolution his father had been chief of police in the neighboring province but he, Milyaga, had not, and had been storing this information in his head, just in case. This enabled Milyaga to entertain the hope that Luzhin might not wish to go as far as a tribunal. Especially since it was essentially Lieutenant Filippov who was to blame for the whole embarrassing business. What could he do, it had to be goodbye, Filippov, though of course he felt a little sorry for the guy. As far as Chonkin was concerned, he, Milyaga, would personally take care of that one.

Having reminded himself of Chonkin, the captain smiled vengefully. He wiped away his tears. Life made sense again, and for that it was well worth it to slog through the rain and the dark.

The captain unglued himself from the wall and took a

step forward. His feet slid off in different directions, then got stuck in the drenched ground. But still he had his good strong boots, he'd get through it somehow.

He had already gone around the airplane when he heard a door squeak behind him. Without a moment's reflection, the captain collapsed into the mud. Somebody had come out onto the porch. But now that he had regained the will to conquer, the captain was prepared to endure worse than this to save himself.

"Can you spot anything?" From somewhere, probably the hut, came Nyura's worried voice.

"Nope, nothing," said Chonkin, much closer by. "Light the lantern, will you?"

"There's no kerosene," answered Nyura. "And if I bring the oil lamp out, the rest of them will run off."

Mud sploshed right by the captain's ear. Any second now Chonkin would step on the captain and all would be lost. If he grabbed Chonkin by the leg, would he fall . . . ?

"So, anything?" called Nyura again.

"Nothing," said Chonkin. "My boots are lousy. No sense in sloshing through the mud in them for nothing. He must be far away by now."

"What's he supposed to do, wait for you? Come on back in, no use your kneading the mud."

Chonkin stood over the captain for another minute or so, and then his steps began slowly to squish off into the distance.

Captain Milyaga took his time. He waited until Chonkin had walked up the steps and clicked the bolt on the door behind him. Then the captain advanced on his hands and knees. Looking back and seeing nothing suspicious, the captain hopped to his feet and jumped through the tangled wickets in a single bound. Then, as if from the dark earth itself, two dark figures in rain capes sprang up before him. The captain was about to cry out but never had time. One of the figures brought the butt of his rifle around and the captain lost consciousness.

33

The regiment's headquarters was located in one of the empty barns on the far side of the village's vegetable gardens. The barn had been divided into two parts. The first part housed the sentries, the staff duty officer, the clerk, and several of those persons who always like to hang around the people in charge.

Sitting on some straw bedding in the corner, the telephone man was muttering under his breath into the phone: "Swallow, Swallow, this is for your mother, this is Baby Eagle, why the hell don't you come in?"

The second half of the barn, separated from the first by a log partition and lit by an oil lamp resting on a crate, housed Regimental Commander Colonel Lapshin and his adjutant, Junior Lieutenant Bukashov.

The colonel was preparing for a conference on strategy at the division commander's when the scouts Sirikh and Filiukov entered carrying something long, muddy, and resembling a log on their shoulders, which they then heaved into the corner onto a pile of moldy straw bedding.

"What is that?" asked the colonel.

"We caught us a prisoner, Comrade Colonel," said Junior Sergeant Sirikh, coming to attention. His right cheek was covered with clay.

The colonel walked over, closer to the thing lying on the straw, and crinkled up his face. "I don't think that's a prisoner," he said after a moment's thought. "I think it's a corpse."

"That's Filiukov for you, Comrade Colonel," said Sirikh with that undue familiarity only a scout would allow himself. "I says to him, Take him careful now, and he just goes ahead with his rifle butt—bam!"

"What's wrong with you, Filiukov?" The colonel shifted his eyes to the other scout.

"I got scared, Comrade Colonel," said Filiukov sincerely. He began telling his story, also with undue familiarity, but his was of a different sort than Sirikh's. Filiukov's was that of the still-unterrified country boy who thinks everyone in the army is the same as he and that a colonel is something like the brigade leader at the kolkhoz. "Listen, this is how it happened, Comrade Colonel. Me and the junior sergeant crept up to some fence. Not that big a fence, one of them wicket birch deals. We drop flat. We lie there an hour, two hours. Nobody's there, it's dark, it's raining." Filiukov clutched his head with his muddy hands and shook it back and forth to express the utter horror of it. "Even though we had our rain capes on, the rain's still leaking from the top, all right, but underneath, our bellies were getting wet all over. Here, look." He rolled up his rain cape and showed his belly, which truly was wet and dirty.

"Why are you telling me all this?" asked the colonel in surprise.

"Hold on. Give me a drag." Without the slightest hesitation, Filiukov practically ripped the cigarette from the colonel's hand. He took several greedy drags, threw the butt to the floor, and ground it out with his heel. "So we're lying there and I says to the junior sergeant, Let's leave. But he says, Let's wait. Then we hear a door opening. Somebody's walking around behind the fence, splashing around in the mud. Then comes a man's voice asking something, then a woman's voice answers him, 'There's no kerosene.' Then he goes back off and nobody comes back. I think to myself, All right, he's gone. Soon as I think that, there he is, climbing out . . ." Filiukov squatted down and, opening his eyes wide, made his face express the ultimate in terror. "And heading right for us. So I grab my rifle and . . ." Filiukov stood back up, whipped the rifle from his shoulder, and threatened the colonel with it.

The colonel jumped to the side. "What are you doing, what are you doing?" he said, eyeing Filiukov suspiciously.

"I'm showing you," said Filiukov, shouldering his rifle. "Have no doubt about it, you can cut off my head if he isn't alive. I'm from the Volga myself, Comrade Colonel. We had Germans by the wagonful living down there. I don't know about any other kind, but I know about the Germans all right. They got plenty of life in them. You hit another guy like that, you kill him. You kill a cat. But a German'll come out alive. And why's that?" Filiukov did not answer his own question, but spread out his hands and pulled in his head, expressing the ultimate in bewilderment over this mystery of nature.

"All the same, you killed that one," said the colonel severely.

"What are you talking about?" said Filiukov, displaying no faith in his own strength. "I tell you, he's alive and breathing." He walked over to the outstretched body and began to press his foot lightly against the stomach. The man's chest actually began heaving slightly, but it was hard to tell whether it was because he was breathing or because Filiukov was pumping him.

"He's breathing his last," retorted the colonel. "Leave him alone, Filiukov. You're both dismissed."

The scouts left.

The colonel stood for a while, observing the prisoner. "Of course they had to drag him through the mud, so I can't make out his uniform or insignia," he muttered aloud. Then he raised his head. "Junior Lieutenant!"

"Sir!" answered Bukashov.

"What language did you study in school?"

"German, Comrade Colonel."

"If the prisoner comes to can you question him?"

Bukashov hesitated. Of course he had taken German, but studied it? That was the subject he used to cut most often to go to the movies. Naturally he remembered something. "Anna und Marta baden" and "Heute ist das Wasser warm." And several individual words as well.

"Well?" the colonel was waiting.

"I'll give it a try, Comrade Colonel."

"Give it a try. There's no interpreter anyway."

The colonel pulled the hood of his rain cape up over his service cap and left.

34

Although a regiment had been assigned to liquidate Chonkin's gang, in view of its importance, Division Commander General Drinov had taken on the overall direction of this operation.

The general had made a fabulous career for himself in a very short span of time. Four years before, he still wore only a single stripe and commanded a company. But then he had one great piece of luck. His battalion commander told him in confidence that you could say anything you liked about Trotsky but still he had been the commander in chief during the Civil War. Perhaps the battalion commander with the long memory might have been swept away no matter what, even without making statements like these, but then it would have been difficult to tell what effect that would have had on the fate of the future general. But everything fell right in place in the best possible manner; Drinov made a report to the Right Place, and he replaced the battalion commander.

From then on, things could not have gone better for him. Two years later, now wearing three stripes on his lapels, he found himself in the war against the White Finns.

There, his talents for commanding were revealed in all their brilliance. Drinov was distinguished by his ability to easily and quickly get his bearings in any, even the most complex, situation, though, on the other hand, of all possible decisions, he invariably made the most stupid one. This did not, however, prevent him from always landing on his feet, and, by the end of the Finnish campaign, he was in Moscow, this time with four stripes on his lapel. In the Kremlin's Georgievsky Hall, Grandpa Kalinin himself shook Drinov's firm hand with both of his and said a few words as he presented him with the Combat Order of the Red Banner.

Drinov had been made a general quite recently for his outstanding achievements in the field of military science, to wit—during field exercises he had ordered that the men of his own unit be fired upon with live fragmentation shells for a maximal approximation of battle conditions. Drinov maintained that during such training it was only the bad soldiers who got killed, those who did not know how to entrench themselves. On the whole, Drinov saw no use for soldiers who did not know how to entrench themselves. Drinov himself was very fond of being well entrenched.

While the regiment was taking up its attack positions, the soldiers of a separate field-engineer battalion had demolished someone's bathhouse and built a three-layer dugout from the logs. Colonel Lapshin arrived, and having presented his pass to the sentry by the entrance, the colonel went down the four wooden steps and then slammed the sodden doors behind him. Cigarette smoke filled the dugout, billowing up as if something were on fire. A zinc trough, most likely from the recently demolished bathhouse, stood in the center of the room, catching the thick muddy drops that fell from the ceiling.

Several men in rain capes were bunched around a table that had been knocked together from unplaned wood; Drinov's sheepskin hat swayed above all the other heads.

"Request permission to be present, Comrade General." Calmly, with that familiarity only those close in rank can allow themselves, the colonel tossed his hand casually up to his cap in a salute.

"Ah, it's you, Lapshin," said the general, catching sight of him through the waves of smoke. "Granted, granted. Otherwise we'd have the men assembled and the commander missing."

When he'd approached the table, Lapshin could make out all three of his battalion commanders, the chief of staff, the commander of the artillery division, and an official from SMERSH, a small, plain-looking man. Huddled over the table, they had been discussing their combat mission and studying a diagram, which was being explained in a soft voice by a man Lapshin did not recognize. This man was wearing a tarpaulin raincoat with the hood flung back and box-calf boots smeared up to the knees in clay. His dress did not set him much apart from the other officers present, but his crumpled cap betrayed the fact that he was a civilian.

"Introduce yourself." The general nodded to the civilian. "The secretary of the local District Committee."

"Revkin," said the secretary, offering Lapshin his cold hand.

"Lapshin," responded the colonel.

"And so, Lapshin," said the general. "Any news?"

"Sergeant Sirikh and Private Filiukov have just returned from reconnaissance," the colonel reported listlessly.

"Yes and so?"

"They brought in a prisoner."

"What does he say?" The general was intrigued.

"He isn't saying anything, Comrade General."

"What do you mean, he isn't?" The general was outraged. "Make him talk!"

"Difficult to do." Lapshin smiled. "He's unconscious. When they were taking him, the scouts hit him too hard with their rifle butts."

"There, you see!" The general banged his fist on the table. He was beginning to grow angry. "At a time when we need intelligence so badly, they knock out a valuable prisoner with their rifle butts. Who went out on reconnaissance?"

"Sirikh and Filiukov, Comrade General."

"Sirikh to be shot!"

"But it was Filiukov who hit him, Comrade General."

"Filiukov to be shot."

"Comrade General." The colonel attempted to intercede for his scout. "Filiukov has two children."

The general drew himself up straight, his eyes sparkling with anger. "It seems to me, Comrade Colonel, that I ordered Filiukov shot and not his children."

The official from SMERSH smiled. He valued a good sense of humor. The colonel, as well, knew his way around the general's humor. He placed his hand to his cap in a salute and said obediently: "Yes, Comrade General, Filiu-kov to be shot."

"Well, looks like we've finally gotten together on that one," said the general, satisfied, and again with a touch of humor. After all, the colonel was supposed to answer, "Yes, sir!" in a military fashion and not haggle with the general like an old market woman. "Move up a little closer to the table," said the general, quite calmly now.

The officers moved aside, making room for the colonel.

A rough map of the village of Krasnoye and the adjoining area had been sketched out in pencil on a large sheet of tracing paper that lay on top of a two-inch-scale map. The houses were represented by little squares. Two of the squares in the middle had been marked with crosses.

"Take a look. He says"—the general indicated Revkin—"that here"—he jabbed the pencil in one of the squares—"and here"—he jabbed the other—"is where the kolkhoz office and the schoolhouse are located. One would suppose the enemy has quartered his main forces in these two buildings, the largest available dwellings. And so the first battalion will strike from here to here." The general drew a broad curving arrow whose point stopped against the small square representing the kolkhoz office. "The second battalion will strike here." The second arrow went to the schoolhouse. "And the third battalion . . ."

All right, thought Colonel Lapshin, watching the arrows. Maybe we can get Filiukov through all this yet. The main thing is to say "Yes, sir!" when you're supposed to, then afterward you can disregard the order.

35

Captain Milyaga was not able to open his eyes for a long time after regaining consciousness. His head splitting with pain, the captain tried to remember where he'd gotten into such a bad fight and who with, but could not remember anything. He shook his head, opened his eyes, but then closed them again as soon as he saw a totally unexpected sight. He was in some sort of barn. A blond youth about twenty years old, wearing a rain cape, was sitting on a shell crate in the far corner writing something, map case and paper on his knee. Another man was sitting with his back to the captain, in the other corner by the half-open door. The captain's eyes began darting about the room. The whole thing made no sense. Then, from somewhere in the depths of his brain, there emerged the consciousness that he had been going somewhere and had not gotten there. There was some soldier, some woman . . . Ah, yes, Chonkin. Now it all came back to him, except for the very last minutes. He recalled asking permission to go to the outhouse, cutting the rope, and tying up the hog in his place. Then he had crawled across the garden, it had been raining, it was muddy. Muddy. The captain felt himself. His field shirt and pants actually were covered with mud, which had, however, already begun drying out. But what had happened next? And how did he end up here? And who were these people? The captain began to take a closer look at the blond, who was obviously a soldier. Judging by the setup, this was some kind of field unit. But how could it be a field unit if the front was so far away? He couldn't have been crawling through that garden so very long ago if the mud hadn't had time to dry yet. Could they have brought him here on an airplane or something? The captain continued to observe the blond soldier from behind his half-closed eyes. The soldier looked up from his paper and glanced at the captain. Their eyes met. The soldier smiled.

"Guten Morgen," he said suddenly.

The captain lowered his eyelids and began thinking in a hurry. What did he say? Something strange, something not Russian. Guten Morgen. Sounded like German. A memory floated out from the mists of time. 1918. A Ukrainian clay-walled cottage. A red-haired German who wore eyeglasses had been billeted in their cottage. Every morning he would come in from the next room in his undershirt and say to Milyaga's mother: "Guten Morgen, Frau Milleg," pronouncing their last name in the German manner.

The man with the red hair had been a German, that meant he had been speaking German. This one was speaking German too. Since he was speaking German, he must be German. (During his years of service in the Institution, Captain Milyaga had learned to think logically.) This meant that he, Captain Milyaga, had somehow been captured by the Germans. You could wish it weren't so, but the truth had to be looked in the eye (Milyaga's eyes were closed right at this particular moment). From his reading of the newspapers, Captain Milyaga knew the Germans showed no mercy to members of the Institution or to Communists. Milyaga happened to be both. And, as bad luck would have it, his party card had to be right there in his pocket. True, his membership dues hadn't been paid since April, but he didn't think the Germans would start splitting hairs.

The captain opened his eyes again and smiled at the young blond soldier as if they were having a pleasant conversation. "Guten Morgen, Herr," he said, remembering yet another word, though he was not sure this word was entirely proper.

Meanwhile, wracking his memory, Junior Lieutenant

Bukashov had retrieved enough German to compose a simple sentence. "Kommen Sie herr."

"He probably wants me to go over to him," reasoned the captain, noticing that the word "herr" must be completely proper if the blond German used it.

The captain rose, overcame his dizziness, and approached the table, smiling at the German. But the German did not respond and said sullenly: "Sitzen Sie."

The captain understood that he had been invited to sit down, but looking around and seeing nothing that resembled a chair or stool, he thanked the soldier politely by nodding his head and placing the palm of his hand where a person normally touches to signify the heart. The next question "Namen?" made no sense to the captain but, calculating what the first question in an interrogation had to be, he realized it would concern the prisoner's name. This caused him some thought. It was impossible to hide the fact that he belonged to the security forces and the Party; his uniform gave the former away and the first superficial frisk would reveal the latter. Then Milyaga remembered the sentence he had always used to begin his own interrogations: "A sincere confession can improve your fate." Though he knew from his own experience that a sincere confession had never improved anyone's fate, he now had no other hope; he also entertained the faint hope that the Germans were a civilized people and might do things differently.

"Namen?" repeated the junior lieutenant impatiently, uncertain whether he was pronouncing the word correctly. "Du Namen? Sie Namen?"

Milyaga had to answer the question to keep the blond German from getting angry with him. "Ich bin Captain Milyaga," he said hurriedly. "Milleg, Milleg, Fershten?" It was turning out that he did know a little German.

"Captain Milleg." The lieutenant entered the first piece of information into his report of the interrogation. He raised his eyes to the prisoner, without the slightest idea how to ask what branch of the service he was in.

But the prisoner anticipated him and hastened to supply the testimony. "Ich bin ist arbeiten . . . arbeiten, fershten?" Using his hands, the captain pretended to be doing some kind of work, digging a garden or filing something down. "Ich bin ist arbeiten . . ." He considered how to identify the Institution, but then suddenly hit upon an unexpected analogy: "Ich bin arbeiten in Russisch Gestapo."

"Gestapo?" The blond soldier frowned, putting his own interpretation on what the prisoner said. "Du Kommunisten shootirt, bang bang?"

"Ja, ja," the captain confirmed readily. "Und Kommunisten und nonpartyten, all shootirt, bang bang." The captain brandished his right hand, as if shooting a pistol.

Then Milyaga wished to inform his interrogator that he had considerable experience in fighting Communists and that he, Captain Milyaga, could be of service to the German Institution, but he didn't know how to express so complex a thought.

Meanwhile, the junior lieutenant was noting in his report: "While serving in the Gestapo, Captain Milleg executed Communists and non-Party members . . ."

Bukashov could feel the hatred for this Gestapo agent rising in his breast. I'll just shoot him right now, he thought. His hand was already on his holster when the junior lieutenant remembered that he was supposed to be conducting an interrogation and that he had better stay in control of himself. Control regained, he asked the next question: "Vot ist your Ferband dislotsirt?"

The captain looked at the young blond soldier and

smiled, trying to understand, but not understanding. All he could tell was that evidently the question had something to do with a band. "Wass?" he asked.

The junior lieutenant repeated the question. He was not sure that he had phrased it properly and began to lose patience.

Again the captain did not understand, but seeing the young soldier losing his temper, Milyaga decided to proclaim his loyalty: "Es liebe Genosse Hitler." He introduced a new word into a familiar construction. "Heil Hitler! Stalin kaput!"

The junior lieutenant sighed. This Fascist was an outright fanatic. But you couldn't deny him courage. Praises his leader on the way to certain death. Bukashov would have liked to behave like that if he were ever taken prisoner. How many times had Bukashov pictured it, them torturing him, driving needles under his fingernails, burning him, carving a five-pointed star in his back, but he tells them nothing, he just keeps shouting: "Long live Stalin!" But Bukashov was not entirely convinced he would find enough courage in himself and so instead dreamed of perishing on the battlefield with the same cry on his lips.

The junior lieutenant did not react to the German's meaningless outcries and went on with the interrogation, asking his questions in broken German, mixed with Russian. Fortunately, the prisoner understood some Russian and somehow Bukashov managed to squeeze a little something out of him.

The captain took the word "Ferband" to mean the Institution for which he, Milyaga, worked. "There," he said readily, pointing his hand in some direction or other. "Ist Haus, nach Haus ist Chonkin. Fershten?"

"Fershten," said the junior lieutenant, without letting on that it was precisely Chonkin who was of special interest to him.

His forehead contorted with tension and pain, the prisoner continued his statement, struggling to find the right foreign words. "Ist Chonkin und ein, zwei, drei . . . seven . . . seben Russisch Gestapo . . . tied up mit a Strippe, mit a Ropen . . . Fershten?" By means of gestures, the captain tried to depict a number of people tied up together. "Und ein Flug, Airplanen." He waved his arms like a bird.

"Swallow, Swallow!" came a voice from the next room. "Hey, your mother, why don't you come in?"

Captain Milyaga was amazed. He had never suspected that the German language had so much in common with Russian. Or else . . .

But Milyaga did not think this thought through. His head was splitting and a slight nausea was rising in his throat. The captain swallowed his saliva and said to the blond soldier: "Ich bin sicken. Fershten? Mein head, mein Kopf—boom boom." He tapped his fist lightly against the top of his head, then cradled his cheek in the palm of his hand. "Ich bin wanten bye-bye."

Without waiting for permission, trembling from weakness, Milyaga reeled over to the straw bedding, lay down, and once again lost consciousness.

36

The conference at the division commander's was still in progress. There had been only one short break, when the battalion commanders left to transfer their sub-units to the attack positions according to the plan. Having issued the orders to entrench in the new positions, the commanders returned to the dugout.

The problem of arms and ammunition was now under discussion. It appeared that the regiment had only one 45-millimeter cannon and three shells for it, one Maxim-type machine gun and no cartridge belt, two battalion mortars and no mortar shells, two rifles and a limited supply of cartridges for each sub-unit, and one bottle of flammable liquid for every three men.

"It's perfectly clear," said the general, "that arms and ammunition are limited. The factor of surprise will be utilized to the maximum. Ammunition to be used sparingly."

The door opened and a soldier wearing a sopping-wet overcoat entered the dugout. "Comrade General," he shouted out, saluting. "Request permission to address Comrade Colonel."

"Granted," said the general.

Steam coming off his overcoat, the soldier turned to the colonel. "Comrade Colonel, request permission to speak."

"What's that you have there?"

The soldier handed him a letter and, having requested permission to leave, left the dugout.

The colonel ripped the envelope open, read the report, then handed it in silence to the general.

The report read:

To Regimental Commander Colonel Lapshin
from Junior Lieutenant Bukashov
REPORT
I hereby report that I, Junior Lieutenant Bukashov,
have questioned the soldier in the German Army taken
prisoner by scouts Sirikh and Filiukov.

In the course of the questioning the prisoner admitted that he was Gestapo officer Milleg. His service in the Gestapo has been distinguished by its cruelty and mercilessness. He has personally taken part in the mass execution of Communists and of Soviet citizens not belonging to the Party.

At the same time, the prisoner also testified that the headquarters of the so-called Chonkin are located in the farthermost hut, which belonged to the postmistress Belyashova before the occupation and is now defended by a reinforced detachment of Gestapo men, joined together by the tightest of bonds. There is a landing field and an airplane beside the house, apparently used to maintain contact with the regular units of the Nazi Army.

The above-mentioned Milleg avoided more detailed answers. During the questioning he behaved defiantly, like a fanatic. Several times he shouted out Fascist slogans ("Heil Hitler!" in particular), he made revolting statements relating to our country's social and political system. Several of his blasphemous attacks touched on the person of Com. J. V. Stalin.

Junior Lieutenant Bukashov

"Well, now," said the general. "That's what I call valuable information. Junior Lieutenant Bukashov is to be awarded a decoration. The attack positions are to be changed in accordance with the new data. So as not to overextend ourselves, all attack forces are to be concentrated on the headquarters of the so-called Chonkin." He pulled the map over to himself, crossed out the rectangles representing the battalion displacement positions, and moved them to new positions. He crossed out the old arrows and drew new ones. Now all three arrows converged on Nyura Belyashova's hut.

37

After he had questioned the prisoner, Junior Lieutenant Bukashov had composed his report and sent it to the regimental commander with one of the off-duty sentries. Now he had a chance to catch some sleep, but he didn't feel like sleeping and decided to write a letter to his mother. He opened his notebook, pulled over the wick lamp, and, in his still unformed, schoolboyish script, began writing quickly:

My dear, nice, good Mummy:
By the time you receive this letter, your son may no longer be among the living. Summoned by a green flare, I will go into battle today at dawn. This will be my first battle. If it turns out to be my last, I ask you not to grieve. Take comfort in the thought that your son, Junior Lieutenant Bukashov, gave his young life for the motherland, for the Party, for the great Stalin.
Believe me, I will be happy to lose my life if, in any measure, my death washes away the stain of shame forced on us by your former husband, my former father . . .

After writing the word "father," Bukashov became lost in thought. The night of his father's arrest appeared before his eyes in full detail as if it had all happened only the day before. At that time Bukashov was in the eighth grade.

When they came and started banging on the door with their rifle butts, everyone in the apartment was thrown into commotion, but his father had said calmly to his mother: "Hold on. I'll get it. It's for me."

Later, those words, "It's for me," became, in Bukashov's mind, the strongest evidence against his father. They meant that he knew he was guilty because an innocent man would not be capable of such a feeling.

Four men had come. One had a pistol, two had rifles, the fourth, a man with eyeglasses, lived on the floor below them and was there as the witness. The witness trembled with fear and, as it subsequently turned out, with good reason, for he too was arrested somewhat later in connection with Bukashov's father's case.

They ripped open all the feather beds and pillows (feathers kept flying around the courtyard for three days afterward), they broke the furniture apart and smashed the dishes. The one with the pistol kept picking up flower pots, holding them above his head, and shattering them right in the middle of the room, making a pile of broken clay and dirt.

Then they left and took his father with them.

Lyosha Bukashov went on hoping for a while. It was hard for him to grow used to the idea that his father, a Civil War hero, an order bearer who had received an inscribed weapon (a saber with a gold hilt) from the All-Russian Central Executive Committee and who later became director of one of the nation's largest metallurgical plants, had turned out to be nothing but a common spy working in cooperation with the Polish secret police. But, unfortunately, all this was soon to be confirmed. Confronted with the evidence, Bukashov's father testified that he had wanted to put one of the latest-model Martin open-hearth furnaces out of commission. It was impossible for Lyosha not to believe it, since it was his father who provided the testimony. But there was just one thing Lyosha found difficult to accept—why had his father wanted to put that particular furnace out of commission? Could he really have thought the loss of this one furnace would cause the entire Soviet state to collapse? If he had concealed his true nature from the Party, the people, and, finally, from his own family, so cleverly and for so long a time, he couldn't have been that stupid. And he'd had much greater opportunities for sabotage. No, Lyosha could make no sense out of any of it and it was precisely that which tormented him most of all.

Bukashov got up and began pacing the barn. The prisoner was still lying on the straw, his eyes closed, his face pale. There was a smell of hay in the air; somewhere a cricket was chirping. He sat back down, sighed, and wet his indelible-ink pencil with saliva.

Mama dear, perhaps you will condemn me for concealing the truth about my father when entering officers' training school. I know I acted cowardly, but I didn't see any other way out. I wanted to defend the motherland along with my people and was afraid I would not be permitted to . . .

The junior lieutenant laid his pencil aside and grew pensive. He ought to issue some instructions in the event of his death but did not know just what kind to issue. Formerly people made wills, but he had nothing to will anyone. Nevertheless, he wrote:

Mummy, if you see Lena Sinelnikova, tell her that I'm releasing her from the promise she made me (she knows what I mean), and sell my suit, don't save it. The money you get for it will come in handy.

*With this I shall close my letter. There's less than
an hour left before the signal to attack. Farewell, my
dear Mummy. Your loving son, Lyosha.*

After his name, he wrote the date and the time, 4:07.

Junior Lieutenant Bukashov folded his letter up into a
triangle, addressed it, and put it in his left-hand pocket
with his papers. If he came through alive, he'd destroy
the letter; if he lost his life, they'd mail it for him.

It was getting close to dawn, he had to hurry. The junior
lieutenant tore another sheet of paper from his notebook
and wrote a statement to his unit's Party organization. He
did not give the reasons behind his request but wrote
simply and modestly: "If I perish, I ask to be considered
a Communist." Then he signed his name and affixed the
date. Leaving the statement to dry, he went outside to
stretch his legs. It was still dark, but in the far distance a
faint outline could already be distinguished, and somewhere down below a white strip of mist hovered over the
river. The sentry on duty by the entrance to the barn was
smoking, shielding his cigarette with the palm of his
hand. The junior lieutenant was about to rebuke him but
then changed his mind.

What moral right do I have to rebuke a man twice as
old as me? he thought and went back into the barn.

When Bukashov glanced to where he'd left his statement to the Party, he saw that the notebook was there,
but the statement was gone. What the hell is this? thought
the junior lieutenant and started rummaging through his
pockets. He found his military I.D. card. He found the
letter to his mother, and finally he found his photograph
of Lena Sinelnikova. But his statement to the Party was
not there.

Bukashov looked over suspiciously at the prisoner, who was still sleeping in the corner, although he was not as pale as before. But he'd hardly steal the statement, it would be of no use to him. The junior lieutenant took the lantern and began ransacking the immediate area. He peered in every corner, crawled on his knees, turned over all the boxes, but the statement was nowhere to be found.

Bukashov's search was interrupted by sounds coming from outside. He hurried out and saw the division commander standing by the entrance to the barn, his pistol thrust to the sentry's stomach, delivering a speech composed entirely of references to the sentry's mother. Behind the general in the glimmering pre-dawn light could be seen Colonel Lapshin, the official from SMERSH, and a few other dark figures. Holding his rifle tightly, the sentry was staring at the general, his eyes popping with panic. The junior lieutenant drew himself to attention. His appearance distracted the general from the sentry. He shouted: "And who is this one?"

"Junior Lieutenant Bukashov," Bukashov reported, fearfully.

"My adjutant," clarified Lapshin.

"What's the matter with you, junior, you son-of-a-bitch, didn't you see this stupid bastard of yours smoking at his post?"

"I am to blame, Comrade General of the Army!" The sentry had finally regained control of himself and immediately raised Drinov by three ranks.

This was crude flattery, but Drinov was crude too. He relented and muttered: "To blame, your mother's to blame. You'll atone for your guilt in battle. Comrade Revkin, secretary of the District Committee, is with us today." He pointed to the man standing behind the official from SMERSH. "He'll see all this and then he's going to say,

'Oh, the way they do things in the army.' One lout like this can ruin all our camouflage and get a whole division wiped out. So, junior, all quiet?"

"All quiet, Comrade General!"

"All right then, let's go inside."

38

Captain Milyaga was awakened by a sound whose significance he could not grasp. He raised himself up on one elbow. There was no one in the barn. The blond soldier who'd been sitting at the table had taken off somewhere. Maybe he ought to take off too. He looked around and spied a small window close to the ceiling. There had also been a small window right by the ceiling in Nyura Belyashova's shed. If he put all those boxes one on top of the other . . .

Five men entered the barn. The first was big and hulking and had a brick-red face; he was followed by a thin man, then by one in high boots, then by a plain-looking man whom the captain liked at first sight, and finally by the young blond soldier. The one wearing the high boots interested the captain immediately. His face was painfully familiar. Of course, it was Secretary Revkin. The Germans could not have any idea who he was or else they wouldn't be treating him like that. At that very moment the captain saw the way to salvation. He would render the Germans such a great service that they might even forget about shooting him. He jumped up and made straight for Revkin. Revkin halted in bewilderment. The young soldier went for his holster.

"Afanasy Petrovich?" Revkin finally managed to ask uncertainly. "Comrade Milyaga?"

"The wolf is comrade to you!" Milyaga smiled and

turned to the tall man, who it seemed to him was the person in charge there. "Please, bitte, hear my statement, this Schwein ist Secretary of die Districten Committen, Revkin, Districten Führer, Fershten?"

"Afanasy Petrovich," said Revkin, even more amazed now. "What's the matter with you, old man? Get hold of yourself."

"Now it's them that's going to get hold of you. And they'll let you have it too," promised Milyaga.

Thoroughly bewildered, Revkin looked over to the general, who spread his hands and shook his head.

"What the hell is this, you son-of-a-bitch?" exclaimed the general in surprise.

Hearing this familiar phrase once again threw Milyaga into confusion. He looked at the military men, shifting his gaze from one to the other, unable to make any sense out of what was happening. But a faint idea was beginning to glimmer in his head. At that very moment, however, several men with submachine guns entered the room. The large stars on their helmets glistened with rain. The answer began to dawn in the captain's clouded mind.

"Who is this?" asked the tall one in perfect Russian.

"The prisoner, Comrade General." Bukashov came forward. "A captain in the Gestapo."

"So that's the one?" asked the general, recalling the report.

"What are you talking about, Gestapo?" objected Revkin and offered a brief explanation concerning the person of Captain Milyaga.

"But it was me who questioned him." Bukashov grew confused. "He told me he had shot Communists and non-Party members."

"I can't make any goddamn sense of it," said Drinov,

thoroughly confused. "Maybe he'll tell us himself. Who are you?" he asked Milyaga directly.

Milyaga was lost, stunned, crushed. Who was who here? He couldn't make heads or tails of anything. Who were these people? And who was he?

"Ich bin . . ."

"There, you see." The general turned to Revkin. "I told you he was a German."

"Nein, nein!" Milyaga began to shout in terror, mixing up all the words he knew from every language. "I'm nyet German, I'm nichts German. Me russky, Comrade General."

"What the hell kind of Russian are you when you can't even speak the language?"

"I can," said Milyaga, laying his hand on his heart and beginning a fervent attempt to convince them. "I can. I even can very." And in order to convince the general, he shouted out: "Long live Comrade Hitler!"

Of course that was not the name he had meant to say. It was just a mistake. A tragic mistake. But the grave state in which he'd been since his capture had caused everything to get jumbled in Milyaga's poor, banged-up head. After shouting that last phrase, the captain clutched his head in his hands, fell to the floor, and began rolling on the ground, fully aware they would not forgive him for this and that he would not have forgiven it himself.

"To be shot!" said the general with a characteristic wave of the hand.

Two soldiers from the general's escort picked the captain up under his arms and began dragging him from the room. The captain resisted, shouting words of some sort, a mishmash of Russian and German (it turned out he knew that foreign language a little too well), the tips of his muddy, box-calf boots cutting two winding furrows across the chaff-strewn dirt.

Many hearts were constricted with pity as Captain Milyaga was dragged away. Even Junior Lieutenant Bukashov felt some pity, though rationally he knew that the captain deserved his fate.

His eyes accompanying his colleague in his final moments, the official from SMERSH thought to himself: You're a fool, Captain! Ech, what a fool!

And indeed, Captain Milyaga, until recently the terror of the district, perished like a fool, from nothing more than a misunderstanding. After all, had he gotten his bearings while being questioned and realized that he was among friends, would he have actually started talking about a Russian Gestapo? Would he have actually started shouting "Heil Hitler!" "Stalin kaput!" and other such anti-Soviet slogans? Not on his life! He had always considered himself a first-class patriot. It was entirely possible that, having reached the rank of general, he would have retired on a good pension, taken his well-deserved rest, and played dominoes with his fellow pensioners. In all likelihood he would have given lectures in meeting halls, instructing youth in patriotism, civilized behavior in daily life, and intolerance for every manifestation of foreign ideology.

39

Chonkin did not know what kind of danger was hanging over him, but he had a premonition of trouble in connection with Captain Milyaga's escape.

For that reason, shortly before dawn, taking advantage of the fact that both the prisoners and Nyura were in the deep sleep that precedes daybreak, Chonkin opened his knapsack, put on clean underwear, and then began rummaging through his possessions and sorting them out. In case anything happened, he wanted to leave Nyura something to remember him by.

Chonkin's possessions did not amount to much. Besides his underwear, there was a change of flannel winter foot cloths, a needle and thread, the stub of an indelible-ink pencil, and, wrapped up in a piece of newspaper, six photographs of himself from the waist up. His fellow soldiers had their photographs taken to cheer up families and girl friends, but Chonkin had no one to cheer up. And so all six photos had remained in his possession. He pulled the top one out of the pack and held it up to the lamp. Gazing at his likeness, Chonkin was, on the whole, rather pleased.

Quartermaster Sergeant Trofimovich, who picked up a little money on the side taking pictures, had portrayed Chonkin with the aid of a special background which depicted tanks rolling downhill while planes zoomed into the sky. Hovering over Chonkin's head like a halo was the inscription: *Greetings from the Red Army.*

Finding a place for himself at the very edge of the table, he licked his pencil for a long time as he considered what to write. Then he remembered the inscription that Trofimovich had once recommended to him. Sticking out his tongue, he began laboriously tracing out the uneven letters, almost printing them:

May a tender gaze light your eyes
as they touch on this replica of me.
Perhaps in your mind shall rise
a memory of the one you see.

He thought a bit, then added: "To Nyura B. from Vanya C., in their days of life together."

He hid the pencil in his pocket and placed the photograph on the windowsill.

It was growing light outside and the rain seemed to have stopped. It was time to wake Nyura and get a few winks himself; soon he'd have to be taking the prisoners out to work and there, in the open field, he'd have to keep his eyes peeled so that none of them escaped as their boss had.

He felt sorry about waking Nyura. He was feeling sorry anyway. All the time they'd been together, she'd gone through so much on account of him, even all the gossip that went around, and she never once complained. True, one time she did hint shyly that it wouldn't hurt to make it official but, without his commanding officer's permission, a soldier in the Red Army could not get married. Which was so, of course, but to be honest about it, it wasn't the permission, it was that, taking all the angles into account. Chonkin just couldn't make up his mind.

Ivan walked over to Nyura and touched her lightly on the shoulder. "Nyurka, hey, Nyurka," he said fondly.

"Huh? What?" Nyura woke with a start and looked at him with eyes still vacant from sleep.

"Listen, could you take my place for a little while," he asked. "I'm so sleepy, I can't keep my eyes open."

Nyura dutifully got out of bed, stuck her feet in her boots, took the rifle, and sat down by the door.

Without taking off his clothes, Ivan lay down where she'd been sleeping. The pillow was still warm from Nyura. He closed his eyes, and just as his consciousness started to lose its way between dream and reality, he heard some sort of strange sipping sound, something gasping followed by the clinking of glass. Ivan came to immediately and sat up in bed. Svintsov and Edrenkov had woken up. Nyura was still sitting by the door, but her face expressed concern.

"Nyurka," Ivan called in a whisper.

"Huh?" she answered in a whisper.

"What was that?"

"Sounds like shooting."

Shots suddenly rapped out again, but this time they seemed to come from the other direction. Chonkin shuddered.

"Thy will be done!" Nyura breathed out in a whisper.

Now the other prisoners woke up. Only Lieutenant Filippov was still smacking his lips in his sleep. Svintsov got up on one elbow and shifted his gaze from Nyura to Chonkin and then back.

"Nyurka," said Ivan, hastily lacing his boots. "Give me the rifle and you get yourself a revolver from the bag, the biggest one there."

Chonkin went outside without putting on his puttees. It was quiet and muddy but the rain had stopped. Dawn had not quite broken, though the visibility was already pretty good. The airplane, its awkward wings spread, was still in place.

Chonkin looked around and was struck by a strange sight.

White snowdrifts were swirling about two hundred meters away on the other side of the vegetable patches.

"What the hell is that?" marveled Chonkin. "Where's snow coming from in weather like this?"

He observed that these snowdrifts were swirling in his direction. Now Chonkin was even more amazed and stared at them all the harder. It was only then that he realized that these weren't snowdrifts at all but a mass of people crawling in a line toward him, Chonkin. What he did not know was that this was the strike force whose mission was to hurl bottles of flammable liquid at the enemy as a continuation of the artillery barrage. When they were being outfitted, there had not been enough overcoats at the depot and the soldiers had been issued winter camouflage cloaks, which they were now using because of the bad weather. Germans! thought Chonkin. At that very moment a rifle shot rang out, and a bullet whizzed right past Chonkin's ear. He fell to the ground. Crawling through the mud to the strut on the right-hand side of the chassis, he positioned his rifle between the strut and the wheel.

"Hey you, surrender!" came a shout from the white cloaks in the distance.

"Russians don't surrender!" Chonkin was about to shout, but felt too embarrassed. Instead of answering, he pressed his cheek against the butt of his rifle and fired once without taking aim. That started it. Sporadic fire came banging at him from the enemy's side and bullets went whistling over Chonkin's head. Most of them flew right by, but several hit the plane, ripping open the paneling or flattening out with a clang as they struck the motor. Chonkin buried his face in the ground and, saving his cartridges, fired every once in a while, without looking to see where. He used up his first clip, then jammed in a second. Bullets continued to whistle by, some of them quite low. If only the sergeant had issued me a helmet, thought Chonkin longingly, but he had no time to take his thought any further. Something soft had plopped down beside him, startling him. He turned his head slightly and opened one eye. It was Nyura lying there beside him. Flattened against the ground like he was, she was firing two pistols in the air at the same time. The bag with the rest of the pistols was lying beside her in reserve.

"Nyurka." Chonkin nudged his friend.

"Huh?"

"How come you left them?"

"Don't worry," said Nyura, pulling two triggers at the same time. "I made them go down in the cellar, then I nailed the trap door shut over them. Oi, look!"

Chonkin lifted his head. The whites were now making short rushes forward.

"We'll never be able to handle them this way, Nyurka," said Chonkin.

"You know how to use a machine gun?" asked Nyura.

"Sure, but where can you get one?"

"In the cockpit, of course."

"Oi, why didn't I think of that!" Chonkin jumped up, and banged his head against the wing. Hiding behind the fuselage, he ripped off a few strips of the tarpaulin, climbed up onto the wing, and was in the rear cockpit before the whites had time to react. There actually was a machine-gun mount and a machine gun with a full unit of fire. Chonkin grabbed hold of the handles, but the machine gun would not swivel. The mount had rusted from disuse and the rain.

Chonkin tried to loosen it with his shoulder but it wouldn't give.

Just then something heavy fell on the upper wing, though no shot had been fired. Then another something, and another. They began knocking against the wings and all around the plane, the sound of breaking glass kept ringing out, and there was a sharp smell like kerosene in the air. Chonkin poked out his head and caught sight of a cloud of bottles full of yellow liquid flying right at him from behind the fence. The majority of the bottles were plopping in the mud, but several were striking the plane, rolling down the wings, and smashing against the motor. (Afterward it turned out that no one had notified the soldiers of the strike force that the bottles of flammable liquid had to be ignited before they were thrown, and the soldiers were just hurling them as is.)

Nyura appeared on the wing beside him.

"Nyurka, keep your head down," shouted Chonkin. "They'll kill you."

"What the hell are they throwing bottles for?" Nyura shouted in Ivan's ear, firing a pistol into the air with one hand.

"Don't worry, Nyurka, we'll get the deposit back later," said Chonkin, finding the strength for a joke. Then he gave her an order. "I got it, Nyurka, you grab the plane by the tail and wiggle it back and forth. Got that?"

"Got it!" shouted Nyura, crawling down from the wing on her stomach.

40

General Drinov was sitting in his dugout, three floors down, following the action through a periscope. It was not that he was cowardly (he had already proven his courage many times over), he simply considered that a general's rank gave him the privilege of sitting in dugouts and traveling exclusively in armored carriers. Through the periscope he saw his troops advancing in the direction of the farthest hut, first at a crawl, then in short forward rushes. Their fire was being returned but not heavily. The general ordered the telephone man to connect him with the commander of the attack battalion, and he communicated the order to begin the attack.

"Yes, Comrade One!" the battalion commander answered.

Soon thereafter, increased movement could be observed in the attack line.

The soldiers of the strike force, wearing their white cloaks, had crept right up to the fence. The general could see each soldier in turn raise himself up a little from the ground and fling his arm. "They're throwing the bottles now," surmised the general.

But why wasn't there any flame?

The general was again connected with the battalion commander. "Why aren't the bottles on fire?"

"I don't understand it myself, Comrade One."

"Aren't they lighting them with matches?" asked the general, raising his voice.

The battalion commander's heavy breathing could be heard through the phone.

"I'm asking you," said Drinov, without waiting for a reply. "Are they lighting the bottles or aren't they?"

"No, Comrade General."

"Why not?"

"I didn't know you were supposed to," the battalion commander confessed after a moment's silence.

"You'll learn all about it at your court-martial," promised the general. "Which commanding officer holds the same rank as you?"

"Junior Lieutenant Bukashov."

"Transfer the command of the battalion to him and place yourself under arrest."

"Yes, Comrade One" came the doleful reply.

At that moment a machine gun began chattering. Caught by surprise, the general flung the receiver aside and rushed to his periscope.

He could see that the attack line had dropped flat while the soldiers of the strike force, having pressed themselves to the ground, were crawling back in retreat. Their cloaks were no longer so white, or, to put it more precisely, were no longer white at all, and thus were now entirely suitable for camouflage.

Moving the periscope a little to the left, the general could see that the machine-gun fire was coming from the airplane, which was rotating in place, moved by some unknown force.

"What the hell is going on?" marveled the general. Then, after adjusting the focus, he marveled all the more. Some person, clearly of the female sex, wearing a flower-print dress, an unbuttoned quilted jacket, and a kerchief that had fallen down onto her shoulders, was lugging the plane back and forth. Now the plane's side was turned toward him and the general could see distinctly the red star on the tail. "Not one of ours?" flashed through the general's brain. No, it couldn't be. Typical enemy trick. That's why the woman was turning it like that, to trick us. He went back to the telephone again and summoned the regimental commander.

"Listen, Number Two," said the general, "this is Number One speaking! How many shells left in the cannon?"

"One, Comrade One."

"Very good," said Number One. "Order the gun dragged over to that outhouse with the foreign writing on it and have it fired point-blank at that plane."

"But there's a machine gun out there, Comrade One."

"So, what about it?"

"It won't allow us to approach. It's firing. People will get killed."

"Get killed!" roared the general. "Oh, so we've got ourselves a humanist here. This is war, people get killed. Bring up that gun, that's an order!"

"Yes, Comrade One."

At that moment the machine gun fell silent.

Having repelled the attack, Chonkin took his hands off the triggers. The silence began ringing in his ears immediately. There wasn't any fire coming from the enemy's side either.

"Nyurka!" called Ivan, turning.

"What?" Nyura was leaning against the tail, panting, her face red and wet, as if she'd just come from the bathhouse.

"Alive, huh?" Chonkin smiled at her. "All right, take a breather."

It was already fully light and Chonkin had no trouble seeing both the soldiers in the muddy cloaks, who had hurled the bottles, and the other ones in the gray overcoats, who were much greater in number. All of them were lying on the ground, showing no signs of life, and even the feeling of danger seemed to have begun to pass.

Somewhere a rooster began to crow loudly; he was answered by a second rooster, then a third . . .

Ah, the voices on them, thought Chonkin, not noticing the gunners dragging the 45-millimeter gun, hidden from view by Gladishev's outhouse, on which the English words "water closet" were written.

"Nyurka," said Ivan fondly. "You rested a little?"

"Why?" Nyura wiped her face with the tip of her kerchief.

"Could you bring me some water. I'm thirsty. Run quick or they might wing you."

Doubled over, Nyura dashed to the hut.

A belated shot rang out, but Nyura was already around the corner.

The first thing Nyura did in the hut was to check the

cellar door, but everything was fine in that respect, the prisoners were still down there and not showing their noses.

Nyura had just begun ladling water from the bucket when an explosion of such deafening power resounded that the floor capsized beneath her feet; as she fell, she heard the ring of broken glass flying.

41

It had been a very good shot. The sole shell had obligingly hit right on target. The soldiers were still pressed flat to the ground awaiting the enemy's response. No response came.

At that point Junior Lieutenant Bukashov, temporarily acting as commander of the first battalion, got up on his hands and knees.

"For the motherland!" he shouted, his voice hoarse with excitement. "For Stalin! Hurrah!"

He jumped to his feet and began running across the wet grass, waving his pistol in the air.

His heart stopped for an instant as he felt himself all alone, with no one in back of him. But at the next instant he heard a mighty "Hurrah!" and the sound of dozens of feet tramping behind him. Then he noticed that the second battalion was running down the road in a broken line, also shouting "Hurrah!" while the third battalion, having skirted the village from below, was now approaching from the river side.

Junior Lieutenant Bukashov and his eagles were the first to jump over the fence and burst into the vegetable garden. What he saw there seemed beyond belief to him. He did not see heaps of enemy bodies, he did not see enemy soldiers surrendering in panic. He saw a smashed airplane, whose right upper wing had been cut by a shell fragment and was now dangling by thin cables, and whose tail lay scattered off to one side.

Not far from the airplane a Red Army soldier was lying on the churned-up ground while a woman in an unbuttoned quilt jacket, her hair disheveled, was sobbing inconsolably over him.

Bukashov came to a halt. The troops running up behind him came to a halt as well. The ones in back got up on tiptoe to see what was happening down in front. The junior lieutenant, marking time in confusion, removed the helmet from his head. The other soldiers followed his example.

Colonel Lapshin walked up and he too removed his helmet. "What is that soldier's name?" he asked the woman.

"Chonkin, Vanya, my husband," said Nyura, drowning in tears.

The armored carrier rumbled up to the scene. The submachine gunners hopped out and began to jostle the soldiers aside, clearing a path for the general, who was struggling to get out of the carrier. They removed part of the fence so that the general would not have to lift his feet from the ground. His hands crossed behind his back, the general walked leisurely over to the airplane. Catching sight of Chonkin lying on the ground, he slowly removed his sheepskin hat.

Colonel Lapshin ran over to the general.

"Comrade General," he reported, "the mission of liquidating Chonkin's gang has been accomplished."

"So that is Chonkin?" asked Drinov.

"Yes, Comrade General, that's Chonkin."

"So where is his gang?"

The colonel began turning his head in confusion. At

that moment the door to the hut opened and several armed soldiers led out a group of men in gray coats, all tied together.

"That's them, that's the gang," said one of the soldiers from behind.

"What do you mean, gang?" Revkin popped into the picture. "Those are our comrades."

"Who called them a gang?" asked the general and stared at the soldiers, who now huddled together. Confusion ran through the ranks. The soldiers moved back, each one trying to hide behind the other's back.

"Untie them!" the general ordered Colonel Lapshin.

"Untie them!" the colonel ordered Junior Lieutenant Bukashov.

"Untie them!" Bukashov ordered the soldiers.

"But, meanwhile, where is the gang?" asked the general, turning his entire body around to face Revkin, who was standing behind him.

"You'll have to ask him," said Revkin, and he pointed to Chairman Golubev, who had just driven up in his two-wheeled cart. "Ivan Timofeyevich," Revkin shouted out to him, "so where's the gang?"

Golubev hitched his horse to the fence and walked over to them.

"What gang?" he asked, gazing with pity on his drinking buddy of the day before.

"What do you mean?" Revkin was beginning to grow alarmed. "Remember, I was talking to you on the phone, asking you about my comrades here and who'd arrested them. And you told me—Chonkin and his gang."

"I didn't say gang." Golubev frowned. "I said girl. That one there, Nyura."

Hearing her own name, Nyura began sobbing all the

more. A hot tear fell on Chonkin's face. Chonkin quivered and opened his eyes, for he had not been killed; he had only had a slight concussion.

"He's alive! Alive!" Voices stirred among the soldiers.

"Vanechka!" cried Nyura. "You're alive!" She began covering his face with kisses.

Chonkin rubbed his temple. "I guess I really slept," he said uncertainly and then caught sight of the many curious faces looking down at him. Chonkin frowned and rested his gaze on one of the men standing over him, the one holding his sheepskin hat in his hand. "Who's that?" he asked Nyura.

"The devil knows," answered Nyura. "Some big shot. I can't tell them apart."

"But that's a general, Nyurka," said Ivan, after a moment's thought.

"That's right, son, I'm a general," said the man with the sheepskin hat fondly.

Chonkin looked up at him mistrustfully. "Nyurka," he asked emotionally. "I couldn't be dreaming all this, could I?"

"No, Vanya, this isn't any dream."

Chonkin did not believe her especially, but he thought that a general was a general, and ought to be treated accordingly, even in a dream. Fumbling with one hand on the ground beside him, he found his forage cap and pulled it down to his ears. He got up on shaky legs and, feeling slightly nauseous and dizzy, he saluted, his fingers spread wide apart against his temple.

"Comrade General," he reported, swallowing his saliva, "during your absence there were no incidents . . ."

Not knowing what else to say, Chonkin fell silent and, blinking rapidly, stared at the general.

"Listen, son," said the general, putting his sheepskin hat back on. "You mean to tell me you fought a whole regiment all by yourself?"

"I wasn't by myself, Comrade General." Chonkin pulled in his stomach and threw out his chest.

"Ah, so then you weren't all by yourself," said the general, gladdened. "So who were you with then?"

"With Nyurka, Comrade General!" Chonkin bellowed as he came back to his senses.

Laughter rang out from the soldiers.

"Who's laughing there?" The general ran his eyes angrily down the ranks. The laughter died at once. "There's nothing to laugh at here, you sons-of-bitches!" continued the general, gradually recalling and employing all the choicest expressions he knew. "One goddamn soldier with a gun, bang bang bang, and a whole regiment can't deal with him. And you, Chonkin, I'll tell you straight off, you may look like a dolt but you're a hero. On behalf of the command, goddamn it, I declare our gratitude to you and present you with this decoration."

The general reached inside his rain cape, pulled off one of his own decorations, and fastened it to Chonkin's field shirt. Drawing himself up to full attention, Chonkin squinted down at the decoration, then shifted his gaze to Nyura. He thought how wonderful it would be to have his picture taken now, for afterwards no one was going to believe that the general himself had presented him with the decoration. He thought of Samushkin, Sergeant Peskov, Quartermaster Trofimovich—if they could only see him now!

"Comrade General, I request permission to address you!" Lieutenant Filippov saluted smartly.

The general started and looked over at the lieutenant in none too friendly a fashion.

"All right, speak," said the general reluctantly.

"Please familiarize yourself with this document!" The lieutenant unfolded a sheet of paper with a small hole in the lower-right-hand corner. The general took the paper and slowly began to read it. The more he read, the more he frowned. It was a warrant. A warrant for the arrest of the traitor to the motherland: Chonkin, Ivan Vasilyevich.

"But where's the seal?" asked the general, hoping that the warrant had not been drawn up in a legal manner.

"The seal was shot away during the battle," said the lieutenant with dignity, dropping his eyes.

"Well, then," said the general in some confusion. "Well, then . . . If that's so, then of course . . . I have no grounds not to believe it: Act in accordance with the warrant." The general stepped back, making room for the lieutenant. The lieutenant strode over to Chonkin and hooked two fingers onto the freshly presented decoration as if he were pulling out a nail. Chonkin stepped back instinctively, but it was too late. With one tug of his hand the lieutenant ripped off the decoration, along with a piece of Chonkin's field shirt.

"Svintsov! Khabibullin!" came the command. "Take the prisoner!"

They grabbed Chonkin by the elbows. A murmur passed through the ranks of soldiers. They had not understood any of it.

Remembering the commander's role as educator, General Drinov turned to the soldiers and declared: "Comrade soldiers, my order that Chonkin be decorated has been rescinded. Private Chonkin has turned out to be a traitor to the motherland. He pretended to be a hero in order to worm his way into our confidence. Is that clear?"

"Clear!" shouted the soldiers without much conviction.

"Colonel Lapshin," said the general. "Form the regiment and conduct them to the echelon embarkation point."

"Yes, Comrade General!"

Colonel Lapshin ran out onto the road and, standing with his back to the village, put his arms by his sides.

"Regiment!" he shouted at the top of his lungs. "By battalions, in columns, four abreast!"

While the regiment was forming on the road, the general and Revkin climbed into the armored carrier and drove away. Golubev drove away as well, before something happened to him too.

Finally the regiment formed, occupying the entire road from one end of the village to the other.

"Regiment, dress!" commanded the colonel. "Attention! Now, singing, forward . . ." the colonel prolonged the pause ". . . march!"

Boots rumbled on the damp road. The lead singer's high voice soared up from within the formation:

A Cossack galloped through the valley,
through the Caucasian lands . . .

Hundreds of throats joined in the song.

Boys from all over the village ran alongside the formation and tried to march in step with them. The women waved their handkerchiefs and wiped away their tears.

A lame nag came up behind the regiment, dragging the 45-millimeter gun, and behind the cannon came Ilya Zhikin, the Civil War veteran, wheeling himself along on his board and casters. When he had wheeled himself to the center of the village, Zhikin gave up on it and turned back.

Soon after the regiment left, the residents of Krasnoye saw the one-and-a-half-ton truck drive out of Chonkin's yard.

The lieutenant was sitting in the cab beside the driver. In the back of the truck, four men were holding Chonkin by the arms, not that he was struggling to break loose.

Sobbing and stumbling, Nyura ran after the truck. Her kerchief had fallen onto her shoulders, her hair was flying.

"Vanya!" cried Nyura, choking on her sobs. "Vanechka!" She reached her arms out to the truck as she ran.

To cut this disgraceful scene short, the lieutenant ordered the driver to go faster. The driver stepped on the gas. Nyura could not compete with a truck, and stumbling one last time, she fell to the ground. But even there on the ground she kept reaching her arms out toward the swiftly departing truck . . . Chonkin's heart began to ache with pity for Nyura. He struggled but couldn't quite break free, they were holding him too tightly.

"Nyurka!" he shouted, shaking his head desperately. "Don't cry, Nyurka! I'll be back!"

42

At sunset of that same day, the warehouseman Gladishev came out of his house with the intention of examining the site of the recent battle. When he walked through the plowed field on the other side of the hillock, about a kilometer and a half from the village, he came upon a dead horse that had been killed by a stray bullet. At first Gladishev thought the horse wasn't from their parts, but when he moved closer to it he recognized Osoaviakhim. Evidently the gelding had been killed right on the spot—there was a black ragged wound by its ear and a line of congealed blood ran from the ear to the lips. Gladishev grinned as he stood over the dead gelding. Why hide it? He really had believed his strange dream. Not that he had believed it entirely, but he had given it some credence. Everything had happened so coincidentally that it had been difficult for him not to waver in his anti-mystical convictions. If he were ever to tell anyone about it, the shame and the laughter, the shame . . .

Suddenly Gladishev noticed that there was no shoe on the gelding's front hoof.

"That's the limit," he muttered. Then, bending down, he made a second discovery. There was a scrap of paper mashed to the ground beneath the horse's hoof. Seized by a premonition of something extraordinary, Gladishev grabbed the piece of paper, brought it up close to his eyes, and froze, dumbfounded.

In spite of the gathering dusk and his none-too-sharp eyesight, the born breeder was able to make out the large wavering script beneath the caked-on mud and bloodstains: "If I perish, I ask to be considered a Communist."

"Good Lord!" shrieked Gladishev, and for the first time in many years, he crossed himself.

1963–1970

EUROPEAN CLASSICS

Honoré de Balzac	*The Bureaucrats*
Heinrich Böll	*Absent without Leave* *And Never Said a Word* *And Where Were You, Adam?* *The Bread of Those Early Years* *End of a Mission* *Irish Journal* *Missing Persons and Other Essays* *A Soldier's Legacy* *The Train Was on Time* *Women in a River Landscape*
Madeleine Bourdouxhe	*La Femme de Gilles*
Lydia Chukovskaya	*Sofia Petrovna*
Grazia Deledda	*After the Divorce* *Elias Portolu*
Aleksandr Druzhinin	*Polinka Saks • The Story of Aleksei Dmitrich*
Venedikt Erofeev	*Moscow to the End of the Line*
Konstantin Fedin	*Cities and Years*
Fyodor Vasilievich Gladkov	*Cement*
I. Grekova	*The Ship of Widows*
Marek Hlasko	*The Eighth Day of the Week*
Bohumil Hrabal	*Closely Watched Trains*
Erich Kästner	*Fabian: The Story of a Moralist*
Ignacy Krasicki	*The Adventures of Mr. Nicholas Wisdom*
Miroslav Krleža	*The Return of Philip Latinowicz*
Karin Michaëlis	*The Dangerous Age*
Andrey Platonov	*The Foundation Pit*
Arthur Schnitzler	*The Road to the Open*
Ludvík Vaculík	*The Axe*
Vladimir Voinovich	*The Life & Extraordinary Adventures of Private Ivan Chonkin* *Pretender to the Throne*